Lincoln Peirce

BiG NATE
GENIUS MODE

HARPER

An Imprint of HarperCollins*Publishers*

BIG NATE is a registered trademark
of United Feature Syndicate, Inc.

These comic strips first appeared in newspapers
from January 11, 2009, through August 9, 2009.

Big Nate: Genius Mode
Copyright © 2013 by United Feature Syndicate, Inc.
All rights reserved. Printed in the United States of America.
No part of this book may be used or reproduced in any manner
whatsoever without written permission except in the case of brief
quotations embodied in critical articles and reviews. For information
address HarperCollins Children's Books, a division of HarperCollins
Publishers, 10 East 53rd Street, New York, NY 10022.
www.harpercollinschildrens.com
www.bignatebooks.com

Go to www.bignate.com to read the *Big Nate* comic strip.

Library of Congress catalog card number: 2012956502
ISBN 978-0-06-208698-3 (pbk.)

Typography by Andrea Vandergrift
13 14 15 16 17 LP/RRDH 10 9 8 7 6 5 4 3 2 1
❖
First Edition

More

BiG
NATE

adventures from

Lincoln Peirce

Novels:

BIG NATE: IN A CLASS BY HIMSELF

BIG NATE STRIKES AGAIN

BIG NATE ON A ROLL

BIG NATE GOES FOR BROKE

BIG NATE FLIPS OUT

Activity Books:

BIG NATE BOREDOM BUSTER

BIG NATE FUN BLASTER

Comic Compilations:

BIG NATE: WHAT COULD POSSIBLY GO WRONG?

BIG NATE: HERE GOES NOTHING

BIG NATE FROM THE TOP

BIG NATE OUT LOUD

BIG NATE AND FRIENDS

BIG NATE MAKES THE GRADE

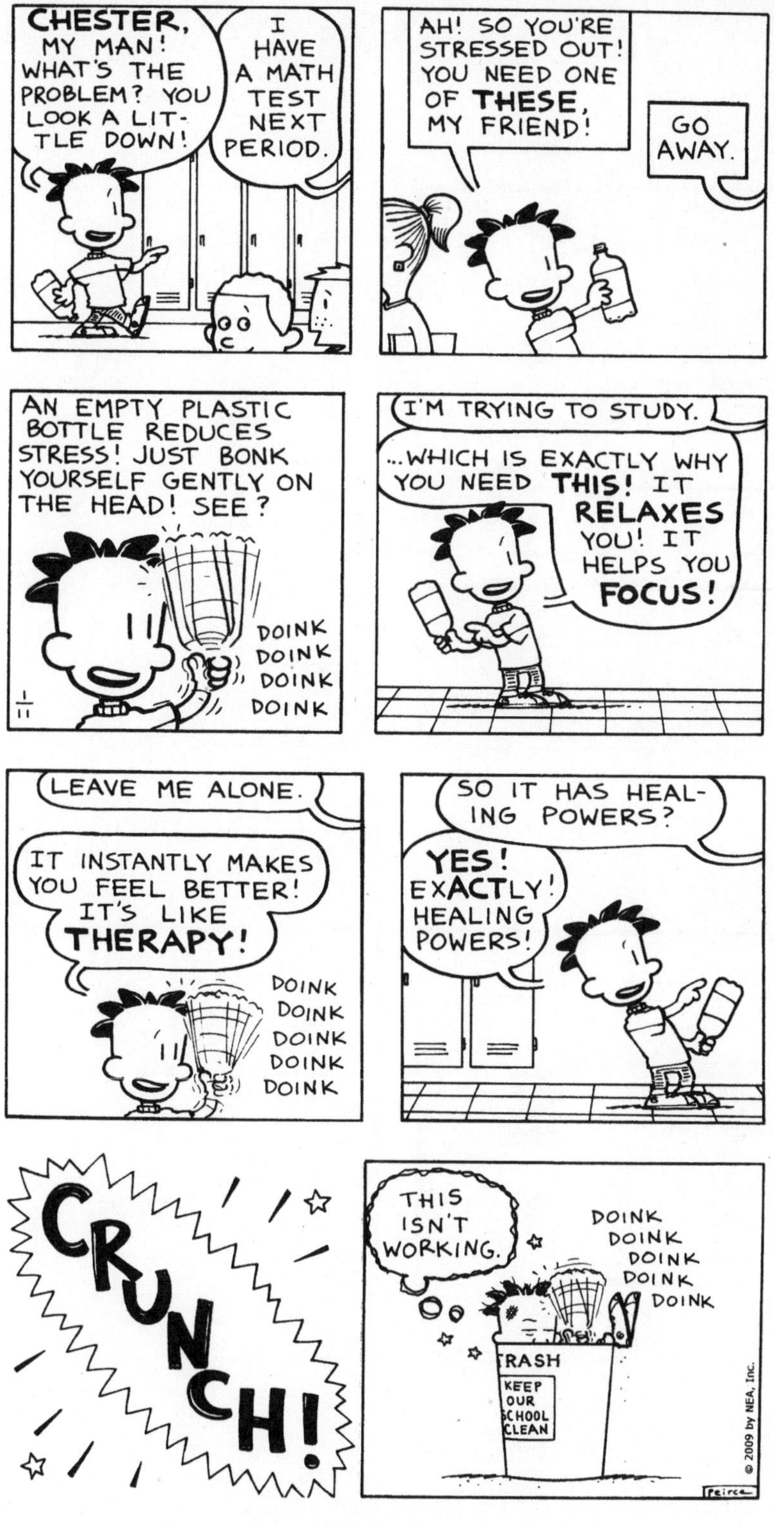

CHESTER, MY MAN! WHAT'S THE PROBLEM? YOU LOOK A LIT-TLE DOWN!
I HAVE A MATH TEST NEXT PERIOD.
AH! SO YOU'RE STRESSED OUT! YOU NEED ONE OF THESE, MY FRIEND!
GO AWAY.
AN EMPTY PLASTIC BOTTLE REDUCES STRESS! JUST BONK YOURSELF GENTLY ON THE HEAD! SEE?
DOINK DOINK DOINK DOINK
I'M TRYING TO STUDY.
...WHICH IS EXACTLY WHY YOU NEED THIS! IT RELAXES YOU! IT HELPS YOU FOCUS!
LEAVE ME ALONE.
IT INSTANTLY MAKES YOU FEEL BETTER! IT'S LIKE THERAPY!
DOINK DOINK DOINK DOINK DOINK
SO IT HAS HEAL-ING POWERS?
YES! EXACTLY! HEALING POWERS!
CRUNCH!
THIS ISN'T WORKING.
DOINK DOINK DOINK DOINK DOINK
TRASH
KEEP OUR SCHOOL CLEAN
© 2009 by NEA, Inc.
Peirce

WHAT'S IN A NAME?

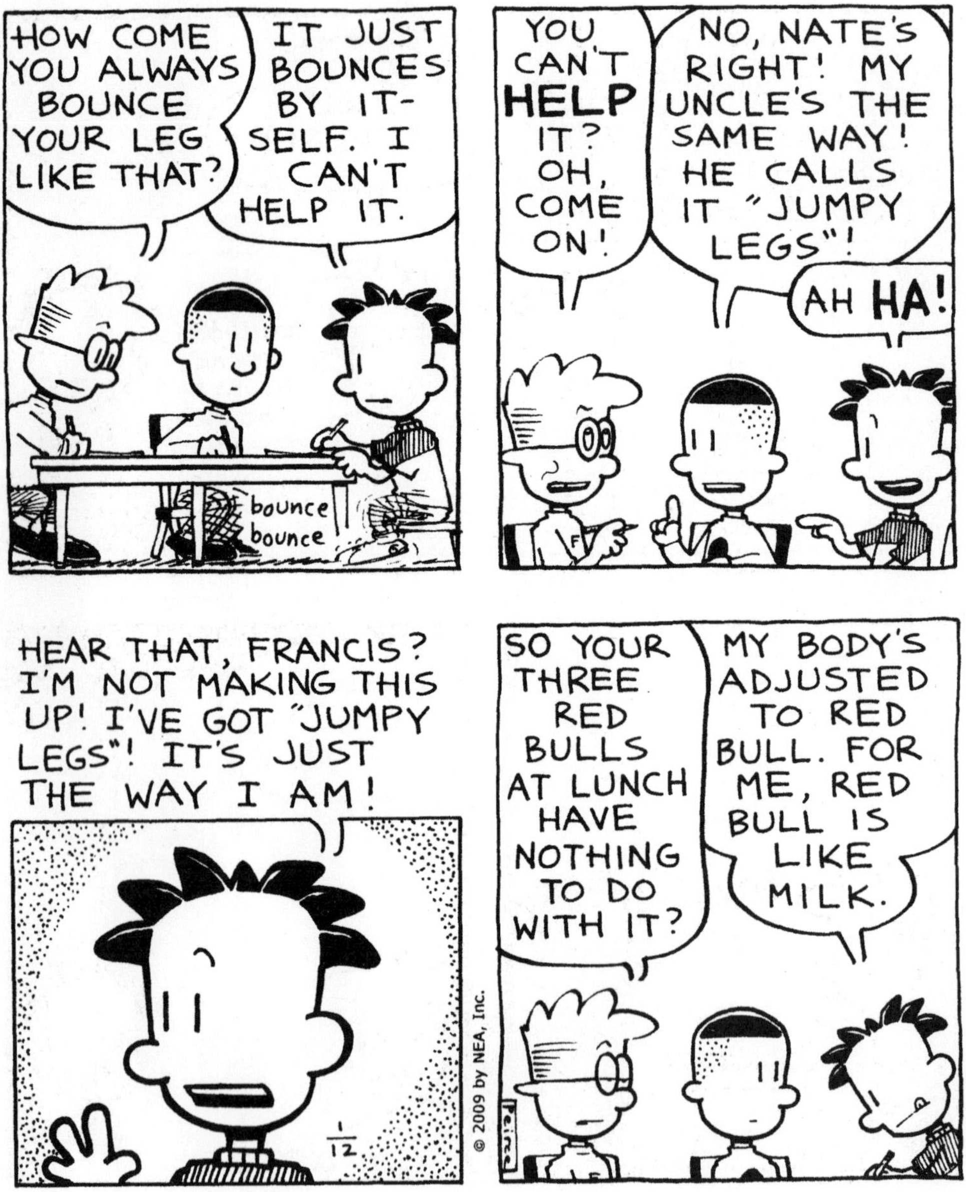
HOW COME YOU ALWAYS BOUNCE YOUR LEG LIKE THAT?
IT JUST BOUNCES BY IT-SELF. I CAN'T HELP IT.
bounce bounce
YOU CAN'T **HELP** IT? OH, COME ON!
NO, NATE'S RIGHT! MY UNCLE'S THE SAME WAY! HE CALLS IT "JUMPY LEGS"!
AH **HA!**
HEAR THAT, FRANCIS? I'M NOT MAKING THIS UP! I'VE GOT "JUMPY LEGS"! IT'S JUST THE WAY I AM!
1/12
© 2009 by NEA, Inc.
SO YOUR THREE RED BULLS AT LUNCH HAVE NOTHING TO DO WITH IT?
MY BODY'S ADJUSTED TO RED BULL. FOR ME, RED BULL IS LIKE MILK.
Peirce

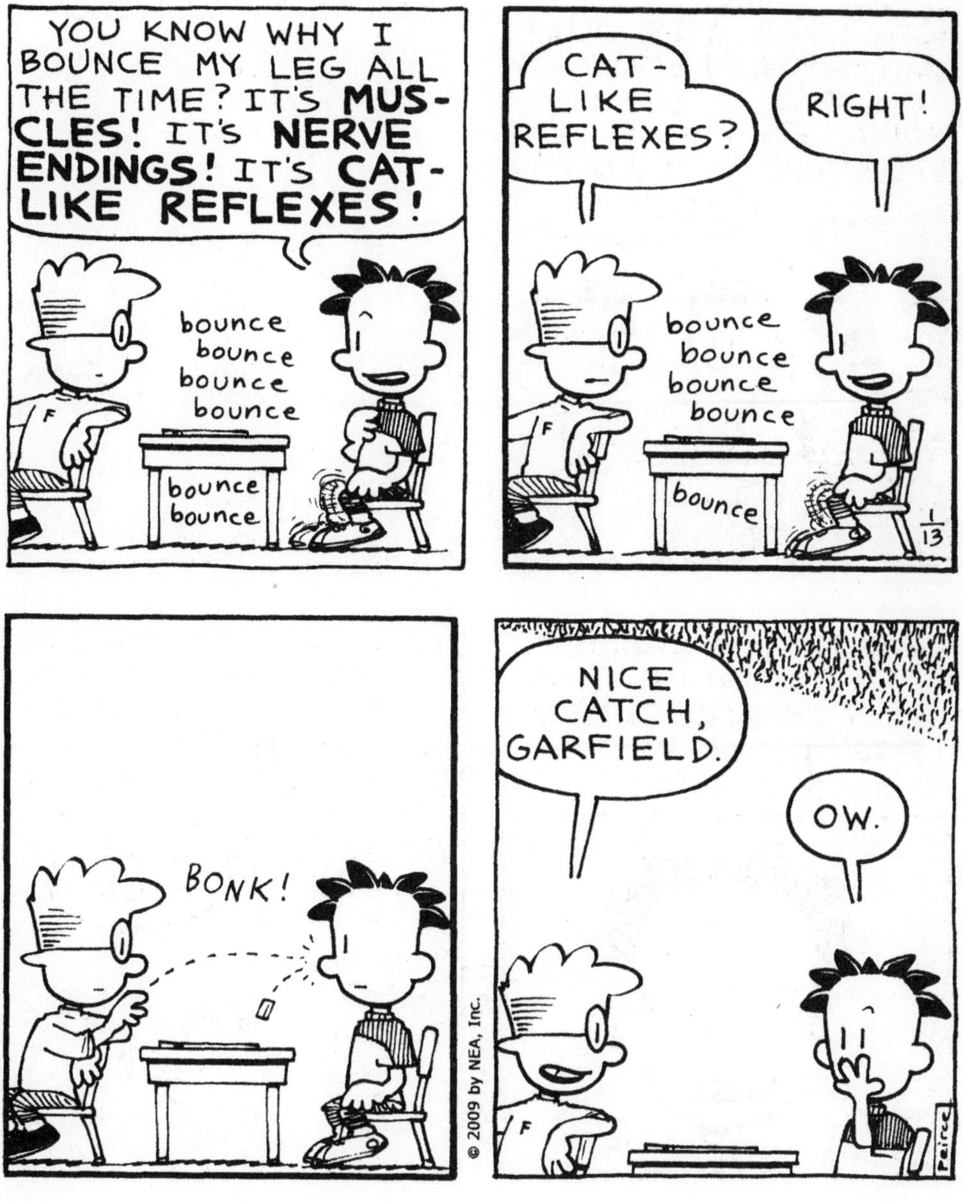

YOU KNOW WHY I BOUNCE MY LEG ALL THE TIME? IT'S **MUSCLES!** IT'S **NERVE ENDINGS!** IT'S **CAT-LIKE REFLEXES!**
bounce bounce bounce bounce
bounce bounce
CAT-LIKE REFLEXES?
RIGHT!
bounce bounce bounce bounce
bounce
1/13
BONK!
© 2009 by NEA, Inc.
NICE CATCH, GARFIELD.
OW.
PEIRCE

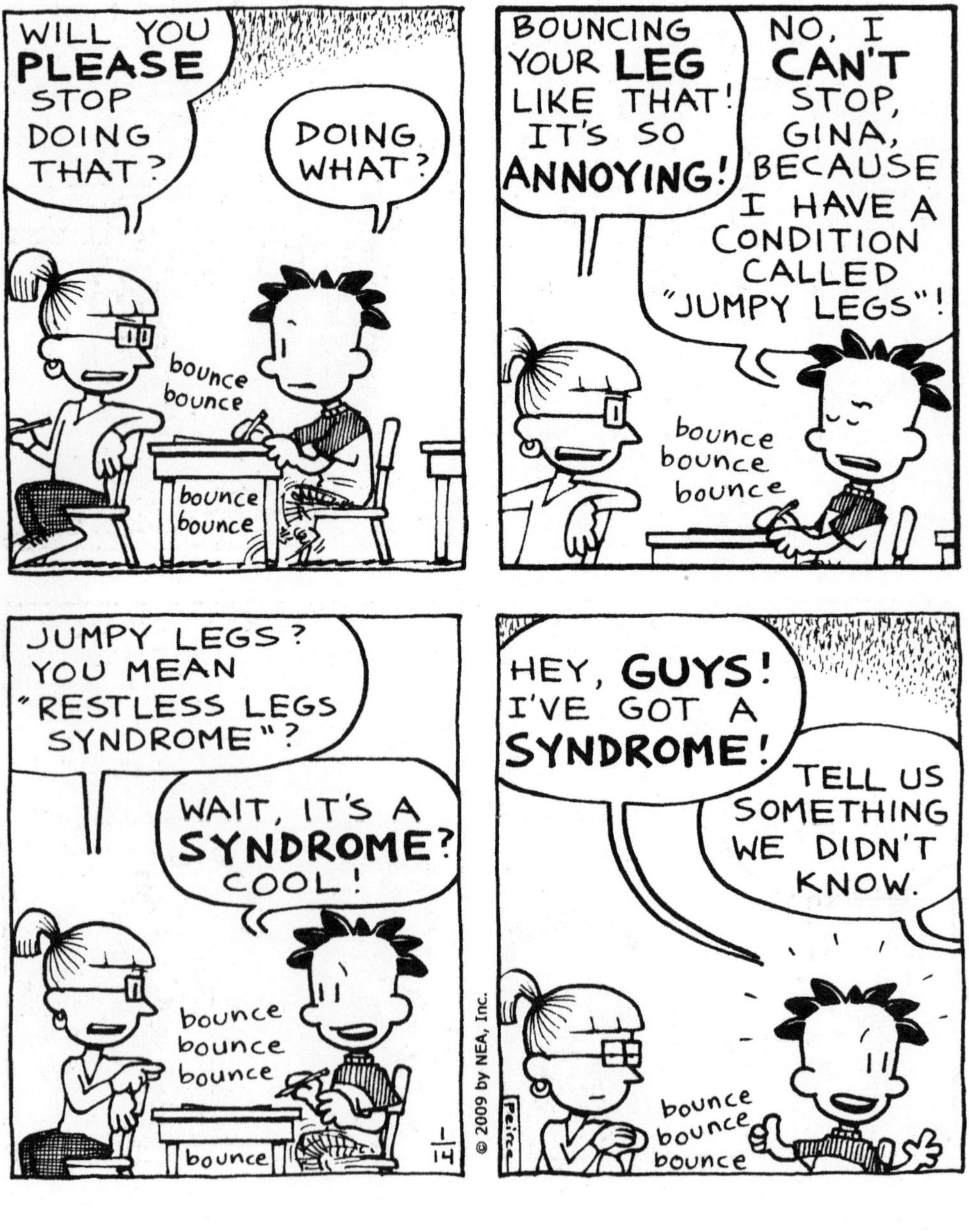
WILL YOU PLEASE STOP DOING THAT?
DOING WHAT?
bounce bounce
bounce bounce
BOUNCING YOUR LEG LIKE THAT! IT'S SO ANNOYING!
NO, I CAN'T STOP, GINA, BECAUSE I HAVE A CONDITION CALLED "JUMPY LEGS"!
bounce bounce bounce
JUMPY LEGS? YOU MEAN "RESTLESS LEGS SYNDROME"?
WAIT, IT'S A SYNDROME? COOL!
bounce bounce bounce
bounce
1/14
© 2009 by NEA, Inc.
Peirce
HEY, GUYS! I'VE GOT A SYNDROME!
TELL US SOMETHING WE DIDN'T KNOW.
bounce bounce bounce

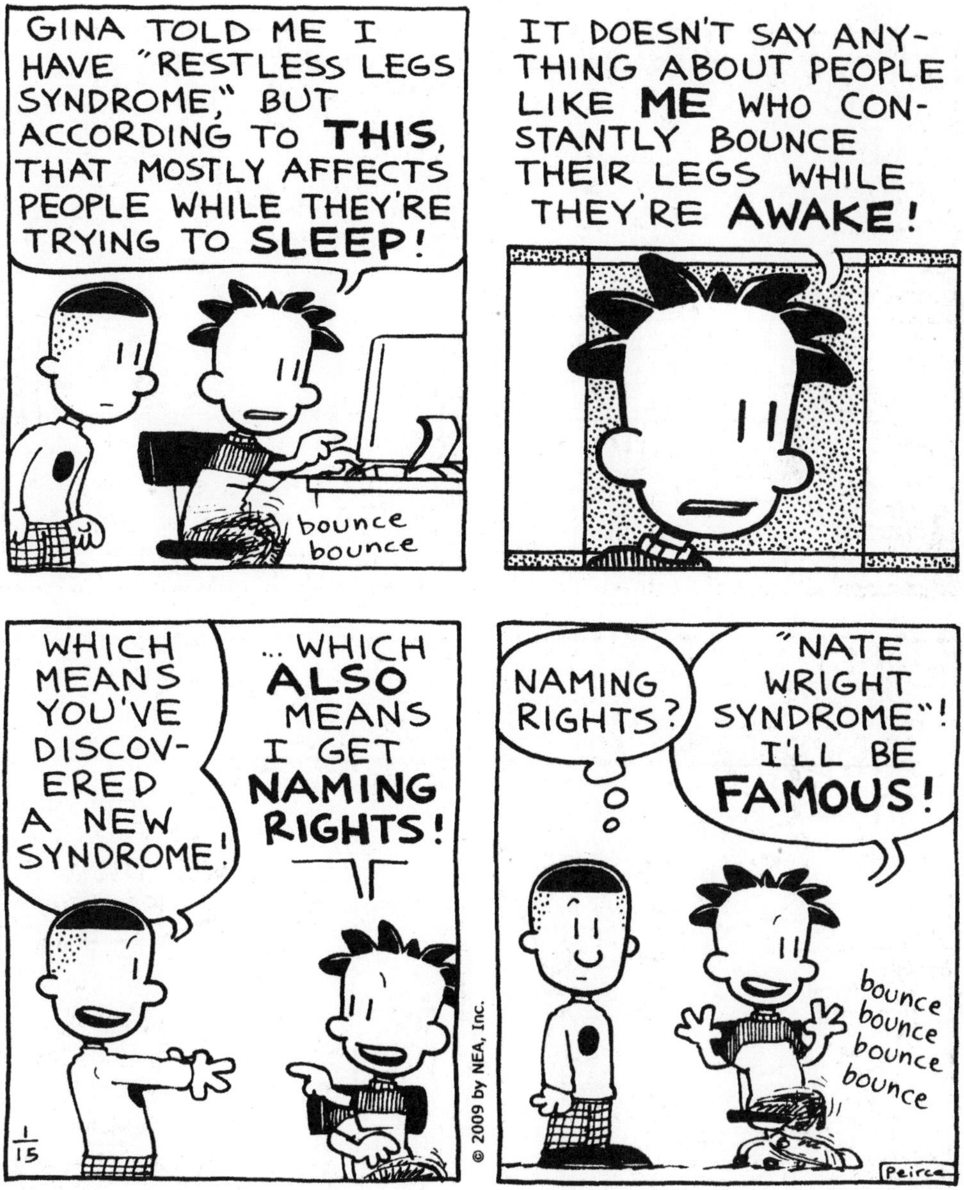
GINA TOLD ME I HAVE "RESTLESS LEGS SYNDROME," BUT ACCORDING TO **THIS**, THAT MOSTLY AFFECTS PEOPLE WHILE THEY'RE TRYING TO **SLEEP**!
bounce bounce
IT DOESN'T SAY ANYTHING ABOUT PEOPLE LIKE **ME** WHO CONSTANTLY BOUNCE THEIR LEGS WHILE THEY'RE **AWAKE**!
WHICH MEANS YOU'VE DISCOVERED A NEW SYNDROME!
...WHICH **ALSO** MEANS I GET **NAMING RIGHTS**!
1/15
© 2009 by NEA, Inc.
NAMING RIGHTS?
"NATE WRIGHT SYNDROME"! I'LL BE **FAMOUS**!
bounce bounce bounce bounce
Peirce

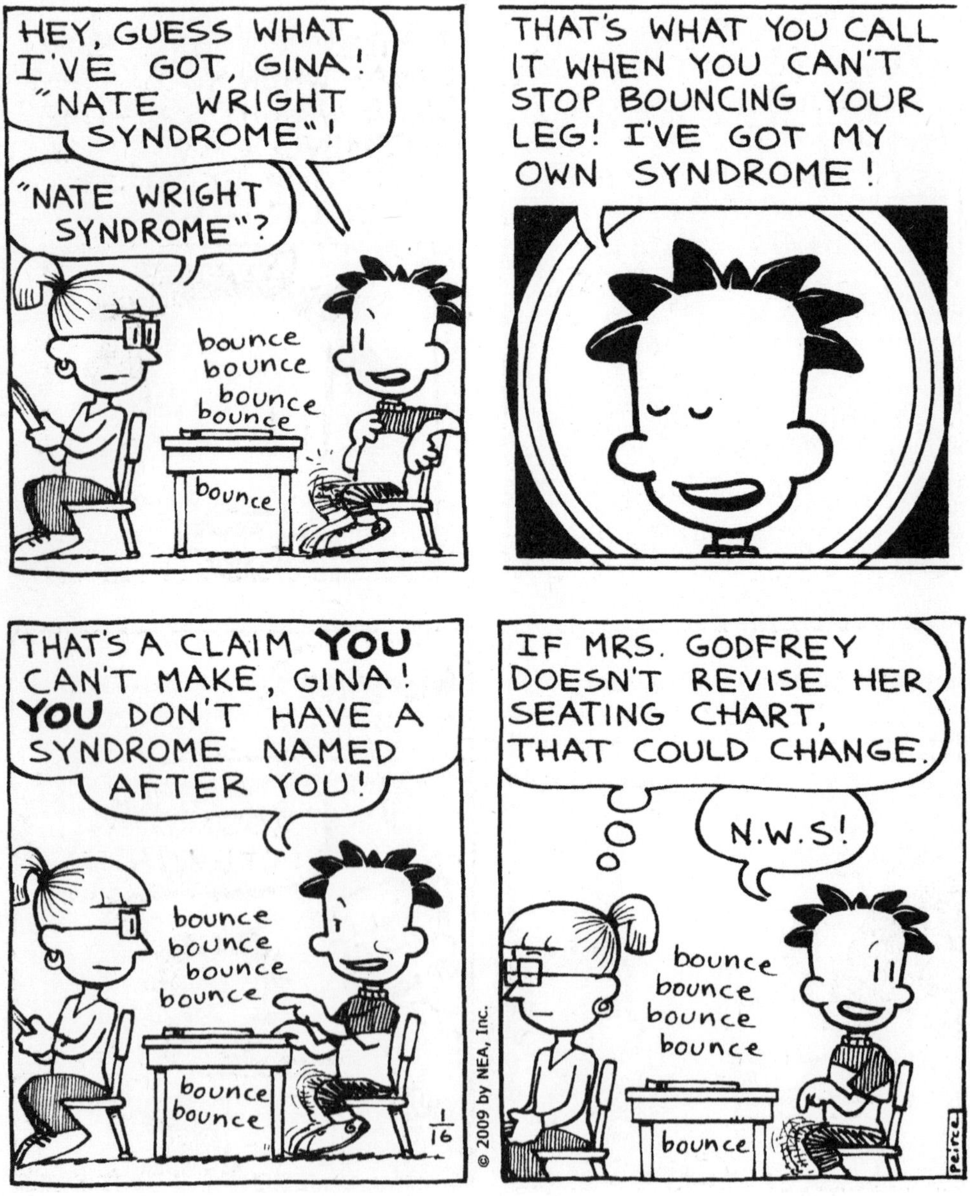
HEY, GUESS WHAT I'VE GOT, GINA! "NATE WRIGHT SYNDROME"!
"NATE WRIGHT SYNDROME"?
bounce
bounce
bounce
bounce
bounce
THAT'S WHAT YOU CALL IT WHEN YOU CAN'T STOP BOUNCING YOUR LEG! I'VE GOT MY OWN SYNDROME!
THAT'S A CLAIM **YOU** CAN'T MAKE, GINA! **YOU** DON'T HAVE A SYNDROME NAMED AFTER YOU!
bounce
bounce
bounce
bounce
bounce
bounce
1/16
© 2009 by NEA, Inc.
IF MRS. GODFREY DOESN'T REVISE HER SEATING CHART, THAT COULD CHANGE.
N.W.S!
bounce
bounce
bounce
bounce
bounce
Peirce

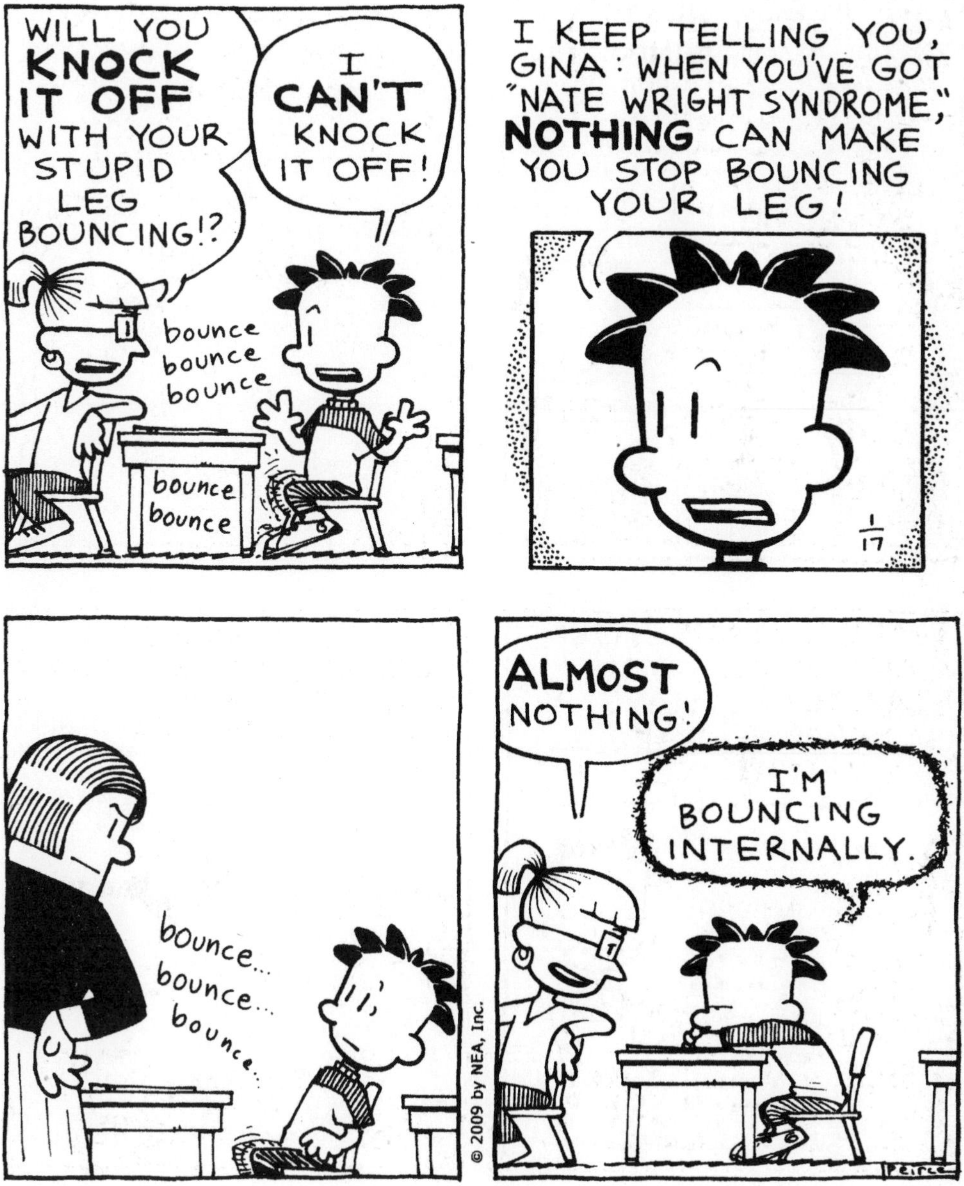
WILL YOU KNOCK IT OFF WITH YOUR STUPID LEG BOUNCING!?
I CAN'T KNOCK IT OFF!
bounce bounce bounce
bounce bounce
I KEEP TELLING YOU, GINA: WHEN YOU'VE GOT "NATE WRIGHT SYNDROME," NOTHING CAN MAKE YOU STOP BOUNCING YOUR LEG!
1/17
bounce... bounce... bounce...
© 2009 by NEA, Inc.
ALMOST NOTHING!
I'M BOUNCING INTERNALLY.
PEIRCE

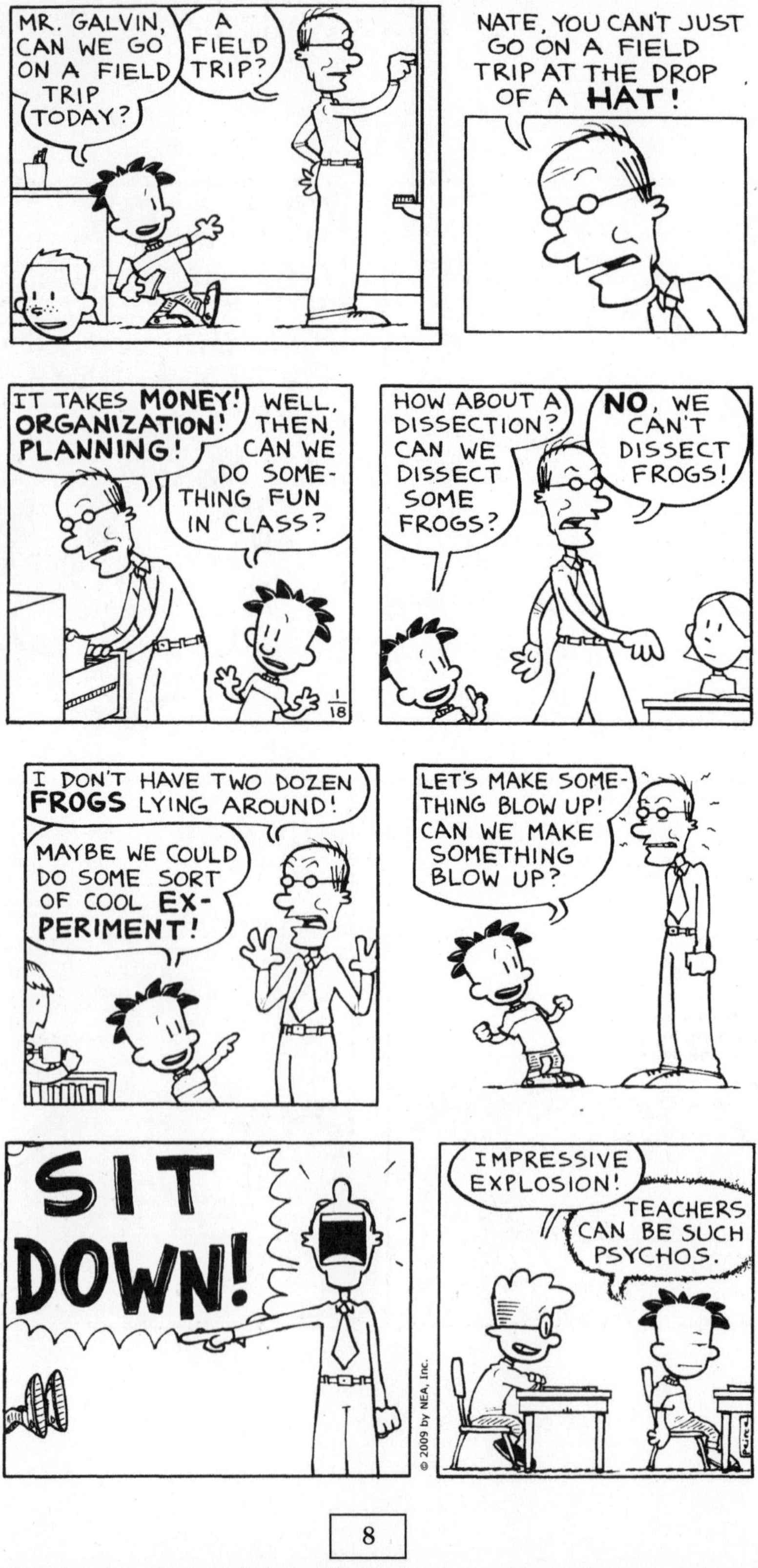
MR. GALVIN, CAN WE GO ON A FIELD TRIP TODAY?
A FIELD TRIP?
NATE, YOU CAN'T JUST GO ON A FIELD TRIP AT THE DROP OF A HAT!
IT TAKES MONEY! ORGANIZATION! PLANNING!
WELL, THEN, CAN WE DO SOME-THING FUN IN CLASS?
1/18
HOW ABOUT A DISSECTION? CAN WE DISSECT SOME FROGS?
NO, WE CAN'T DISSECT FROGS!
I DON'T HAVE TWO DOZEN FROGS LYING AROUND!
MAYBE WE COULD DO SOME SORT OF COOL EX-PERIMENT!
LET'S MAKE SOME-THING BLOW UP! CAN WE MAKE SOMETHING BLOW UP?
SIT DOWN!
© 2009 by NEA, Inc.
IMPRESSIVE EXPLOSION!
TEACHERS CAN BE SUCH PSYCHOS.

OUTRAGED!

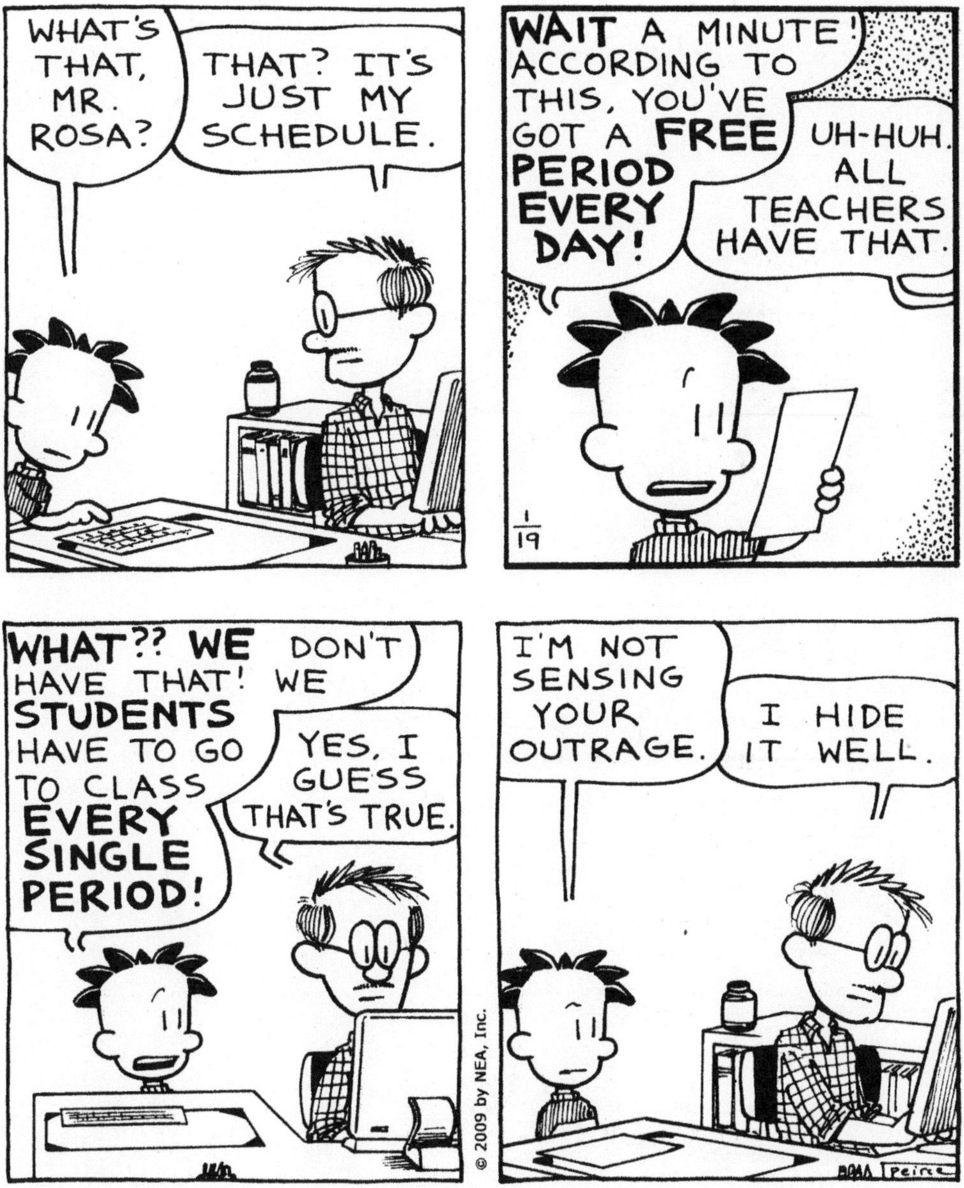
WHAT'S THAT, MR. ROSA?
THAT? IT'S JUST MY SCHEDULE.
WAIT A MINUTE! ACCORDING TO THIS, YOU'VE GOT A FREE PERIOD EVERY DAY!
UH-HUH. ALL TEACHERS HAVE THAT.
1/19
WHAT?? WE DON'T HAVE THAT! WE STUDENTS HAVE TO GO TO CLASS EVERY SINGLE PERIOD!
YES, I GUESS THAT'S TRUE.
I'M NOT SENSING YOUR OUTRAGE.
I HIDE IT WELL.
© 2009 by NEA, Inc.
Peirce

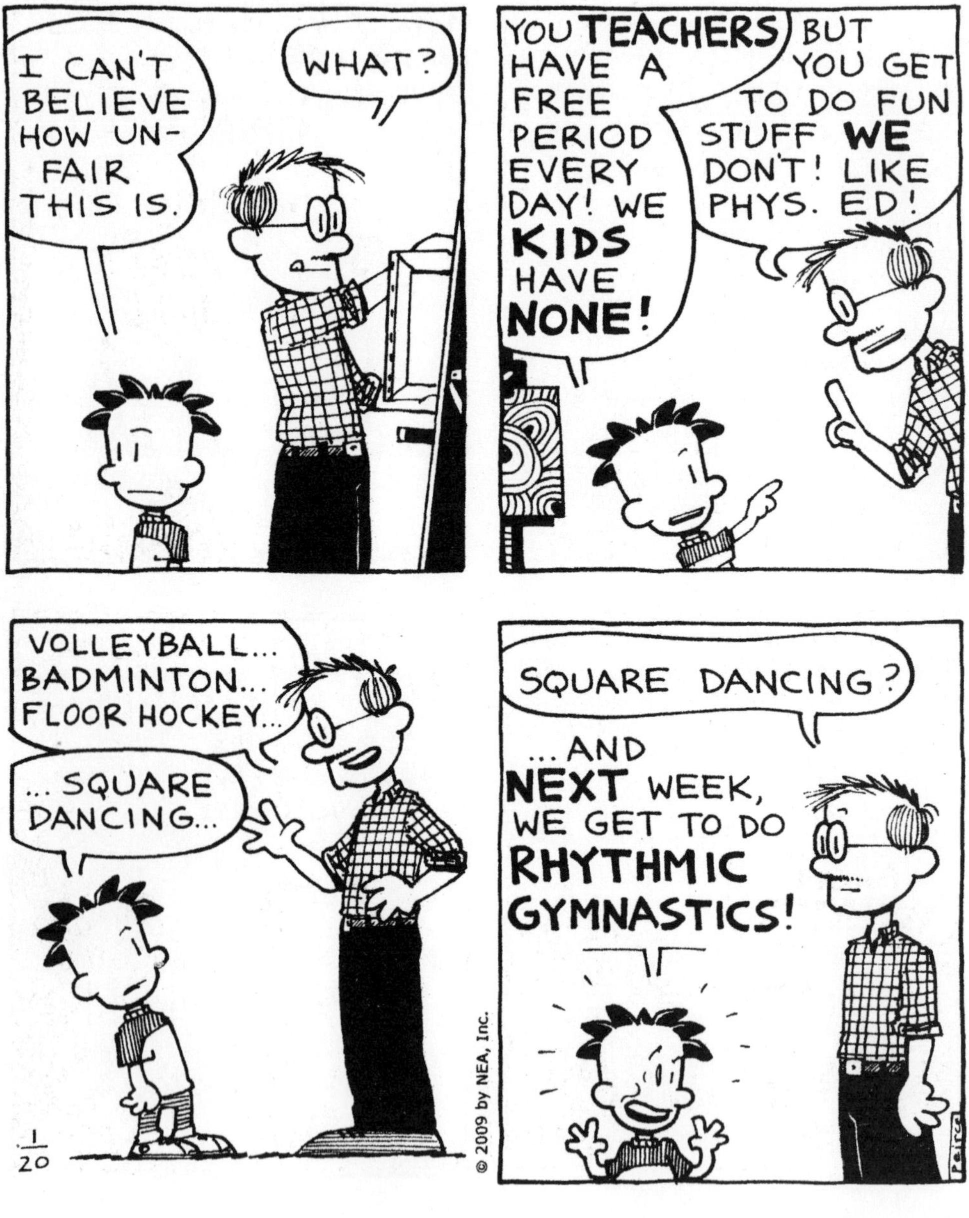
I CAN'T BELIEVE HOW UN-FAIR THIS IS.
WHAT?
YOU TEACHERS HAVE A FREE PERIOD EVERY DAY! WE KIDS HAVE NONE!
BUT YOU GET TO DO FUN STUFF WE DON'T! LIKE PHYS. ED!
VOLLEYBALL... BADMINTON... FLOOR HOCKEY...
... SQUARE DANCING...
1/20
© 2009 by NEA, Inc.
SQUARE DANCING?
... AND NEXT WEEK, WE GET TO DO RHYTHMIC GYMNASTICS!
Peirce

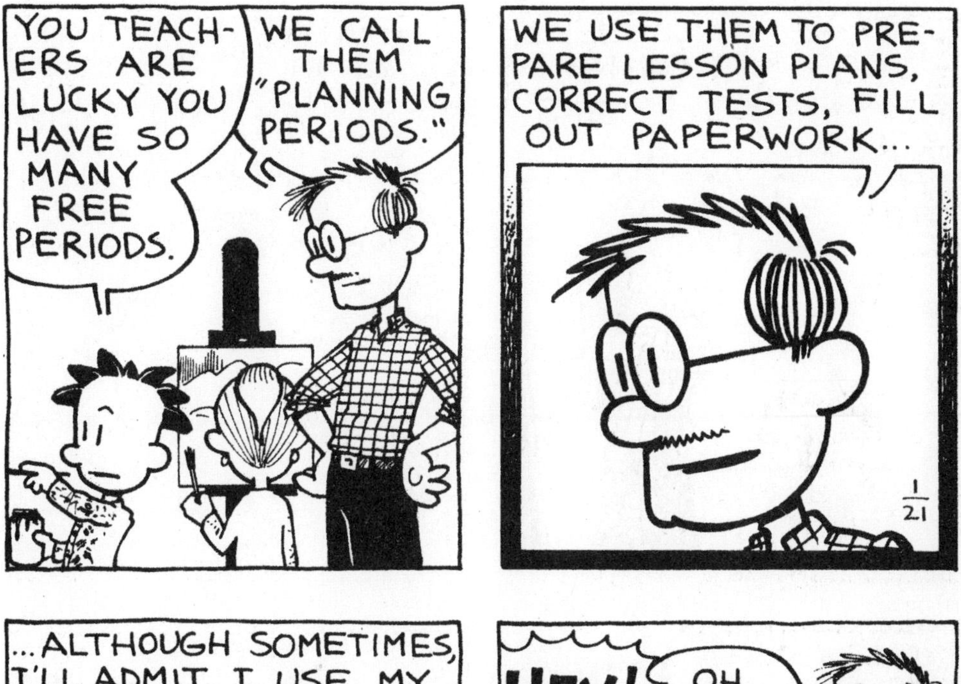
YOU TEACHERS ARE LUCKY YOU HAVE SO MANY FREE PERIODS.
WE CALL THEM "PLANNING PERIODS."
WE USE THEM TO PREPARE LESSON PLANS, CORRECT TESTS, FILL OUT PAPERWORK...
1/21
...ALTHOUGH SOMETIMES, I'LL ADMIT, I USE MY PLANNING PERIOD JUST TO RECOVER.
RECOVER? RECOVER FROM **WHAT**?
SPLOOSH!
HEY!
OH, RELAX, CHAD. IT'S ACRYLIC.
Peirce

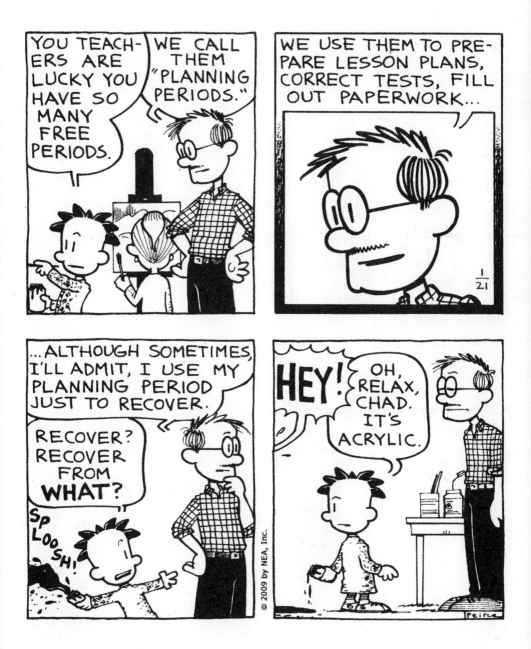

ALL IN

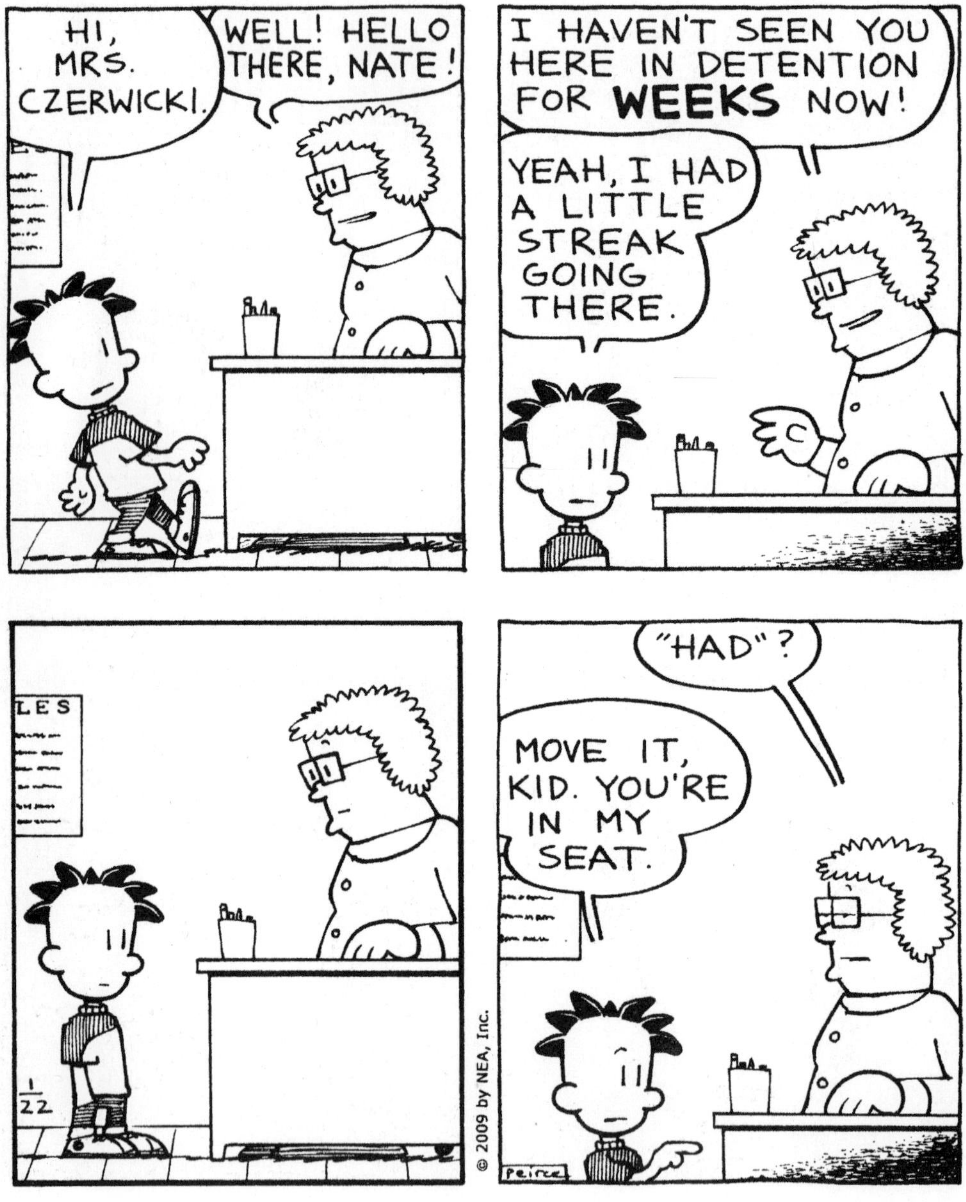
HI, MRS. CZERWICKI.
WELL! HELLO THERE, NATE!
I HAVEN'T SEEN YOU HERE IN DETENTION FOR **WEEKS** NOW!
YEAH, I HAD A LITTLE STREAK GOING THERE.
"HAD"?
MOVE IT, KID. YOU'RE IN MY SEAT.
1/22
© 2009 by NEA, Inc.
Peirce

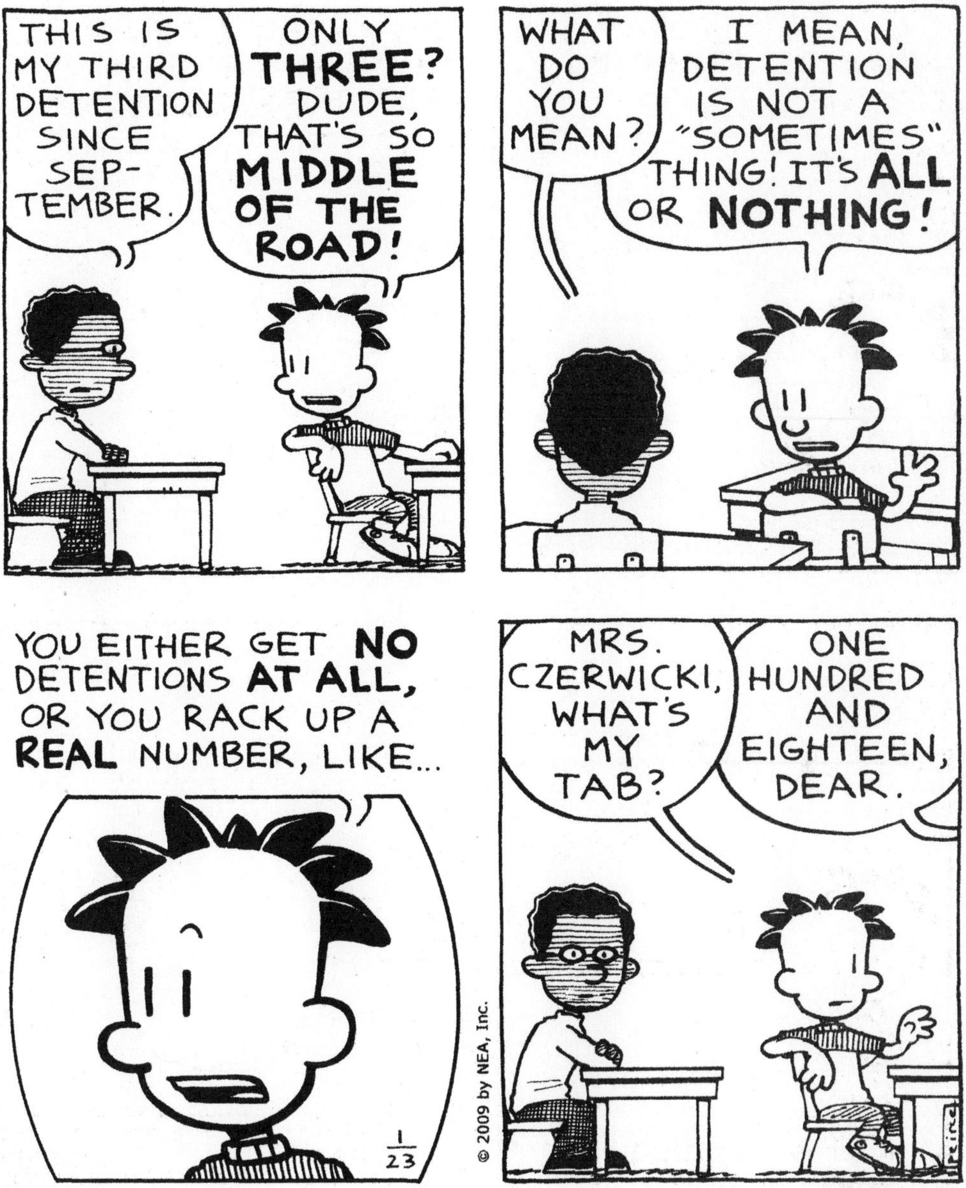
THIS IS MY THIRD DETENTION SINCE SEP-TEMBER.
ONLY THREE? DUDE, THAT'S SO MIDDLE OF THE ROAD!
WHAT DO YOU MEAN?
I MEAN, DETENTION IS NOT A "SOMETIMES" THING! IT'S ALL OR NOTHING!
YOU EITHER GET NO DETENTIONS AT ALL, OR YOU RACK UP A REAL NUMBER, LIKE...
MRS. CZERWICKI, WHAT'S MY TAB?
ONE HUNDRED AND EIGHTEEN, DEAR.
1/23
© 2009 by NEA, Inc.
PEIRCE

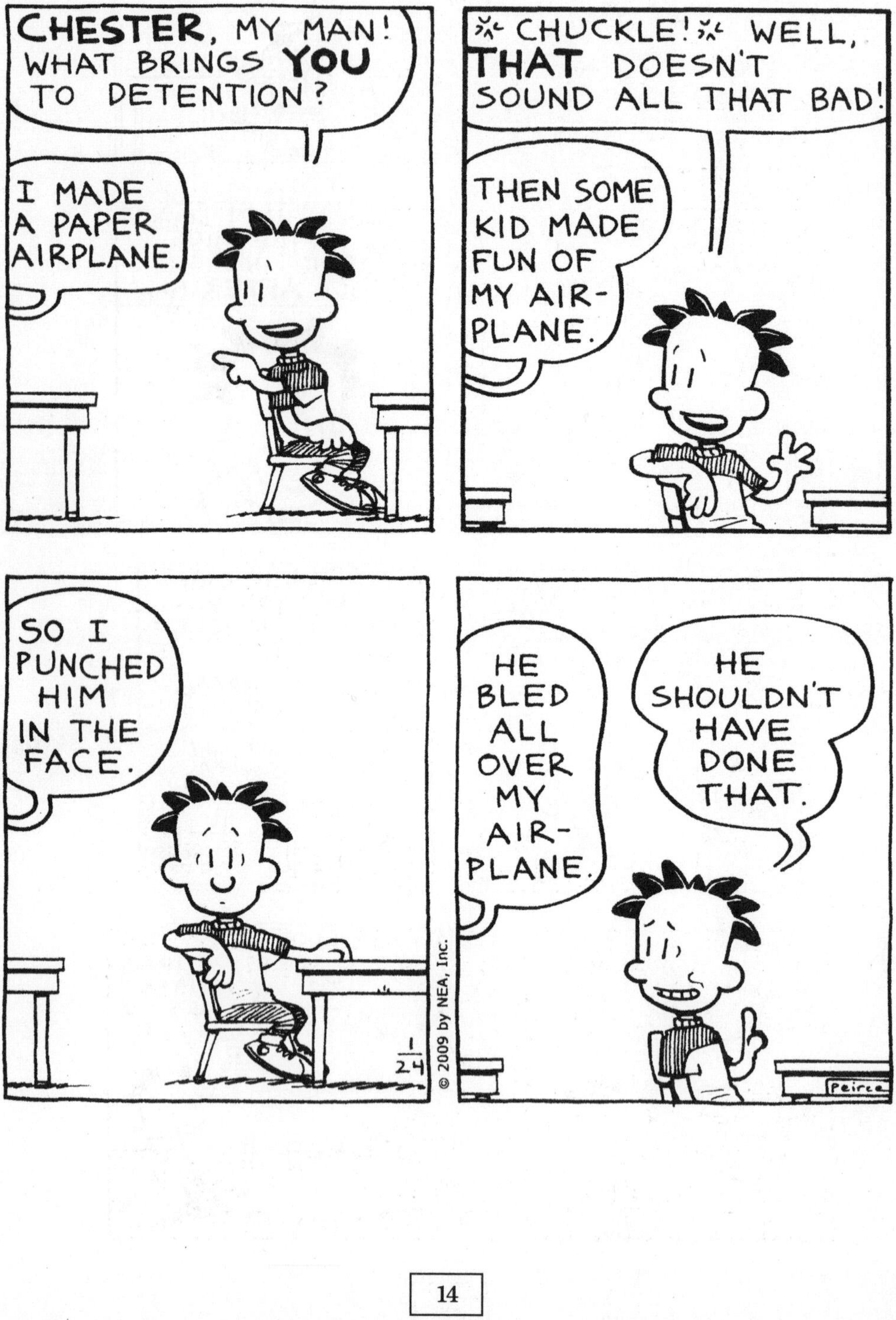
CHESTER, MY MAN! WHAT BRINGS YOU TO DETENTION?
I MADE A PAPER AIRPLANE.
CHUCKLE! WELL, THAT DOESN'T SOUND ALL THAT BAD!
THEN SOME KID MADE FUN OF MY AIR-PLANE.
SO I PUNCHED HIM IN THE FACE.
1/24
© 2009 by NEA, Inc.
HE BLED ALL OVER MY AIR-PLANE.
HE SHOULDN'T HAVE DONE THAT.
Peirce

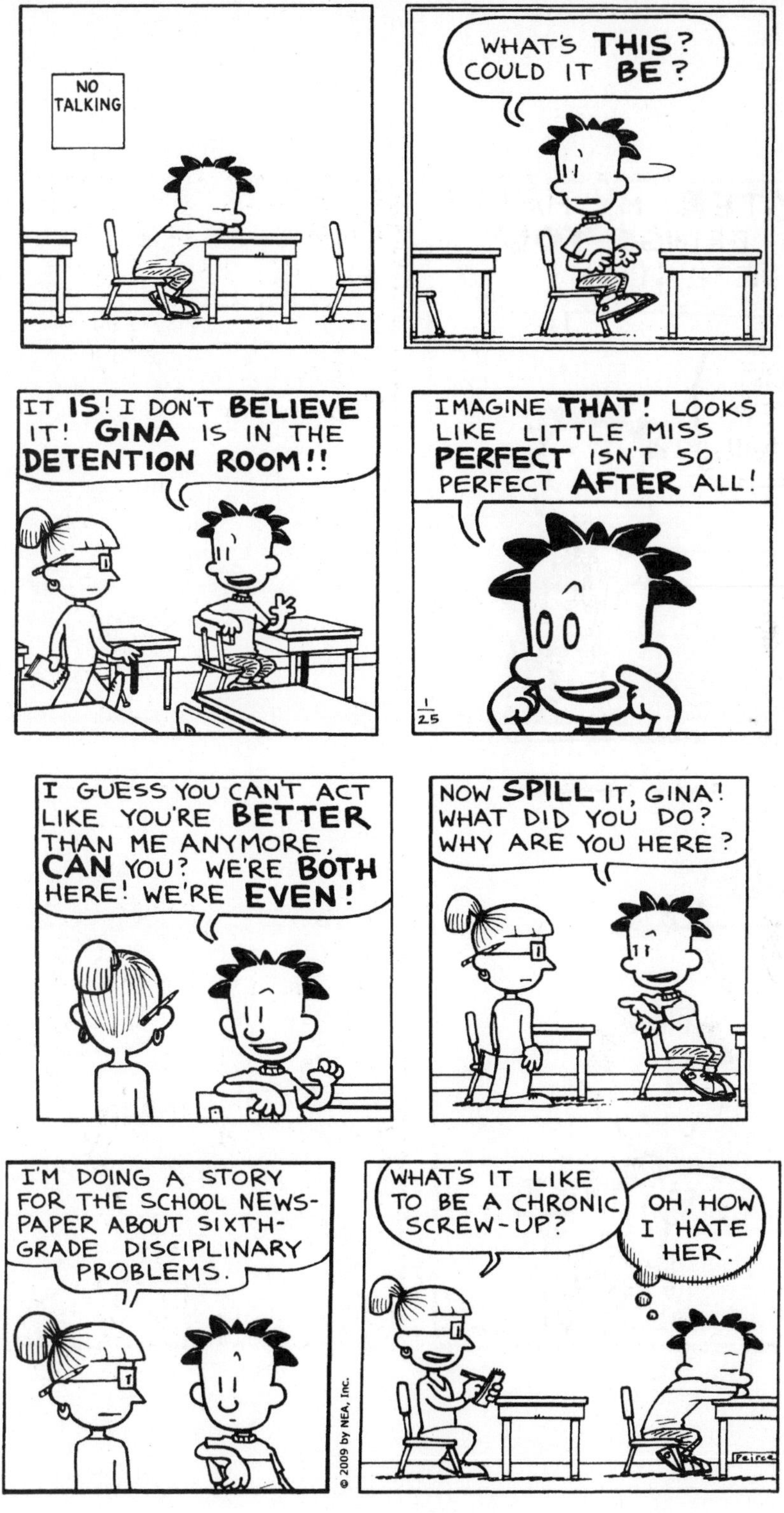
NO TALKING
WHAT'S THIS? COULD IT BE?
IT IS! I DON'T BELIEVE IT! GINA IS IN THE DETENTION ROOM!!
IMAGINE THAT! LOOKS LIKE LITTLE MISS PERFECT ISN'T SO PERFECT AFTER ALL!
1/25
I GUESS YOU CAN'T ACT LIKE YOU'RE BETTER THAN ME ANYMORE, CAN YOU? WE'RE BOTH HERE! WE'RE EVEN!
NOW SPILL IT, GINA! WHAT DID YOU DO? WHY ARE YOU HERE?
I'M DOING A STORY FOR THE SCHOOL NEWS-PAPER ABOUT SIXTH-GRADE DISCIPLINARY PROBLEMS.
© 2009 by NEA, Inc.
WHAT'S IT LIKE TO BE A CHRONIC SCREW-UP?
OH, HOW I HATE HER.
Peirce

SAY CHEESE!

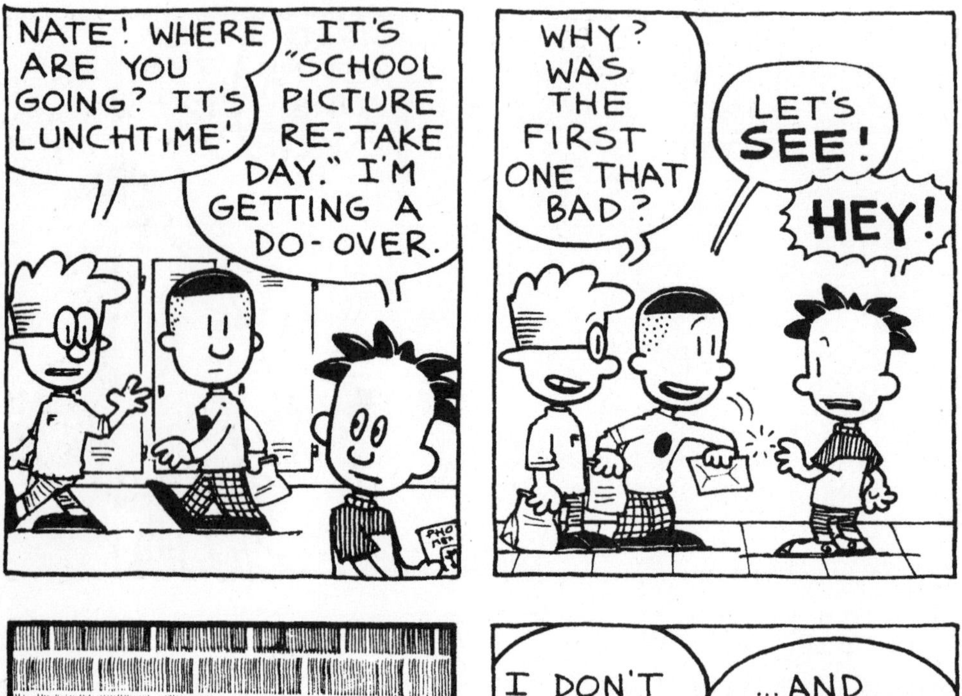
NATE! WHERE ARE YOU GOING? IT'S LUNCHTIME!
IT'S "SCHOOL PICTURE RE-TAKE DAY." I'M GETTING A DO-OVER.
WHY? WAS THE FIRST ONE THAT BAD?
LET'S **SEE!**
HEY!
I DON'T KNOW WHETHER TO LAUGH OR THROW UP.
...AND APPARENTLY, NEITHER DID **YOU!**
1/26
© 2009 by NEA, Inc.
Peirce

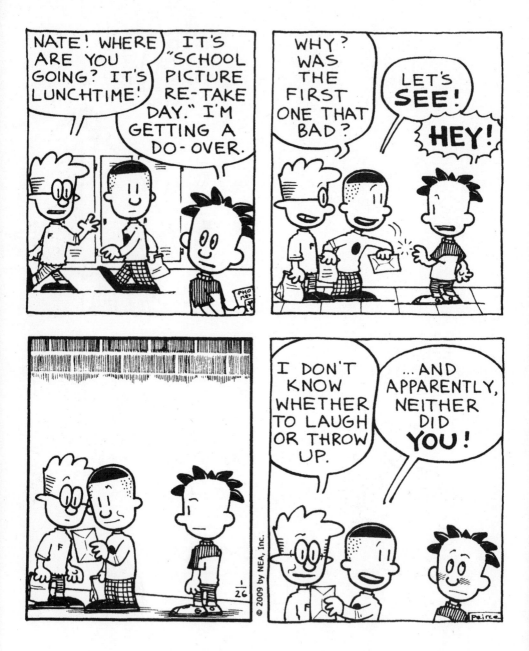

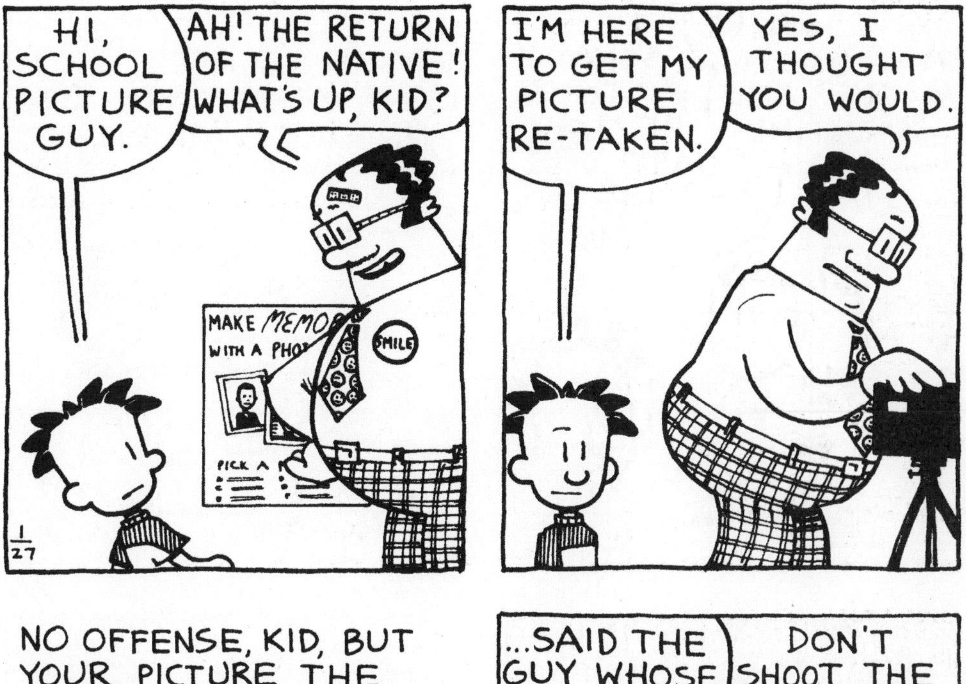
HI, SCHOOL PICTURE GUY.
AH! THE RETURN OF THE NATIVE! WHAT'S UP, KID?
MAKE MEMO
WITH A PHO
SMILE
PICK A
1/27
I'M HERE TO GET MY PICTURE RE-TAKEN.
YES, I THOUGHT YOU WOULD.
NO OFFENSE, KID, BUT YOUR PICTURE THE **FIRST** TIME AROUND WAS A COMPLETE **DISASTER**!!
...SAID THE GUY WHOSE JOB IT IS TO MAKE PEOPLE LOOK **GOOD** IN THEIR PICTURES!
DON'T SHOOT THE MESSENGER, KID. ALL I DO IS PRESS THE BUTTON.
© 2009 by NEA, Inc.
Peirce

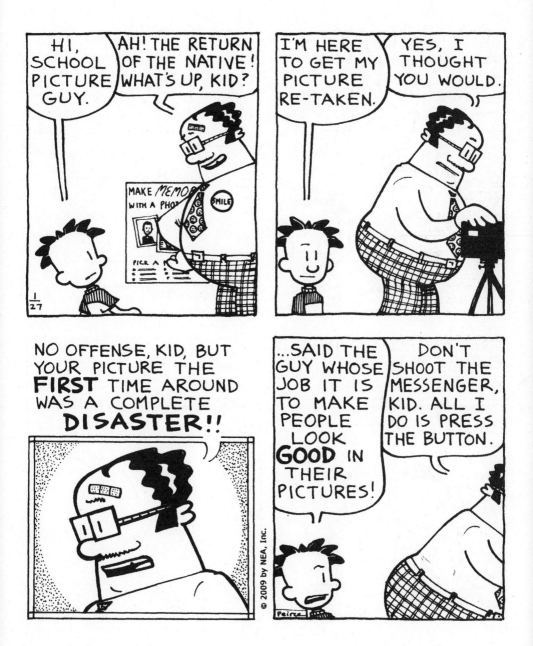

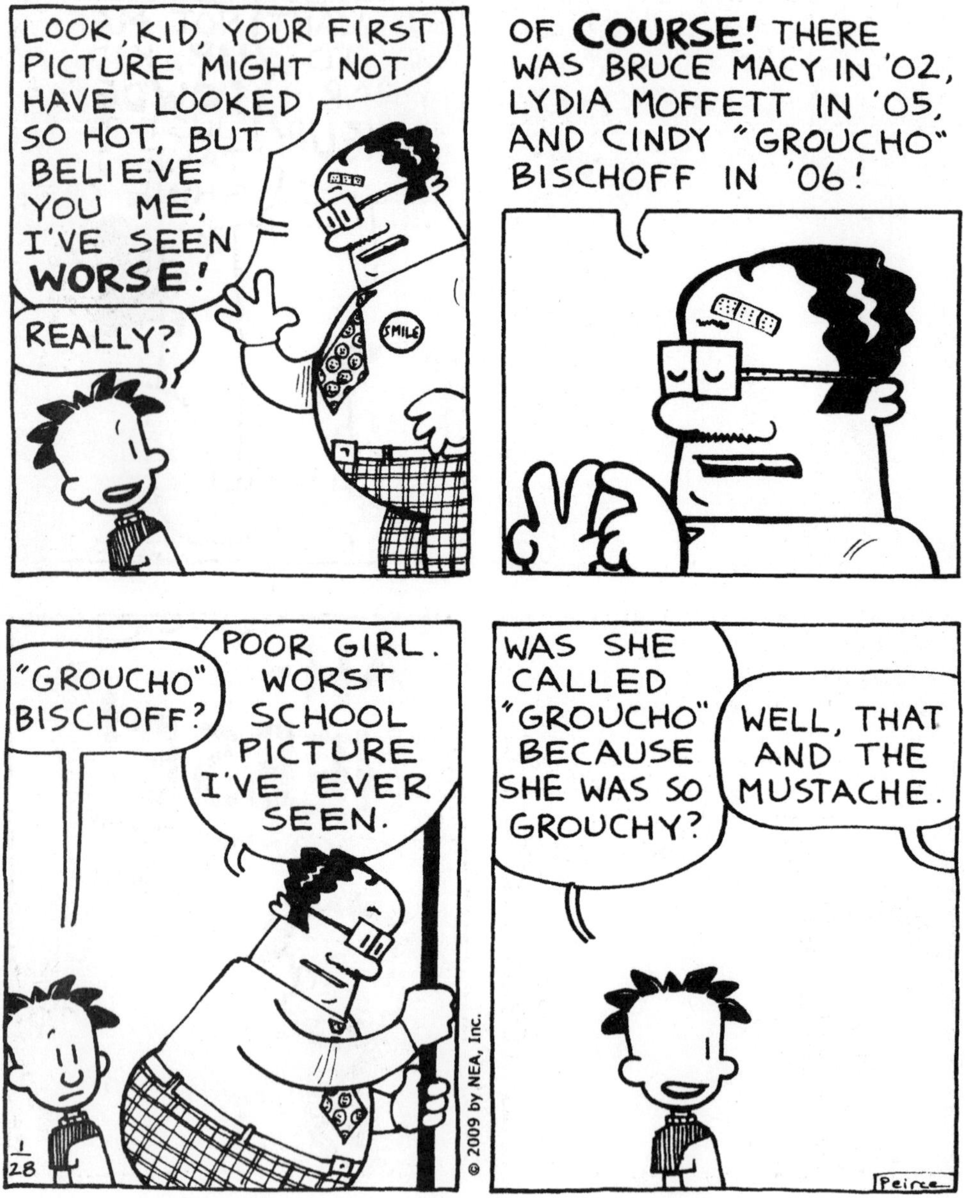
LOOK, KID, YOUR FIRST PICTURE MIGHT NOT HAVE LOOKED SO HOT, BUT BELIEVE YOU ME, I'VE SEEN **WORSE**!
REALLY?
SMILE
OF **COURSE!** THERE WAS BRUCE MACY IN '02, LYDIA MOFFETT IN '05, AND CINDY "GROUCHO" BISCHOFF IN '06!
"GROUCHO" BISCHOFF?
POOR GIRL. WORST SCHOOL PICTURE I'VE EVER SEEN.
1/28
WAS SHE CALLED "GROUCHO" BECAUSE SHE WAS SO GROUCHY?
WELL, THAT AND THE MUSTACHE.
Peirce

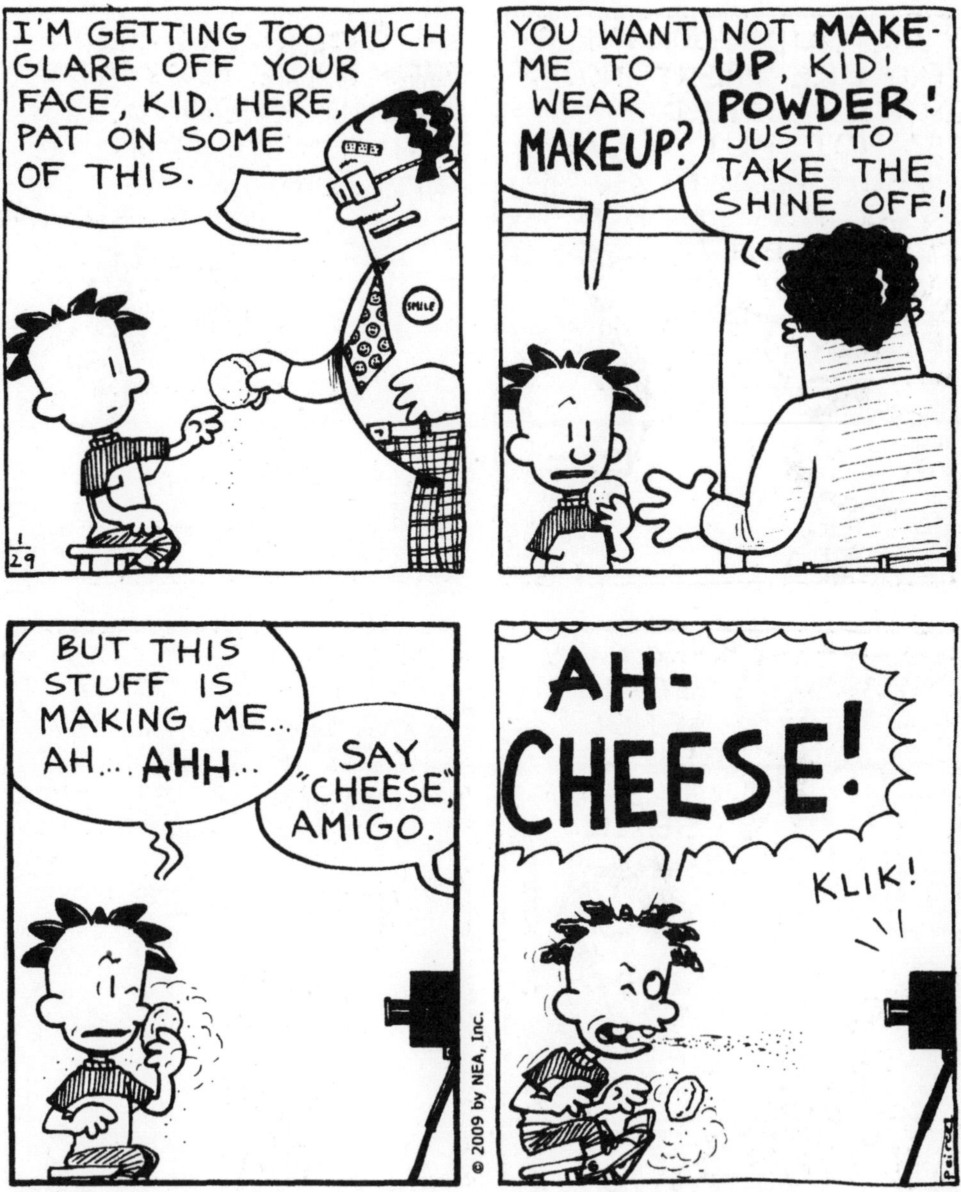
I'M GETTING TOO MUCH GLARE OFF YOUR FACE, KID. HERE, PAT ON SOME OF THIS.
SMILE
1/29
YOU WANT ME TO WEAR MAKEUP?
NOT MAKE-UP, KID! POWDER! JUST TO TAKE THE SHINE OFF!
BUT THIS STUFF IS MAKING ME... AH.... AHH...
SAY "CHEESE," AMIGO.
AH-CHEESE!
KLIK!
© 2009 by NEA, Inc.
PEIRCE

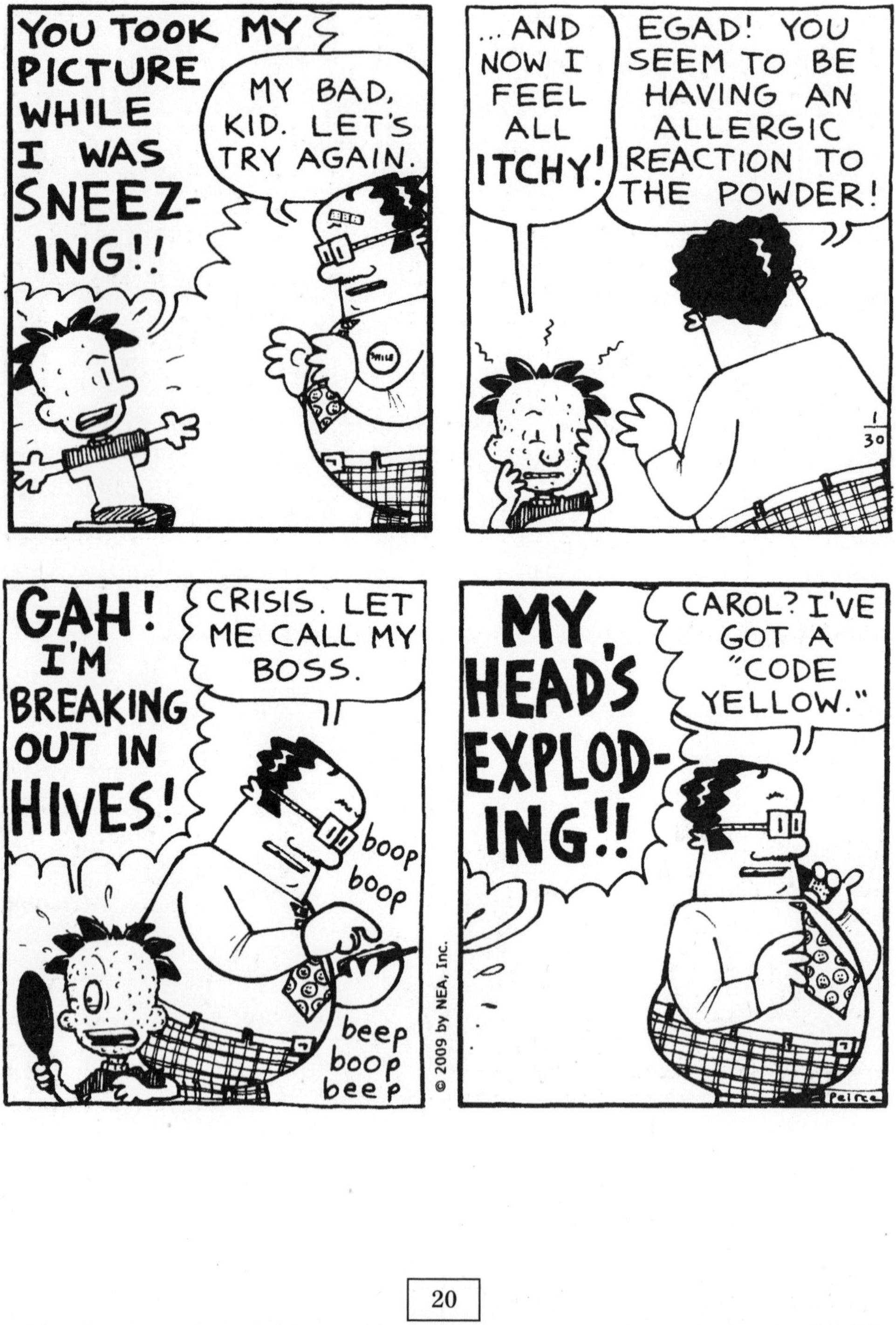
YOU TOOK MY PICTURE WHILE I WAS SNEEZ-ING!!
MY BAD, KID. LET'S TRY AGAIN.
SMILE
...AND NOW I FEEL ALL ITCHY!
EGAD! YOU SEEM TO BE HAVING AN ALLERGIC REACTION TO THE POWDER!
1/30
GAH! I'M BREAKING OUT IN HIVES!
CRISIS. LET ME CALL MY BOSS.
boop boop
beep boop beep
© 2009 by NEA, Inc.
MY HEAD'S EXPLOD-ING!!
CAROL? I'VE GOT A "CODE YELLOW."
Peirce

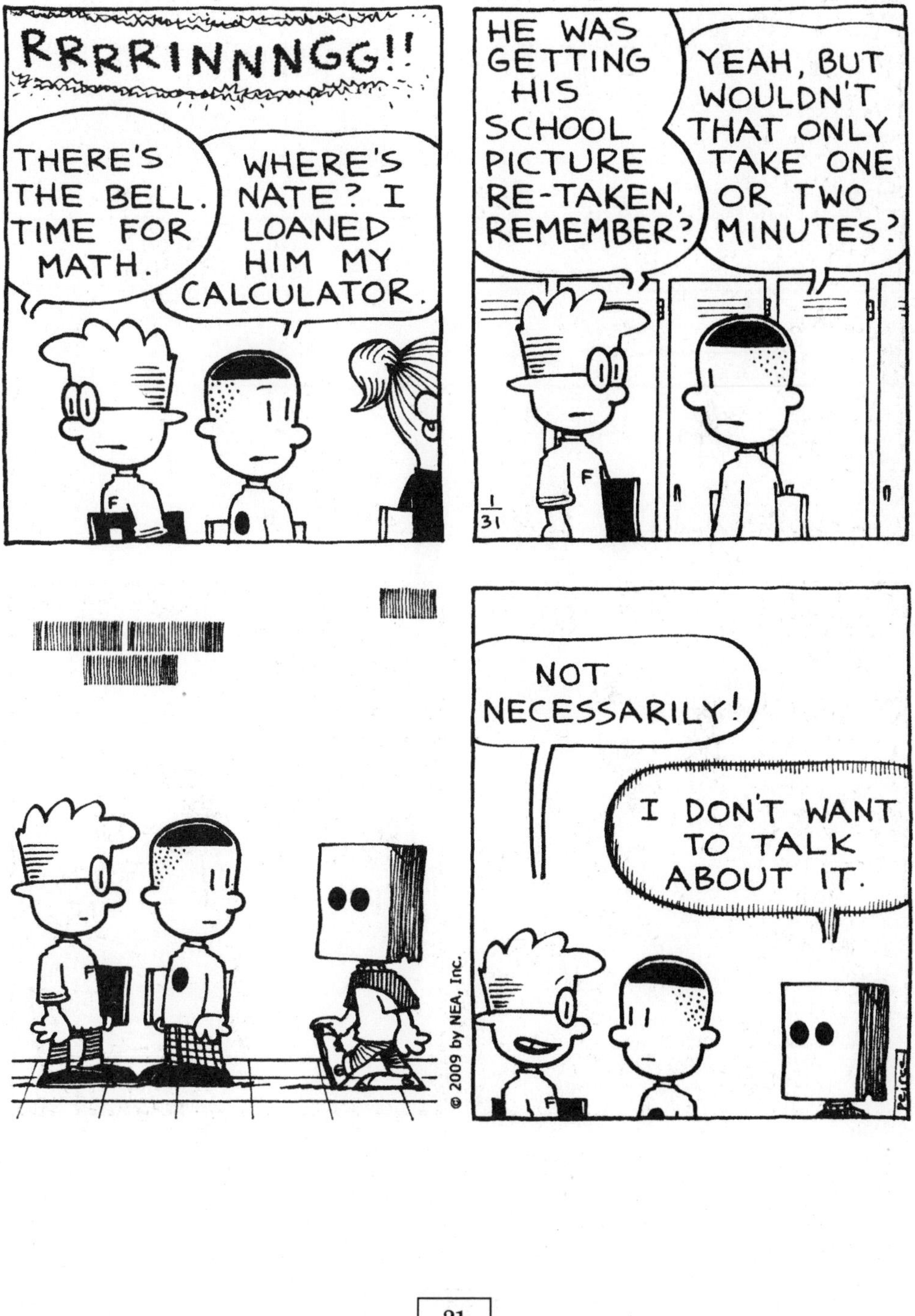
RRRRINNNGG!!
THERE'S THE BELL. TIME FOR MATH.
WHERE'S NATE? I LOANED HIM MY CALCULATOR.
HE WAS GETTING HIS SCHOOL PICTURE RE-TAKEN, REMEMBER?
YEAH, BUT WOULDN'T THAT ONLY TAKE ONE OR TWO MINUTES?
[redacted]
[redacted]
NOT NECESSARILY!
I DON'T WANT TO TALK ABOUT IT.

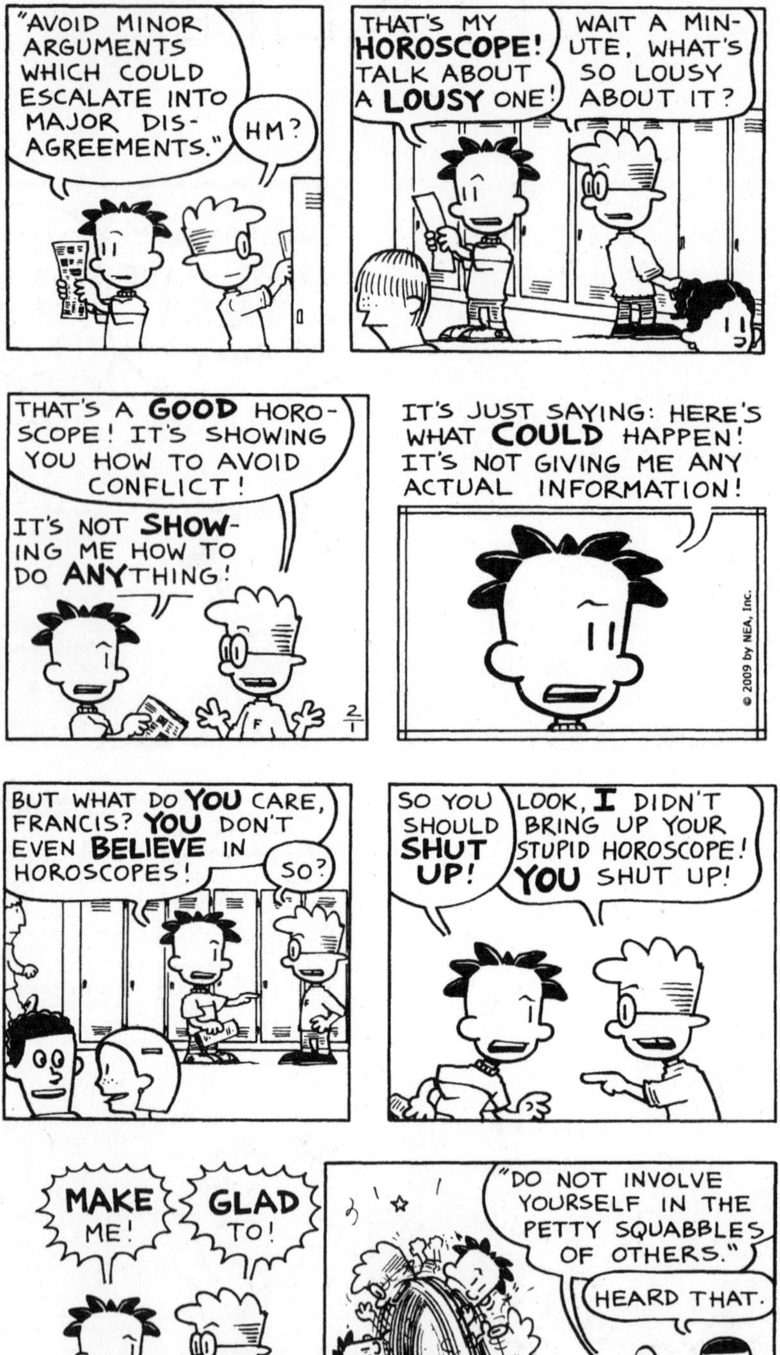
"AVOID MINOR ARGUMENTS WHICH COULD ESCALATE INTO MAJOR DIS-AGREEMENTS."
HM?
THAT'S MY HOROSCOPE! TALK ABOUT A LOUSY ONE!
WAIT A MIN-UTE, WHAT'S SO LOUSY ABOUT IT?
THAT'S A GOOD HORO-SCOPE! IT'S SHOWING YOU HOW TO AVOID CONFLICT!
IT'S NOT SHOW-ING ME HOW TO DO ANYTHING!
2/1
IT'S JUST SAYING: HERE'S WHAT COULD HAPPEN! IT'S NOT GIVING ME ANY ACTUAL INFORMATION!
© 2009 by NEA, Inc.
BUT WHAT DO YOU CARE, FRANCIS? YOU DON'T EVEN BELIEVE IN HOROSCOPES!
SO?
SO YOU SHOULD SHUT UP!
LOOK, I DIDN'T BRING UP YOUR STUPID HOROSCOPE! YOU SHUT UP!
MAKE ME!
GLAD TO!
"DO NOT INVOLVE YOURSELF IN THE PETTY SQUABBLES OF OTHERS."
HEARD THAT.
Peirce

GET A LIFE

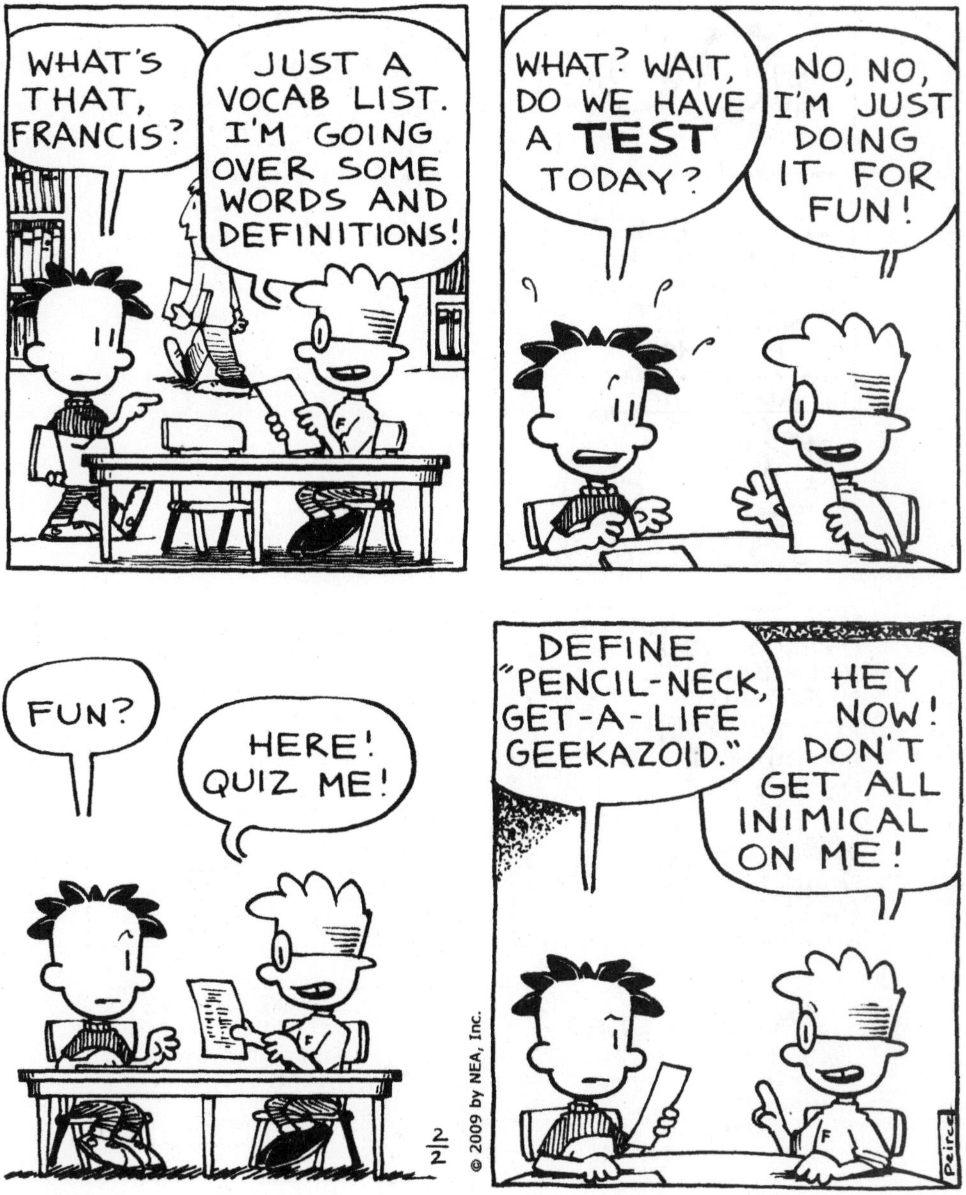

WHAT'S THAT, FRANCIS?
JUST A VOCAB LIST. I'M GOING OVER SOME WORDS AND DEFINITIONS!
WHAT? WAIT, DO WE HAVE A **TEST** TODAY?
NO, NO, I'M JUST DOING IT FOR FUN!
FUN?
HERE! QUIZ ME!
DEFINE "PENCIL-NECK, GET-A-LIFE GEEKAZOID."
HEY NOW! DON'T GET ALL INIMICAL ON ME!
2/2
© 2009 by NEA, Inc.
Peirce

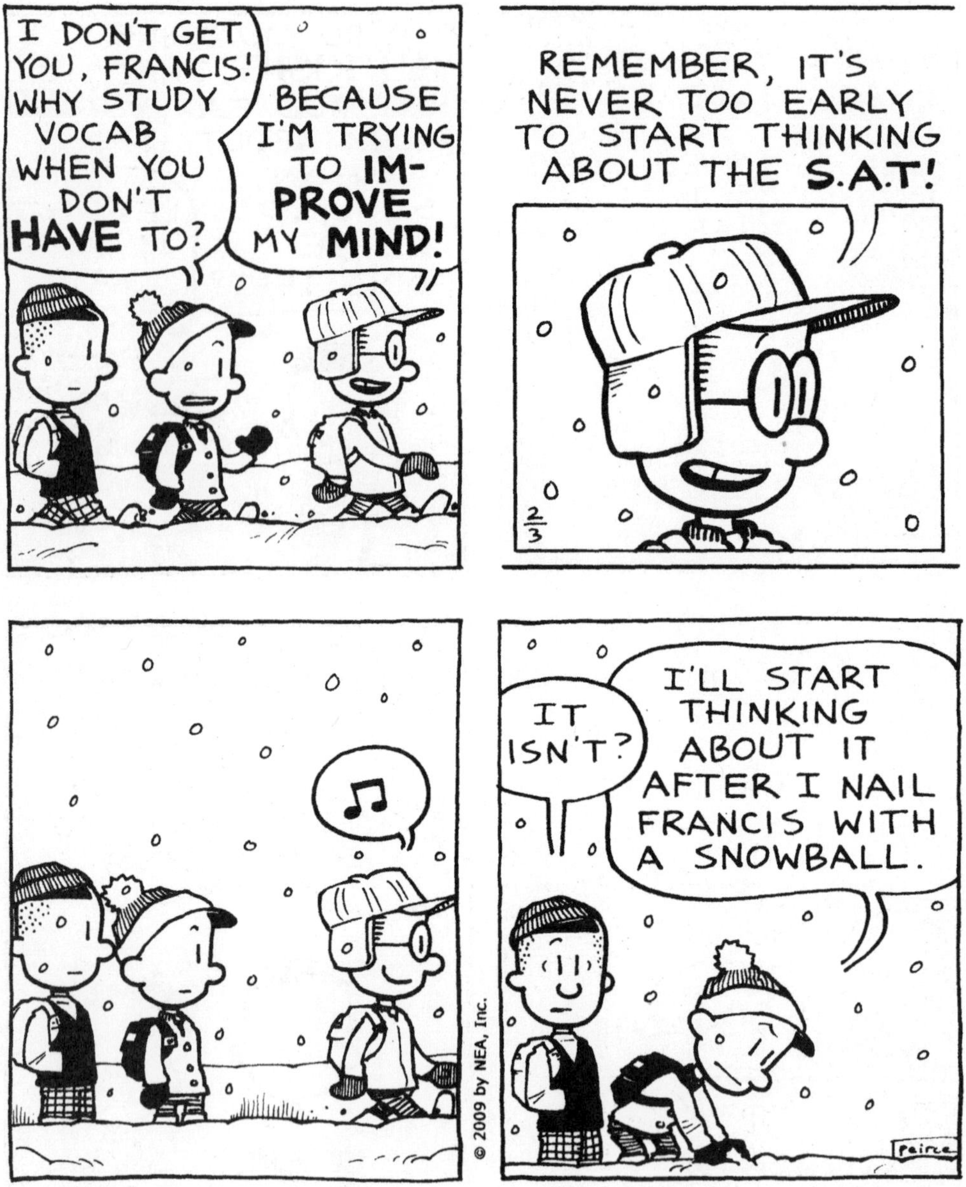
I DON'T GET YOU, FRANCIS! WHY STUDY VOCAB WHEN YOU DON'T **HAVE** TO?
BECAUSE I'M TRYING TO **IM-PROVE** MY **MIND!**
REMEMBER, IT'S NEVER TOO EARLY TO START THINKING ABOUT THE **S.A.T!**
2/3
♫
© 2009 by NEA, Inc.
IT ISN'T?
I'LL START THINKING ABOUT IT AFTER I NAIL FRANCIS WITH A SNOWBALL.
peirce

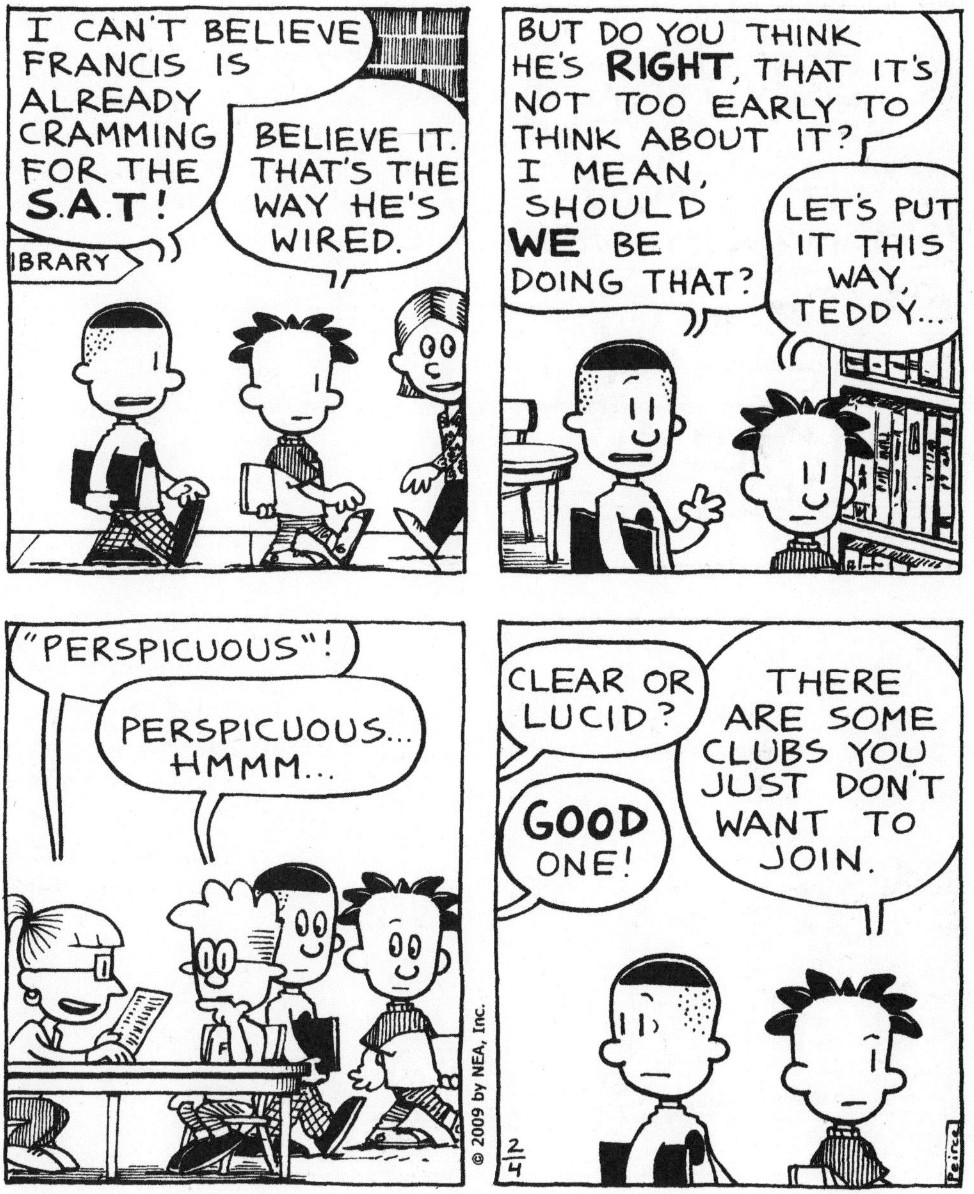
I CAN'T BELIEVE FRANCIS IS ALREADY CRAMMING FOR THE S.A.T!
BELIEVE IT. THAT'S THE WAY HE'S WIRED.
IBRARY
BUT DO YOU THINK HE'S RIGHT, THAT IT'S NOT TOO EARLY TO THINK ABOUT IT? I MEAN, SHOULD WE BE DOING THAT?
LET'S PUT IT THIS WAY, TEDDY...
"PERSPICUOUS"!
PERSPICUOUS... HMMM...
© 2009 by NEA, Inc.
2/4
CLEAR OR LUCID?
THERE ARE SOME CLUBS YOU JUST DON'T WANT TO JOIN.
GOOD ONE!
Peirce

DAD ON ICE

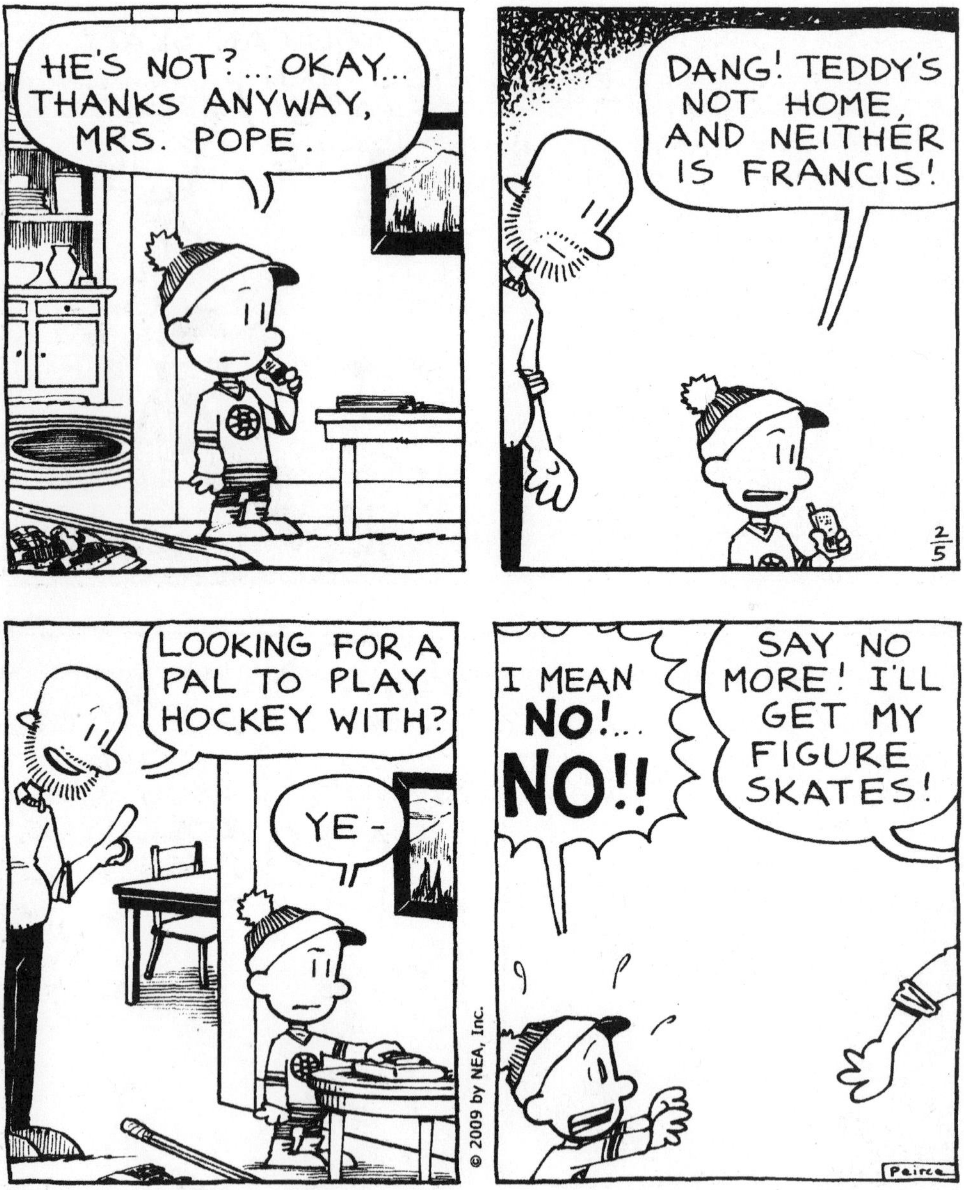

HE'S NOT?... OKAY... THANKS ANYWAY, MRS. POPE.
DANG! TEDDY'S NOT HOME, AND NEITHER IS FRANCIS!
2/5
LOOKING FOR A PAL TO PLAY HOCKEY WITH?
YE-
I MEAN NO!... NO!!
SAY NO MORE! I'LL GET MY FIGURE SKATES!
© 2009 by NEA, Inc.
Peirce

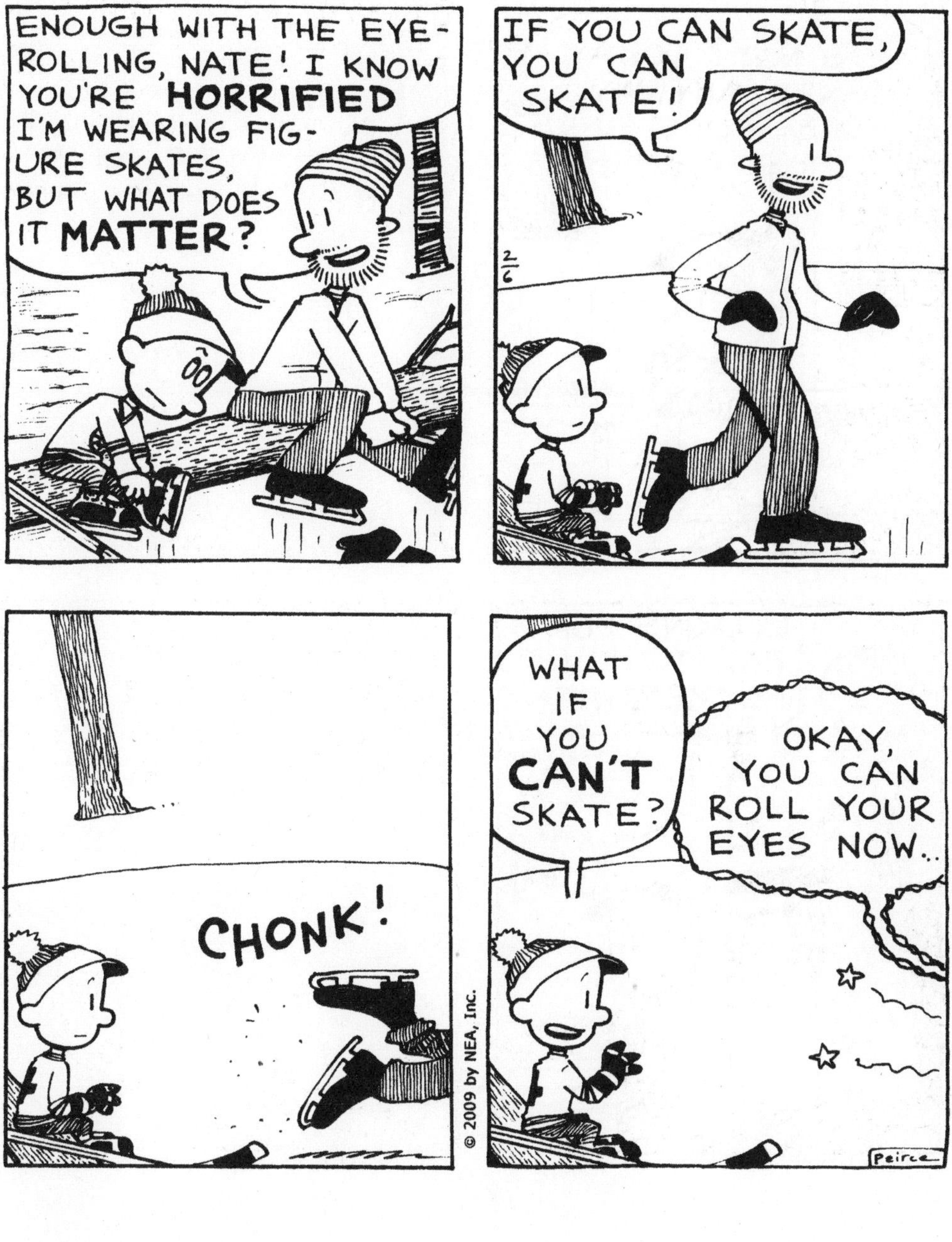
ENOUGH WITH THE EYE-ROLLING, NATE! I KNOW YOU'RE **HORRIFIED** I'M WEARING FIG-URE SKATES, BUT WHAT DOES IT **MATTER**?
IF YOU CAN SKATE, YOU CAN SKATE!
2/6
CHONK!
© 2009 by NEA, Inc.
WHAT IF YOU **CAN'T** SKATE?
OKAY, YOU CAN ROLL YOUR EYES NOW...
Peirce

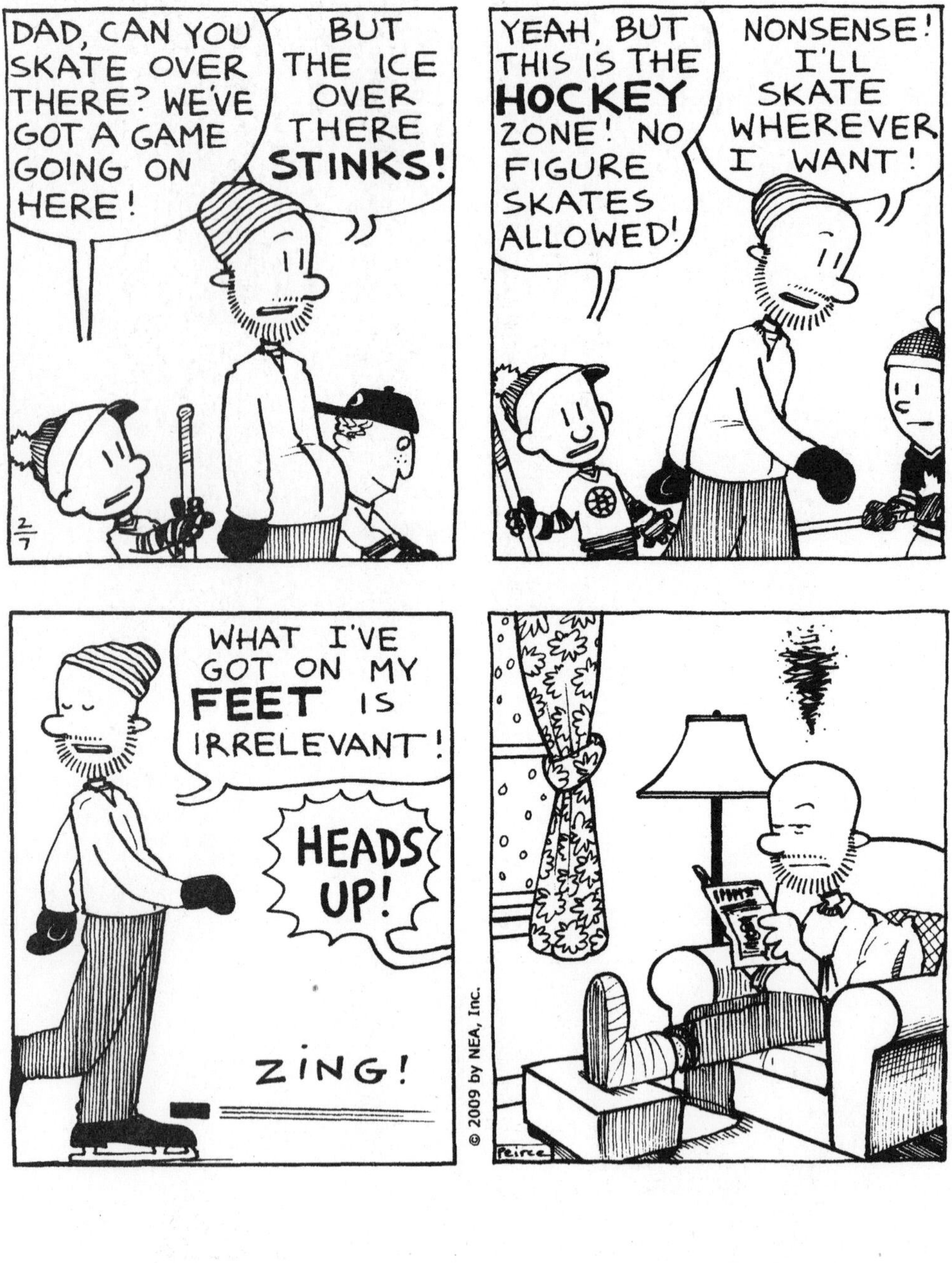
DAD, CAN YOU SKATE OVER THERE? WE'VE GOT A GAME GOING ON HERE!
BUT THE ICE OVER THERE STINKS!
2/7
YEAH, BUT THIS IS THE HOCKEY ZONE! NO FIGURE SKATES ALLOWED!
NONSENSE! I'LL SKATE WHEREVER I WANT!
WHAT I'VE GOT ON MY FEET IS IRRELEVANT!
HEADS UP!
ZING!
© 2009 by NEA, Inc.
Peirce

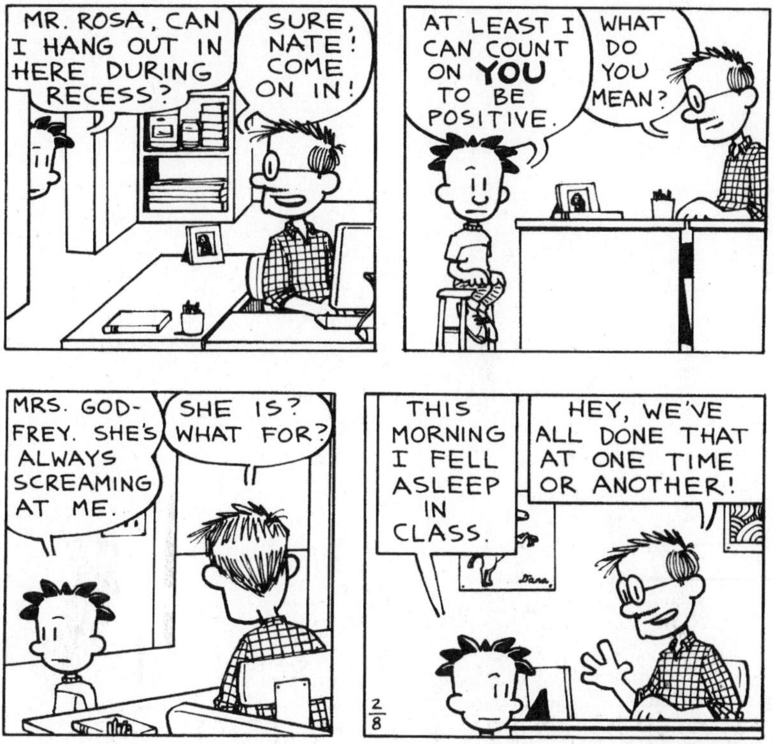
MR. ROSA, CAN I HANG OUT IN HERE DURING RECESS?
SURE, NATE! COME ON IN!
AT LEAST I CAN COUNT ON **YOU** TO BE POSITIVE.
WHAT DO YOU MEAN?
MRS. GODFREY. SHE'S ALWAYS SCREAMING AT ME.
SHE IS? WHAT FOR?
THIS MORNING I FELL ASLEEP IN CLASS.
HEY, WE'VE ALL DONE THAT AT ONE TIME OR ANOTHER!
2/8

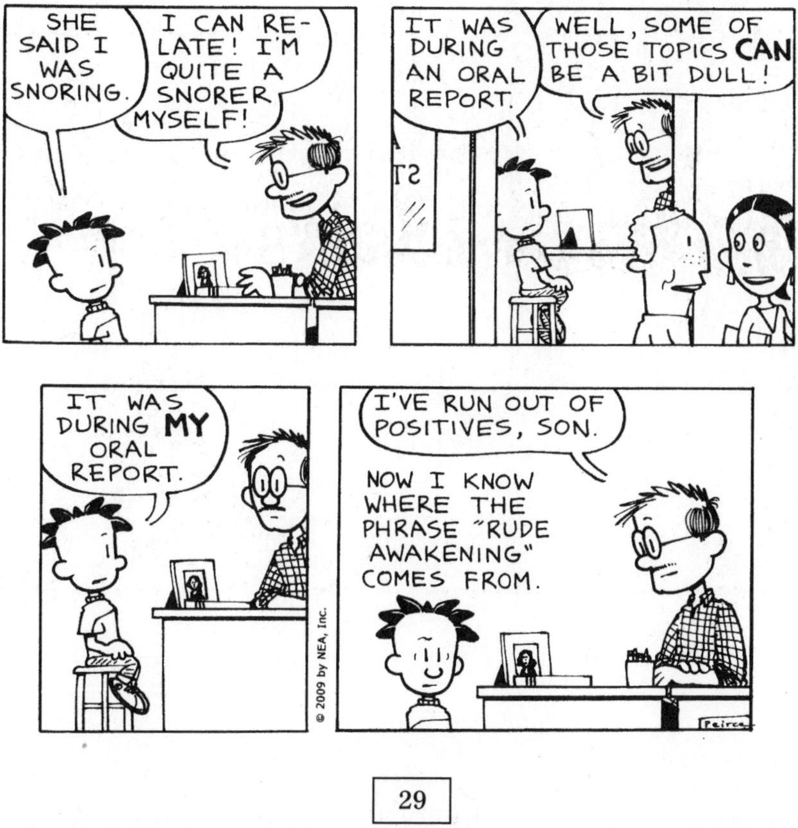
SHE SAID I WAS SNORING.
I CAN RELATE! I'M QUITE A SNORER MYSELF!
IT WAS DURING AN ORAL REPORT.
WELL, SOME OF THOSE TOPICS **CAN** BE A BIT DULL!
IT WAS DURING **MY** ORAL REPORT.
I'VE RUN OUT OF POSITIVES, SON.
NOW I KNOW WHERE THE PHRASE "RUDE AWAKENING" COMES FROM.
Peirce

THE WAY THE COOKIE CRUMBLES

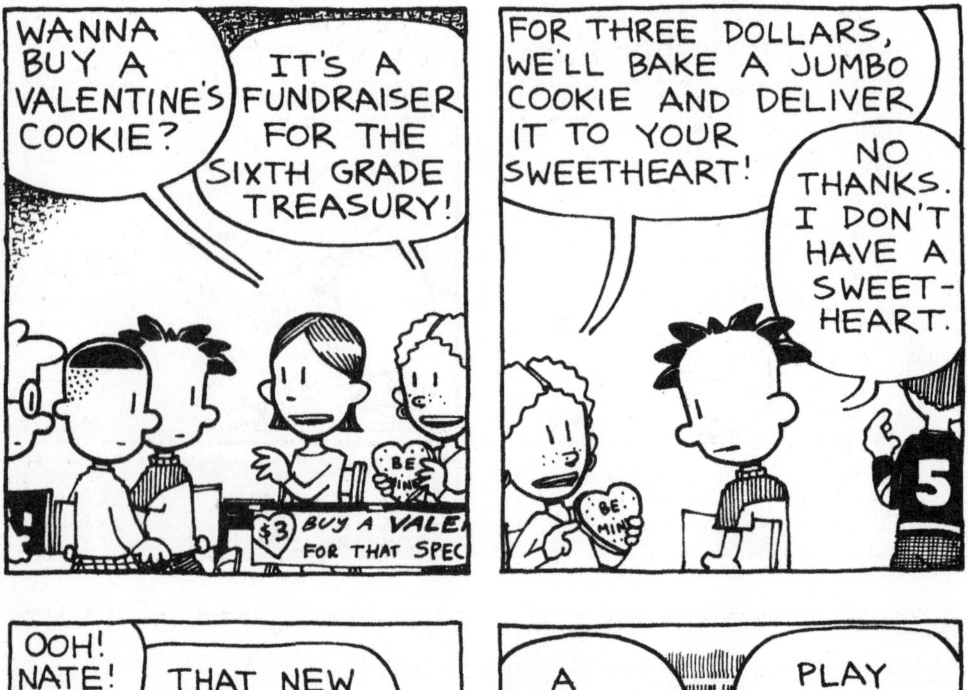
WANNA BUY A VALENTINE'S COOKIE?
IT'S A FUNDRAISER FOR THE SIXTH GRADE TREASURY!
FOR THREE DOLLARS, WE'LL BAKE A JUMBO COOKIE AND DELIVER IT TO YOUR SWEETHEART!
NO THANKS. I DON'T HAVE A SWEET-HEART.
OOH! NATE! WHAT ABOUT **TINA**?
THAT NEW GIRL? I BARELY **KNOW** HER!
...WHICH MEANS **SHE** BARELY KNOWS **YOU**!
A **MAJOR** PLUS!
PLAY TO YOUR STRENGTHS, DUDE!
2/9
Peirce

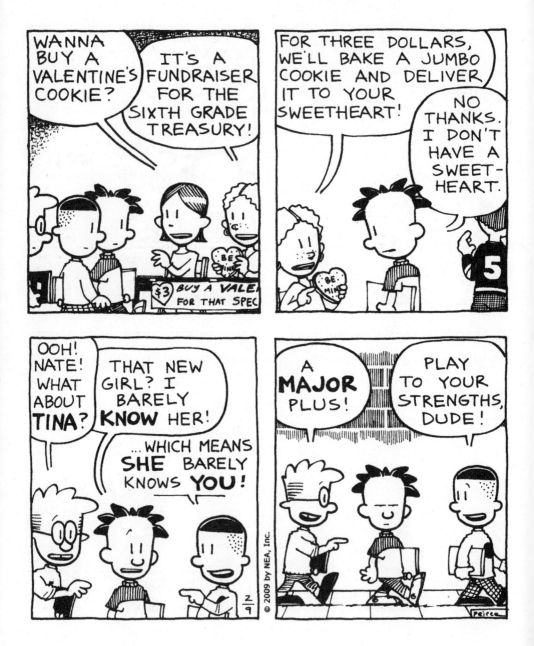

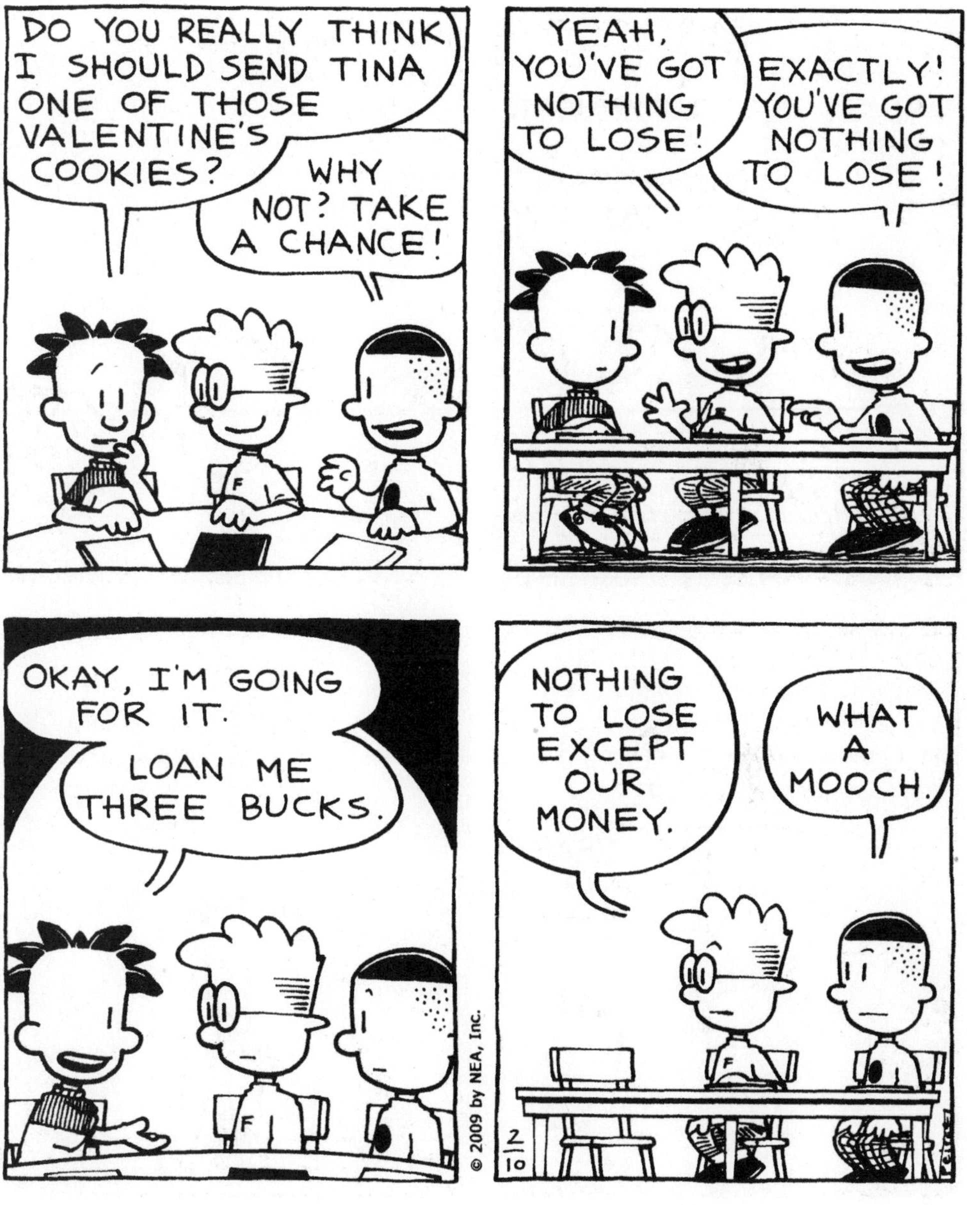
DO YOU REALLY THINK I SHOULD SEND TINA ONE OF THOSE VALENTINE'S COOKIES?
WHY NOT? TAKE A CHANCE!
YEAH, YOU'VE GOT NOTHING TO LOSE!
EXACTLY! YOU'VE GOT NOTHING TO LOSE!
OKAY, I'M GOING FOR IT.
LOAN ME THREE BUCKS.
NOTHING TO LOSE EXCEPT OUR MONEY.
WHAT A MOOCH.
© 2009 by NEA, Inc.
2/10

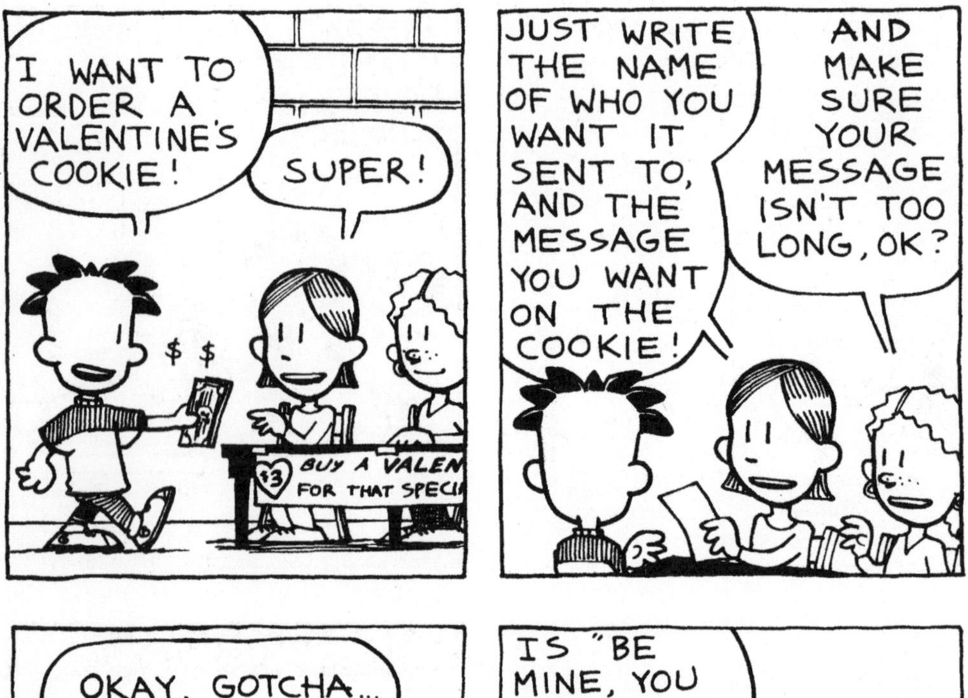
I WANT TO ORDER A VALENTINE'S COOKIE!
SUPER!
$ $
BUY A VALEN
$3
FOR THAT SPECI
JUST WRITE THE NAME OF WHO YOU WANT IT SENT TO, AND THE MESSAGE YOU WANT ON THE COOKIE!
AND MAKE SURE YOUR MESSAGE ISN'T TOO LONG, OK?
OKAY, GOTCHA... HMMMMM...
2/11
© 2009 by NEA, Inc.
IS "BE MINE, YOU FOXALICIOUS TURBO-HOTTIE" TOO LONG?
IT'S TOO STUPID.

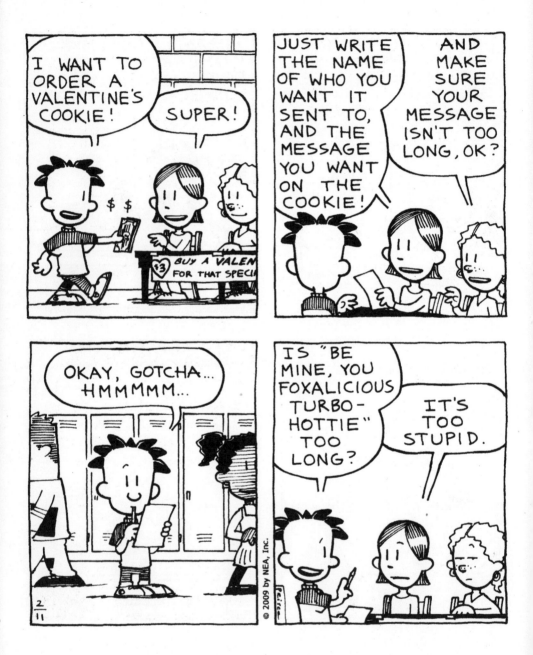

NATE! DID YOU DO IT? DID YOU ORDER A VALENTINE'S COOKIE FOR TINA?
FRANCIS! SSH! SHE'S RIGHT OVER THERE!
I DON'T WANT HER TO HEAR YOU! I DON'T WANT HER TO SUSPECT ANYTHING!
WHEN MY COOKIE GETS DELIVERED, I WANT IT TO BE A TOTAL SURPRISE!
2/12
© 2009 by NEA, Inc.
MEANWHILE...
GINA! VALENTINE'S COOKIE FOR YOU FROM AN ADMIRER!
? ?
Peirce
CONT'D!

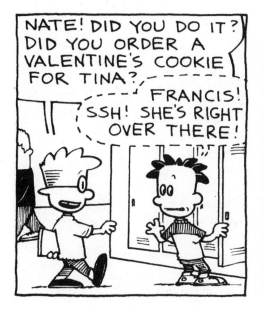

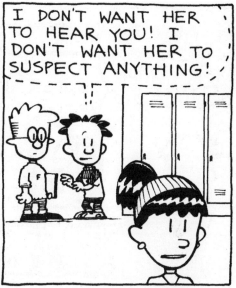

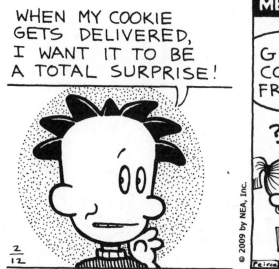

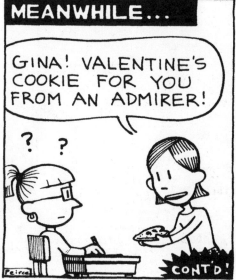

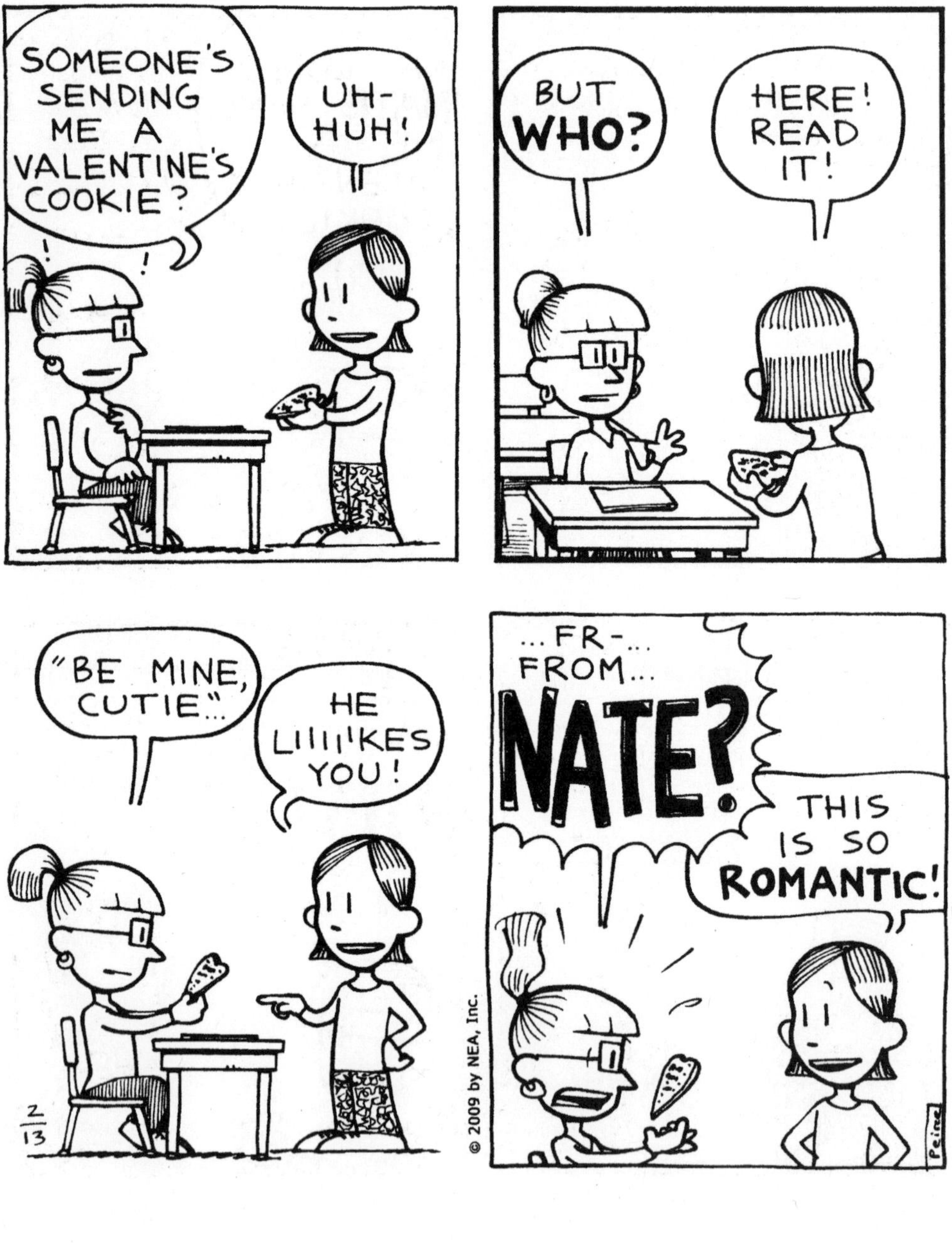
SOMEONE'S SENDING ME A VALENTINE'S COOKIE?
UH-HUH!
BUT WHO?
HERE! READ IT!
"BE MINE, CUTIE."...
HE LIIII'KES YOU!
2/13
© 2009 by NEA, Inc.
...FR-... FROM... NATE?
THIS IS SO ROMANTIC!
Peirce

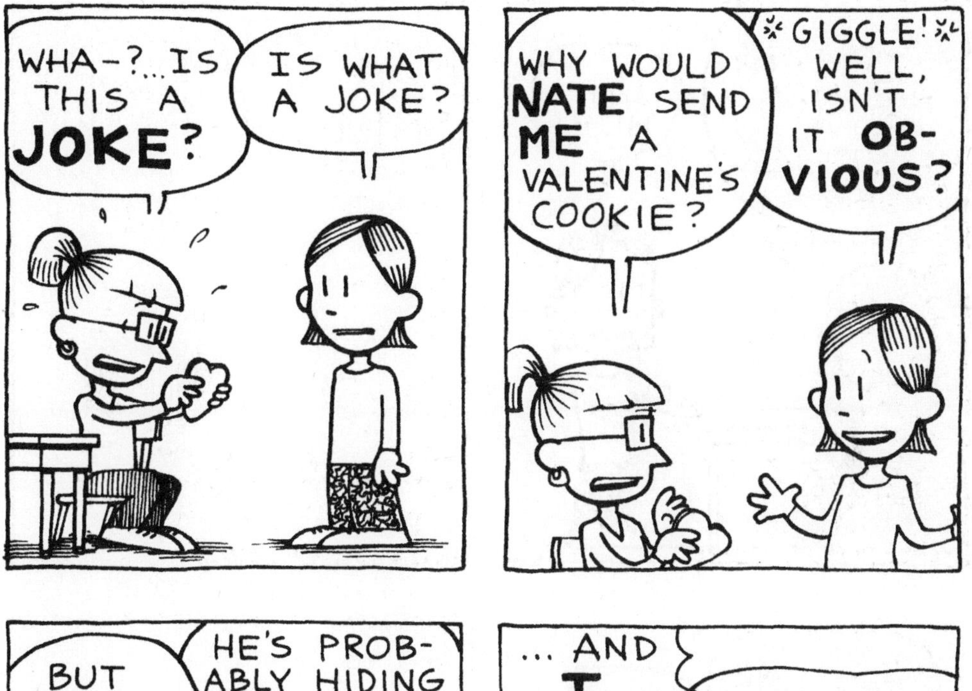

WHA-?... IS THIS A JOKE?
IS WHAT A JOKE?
WHY WOULD NATE SEND ME A VALENTINE'S COOKIE?
GIGGLE! WELL, ISN'T IT OB-VIOUS?
BUT NATE HATES ME!
HE'S PROB-ABLY HIDING HIS TRUE FEELINGS!
2/14
© 2009 by NEA, Inc.
... AND I HATE HIM!
OH. WELL, CAN'T HELP YOU THERE.
Peirce

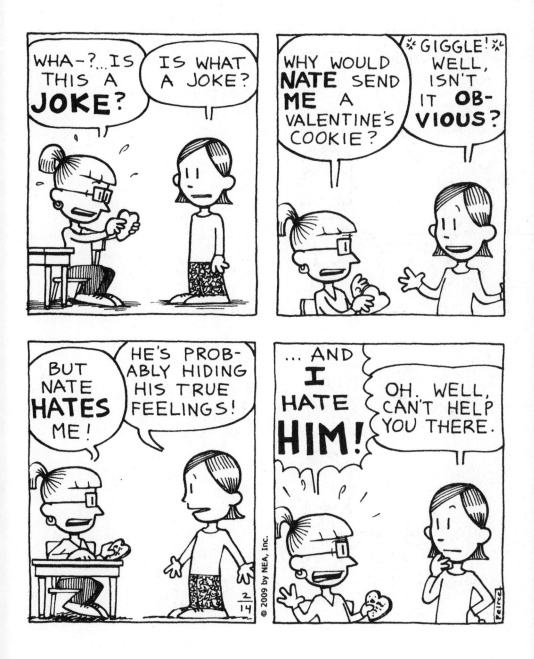

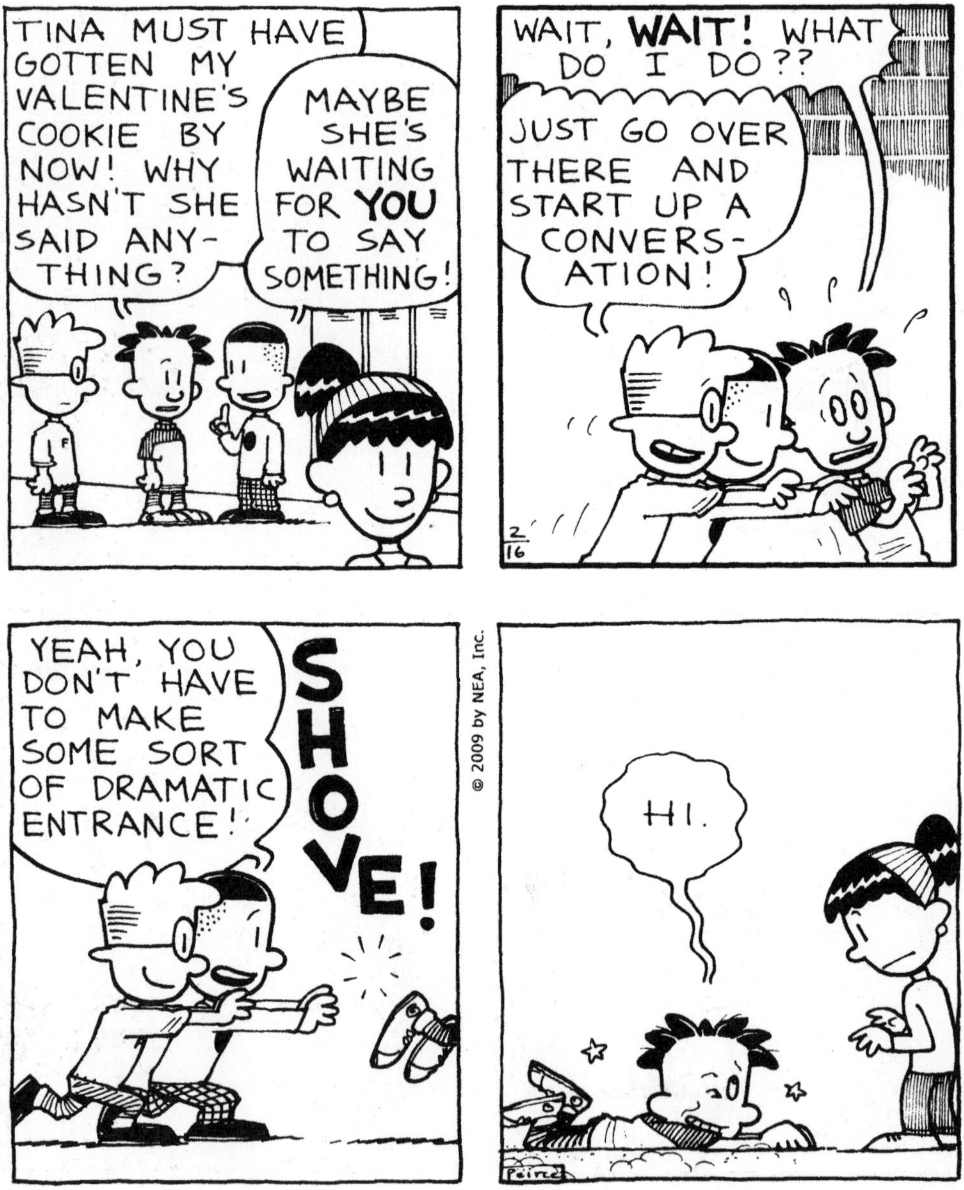

TINA MUST HAVE GOTTEN MY VALENTINE'S COOKIE BY NOW! WHY HASN'T SHE SAID ANYTHING?
MAYBE SHE'S WAITING FOR **YOU** TO SAY SOMETHING!
WAIT, **WAIT!** WHAT DO I DO??
JUST GO OVER THERE AND START UP A CONVERSATION!
2/16
YEAH, YOU DON'T HAVE TO MAKE SOME SORT OF DRAMATIC ENTRANCE!
SHOVE!
HI.
Peirce

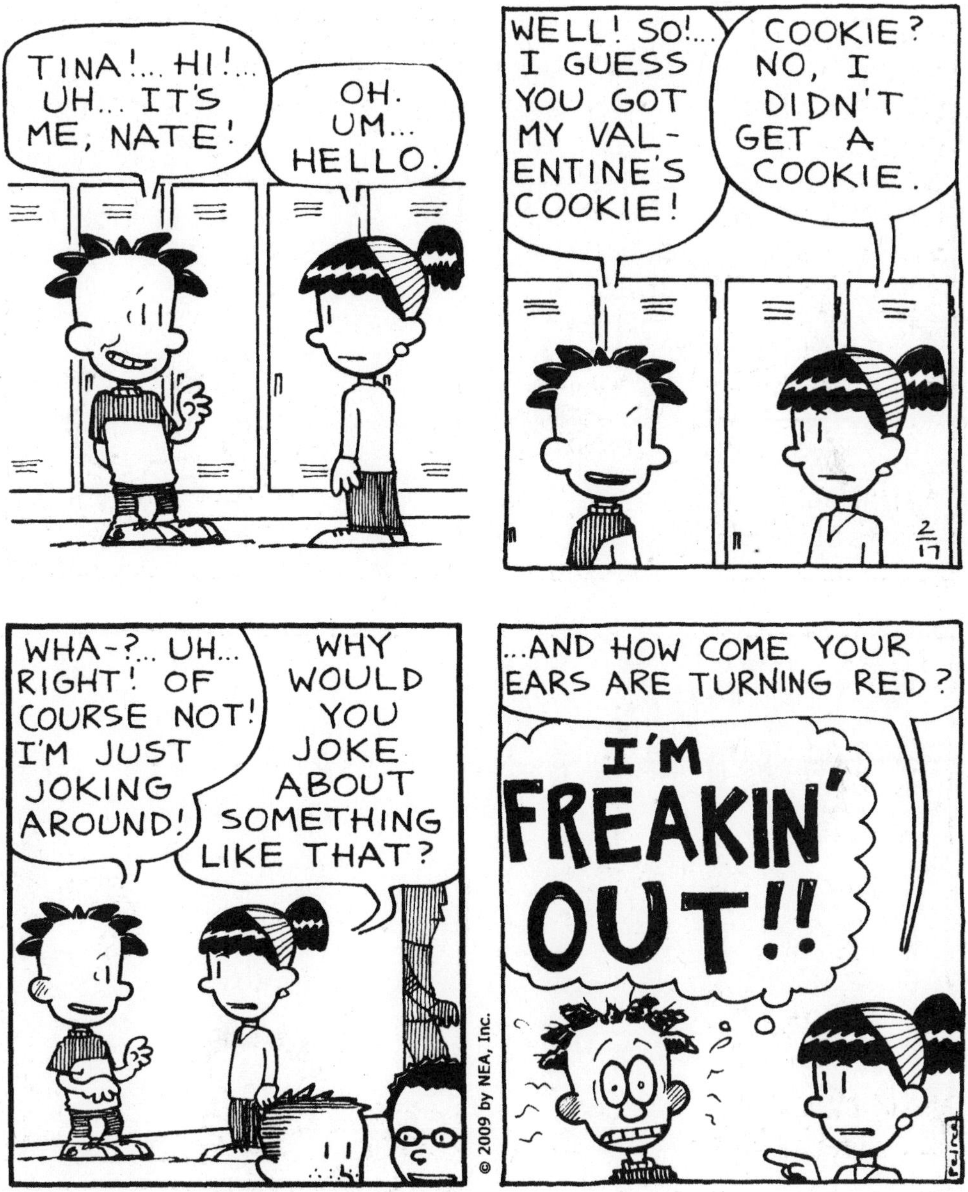
TINA!... HI!... UH... IT'S ME, NATE!
OH. UM... HELLO.
WELL! SO!... I GUESS YOU GOT MY VALENTINE'S COOKIE!
COOKIE? NO, I DIDN'T GET A COOKIE.
2/17
WHA-?... UH... RIGHT! OF COURSE NOT! I'M JUST JOKING AROUND!
WHY WOULD YOU JOKE ABOUT SOMETHING LIKE THAT?
...AND HOW COME YOUR EARS ARE TURNING RED?
I'M FREAKIN' OUT!!

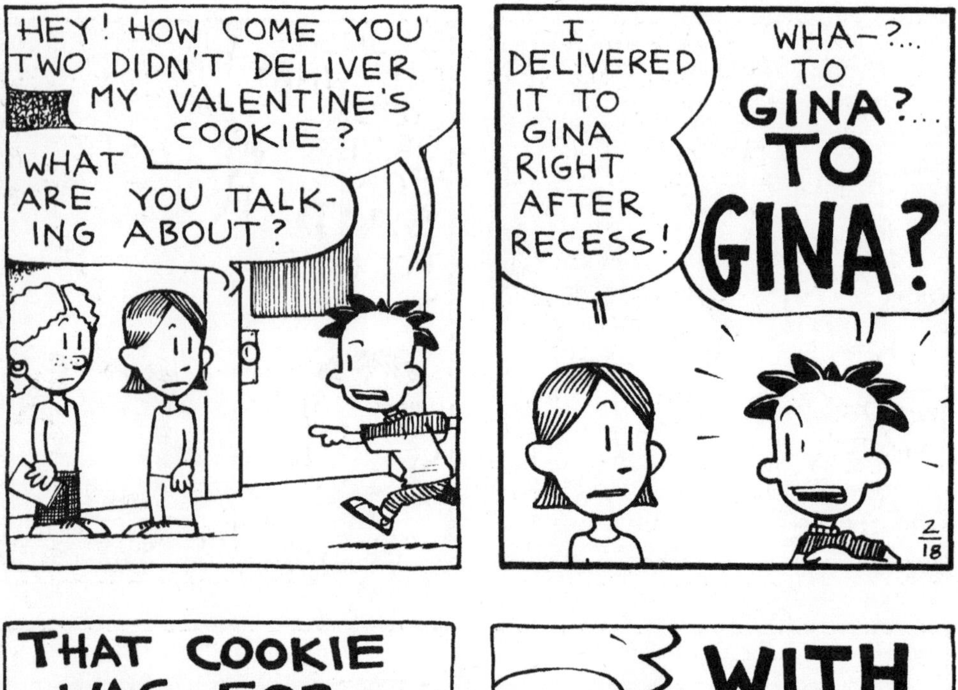
HEY! HOW COME YOU TWO DIDN'T DELIVER MY VALENTINE'S COOKIE?
WHAT ARE YOU TALKING ABOUT?
I DELIVERED IT TO GINA RIGHT AFTER RECESS!
WHA-?... TO GINA?... TO GINA?
2/18
THAT COOKIE WAS FOR TINA!
© 2009 by NEA, Inc.
TINA?
WITH A "T"!
Peirce

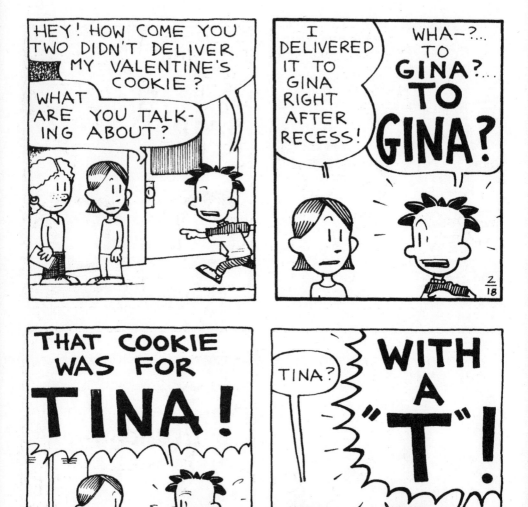

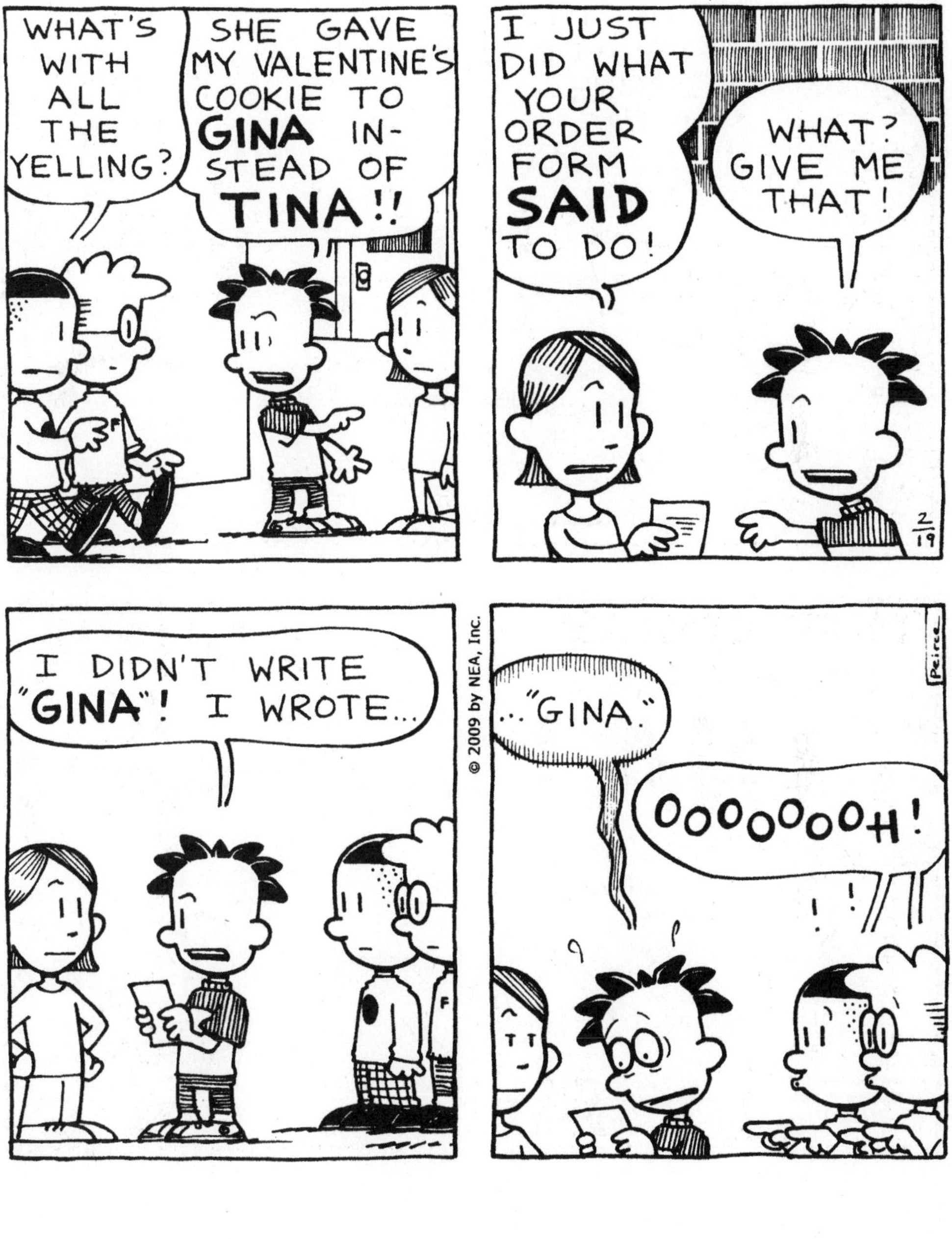
WHAT'S WITH ALL THE YELLING?
SHE GAVE MY VALENTINE'S COOKIE TO GINA INSTEAD OF TINA!!
I JUST DID WHAT YOUR ORDER FORM SAID TO DO!
WHAT? GIVE ME THAT!
2/19
I DIDN'T WRITE "GINA"! I WROTE...
© 2009 by NEA, Inc.
Peirce
..."GINA."
OOOOOOOH!
! !

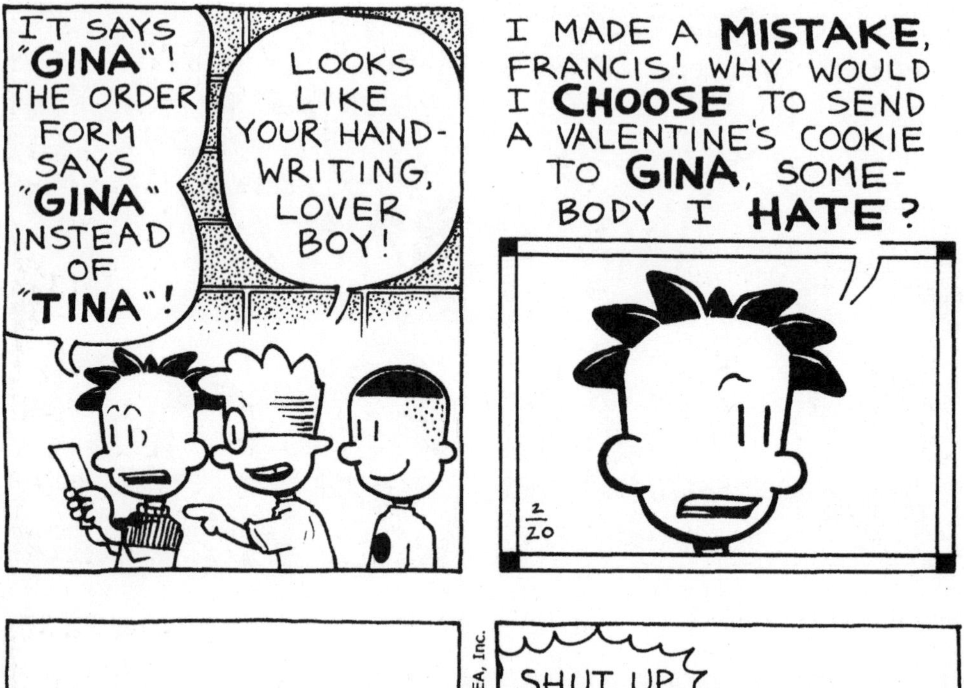
IT SAYS "GINA"! THE ORDER FORM SAYS "GINA" INSTEAD OF "TINA"!
LOOKS LIKE YOUR HAND-WRITING, LOVER BOY!
I MADE A MISTAKE, FRANCIS! WHY WOULD I CHOOSE TO SEND A VALENTINE'S COOKIE TO GINA, SOMEBODY I HATE?
2/20
© 2009 by NEA, Inc.
SHUT UP, SHUT UP, SHUT UP!
"HATE" IN QUOTES!
SNICKER!

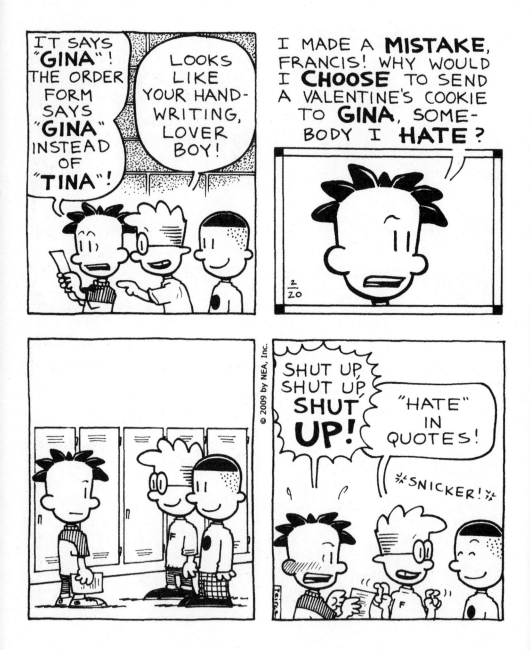

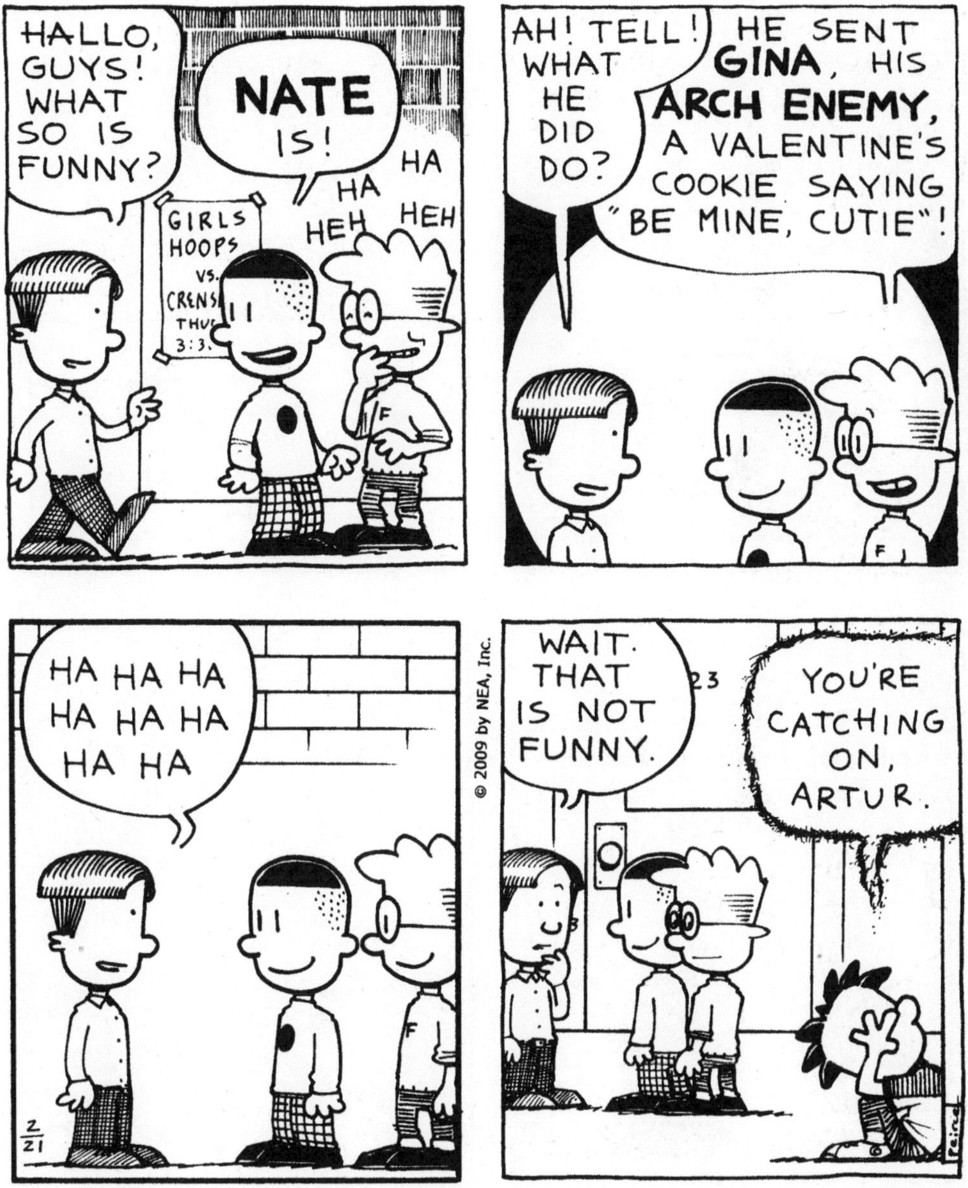
HALLO, GUYS! WHAT SO IS FUNNY?
NATE IS!
HA HA HEH HEH
GIRLS HOOPS VS. CRENS THU 3:3
AH! TELL! WHAT HE DID DO?
HE SENT GINA, HIS ARCH ENEMY, A VALENTINE'S COOKIE SAYING "BE MINE, CUTIE"!
HA HA HA HA HA HA HA HA
WAIT. THAT IS NOT FUNNY.
YOU'RE CATCHING ON, ARTUR.
© 2009 by NEA, Inc.
2/21

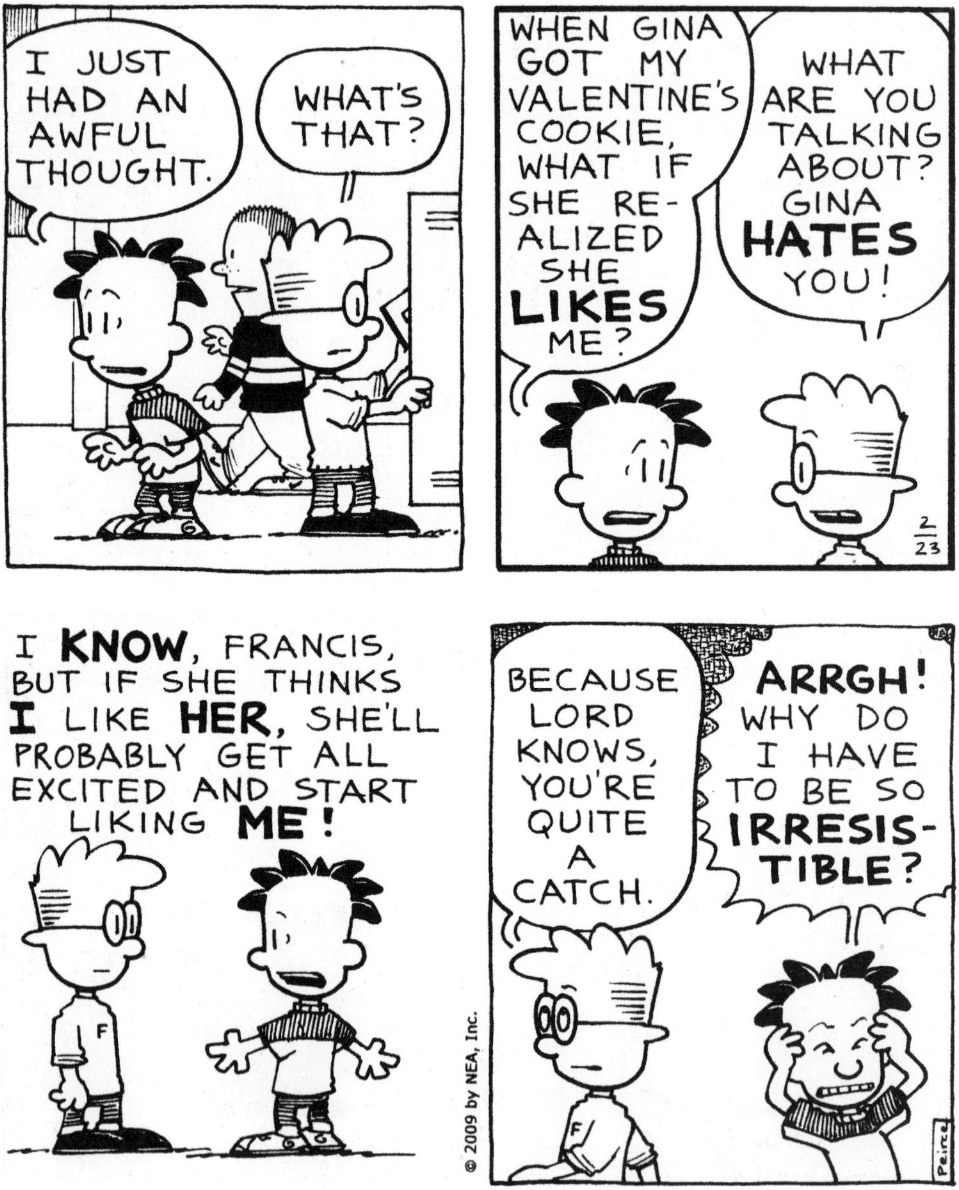
I JUST HAD AN AWFUL THOUGHT.
WHAT'S THAT?
WHEN GINA GOT MY VALENTINE'S COOKIE, WHAT IF SHE RE-ALIZED SHE LIKES ME?
WHAT ARE YOU TALKING ABOUT? GINA HATES YOU!
2/23
I KNOW, FRANCIS, BUT IF SHE THINKS I LIKE HER, SHE'LL PROBABLY GET ALL EXCITED AND START LIKING ME!
BECAUSE LORD KNOWS, YOU'RE QUITE A CATCH.
ARRGH! WHY DO I HAVE TO BE SO IRRESIS-TIBLE?
Peirce

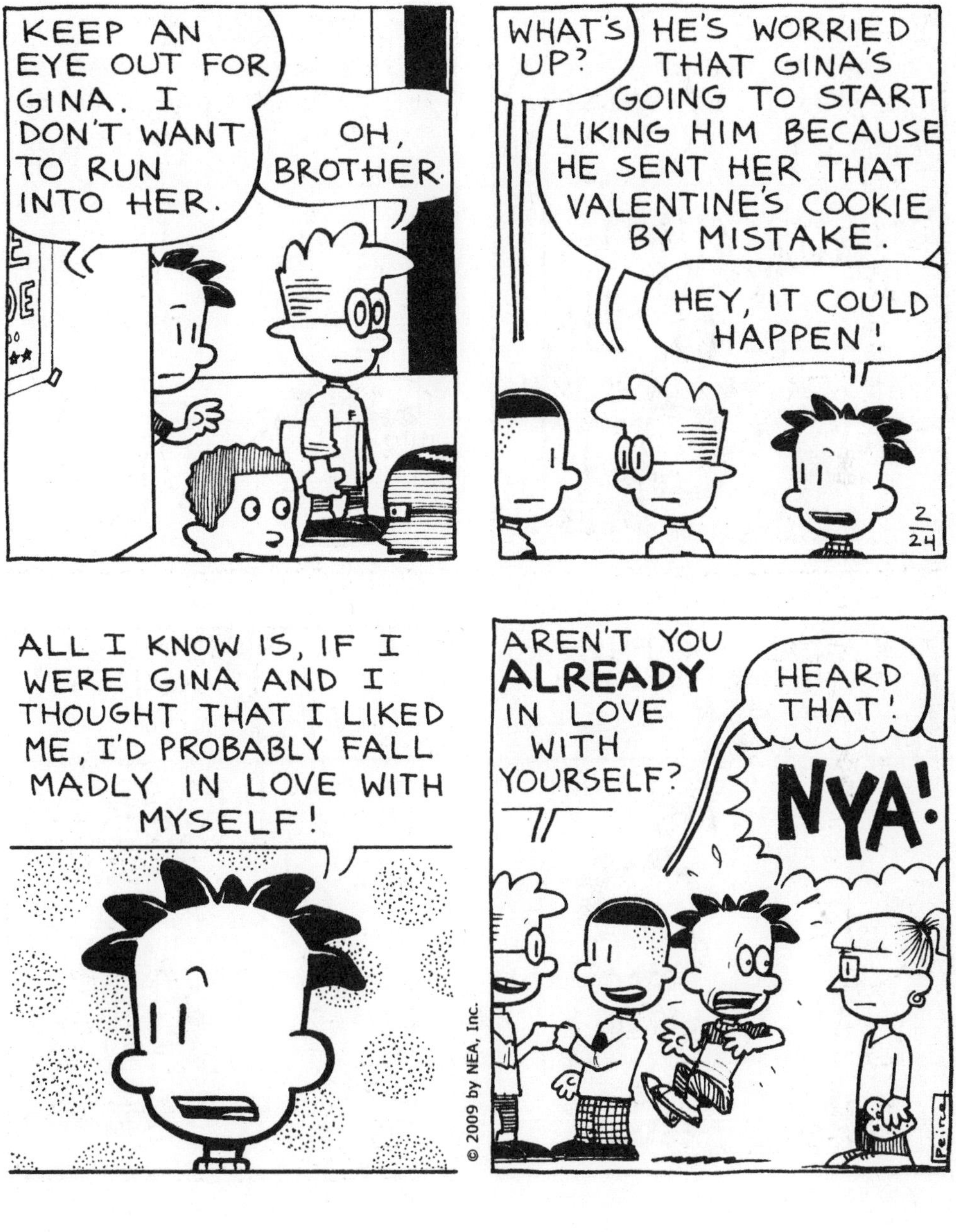
KEEP AN EYE OUT FOR GINA. I DON'T WANT TO RUN INTO HER.
OH, BROTHER.
WHAT'S UP?
HE'S WORRIED THAT GINA'S GOING TO START LIKING HIM BECAUSE HE SENT HER THAT VALENTINE'S COOKIE BY MISTAKE.
HEY, IT COULD HAPPEN!
2/24
ALL I KNOW IS, IF I WERE GINA AND I THOUGHT THAT I LIKED ME, I'D PROBABLY FALL MADLY IN LOVE WITH MYSELF!
AREN'T YOU **ALREADY** IN LOVE WITH YOURSELF?
HEARD THAT!
NYA!
© 2009 by NEA, Inc.
Peirce

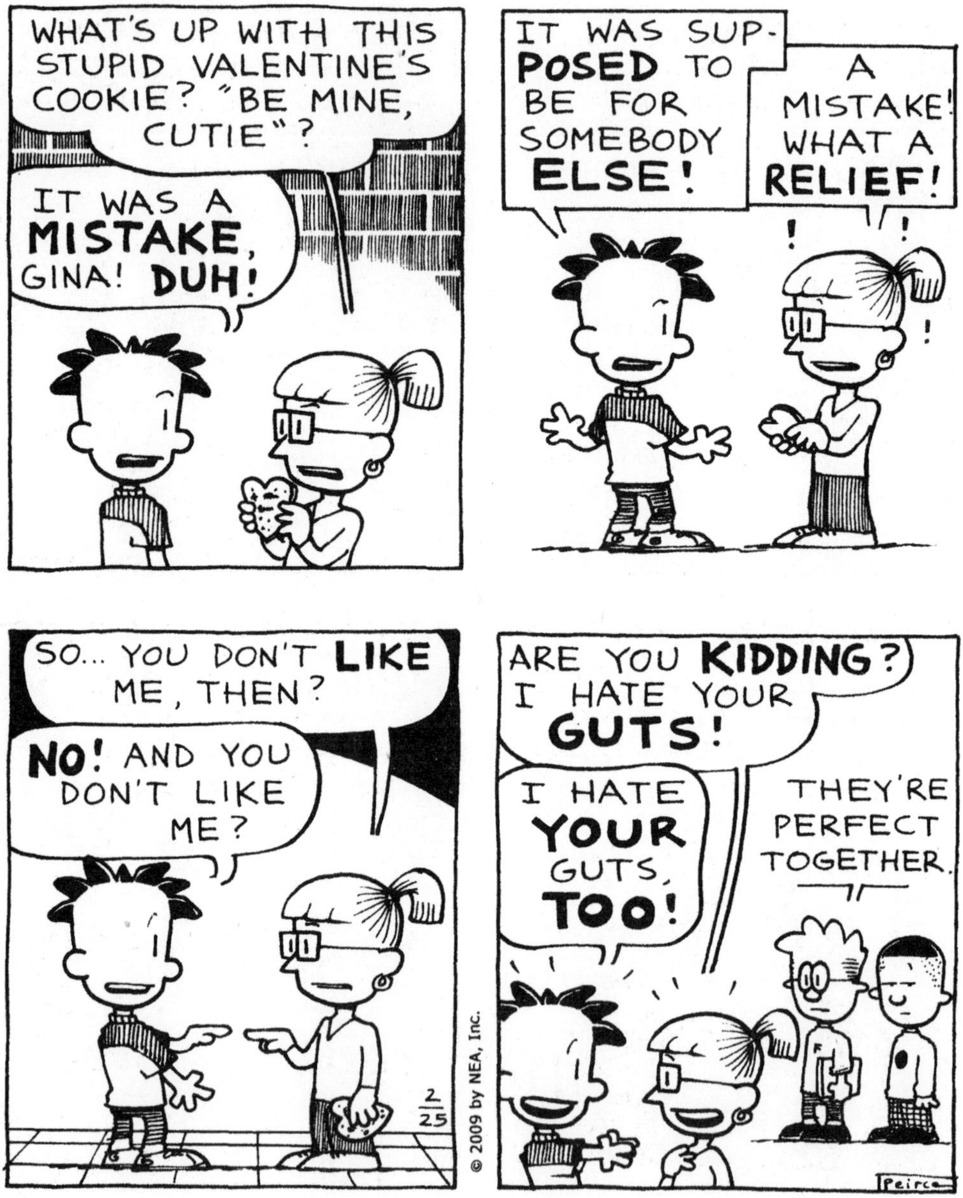
WHAT'S UP WITH THIS STUPID VALENTINE'S COOKIE? "BE MINE, CUTIE"?
IT WAS A MISTAKE, GINA! DUH!
IT WAS SUPPOSED TO BE FOR SOMEBODY ELSE!
A MISTAKE! WHAT A RELIEF!
!
!
!
SO... YOU DON'T LIKE ME, THEN?
NO! AND YOU DON'T LIKE ME?
2/25
© 2009 by NEA, Inc.
ARE YOU KIDDING? I HATE YOUR GUTS!
I HATE YOUR GUTS, TOO!
THEY'RE PERFECT TOGETHER.
Peirce

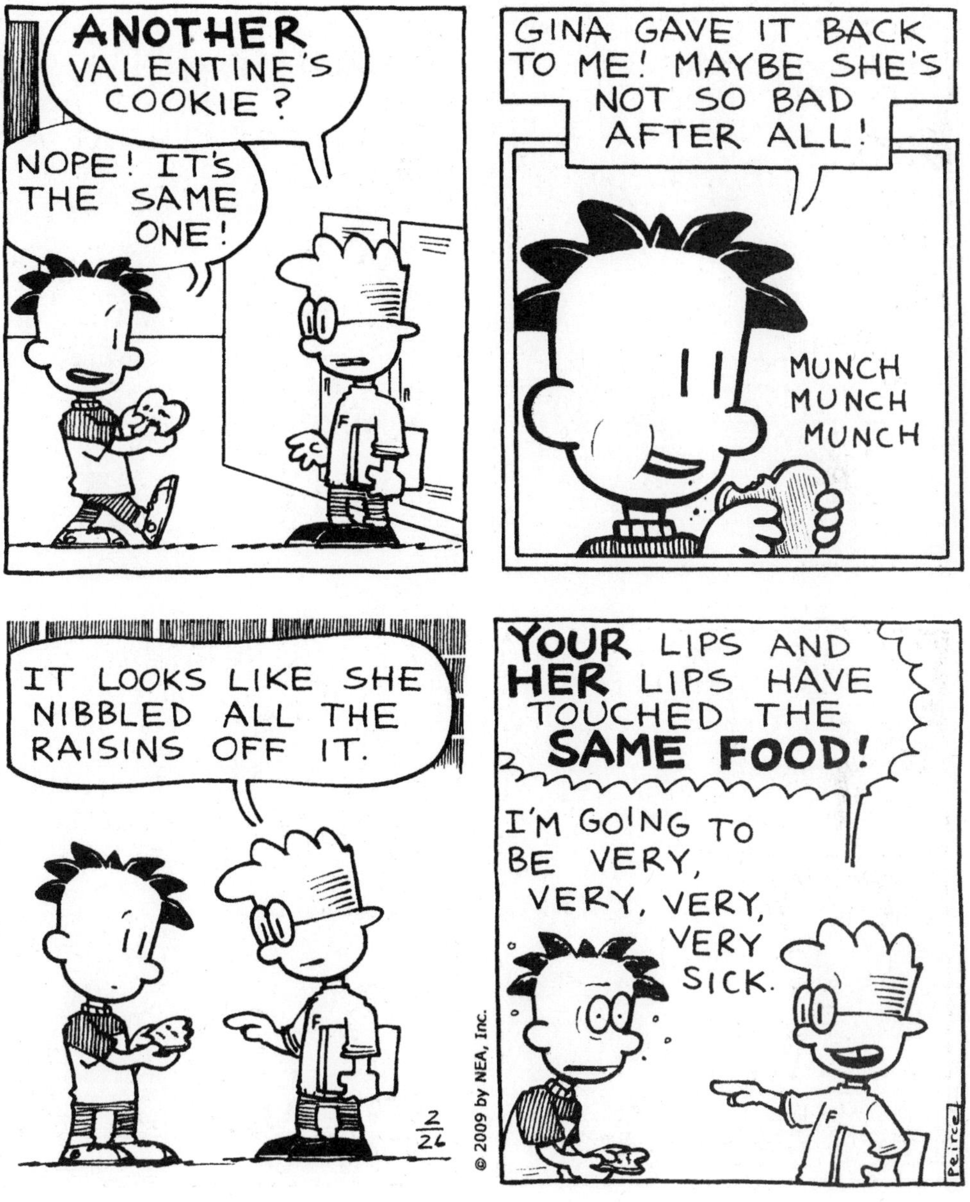
ANOTHER VALENTINE'S COOKIE?
NOPE! IT'S THE SAME ONE!
GINA GAVE IT BACK TO ME! MAYBE SHE'S NOT SO BAD AFTER ALL!
MUNCH MUNCH MUNCH
IT LOOKS LIKE SHE NIBBLED ALL THE RAISINS OFF IT.
2/26
YOUR LIPS AND HER LIPS HAVE TOUCHED THE SAME FOOD!
I'M GOING TO BE VERY, VERY, VERY, VERY VERY SICK.
Peirce

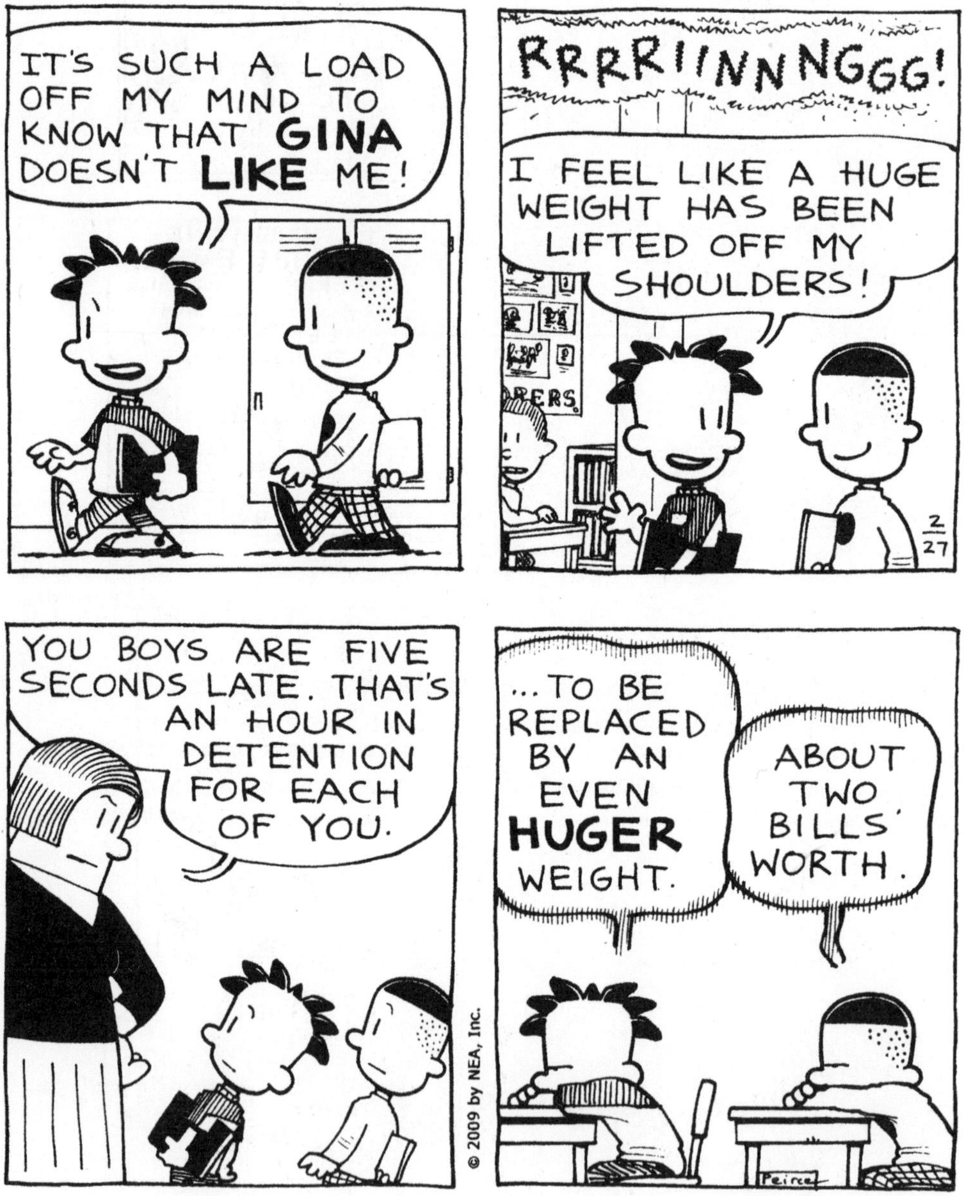
IT'S SUCH A LOAD OFF MY MIND TO KNOW THAT GINA DOESN'T LIKE ME!
RRRRIINNNGGG!
I FEEL LIKE A HUGE WEIGHT HAS BEEN LIFTED OFF MY SHOULDERS!
2/27
YOU BOYS ARE FIVE SECONDS LATE. THAT'S AN HOUR IN DETENTION FOR EACH OF YOU.
...TO BE REPLACED BY AN EVEN HUGER WEIGHT.
ABOUT TWO BILLS' WORTH.
Peirce

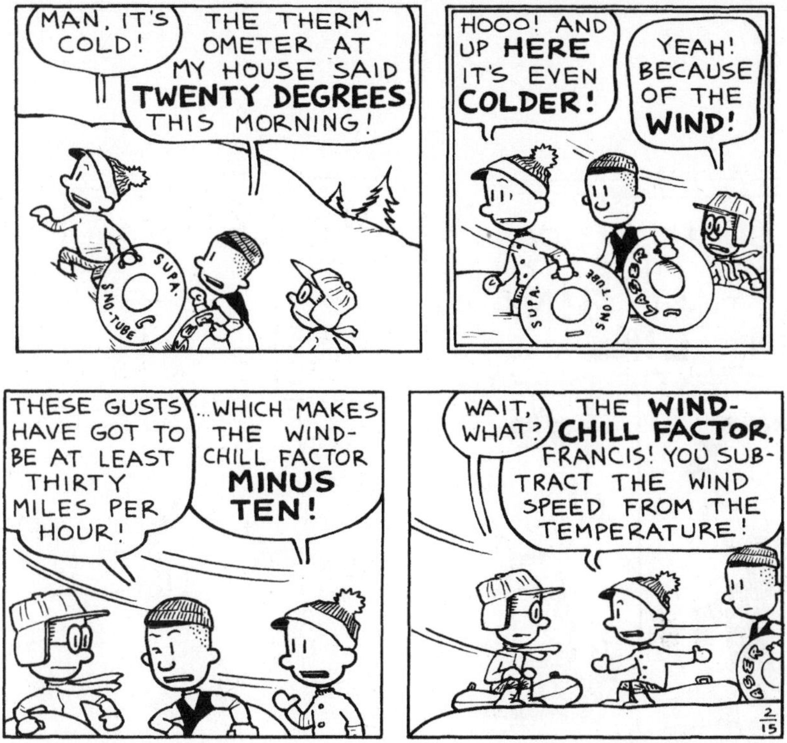
MAN, IT'S COLD!
THE THERMOMETER AT MY HOUSE SAID TWENTY DEGREES THIS MORNING!
SUPA SNO-TUBE
HOOO! AND UP HERE IT'S EVEN COLDER!
YEAH! BECAUSE OF THE WIND!
THESE GUSTS HAVE GOT TO BE AT LEAST THIRTY MILES PER HOUR!
...WHICH MAKES THE WIND-CHILL FACTOR MINUS TEN!
WAIT, WHAT?
THE WIND-CHILL FACTOR, FRANCIS! YOU SUBTRACT THE WIND SPEED FROM THE TEMPERATURE!
2/15

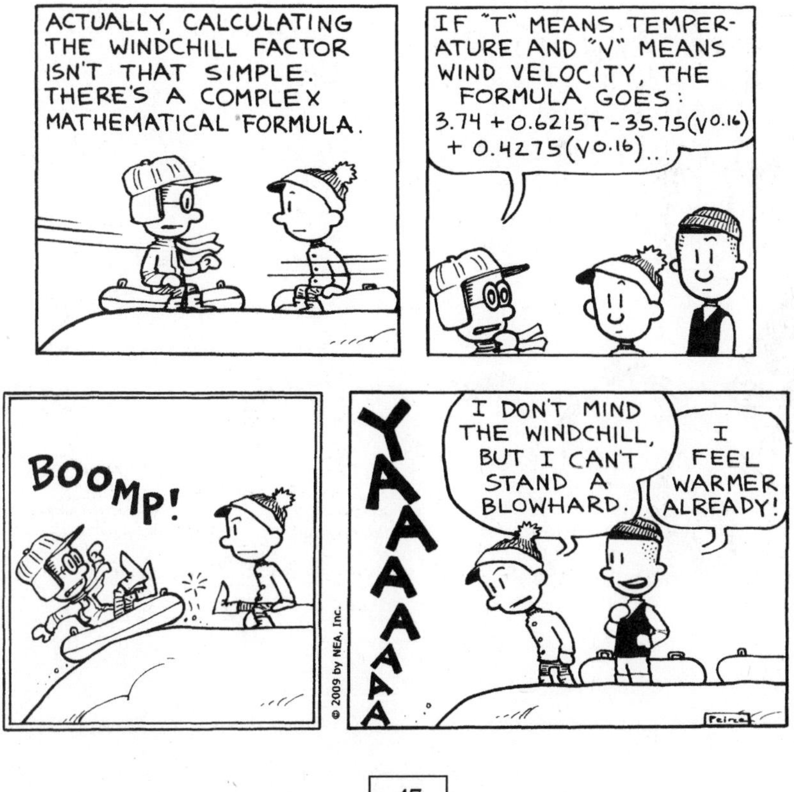
ACTUALLY, CALCULATING THE WINDCHILL FACTOR ISN'T THAT SIMPLE. THERE'S A COMPLEX MATHEMATICAL FORMULA.
IF "T" MEANS TEMPERATURE AND "V" MEANS WIND VELOCITY, THE FORMULA GOES:
3.74 + 0.6215T - 35.75(V0.16) + 0.4275(V0.16)...
BOOMP!
YAAAAAA
I DON'T MIND THE WINDCHILL, BUT I CAN'T STAND A BLOWHARD.
I FEEL WARMER ALREADY!
© 2009 by NEA, Inc.

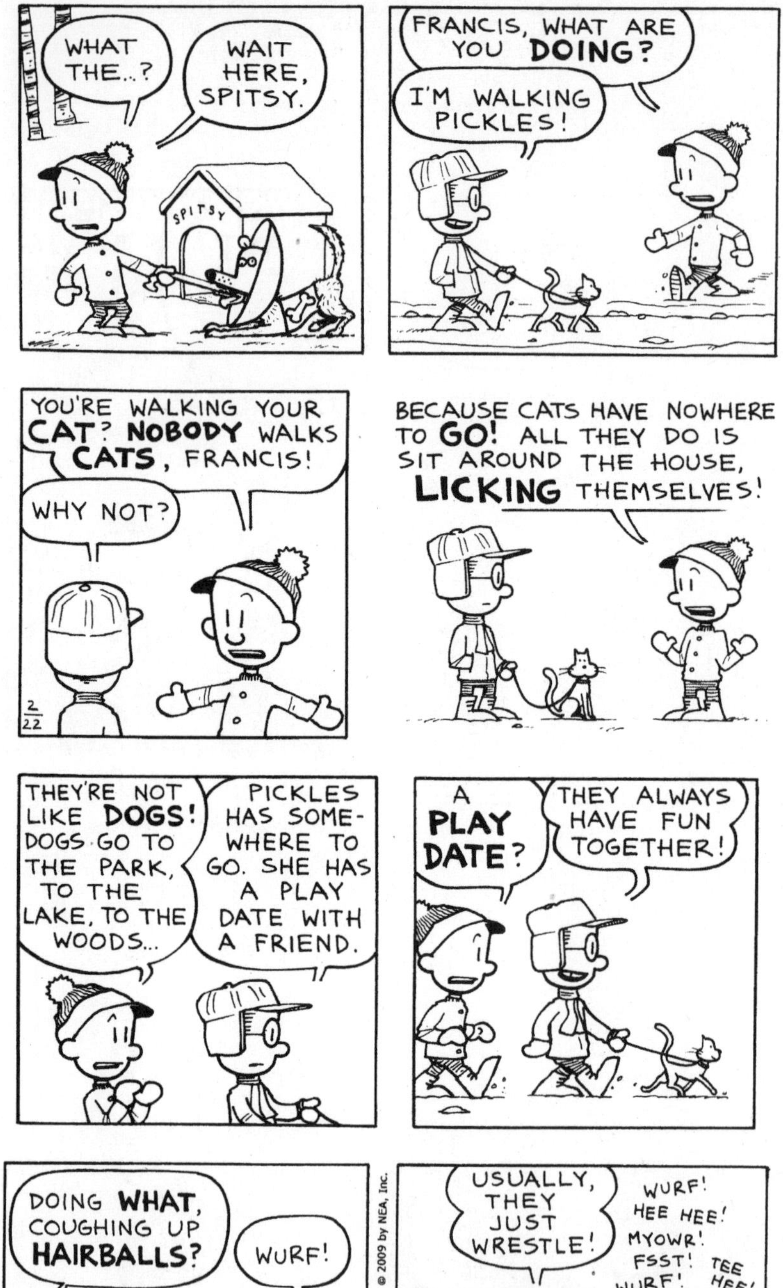
WHAT THE...?
WAIT HERE, SPITSY.
SPITSY
FRANCIS, WHAT ARE YOU DOING?
I'M WALKING PICKLES!
YOU'RE WALKING YOUR CAT? NOBODY WALKS CATS, FRANCIS!
WHY NOT?
2/22
BECAUSE CATS HAVE NOWHERE TO GO! ALL THEY DO IS SIT AROUND THE HOUSE, LICKING THEMSELVES!
THEY'RE NOT LIKE DOGS! DOGS GO TO THE PARK, TO THE LAKE, TO THE WOODS...
PICKLES HAS SOMEWHERE TO GO. SHE HAS A PLAY DATE WITH A FRIEND.
A PLAY DATE?
THEY ALWAYS HAVE FUN TOGETHER!
DOING WHAT, COUGHING UP HAIRBALLS?
WURF!
© 2009 by NEA, Inc.
USUALLY, THEY JUST WRESTLE!
WURF! HEE HEE! MYOWR! FSST! TEE HEE! WURF! ROWR! HEE! RUFF!
Peirce

EASY PEASY

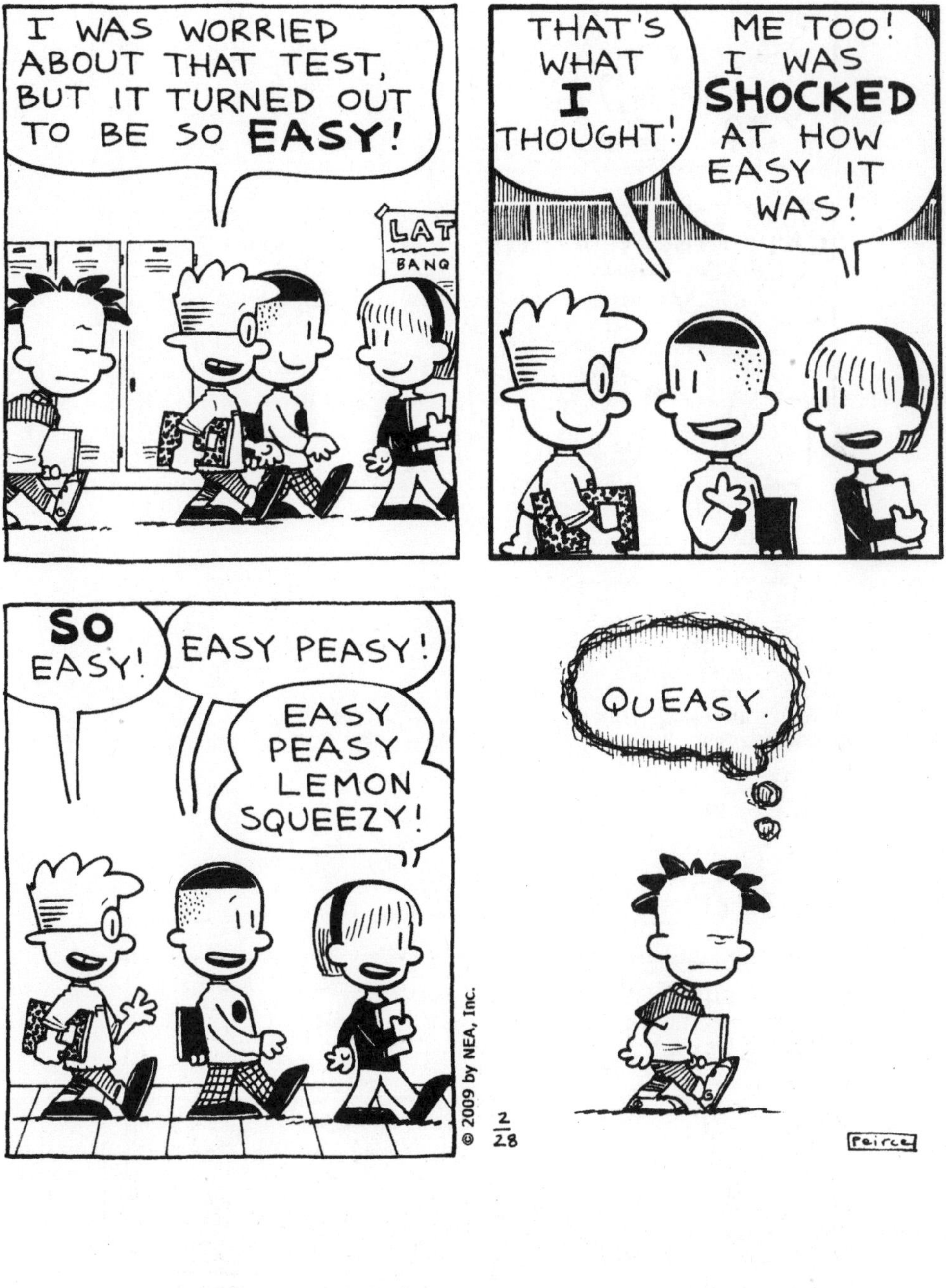
I WAS WORRIED ABOUT THAT TEST, BUT IT TURNED OUT TO BE SO EASY!
LAT
BANQ
THAT'S WHAT I THOUGHT!
ME TOO! I WAS SHOCKED AT HOW EASY IT WAS!
SO EASY!
EASY PEASY!
EASY PEASY LEMON SQUEEZY!
© 2009 by NEA, Inc.
2/28
QUEASY.
peirce

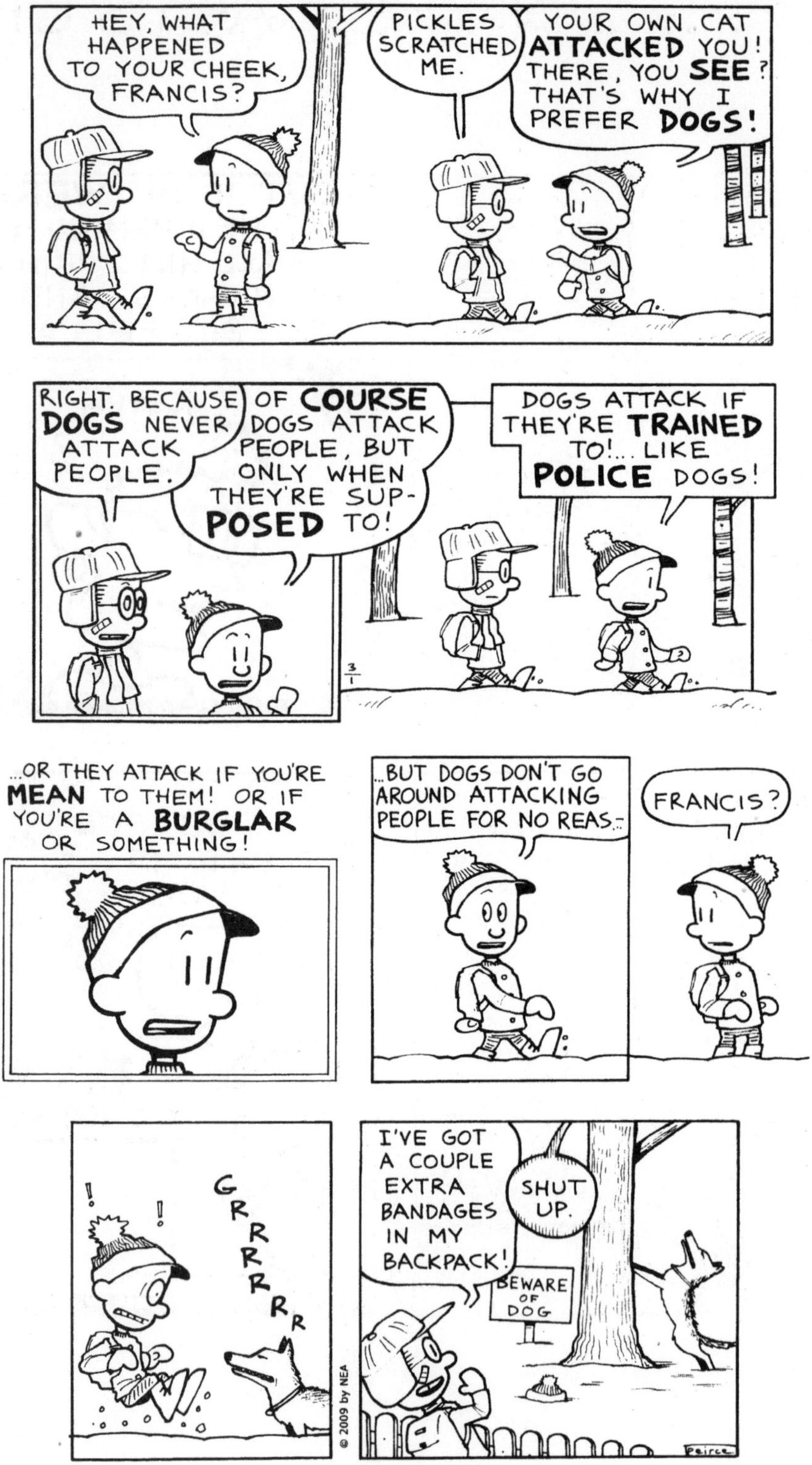
HEY, WHAT HAPPENED TO YOUR CHEEK, FRANCIS?
PICKLES SCRATCHED ME.
YOUR OWN CAT ATTACKED YOU! THERE, YOU SEE? THAT'S WHY I PREFER DOGS!
RIGHT. BECAUSE DOGS NEVER ATTACK PEOPLE.
OF COURSE DOGS ATTACK PEOPLE, BUT ONLY WHEN THEY'RE SUPPOSED TO!
DOGS ATTACK IF THEY'RE TRAINED TO!... LIKE POLICE DOGS!
...OR THEY ATTACK IF YOU'RE MEAN TO THEM! OR IF YOU'RE A BURGLAR OR SOMETHING!
...BUT DOGS DON'T GO AROUND ATTACKING PEOPLE FOR NO REAS–
FRANCIS?
! !
GRRRRRR
© 2009 by NEA
I'VE GOT A COUPLE EXTRA BANDAGES IN MY BACKPACK!
SHUT UP.
BEWARE OF DOG
Peirce

MRS. GODFREY ACTS UP

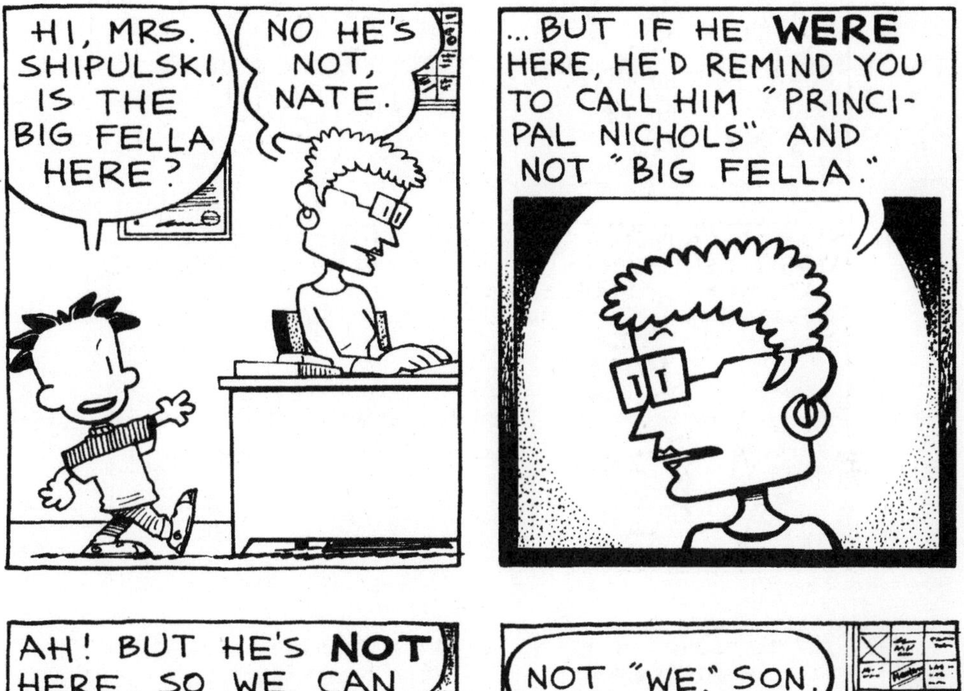
HI, MRS. SHIPULSKI, IS THE BIG FELLA HERE?
NO HE'S NOT, NATE.
...BUT IF HE **WERE** HERE, HE'D REMIND YOU TO CALL HIM "PRINCIPAL NICHOLS" AND NOT "BIG FELLA."
AH! BUT HE'S **NOT** HERE, SO WE CAN CALL HIM WHATEVER WE **WANT**!
3/2
© 2009 by NEA, Inc.
NOT "WE," SON. THERE IS NO "WE."
HOW ABOUT "SHEMP"?
Peirce

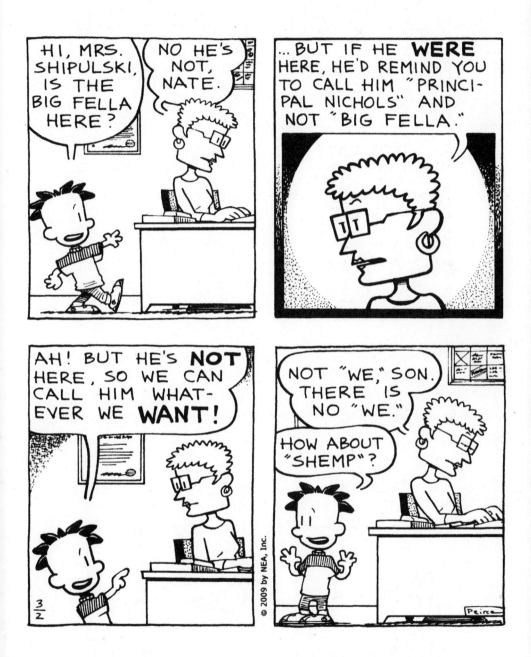

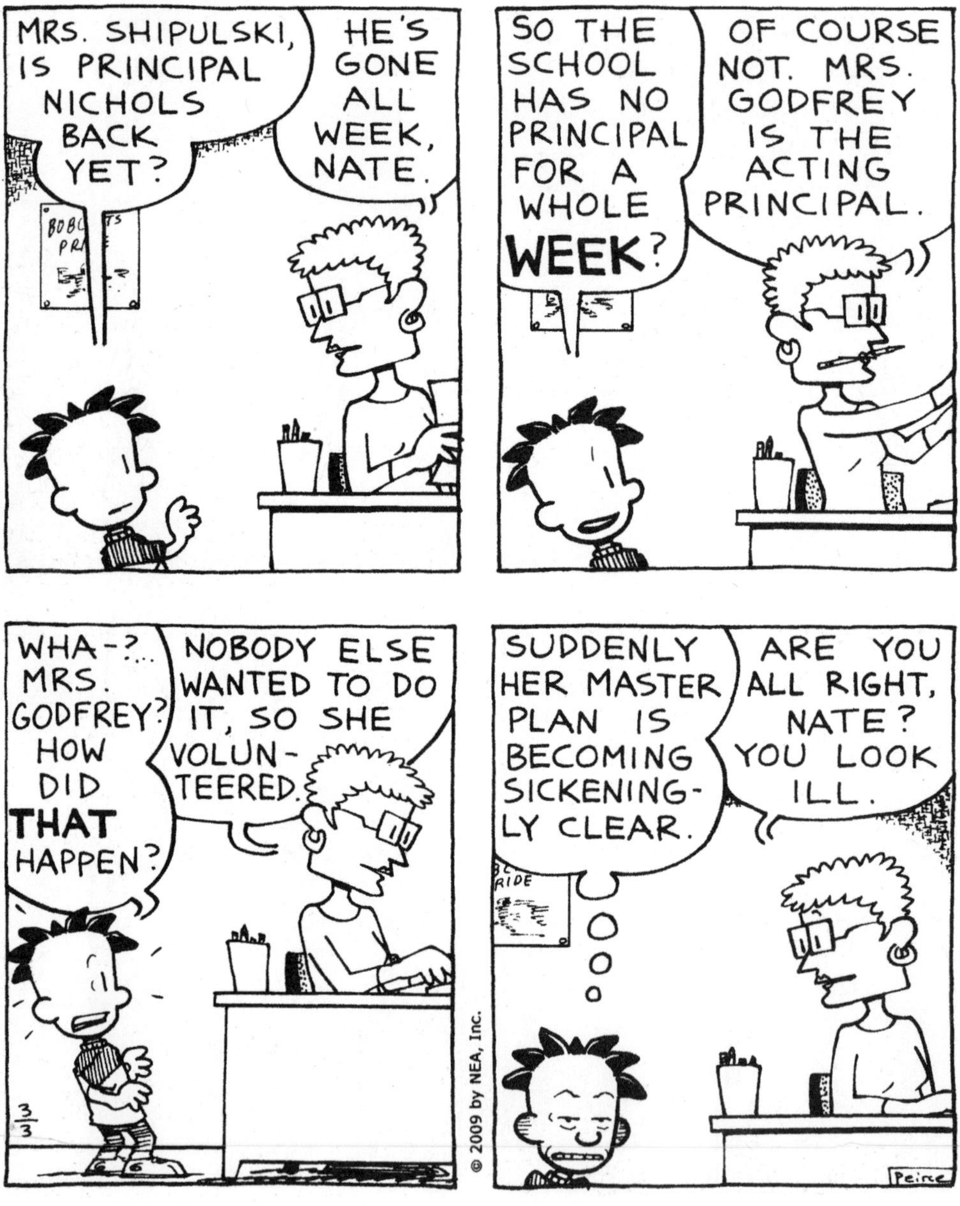
MRS. SHIPULSKI, IS PRINCIPAL NICHOLS BACK YET?
HE'S GONE ALL WEEK, NATE.
SO THE SCHOOL HAS NO PRINCIPAL FOR A WHOLE WEEK?
OF COURSE NOT. MRS. GODFREY IS THE ACTING PRINCIPAL.
WHA-?... MRS. GODFREY? HOW DID THAT HAPPEN?
NOBODY ELSE WANTED TO DO IT, SO SHE VOLUNTEERED.
SUDDENLY HER MASTER PLAN IS BECOMING SICKENINGLY CLEAR.
ARE YOU ALL RIGHT, NATE? YOU LOOK ILL.
3/3
© 2009 by NEA, Inc.
Peirce

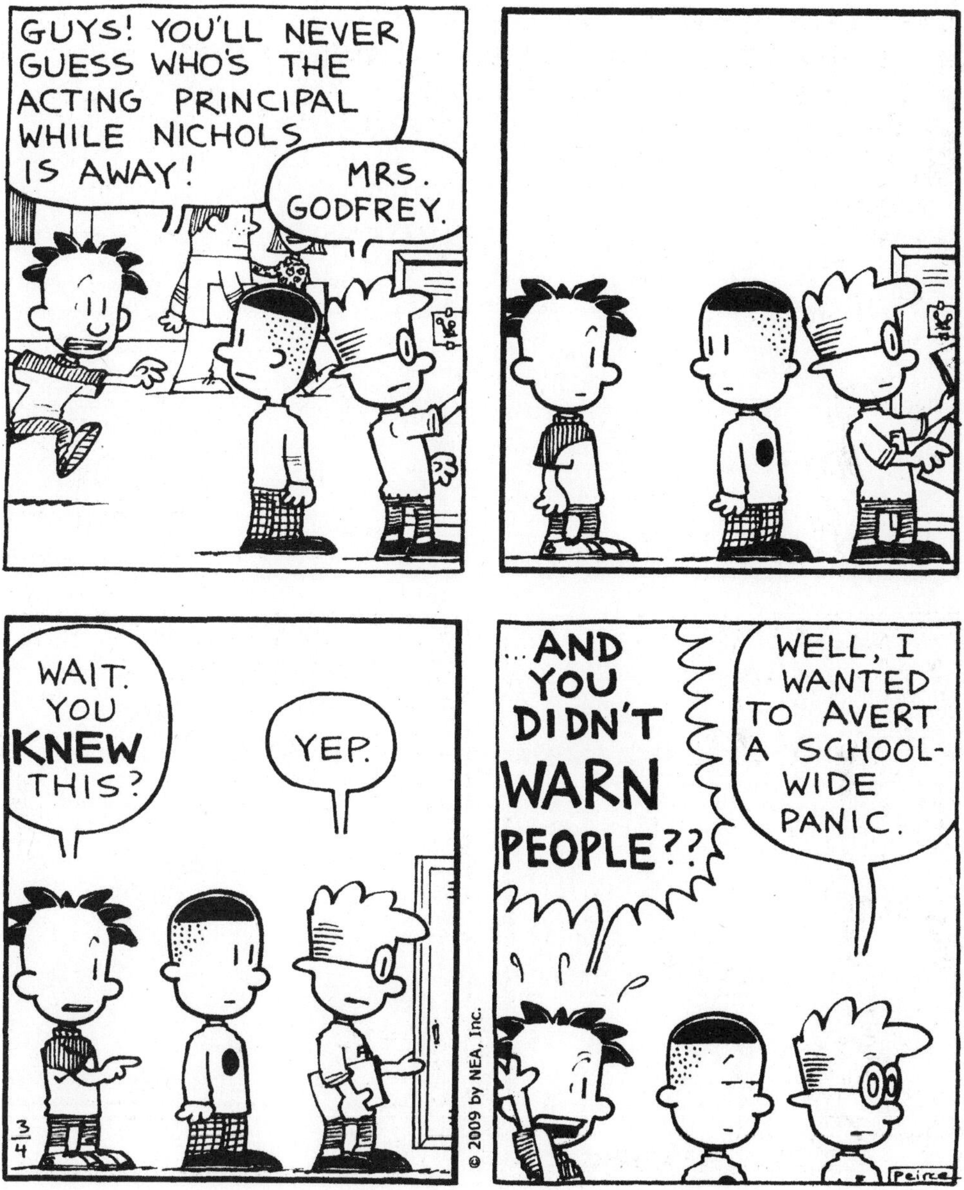
GUYS! YOU'LL NEVER GUESS WHO'S THE ACTING PRINCIPAL WHILE NICHOLS IS AWAY!
MRS. GODFREY.
WAIT. YOU **KNEW** THIS?
YEP.
3/4
© 2009 by NEA, Inc.
...**AND YOU DIDN'T WARN PEOPLE**??
WELL, I WANTED TO AVERT A SCHOOL-WIDE PANIC.
Peirce

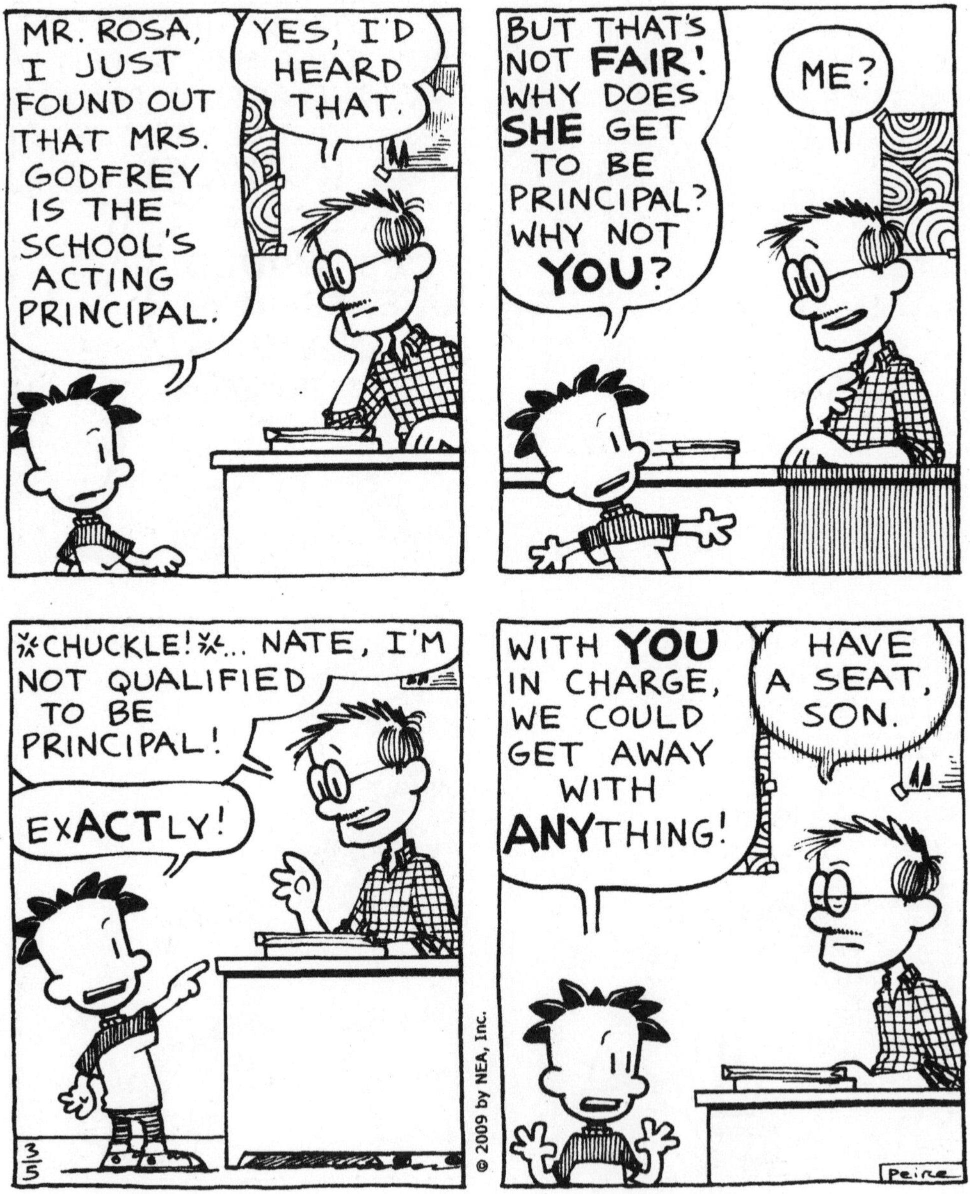
MR. ROSA, I JUST FOUND OUT THAT MRS. GODFREY IS THE SCHOOL'S ACTING PRINCIPAL.
YES, I'D HEARD THAT.
BUT THAT'S NOT FAIR! WHY DOES SHE GET TO BE PRINCIPAL? WHY NOT YOU?
ME?
CHUCKLE!... NATE, I'M NOT QUALIFIED TO BE PRINCIPAL!
ExACTly!
WITH YOU IN CHARGE, WE COULD GET AWAY WITH ANYTHING!
HAVE A SEAT, SON.
3/5
© 2009 by NEA, Inc.
Peirce

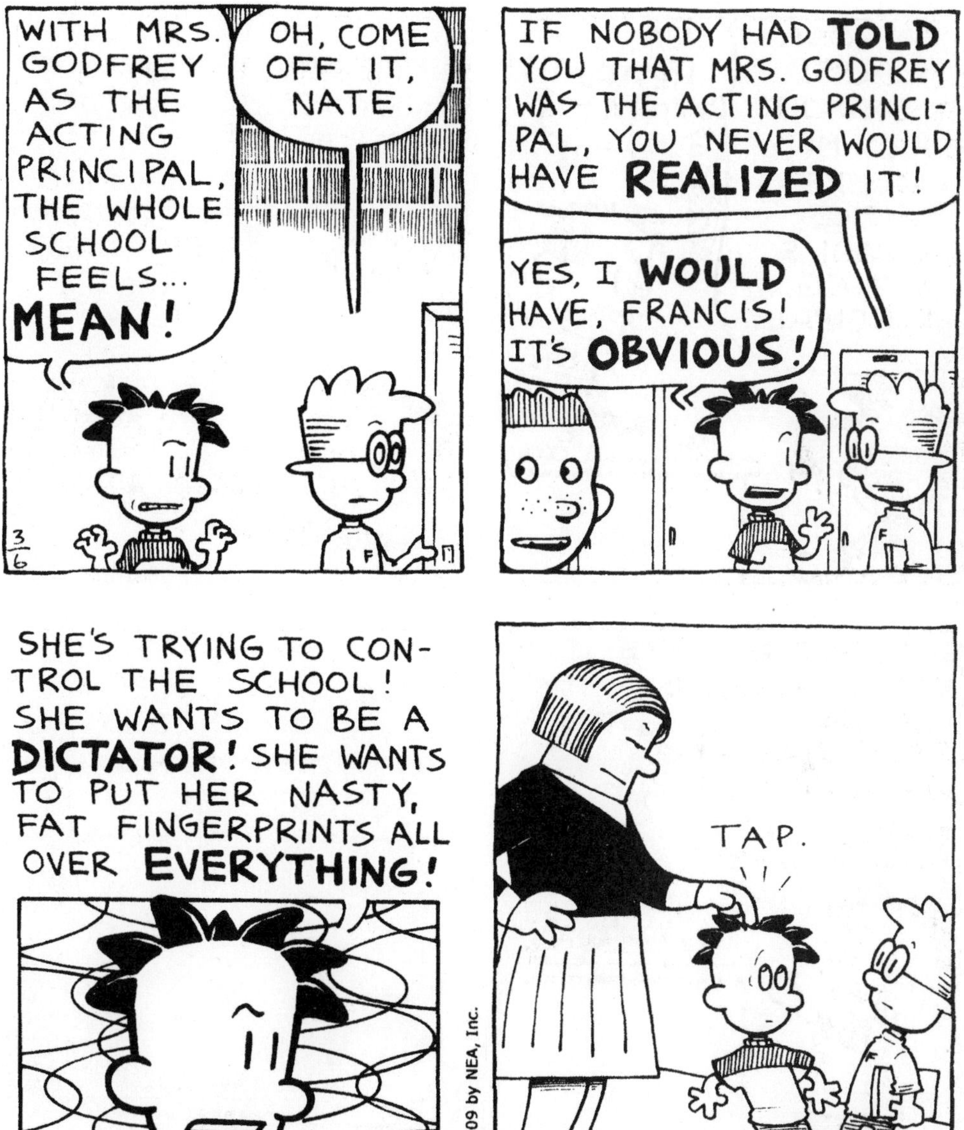
WITH MRS. GODFREY AS THE ACTING PRINCIPAL, THE WHOLE SCHOOL FEELS... MEAN!
OH, COME OFF IT, NATE.
3/6
IF NOBODY HAD TOLD YOU THAT MRS. GODFREY WAS THE ACTING PRINCIPAL, YOU NEVER WOULD HAVE REALIZED IT!
YES, I WOULD HAVE, FRANCIS! IT'S OBVIOUS!
SHE'S TRYING TO CONTROL THE SCHOOL! SHE WANTS TO BE A DICTATOR! SHE WANTS TO PUT HER NASTY, FAT FINGERPRINTS ALL OVER EVERYTHING!
TAP.
Peirce

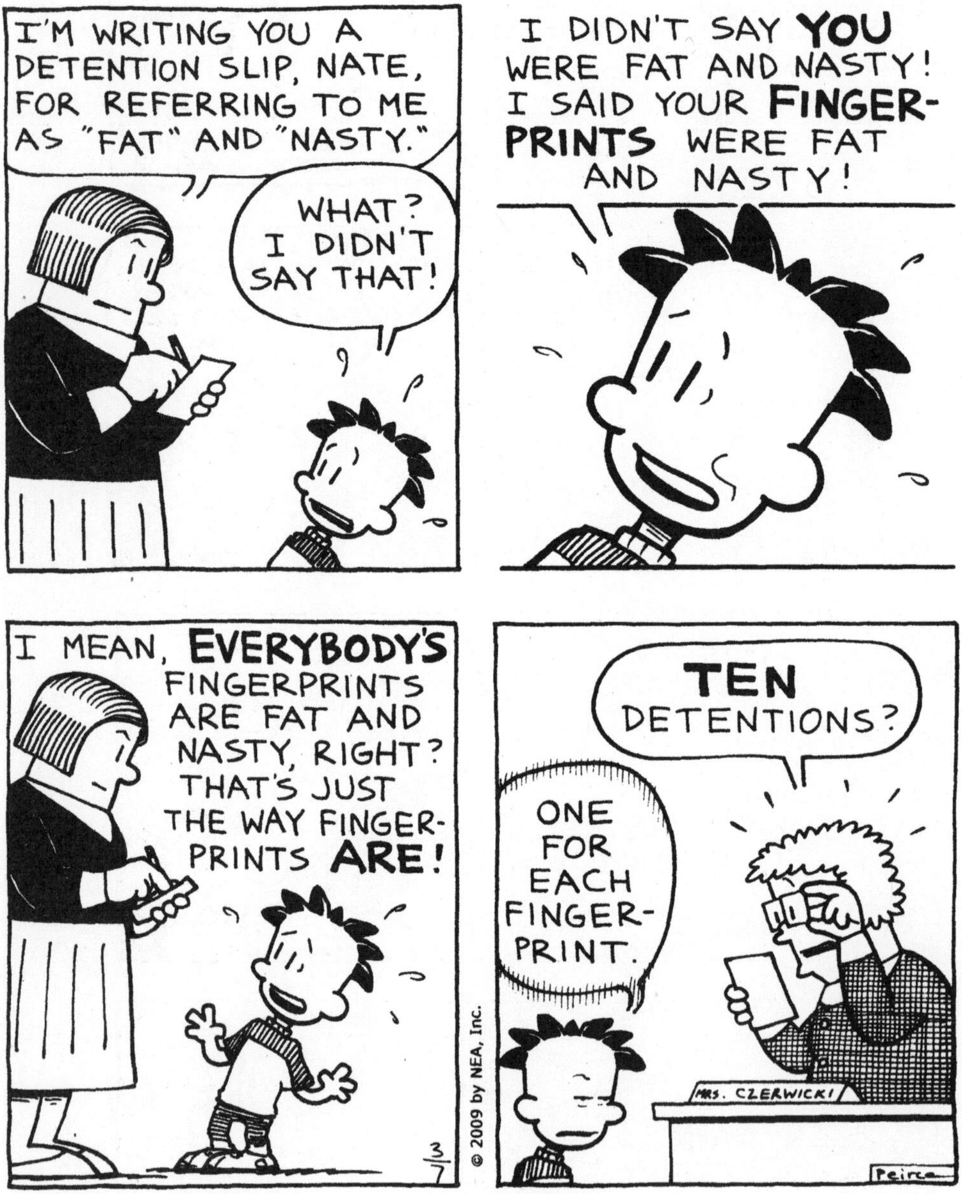
I'M WRITING YOU A DETENTION SLIP, NATE, FOR REFERRING TO ME AS "FAT" AND "NASTY."
WHAT? I DIDN'T SAY THAT!
I DIDN'T SAY **YOU** WERE FAT AND NASTY! I SAID YOUR **FINGER-PRINTS** WERE FAT AND NASTY!
I MEAN, **EVERYBODY'S** FINGERPRINTS ARE FAT AND NASTY, RIGHT? THAT'S JUST THE WAY FINGER-PRINTS **ARE**!
3/7
© 2009 by NEA, Inc.
TEN DETENTIONS?
ONE FOR EACH FINGER-PRINT.
MRS. CZERWICKI
Peirce

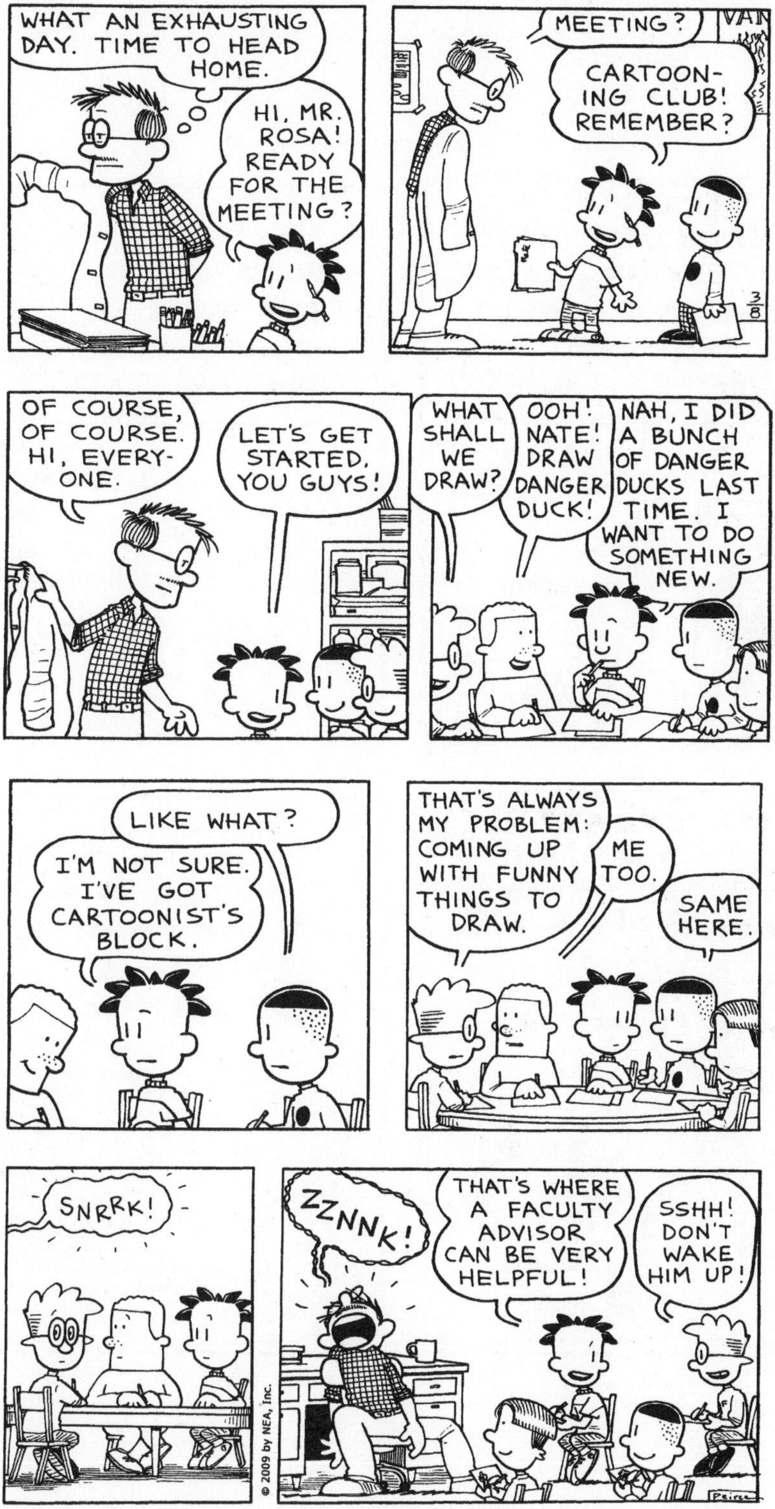
WHAT AN EXHAUSTING DAY. TIME TO HEAD HOME.
HI, MR. ROSA! READY FOR THE MEETING?
MEETING?
CARTOON-ING CLUB! REMEMBER?
3/8
OF COURSE, OF COURSE. HI, EVERY-ONE.
LET'S GET STARTED, YOU GUYS!
WHAT SHALL WE DRAW?
OOH! NATE! DRAW DANGER DUCK!
NAH, I DID A BUNCH OF DANGER DUCKS LAST TIME. I WANT TO DO SOMETHING NEW.
LIKE WHAT?
I'M NOT SURE. I'VE GOT CARTOONIST'S BLOCK.
THAT'S ALWAYS MY PROBLEM: COMING UP WITH FUNNY THINGS TO DRAW.
ME TOO.
SAME HERE.
SNRRK!
© 2009 by NEA, Inc.
ZZNNK!
THAT'S WHERE A FACULTY ADVISOR CAN BE VERY HELPFUL!
SSHH! DON'T WAKE HIM UP!
Peirce

FAME OR LAME?

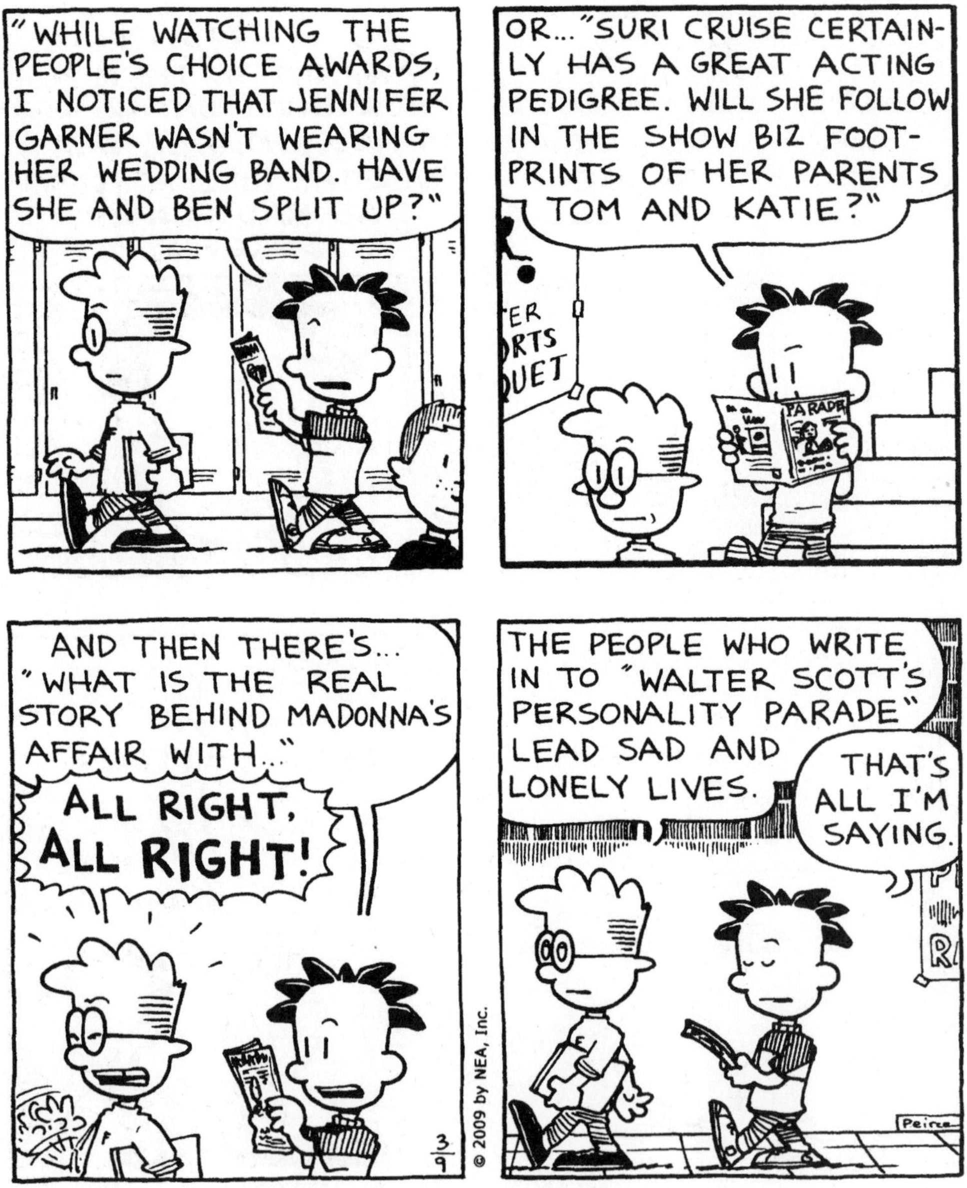
"WHILE WATCHING THE PEOPLE'S CHOICE AWARDS, I NOTICED THAT JENNIFER GARNER WASN'T WEARING HER WEDDING BAND. HAVE SHE AND BEN SPLIT UP?"
OR..."SURI CRUISE CERTAINLY HAS A GREAT ACTING PEDIGREE. WILL SHE FOLLOW IN THE SHOW BIZ FOOTPRINTS OF HER PARENTS TOM AND KATIE?"
PARADE
AND THEN THERE'S... "WHAT IS THE REAL STORY BEHIND MADONNA'S AFFAIR WITH..."
ALL RIGHT, ALL RIGHT!
3/9
© 2009 by NEA, Inc.
THE PEOPLE WHO WRITE IN TO "WALTER SCOTT'S PERSONALITY PARADE" LEAD SAD AND LONELY LIVES.
THAT'S ALL I'M SAYING.
Peirce

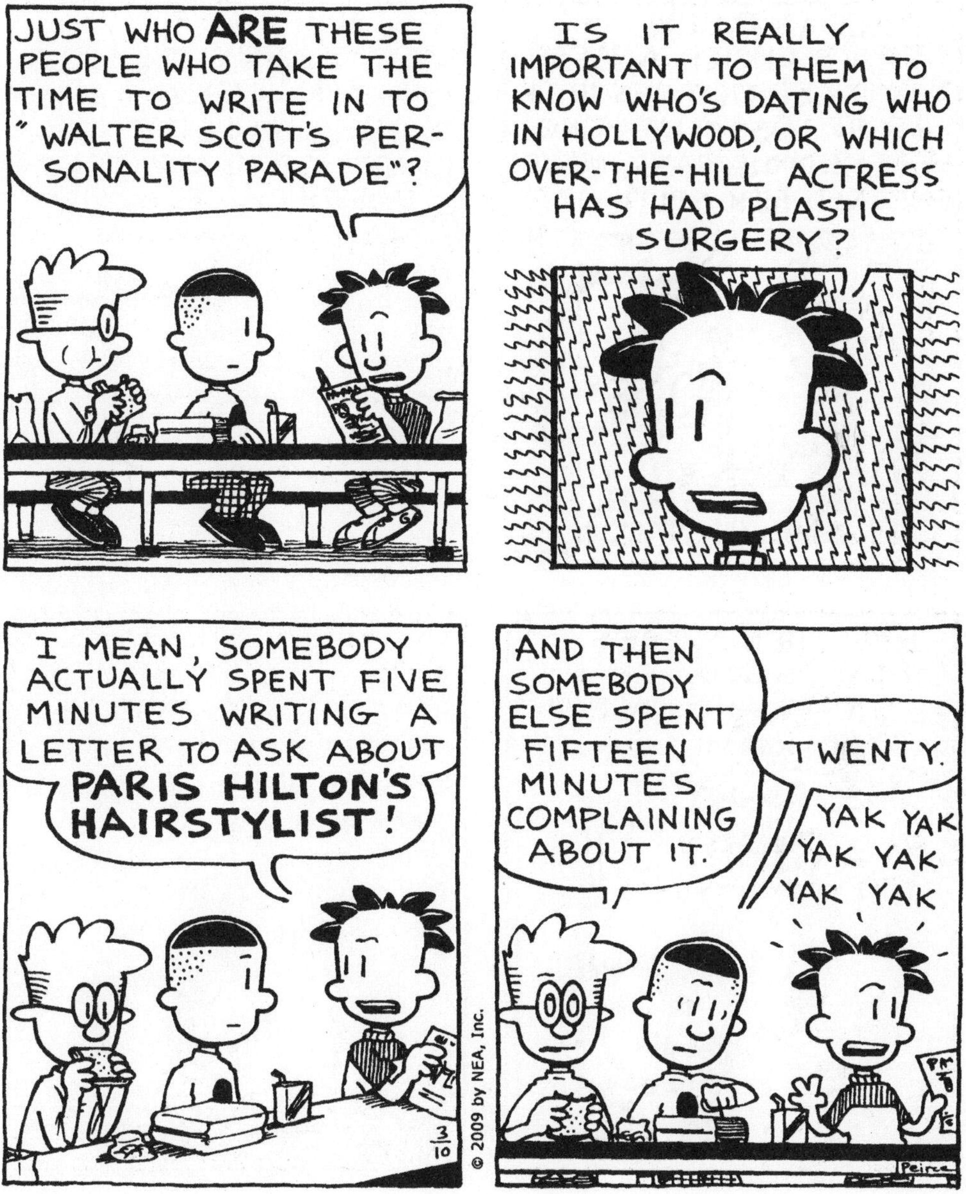
JUST WHO **ARE** THESE PEOPLE WHO TAKE THE TIME TO WRITE IN TO "WALTER SCOTT'S PERSONALITY PARADE"?
IS IT REALLY IMPORTANT TO THEM TO KNOW WHO'S DATING WHO IN HOLLYWOOD, OR WHICH OVER-THE-HILL ACTRESS HAS HAD PLASTIC SURGERY?
I MEAN, SOMEBODY ACTUALLY SPENT FIVE MINUTES WRITING A LETTER TO ASK ABOUT **PARIS HILTON'S HAIRSTYLIST**!
AND THEN SOMEBODY ELSE SPENT FIFTEEN MINUTES COMPLAINING ABOUT IT.
TWENTY.
YAK YAK YAK YAK YAK YAK
Peirce

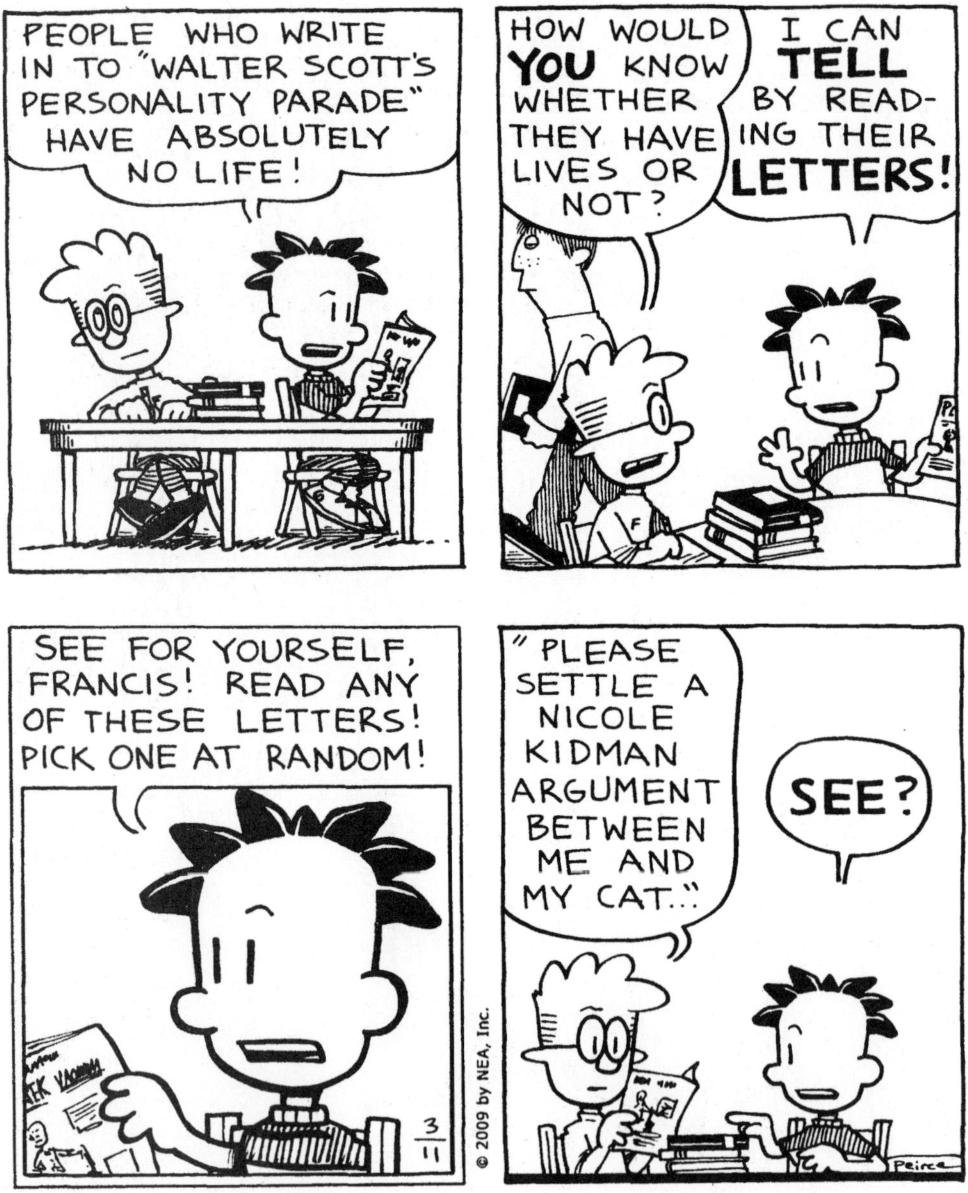
PEOPLE WHO WRITE IN TO "WALTER SCOTT'S PERSONALITY PARADE" HAVE ABSOLUTELY NO LIFE!
HOW WOULD YOU KNOW WHETHER THEY HAVE LIVES OR NOT?
I CAN TELL BY READING THEIR LETTERS!
SEE FOR YOURSELF, FRANCIS! READ ANY OF THESE LETTERS! PICK ONE AT RANDOM!
3/11
© 2009 by NEA, Inc.
"PLEASE SETTLE A NICOLE KIDMAN ARGUMENT BETWEEN ME AND MY CAT..."
SEE?
Peirce

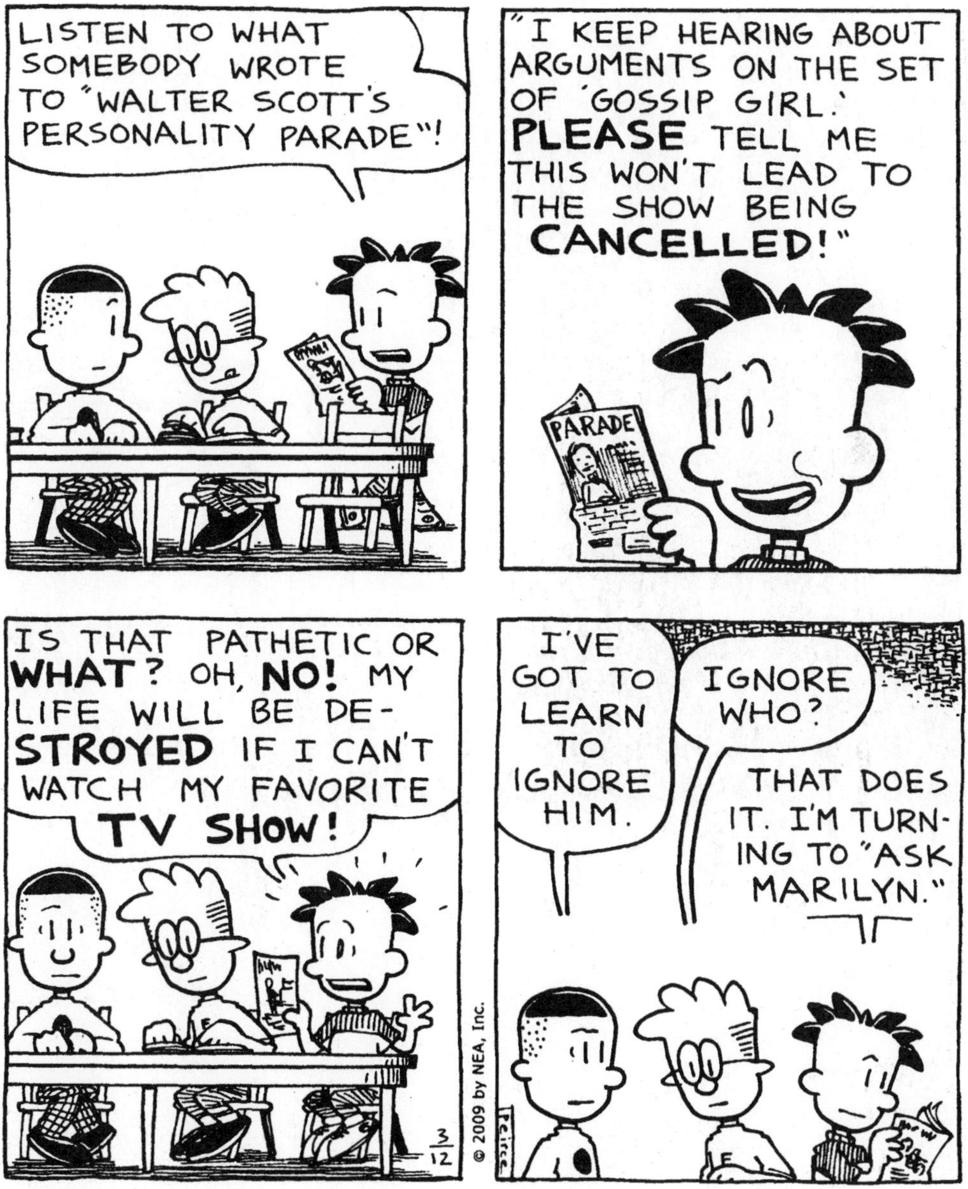
LISTEN TO WHAT SOMEBODY WROTE TO "WALTER SCOTT'S PERSONALITY PARADE"!
"I KEEP HEARING ABOUT ARGUMENTS ON THE SET OF 'GOSSIP GIRL.' PLEASE TELL ME THIS WON'T LEAD TO THE SHOW BEING CANCELLED!"
PARADE
IS THAT PATHETIC OR WHAT? OH, NO! MY LIFE WILL BE DESTROYED IF I CAN'T WATCH MY FAVORITE TV SHOW!
3/12
© 2009 by NEA, Inc.
Peirce
I'VE GOT TO LEARN TO IGNORE HIM.
IGNORE WHO?
THAT DOES IT. I'M TURNING TO "ASK MARILYN."

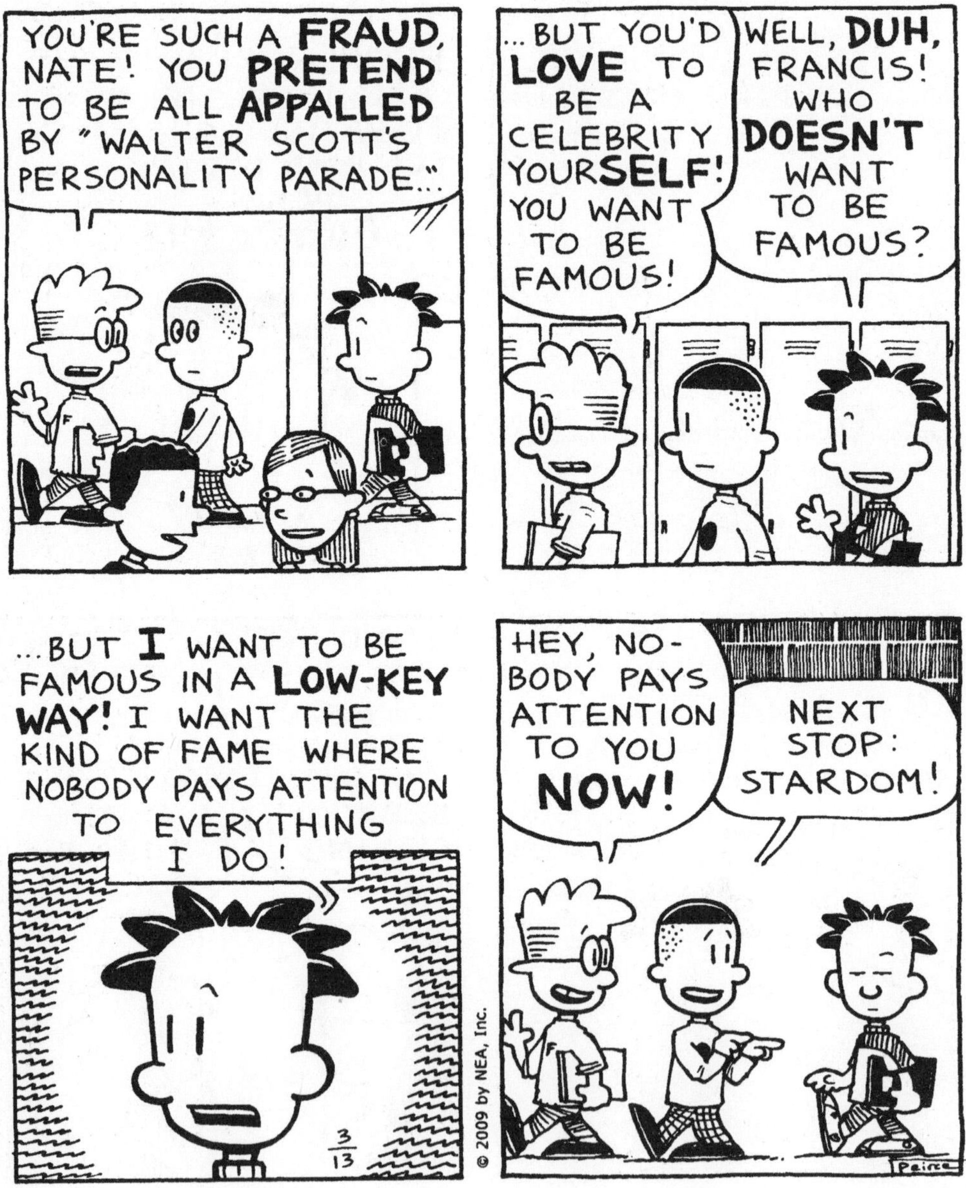
YOU'RE SUCH A FRAUD, NATE! YOU PRETEND TO BE ALL APPALLED BY "WALTER SCOTT'S PERSONALITY PARADE..."
...BUT YOU'D LOVE TO BE A CELEBRITY YOURSELF! YOU WANT TO BE FAMOUS!
WELL, DUH, FRANCIS! WHO DOESN'T WANT TO BE FAMOUS?
...BUT I WANT TO BE FAMOUS IN A LOW-KEY WAY! I WANT THE KIND OF FAME WHERE NOBODY PAYS ATTENTION TO EVERYTHING I DO!
3/13
© 2009 by NEA, Inc.
HEY, NOBODY PAYS ATTENTION TO YOU NOW!
NEXT STOP: STARDOM!
Peirce

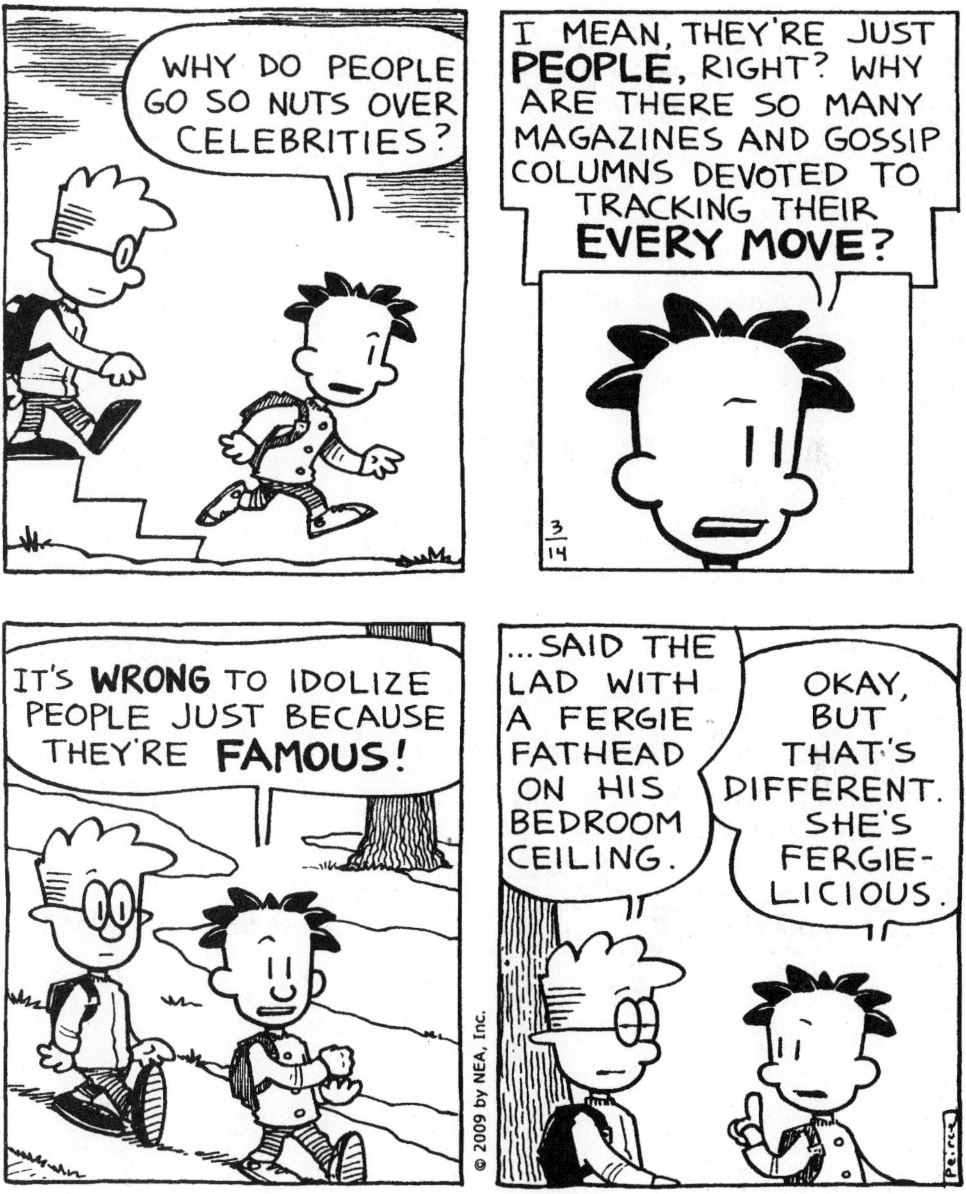
WHY DO PEOPLE GO SO NUTS OVER CELEBRITIES?
I MEAN, THEY'RE JUST PEOPLE, RIGHT? WHY ARE THERE SO MANY MAGAZINES AND GOSSIP COLUMNS DEVOTED TO TRACKING THEIR EVERY MOVE?
3/14
IT'S WRONG TO IDOLIZE PEOPLE JUST BECAUSE THEY'RE FAMOUS!
© 2009 by NEA, Inc.
...SAID THE LAD WITH A FERGIE FATHEAD ON HIS BEDROOM CEILING.
OKAY, BUT THAT'S DIFFERENT. SHE'S FERGIE-LICIOUS.
Peirce

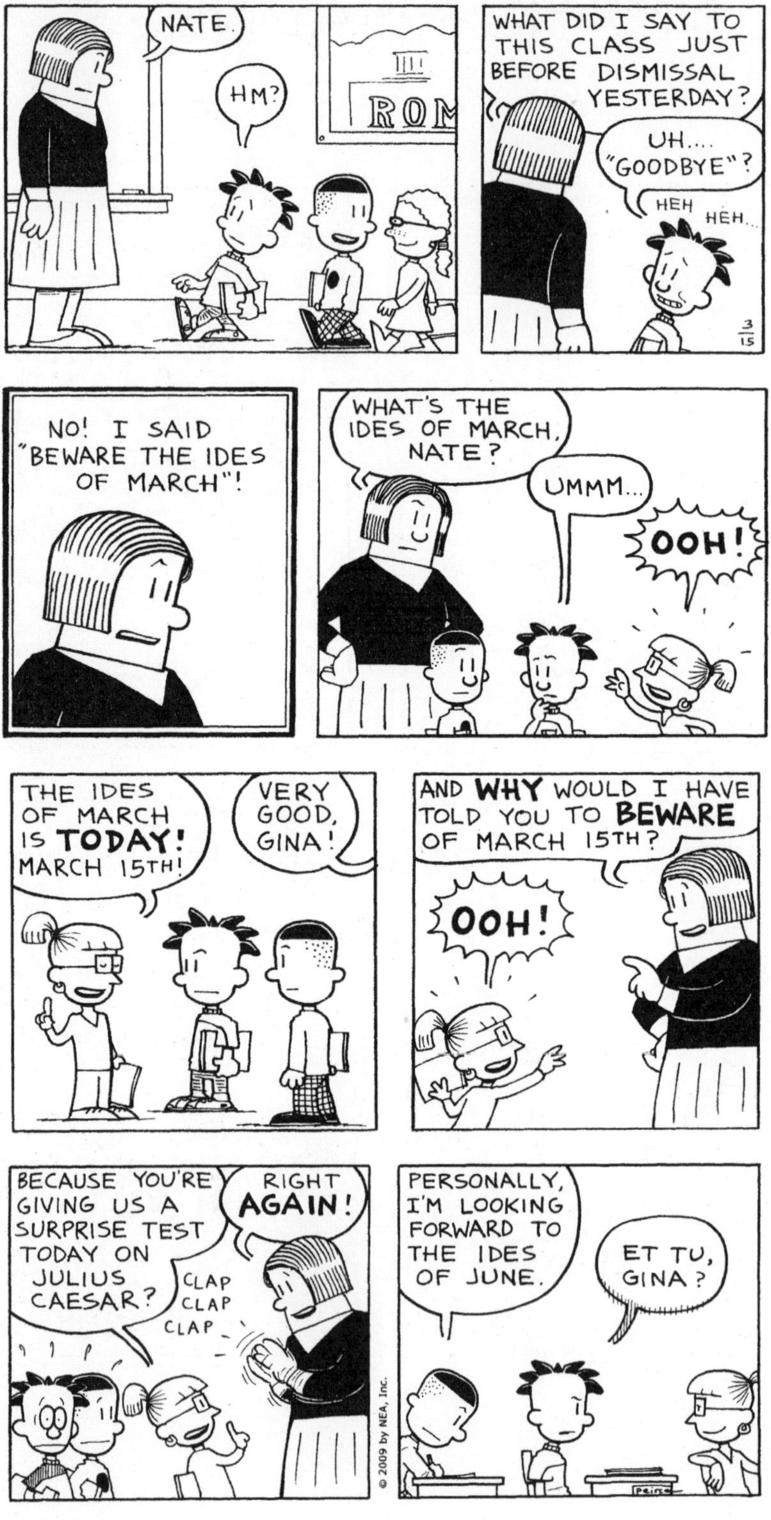
NATE.
HM?
ROM
WHAT DID I SAY TO THIS CLASS JUST BEFORE DISMISSAL YESTERDAY?
UH.... "GOODBYE"?
HEH HEH...
3/15
NO! I SAID "BEWARE THE IDES OF MARCH"!
WHAT'S THE IDES OF MARCH, NATE?
UMMM...
OOH!
THE IDES OF MARCH IS TODAY! MARCH 15TH!
VERY GOOD, GINA!
AND WHY WOULD I HAVE TOLD YOU TO BEWARE OF MARCH 15TH?
OOH!
BECAUSE YOU'RE GIVING US A SURPRISE TEST TODAY ON JULIUS CAESAR?
RIGHT AGAIN!
CLAP CLAP CLAP
© 2009 by NEA, Inc.
PERSONALLY, I'M LOOKING FORWARD TO THE IDES OF JUNE.
ET TU, GINA?
Peirce

MARCH MADNESS

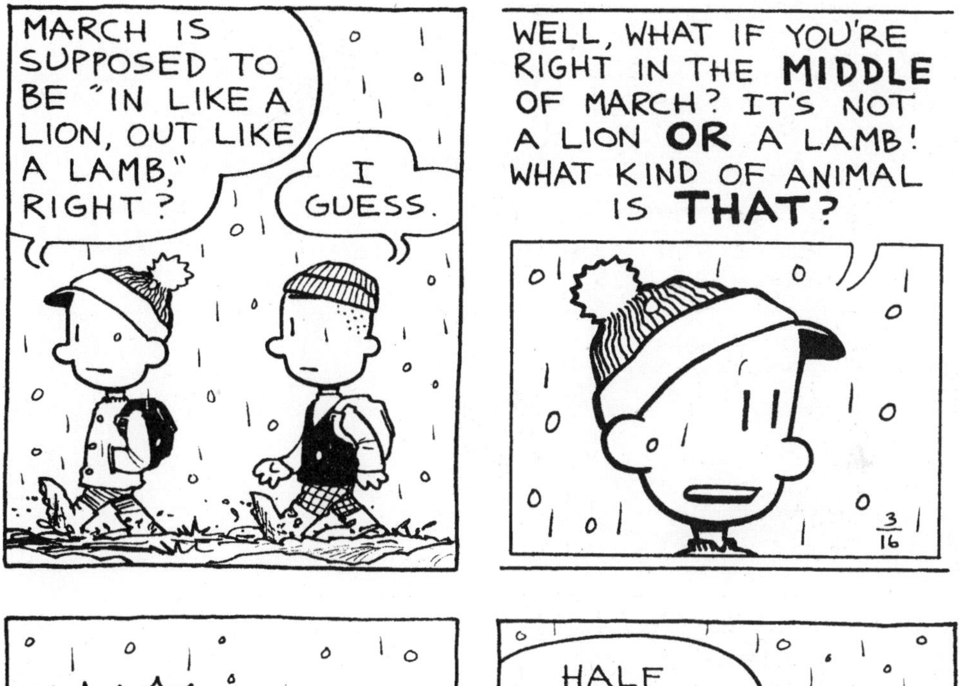
MARCH IS SUPPOSED TO BE "IN LIKE A LION, OUT LIKE A LAMB," RIGHT?
I GUESS.
WELL, WHAT IF YOU'RE RIGHT IN THE **MIDDLE** OF MARCH? IT'S NOT A LION **OR** A LAMB! WHAT KIND OF ANIMAL IS **THAT**?
3/16
WURF!
HALF MUTT, HALF LINEBACKER!
WAG WAG WAG WAG WAG
SPITSY, YOU IDIOT.
Peirce

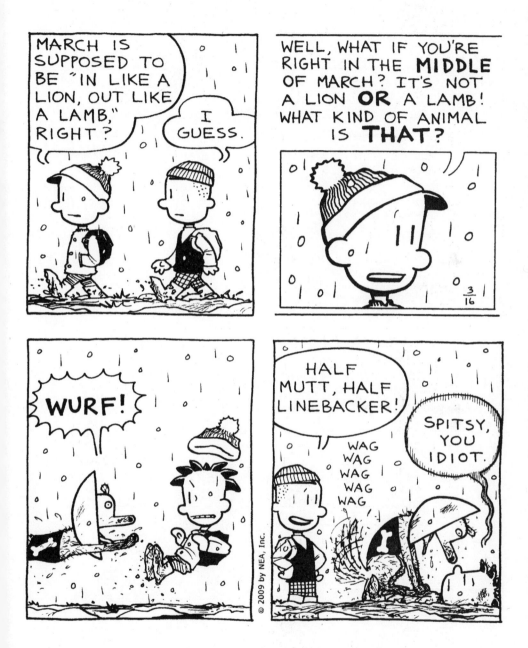

IS IT SPRING YET?

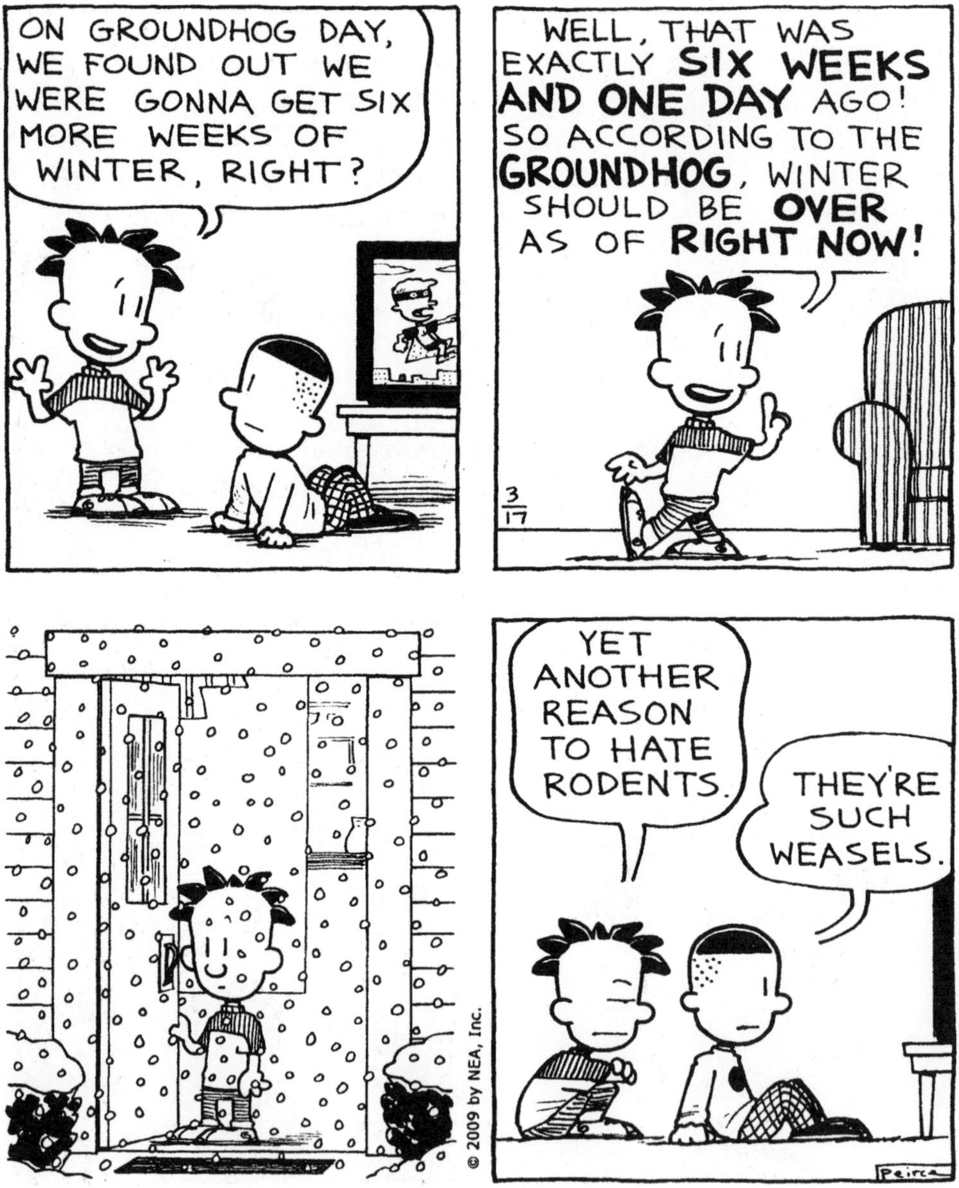
ON GROUNDHOG DAY, WE FOUND OUT WE WERE GONNA GET SIX MORE WEEKS OF WINTER, RIGHT?
WELL, THAT WAS EXACTLY SIX WEEKS AND ONE DAY AGO! SO ACCORDING TO THE GROUNDHOG, WINTER SHOULD BE OVER AS OF RIGHT NOW!
3
17
YET ANOTHER REASON TO HATE RODENTS.
THEY'RE SUCH WEASELS.
Peirce

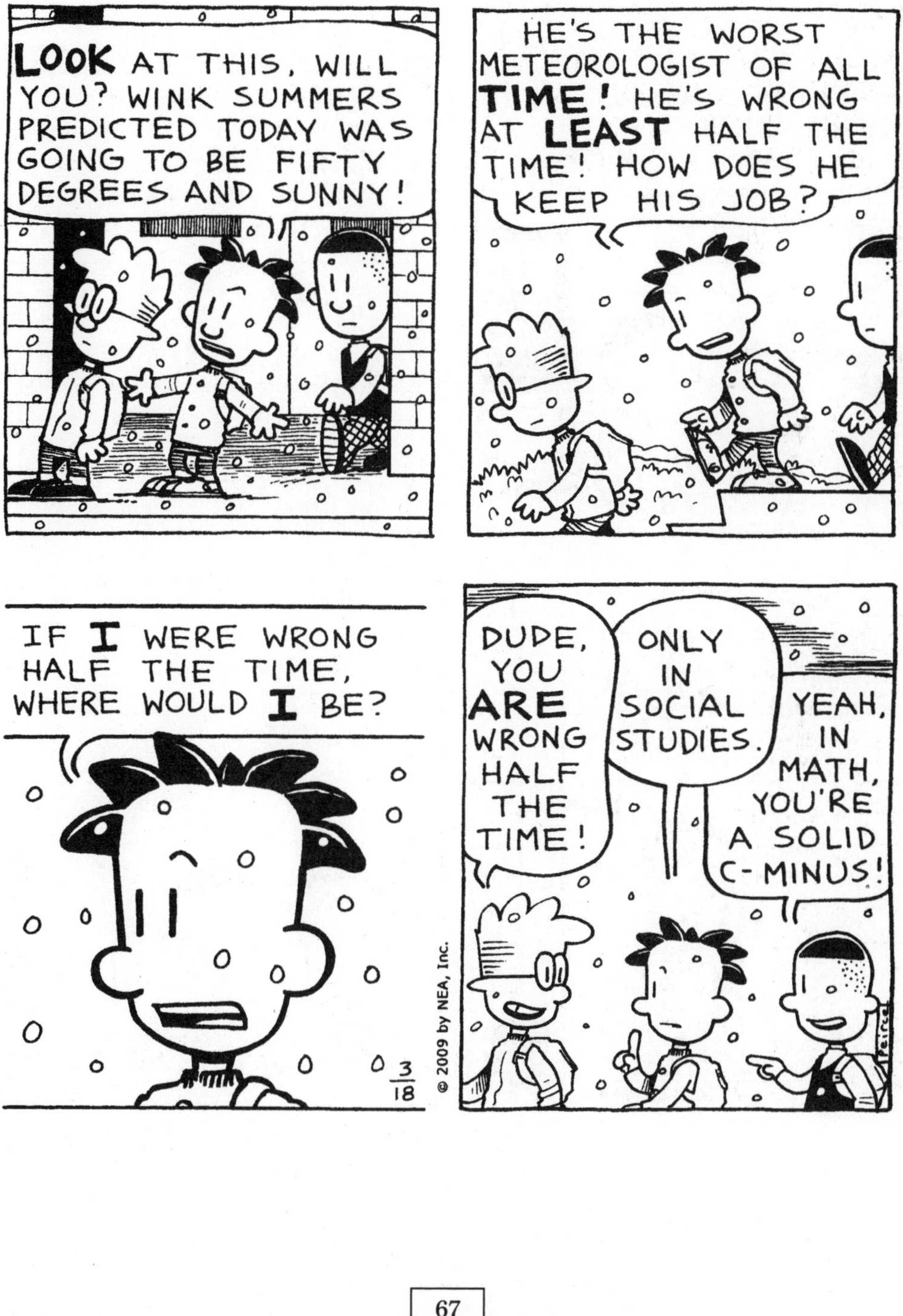
LOOK AT THIS, WILL YOU? WINK SUMMERS PREDICTED TODAY WAS GOING TO BE FIFTY DEGREES AND SUNNY!
HE'S THE WORST METEOROLOGIST OF ALL TIME! HE'S WRONG AT LEAST HALF THE TIME! HOW DOES HE KEEP HIS JOB?
IF I WERE WRONG HALF THE TIME, WHERE WOULD I BE?
DUDE, YOU ARE WRONG HALF THE TIME!
ONLY IN SOCIAL STUDIES.
YEAH, IN MATH, YOU'RE A SOLID C-MINUS!
3/18
© 2009 by NEA, Inc.
Peirce

TAKE OFF

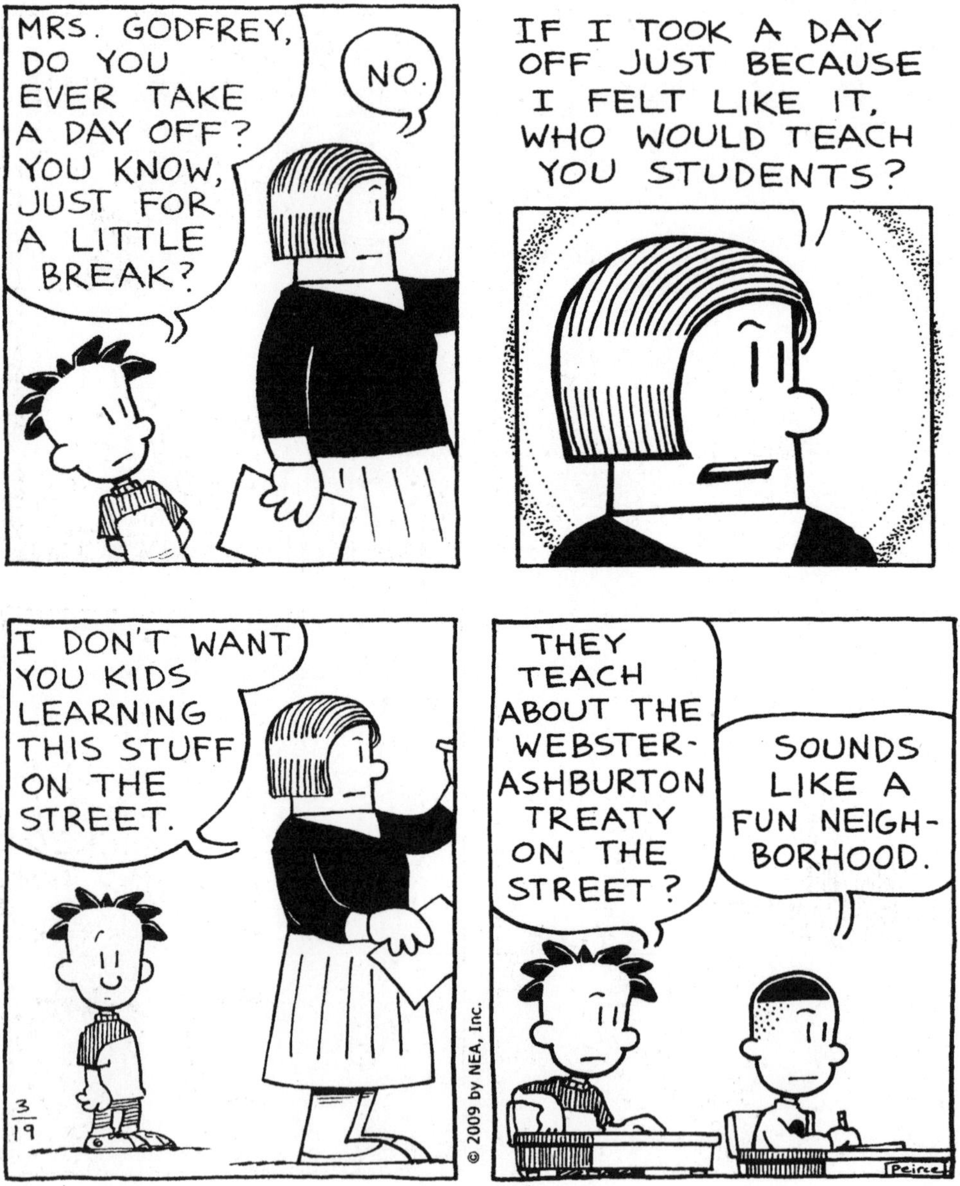
MRS. GODFREY, DO YOU EVER TAKE A DAY OFF? YOU KNOW, JUST FOR A LITTLE BREAK?
NO.
IF I TOOK A DAY OFF JUST BECAUSE I FELT LIKE IT, WHO WOULD TEACH YOU STUDENTS?
I DON'T WANT YOU KIDS LEARNING THIS STUFF ON THE STREET.
THEY TEACH ABOUT THE WEBSTER-ASHBURTON TREATY ON THE STREET?
SOUNDS LIKE A FUN NEIGH-BORHOOD.
3/19
© 2009 by NEA, Inc.
Peirce

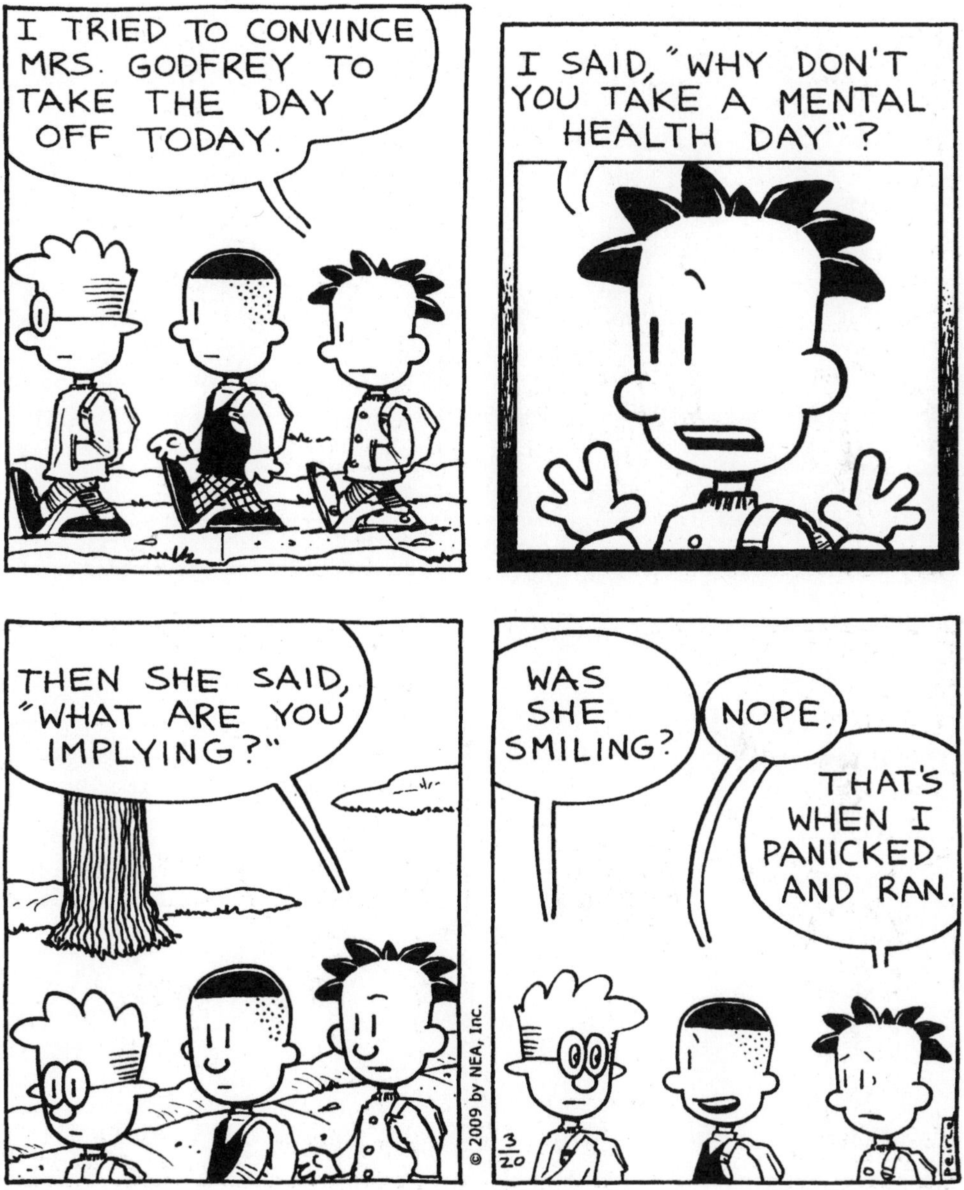
I TRIED TO CONVINCE MRS. GODFREY TO TAKE THE DAY OFF TODAY.
I SAID, "WHY DON'T YOU TAKE A MENTAL HEALTH DAY"?
THEN SHE SAID, "WHAT ARE YOU IMPLYING?"
WAS SHE SMILING?
NOPE.
THAT'S WHEN I PANICKED AND RAN.
© 2009 by NEA, Inc.
3/20
PEIRCE

WAIT 'TIL YOU SEE HIS MATH GRADE

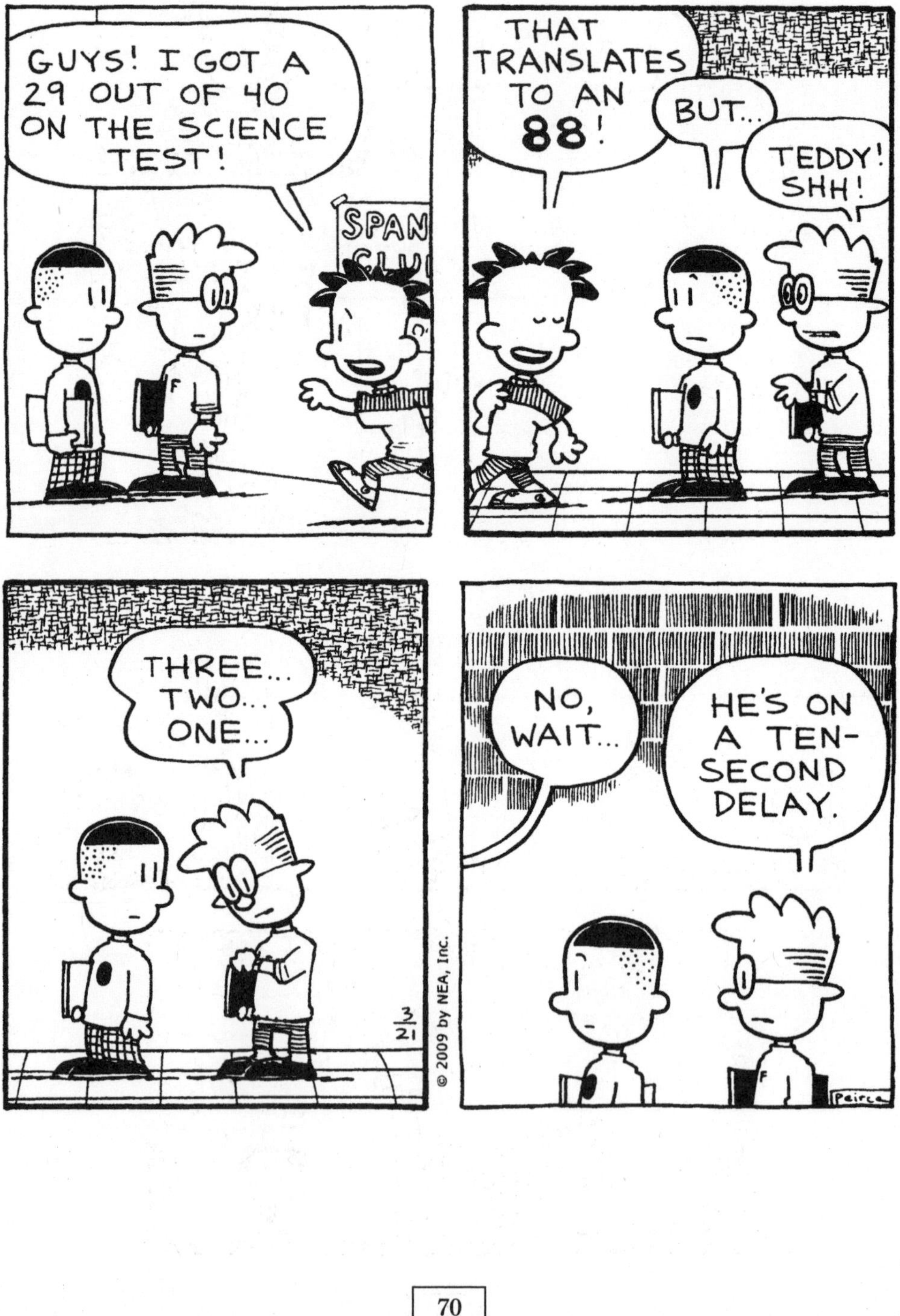
GUYS! I GOT A 29 OUT OF 40 ON THE SCIENCE TEST!
SPAN CLU
THAT TRANSLATES TO AN 88!
BUT...
TEDDY! SHH!
THREE... TWO... ONE...
3/21
© 2009 by NEA, Inc.
NO, WAIT...
HE'S ON A TEN-SECOND DELAY.
Peirce

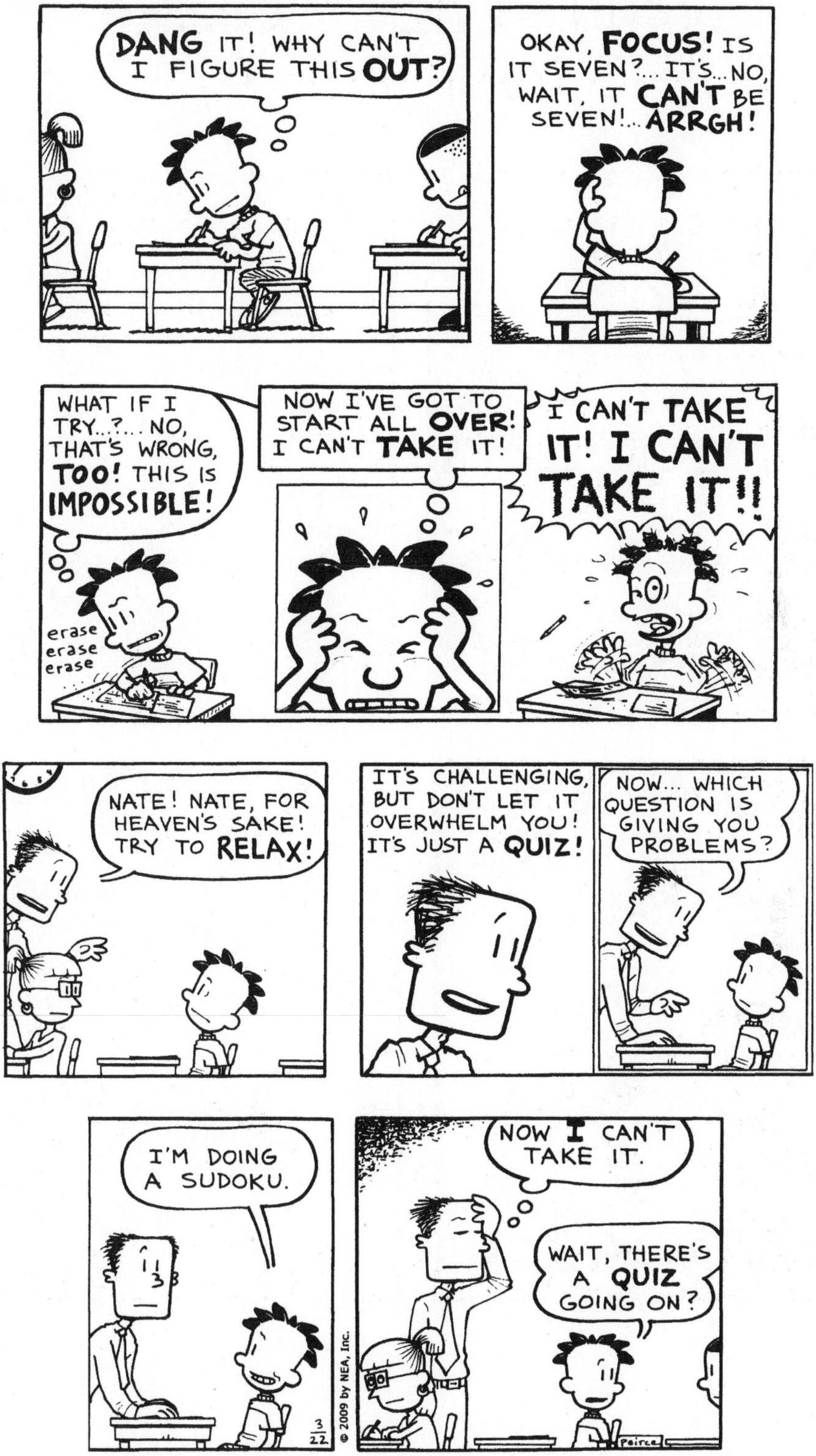
DANG IT! WHY CAN'T I FIGURE THIS OUT?
OKAY, FOCUS! IS IT SEVEN?... IT'S... NO, WAIT, IT CAN'T BE SEVEN!... ARRGH!
WHAT IF I TRY...?... NO, THAT'S WRONG, TOO! THIS IS IMPOSSIBLE!
erase erase erase
NOW I'VE GOT TO START ALL OVER! I CAN'T TAKE IT!
I CAN'T TAKE IT! I CAN'T TAKE IT!!
NATE! NATE, FOR HEAVEN'S SAKE! TRY TO RELAX!
IT'S CHALLENGING, BUT DON'T LET IT OVERWHELM YOU! IT'S JUST A QUIZ!
NOW... WHICH QUESTION IS GIVING YOU PROBLEMS?
I'M DOING A SUDOKU.
3/22
© 2009 by NEA, Inc.
NOW I CAN'T TAKE IT.
WAIT, THERE'S A QUIZ GOING ON?
Peirce

GOOD BREEDING

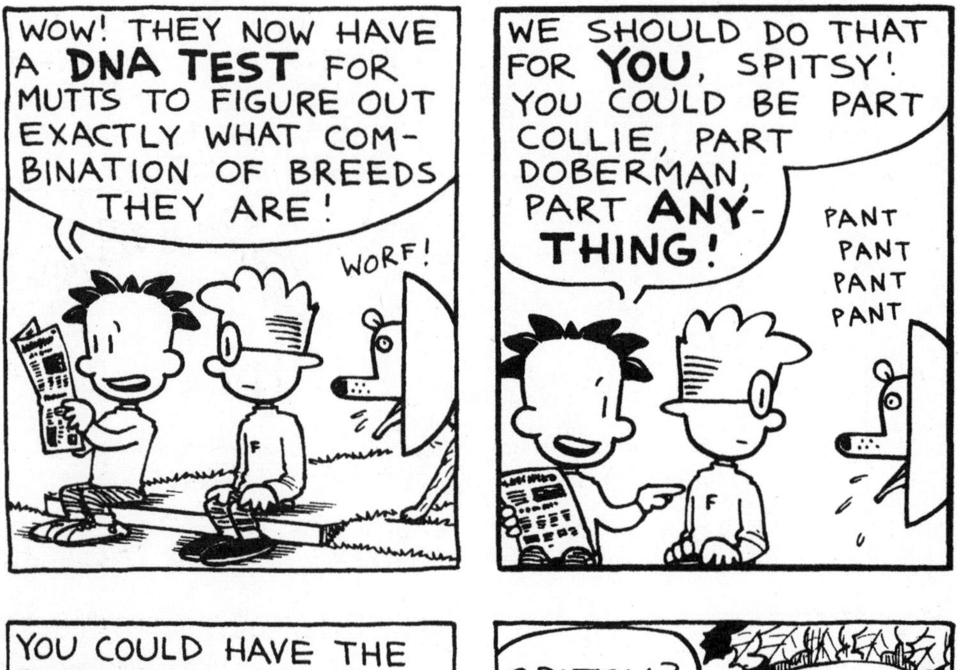
WOW! THEY NOW HAVE A DNA TEST FOR MUTTS TO FIGURE OUT EXACTLY WHAT COMBINATION OF BREEDS THEY ARE!
WORF!
WE SHOULD DO THAT FOR YOU, SPITSY! YOU COULD BE PART COLLIE, PART DOBERMAN, PART ANYTHING!
PANT PANT PANT PANT
YOU COULD HAVE THE BLOODLINES OF A CHAMPION! YOU MIGHT VERY WELL HAVE DESCENDED FROM CANINE ROYALTY!
3/23
© 2009 by NEA, Inc.
SPITSY?
HE'S EATING CAT POOP AGAIN.
Peirce

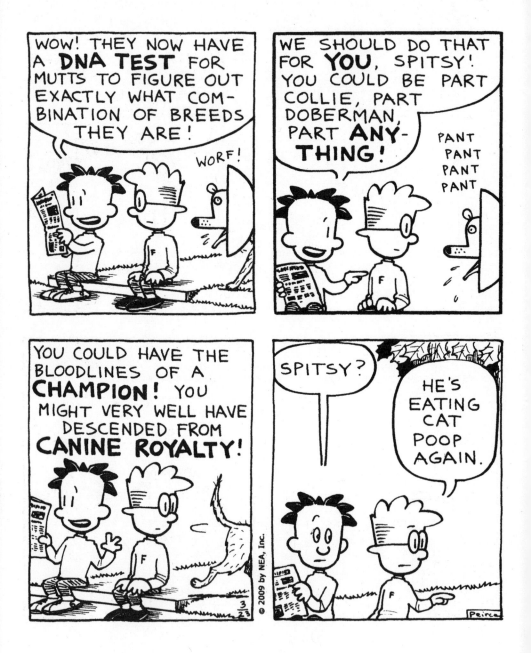

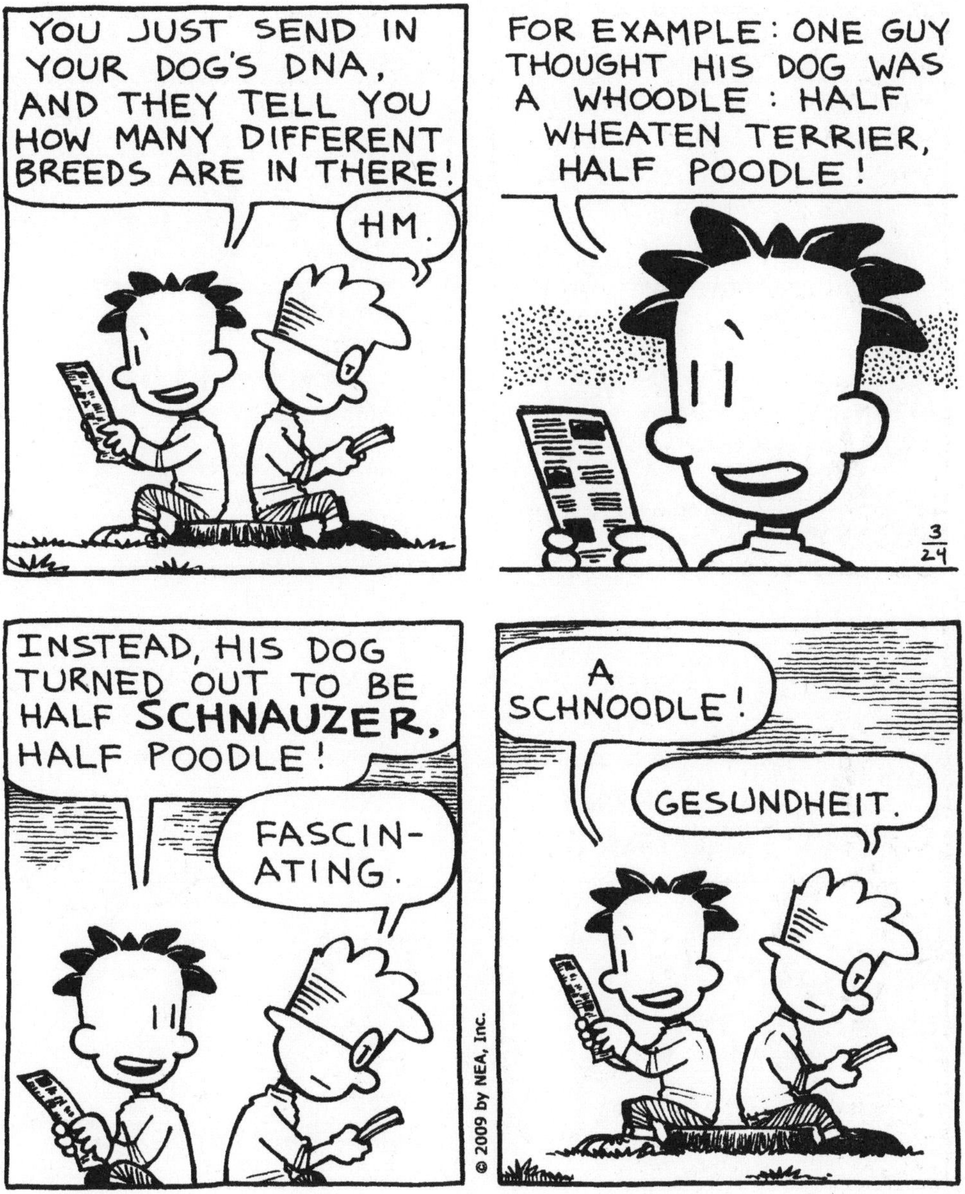
YOU JUST SEND IN YOUR DOG'S DNA, AND THEY TELL YOU HOW MANY DIFFERENT BREEDS ARE IN THERE!
HM.
FOR EXAMPLE: ONE GUY THOUGHT HIS DOG WAS A WHOODLE: HALF WHEATEN TERRIER, HALF POODLE!
3/24
INSTEAD, HIS DOG TURNED OUT TO BE HALF SCHNAUZER, HALF POODLE!
FASCIN-ATING.
© 2009 by NEA, Inc.
A SCHNOODLE!
GESUNDHEIT.

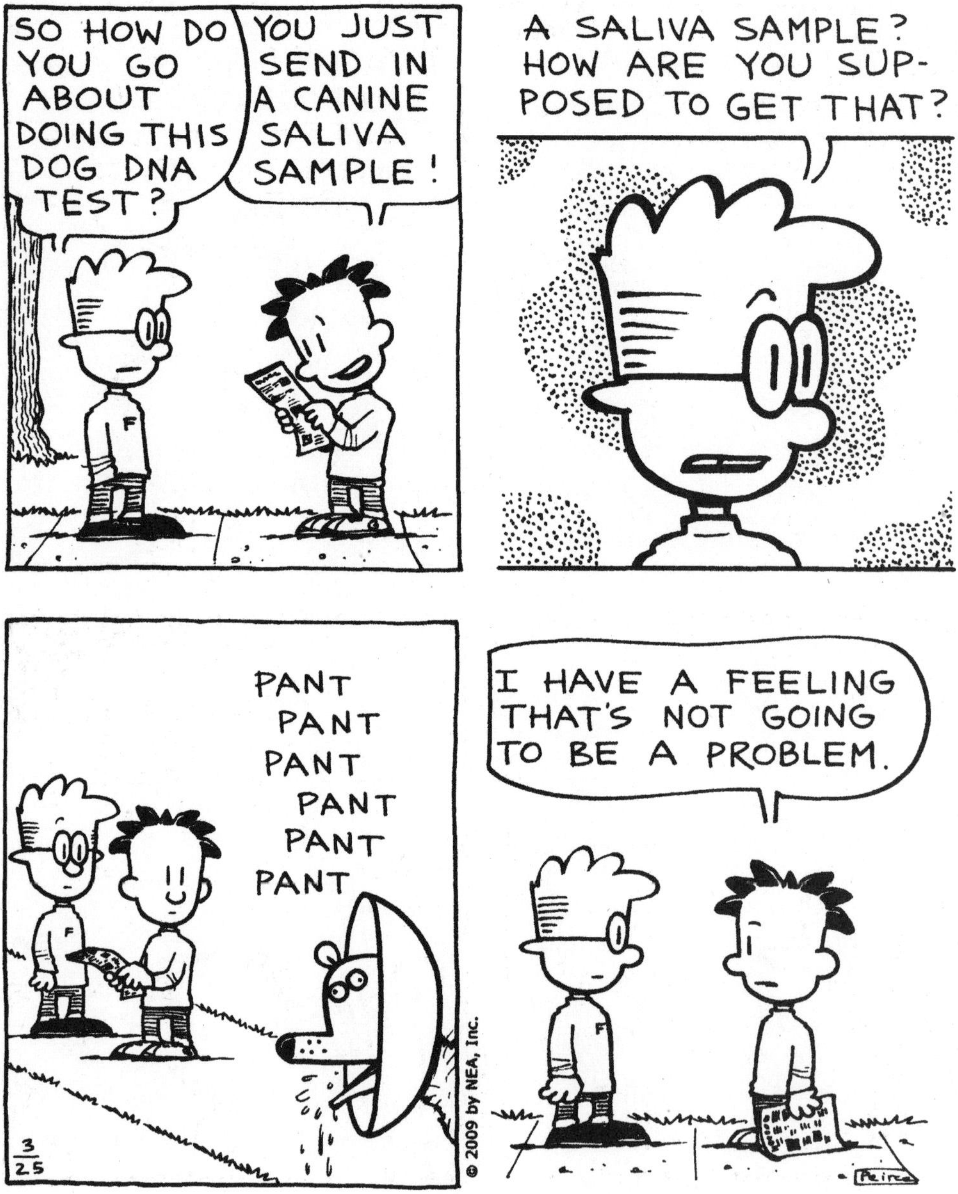
SO HOW DO YOU GO ABOUT DOING THIS DOG DNA TEST?
YOU JUST SEND IN A CANINE SALIVA SAMPLE!
A SALIVA SAMPLE? HOW ARE YOU SUPPOSED TO GET THAT?
PANT PANT PANT PANT PANT PANT
3/25
© 2009 by NEA, Inc.
I HAVE A FEELING THAT'S NOT GOING TO BE A PROBLEM.
Peirce

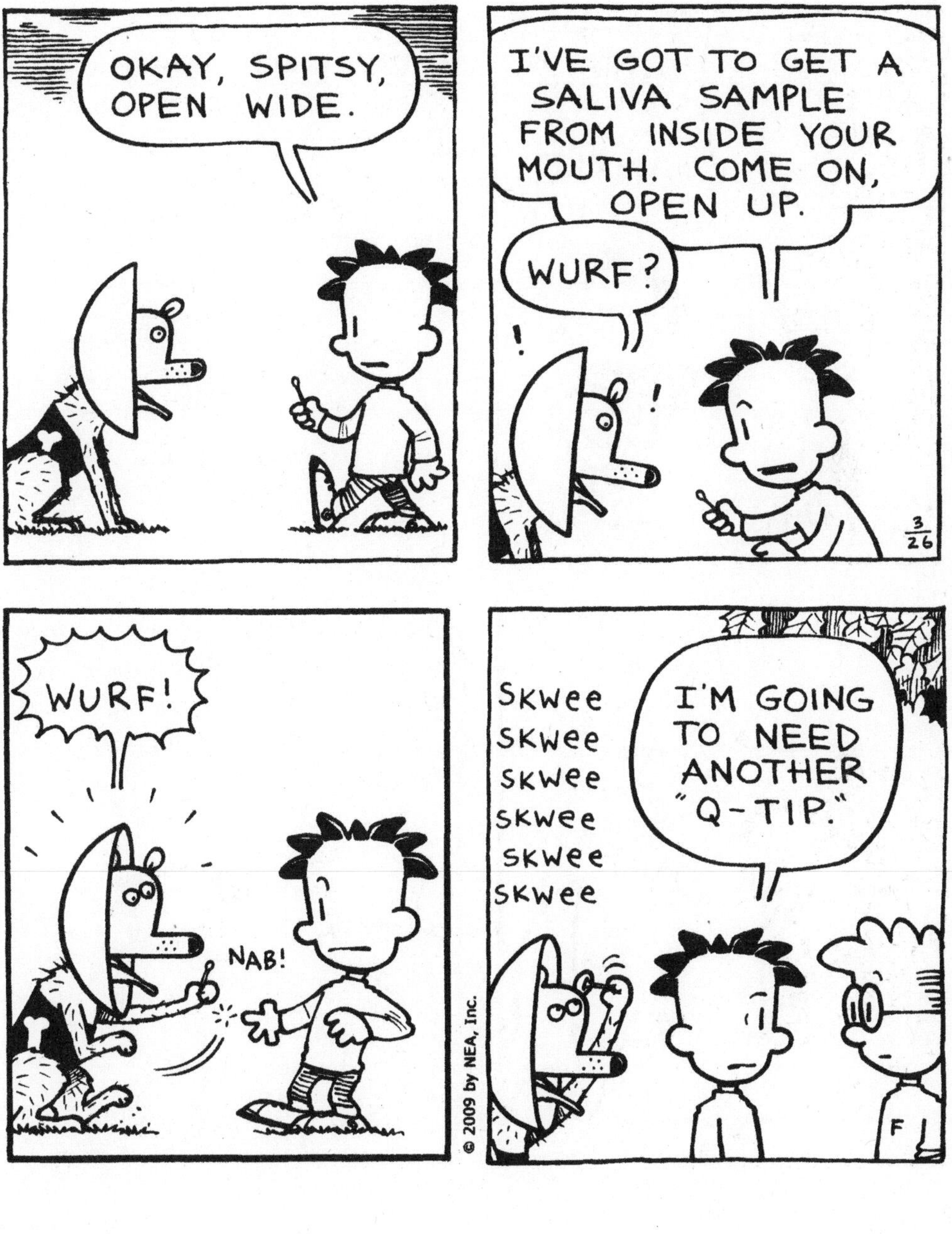
OKAY, SPITSY, OPEN WIDE.
I'VE GOT TO GET A SALIVA SAMPLE FROM INSIDE YOUR MOUTH. COME ON, OPEN UP.
WURF?
!
!
3/26
WURF!
NAB!
SKWEE SKWEE SKWEE SKWEE SKWEE SKWEE
I'M GOING TO NEED ANOTHER "Q-TIP."
F

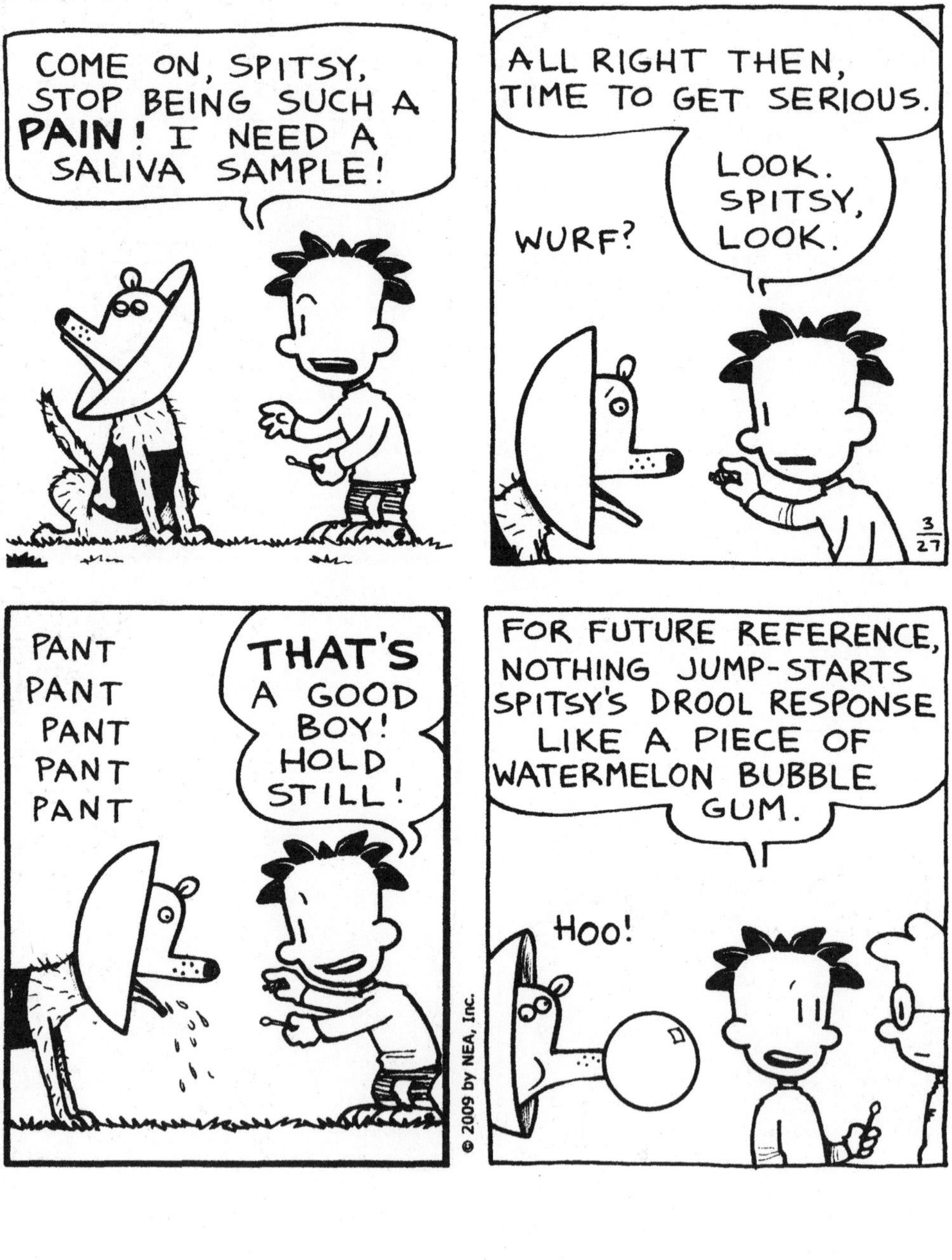
COME ON, SPITSY, STOP BEING SUCH A **PAIN**! I NEED A SALIVA SAMPLE!
ALL RIGHT THEN, TIME TO GET SERIOUS.
WURF?
LOOK. SPITSY, LOOK.
3/27
PANT PANT PANT PANT PANT
THAT'S A GOOD BOY! HOLD STILL!
© 2009 by NEA, Inc.
FOR FUTURE REFERENCE, NOTHING JUMP-STARTS SPITSY'S DROOL RESPONSE LIKE A PIECE OF WATERMELON BUBBLE GUM.
HOO!

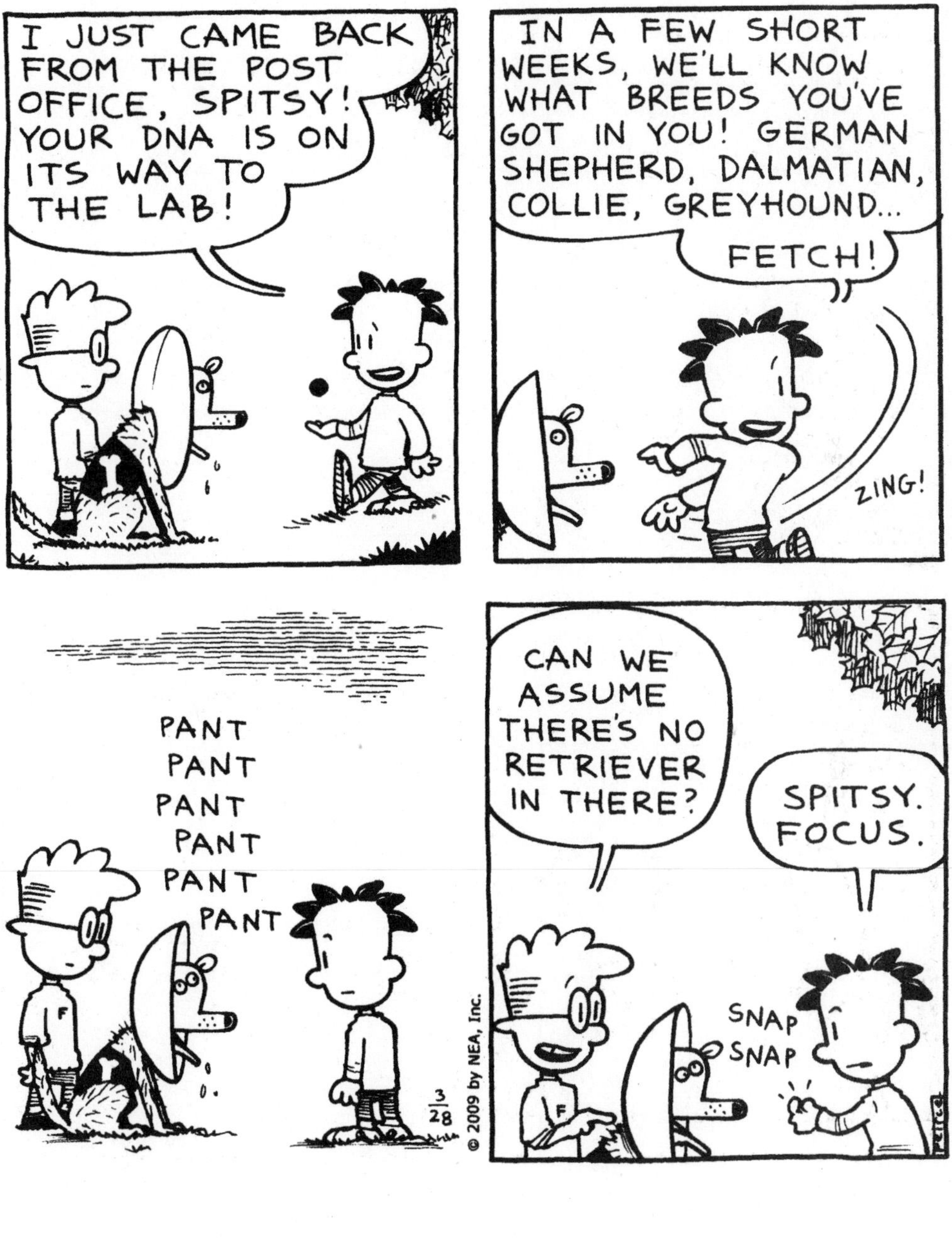
I JUST CAME BACK FROM THE POST OFFICE, SPITSY! YOUR DNA IS ON ITS WAY TO THE LAB!
IN A FEW SHORT WEEKS, WE'LL KNOW WHAT BREEDS YOU'VE GOT IN YOU! GERMAN SHEPHERD, DALMATIAN, COLLIE, GREYHOUND...
FETCH!
ZING!
PANT
PANT
PANT
PANT
PANT
PANT
3
28
© 2009 by NEA, Inc.
CAN WE ASSUME THERE'S NO RETRIEVER IN THERE?
SPITSY. FOCUS.
SNAP
SNAP

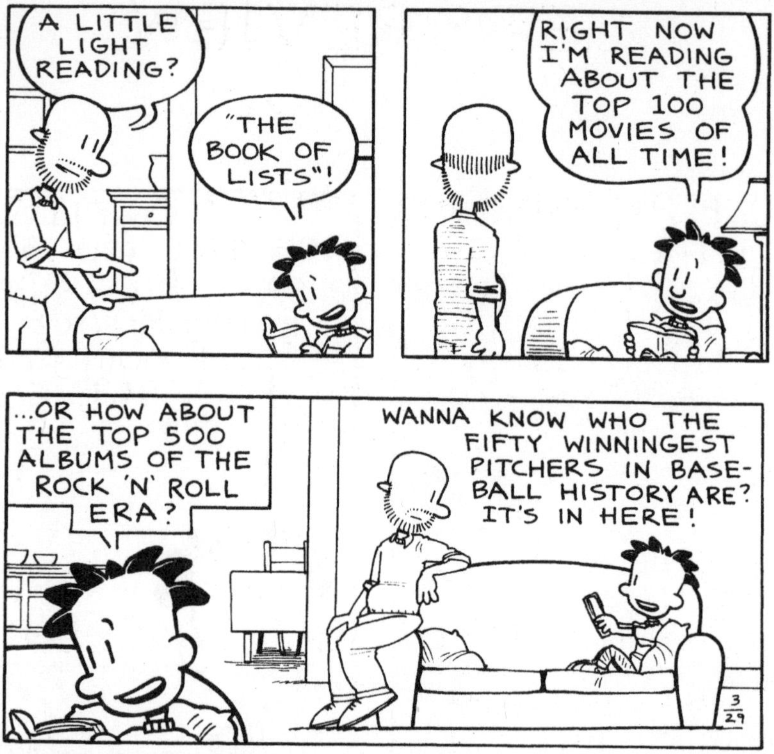
A LITTLE LIGHT READING?
"THE BOOK OF LISTS"!
RIGHT NOW I'M READING ABOUT THE TOP 100 MOVIES OF ALL TIME!
...OR HOW ABOUT THE TOP 500 ALBUMS OF THE ROCK 'N' ROLL ERA?
WANNA KNOW WHO THE FIFTY WINNINGEST PITCHERS IN BASE-BALL HISTORY ARE? IT'S IN HERE!
3/29

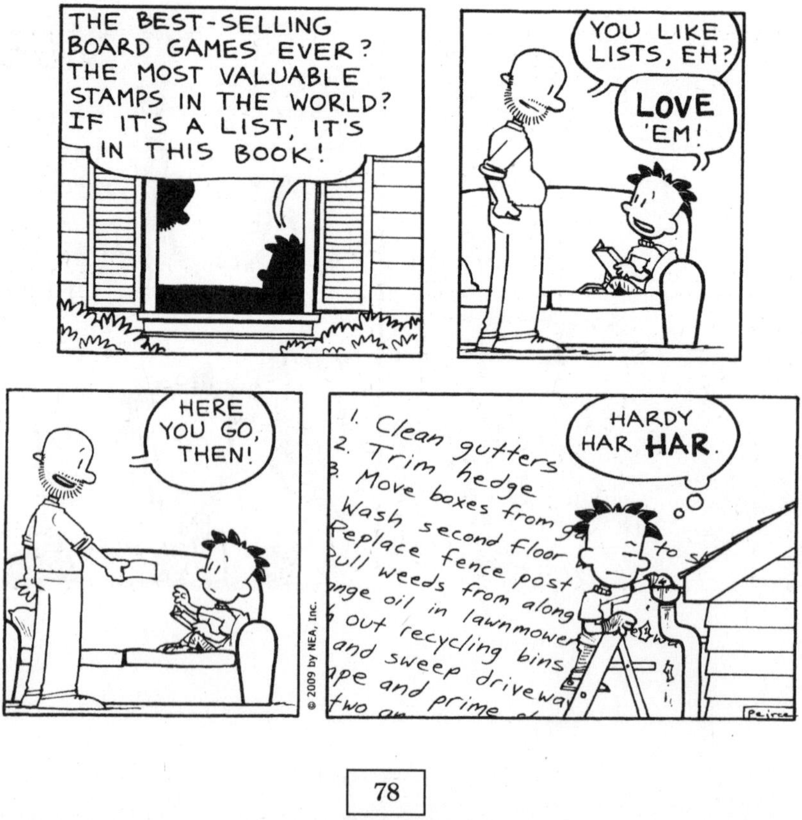
THE BEST-SELLING BOARD GAMES EVER? THE MOST VALUABLE STAMPS IN THE WORLD? IF IT'S A LIST, IT'S IN THIS BOOK!
YOU LIKE LISTS, EH?
LOVE 'EM!
HERE YOU GO, THEN!
1. Clean gutters
2. Trim hedge
Move boxes from
Wash second floor
Replace fence post
Pull weeds from along
oil in lawnmower
out recycling bins
and sweep driveway
HARDY HAR **HAR**.
Peirce

LET'S REVIEW

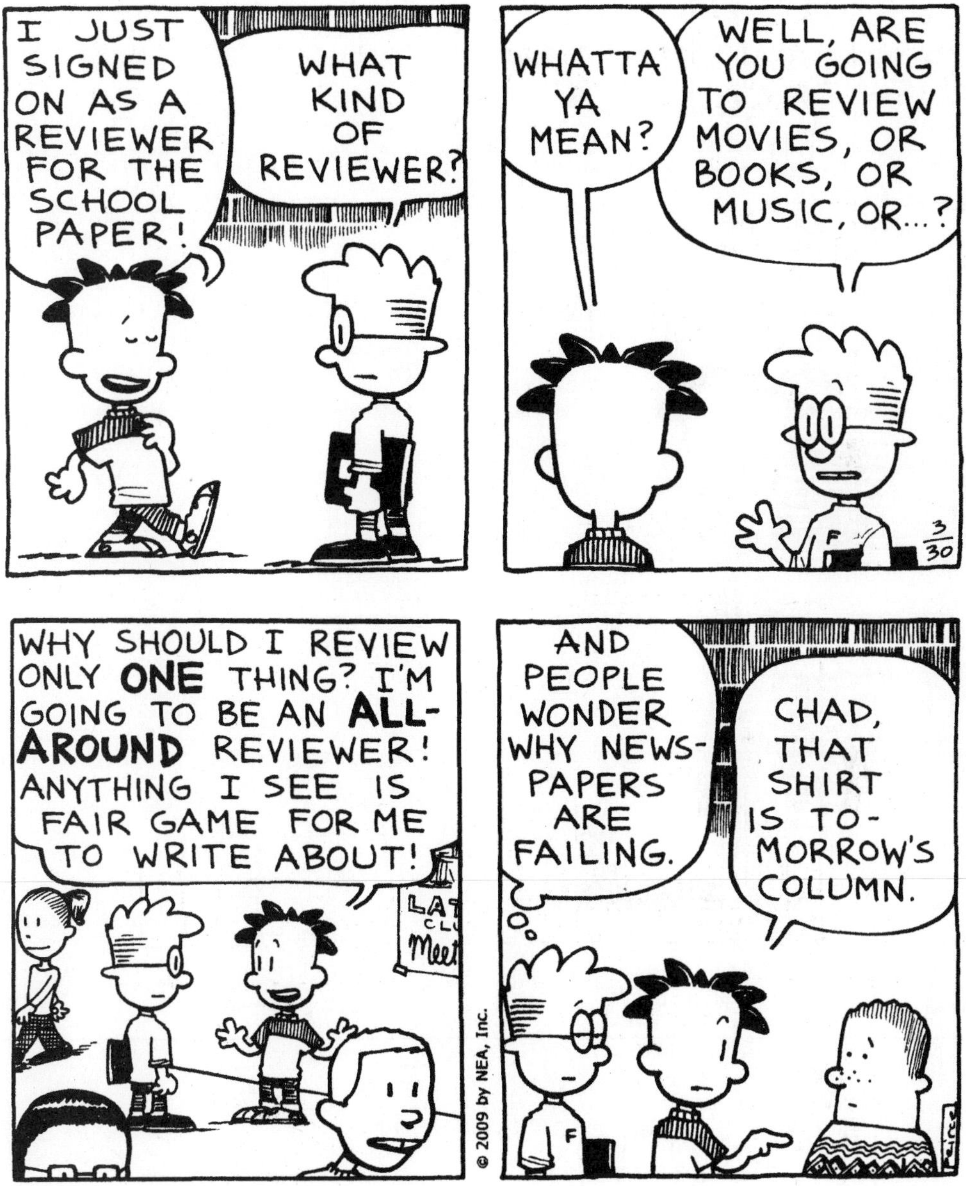

I JUST SIGNED ON AS A REVIEWER FOR THE SCHOOL PAPER!
WHAT KIND OF REVIEWER?
WHATTA YA MEAN?
WELL, ARE YOU GOING TO REVIEW MOVIES, OR BOOKS, OR MUSIC, OR...?
3/30
WHY SHOULD I REVIEW ONLY **ONE** THING? I'M GOING TO BE AN **ALL-AROUND** REVIEWER! ANYTHING I SEE IS FAIR GAME FOR ME TO WRITE ABOUT!
AND PEOPLE WONDER WHY NEWSPAPERS ARE FAILING.
CHAD, THAT SHIRT IS TOMORROW'S COLUMN.
© 2009 by NEA, Inc.

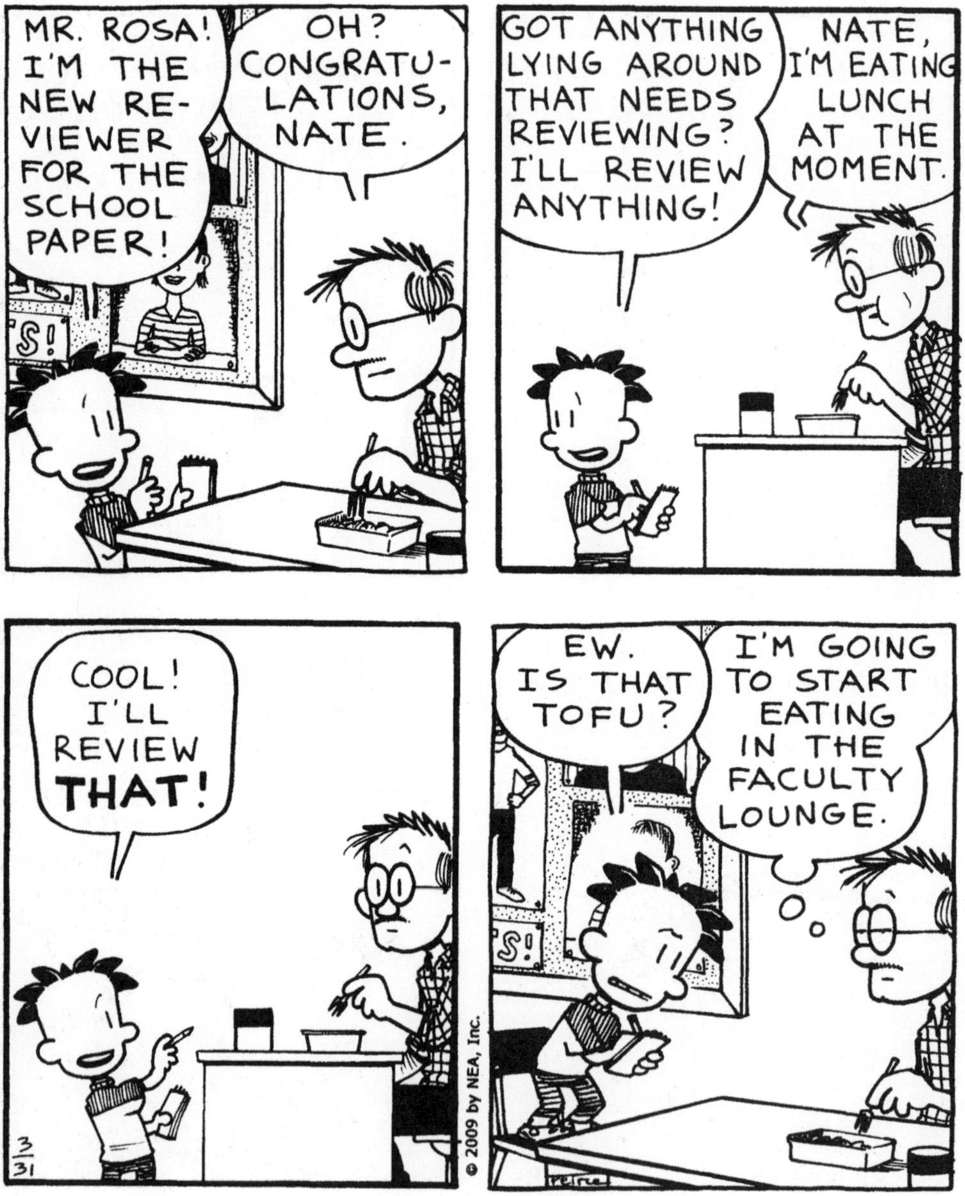
MR. ROSA! I'M THE NEW RE-VIEWER FOR THE SCHOOL PAPER!
OH? CONGRATU-LATIONS, NATE.
GOT ANYTHING LYING AROUND THAT NEEDS REVIEWING? I'LL REVIEW ANYTHING!
NATE, I'M EATING LUNCH AT THE MOMENT.
COOL! I'LL REVIEW **THAT**!
3/31
© 2009 by NEA, Inc.
EW. IS THAT TOFU?
I'M GOING TO START EATING IN THE FACULTY LOUNGE.

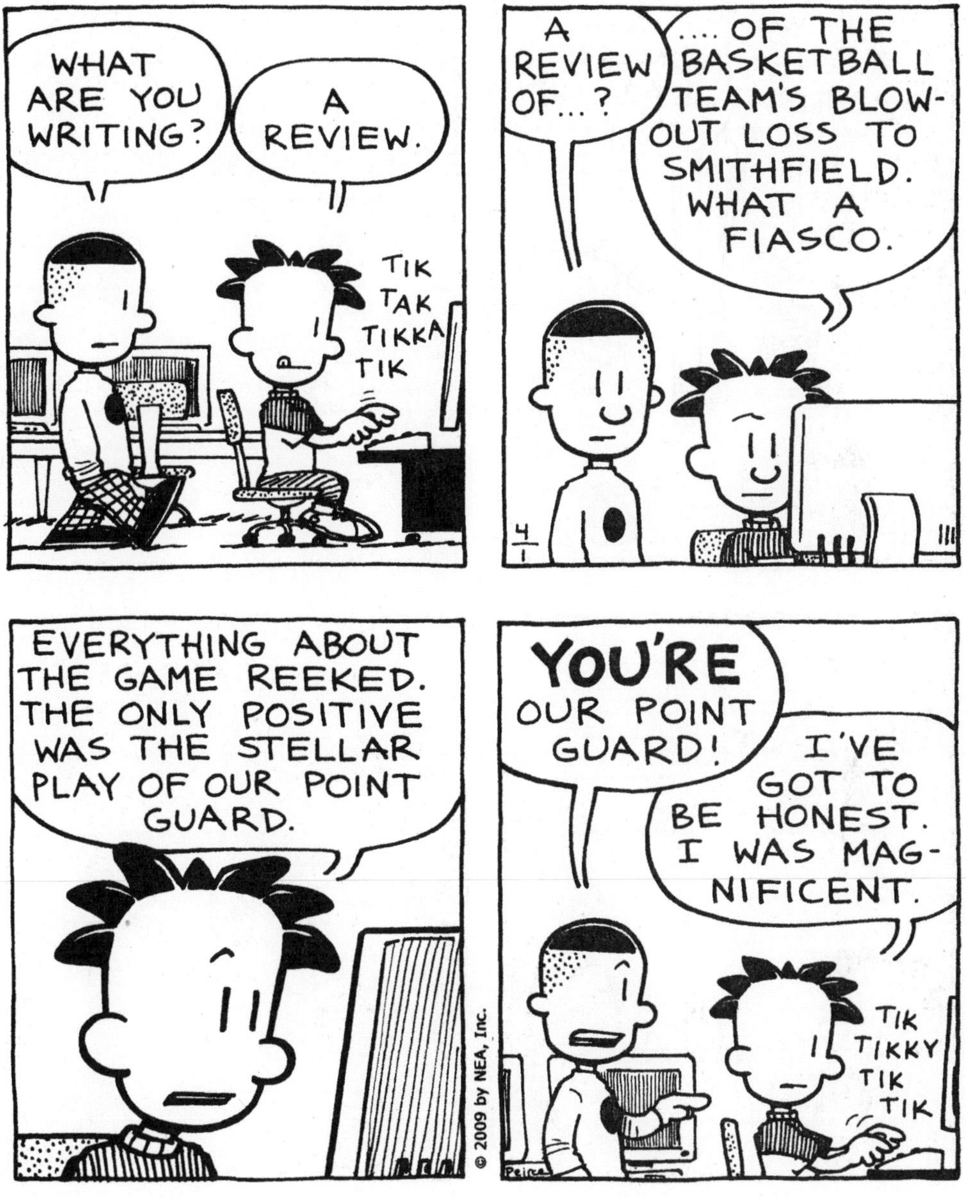
WHAT ARE YOU WRITING?
A REVIEW.
TIK TAK TIKKA TIK
A REVIEW OF...?
.... OF THE BASKETBALL TEAM'S BLOW-OUT LOSS TO SMITHFIELD. WHAT A FIASCO.
4/1
EVERYTHING ABOUT THE GAME REEKED. THE ONLY POSITIVE WAS THE STELLAR PLAY OF OUR POINT GUARD.
YOU'RE OUR POINT GUARD!
I'VE GOT TO BE HONEST. I WAS MAG-NIFICENT.
TIK TIKKY TIK TIK
Peirce
© 2009 by NEA, Inc.

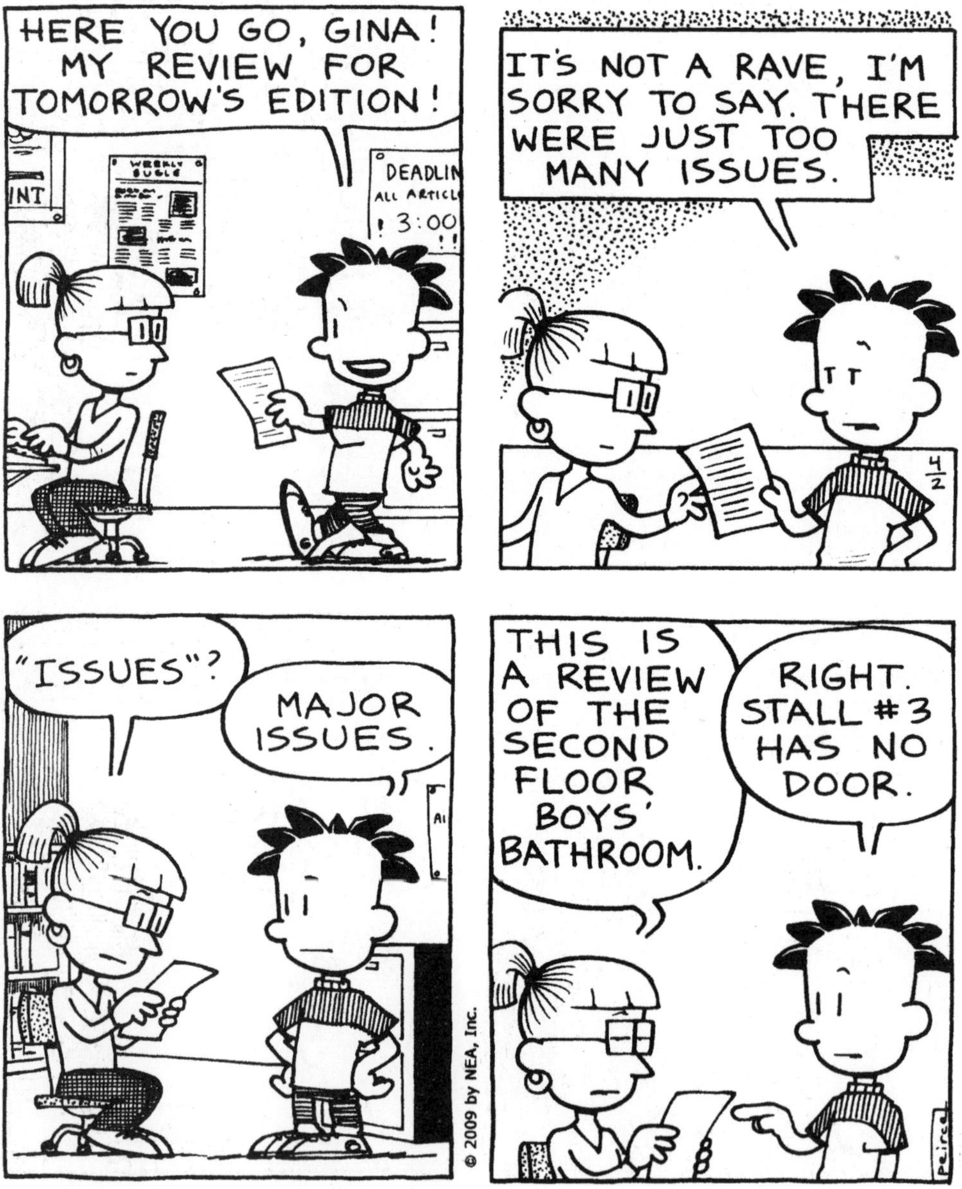
HERE YOU GO, GINA! MY REVIEW FOR TOMORROW'S EDITION!
IT'S NOT A RAVE, I'M SORRY TO SAY. THERE WERE JUST TOO MANY ISSUES.
"ISSUES"?
MAJOR ISSUES.
THIS IS A REVIEW OF THE SECOND FLOOR BOYS' BATHROOM.
RIGHT. STALL #3 HAS NO DOOR.
© 2009 by NEA, Inc.

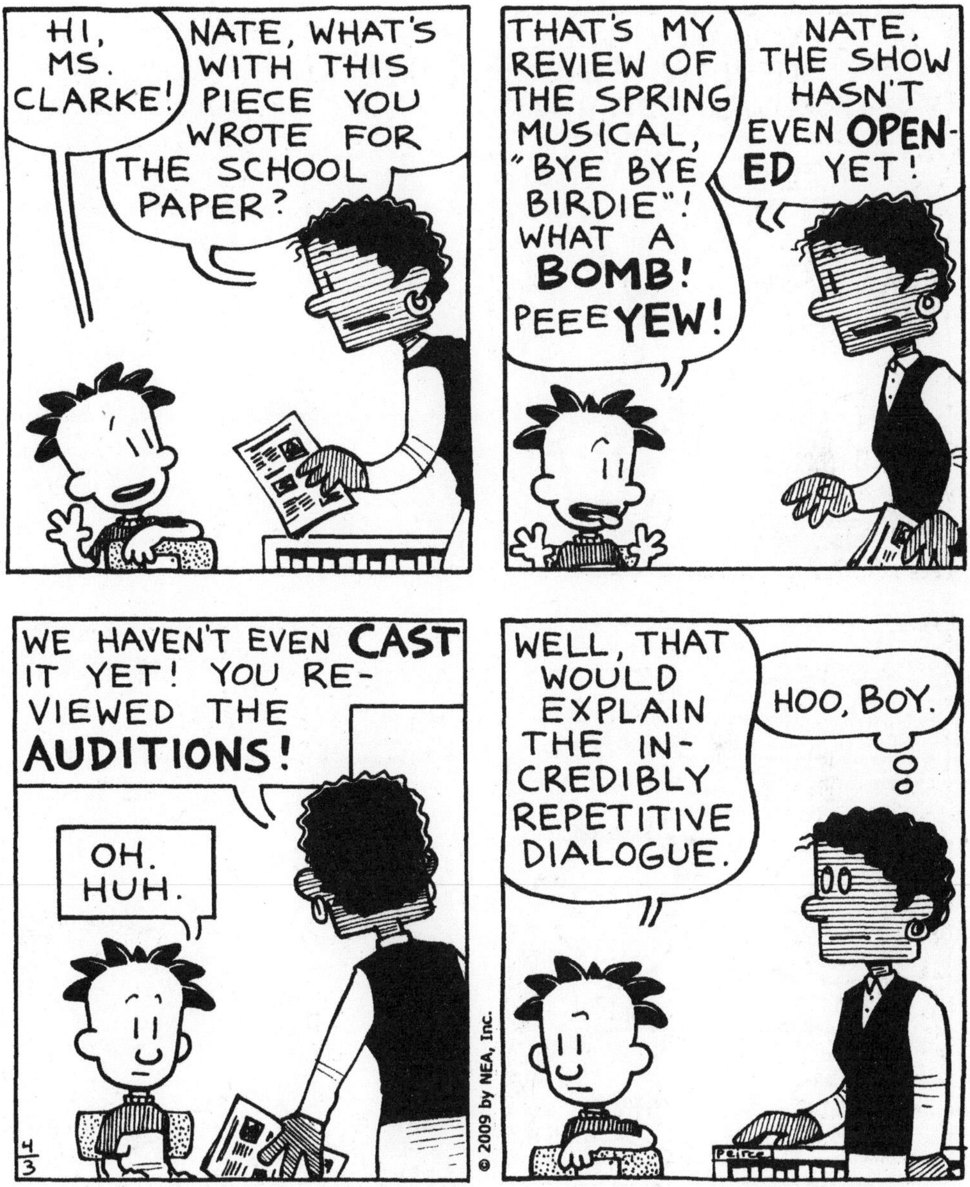
HI, MS. CLARKE!
NATE, WHAT'S WITH THIS PIECE YOU WROTE FOR THE SCHOOL PAPER?
THAT'S MY REVIEW OF THE SPRING MUSICAL, "BYE BYE BIRDIE"! WHAT A BOMB! PEEEYEW!
NATE, THE SHOW HASN'T EVEN OPENED YET!
WE HAVEN'T EVEN CAST IT YET! YOU REVIEWED THE AUDITIONS!
OH. HUH.
WELL, THAT WOULD EXPLAIN THE INCREDIBLY REPETITIVE DIALOGUE.
HOO, BOY.
4/3
© 2009 by NEA, Inc.

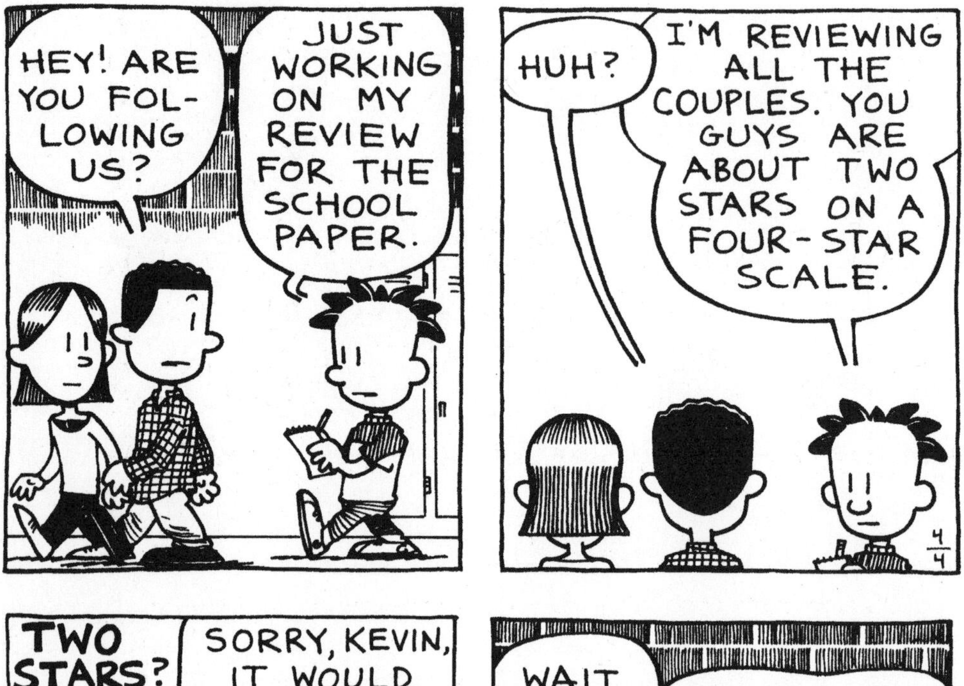
HEY! ARE YOU FOL-LOWING US?
JUST WORKING ON MY REVIEW FOR THE SCHOOL PAPER.
HUH?
I'M REVIEWING ALL THE COUPLES. YOU GUYS ARE ABOUT TWO STARS ON A FOUR-STAR SCALE.
4/4
TWO STARS? C'MON. WE'VE BEEN GOING OUT SINCE SEP-TEMBER!
SORRY, KEVIN, IT WOULD BE HIGHER IF SHANA WEREN'T PLAN-NING TO DUMP YOU FOR JASON.
© 2009 by NEA, Inc.
WAIT, WHAT?
OOP, I'VE GOT A DEADLINE. TOODLES.
Peirce

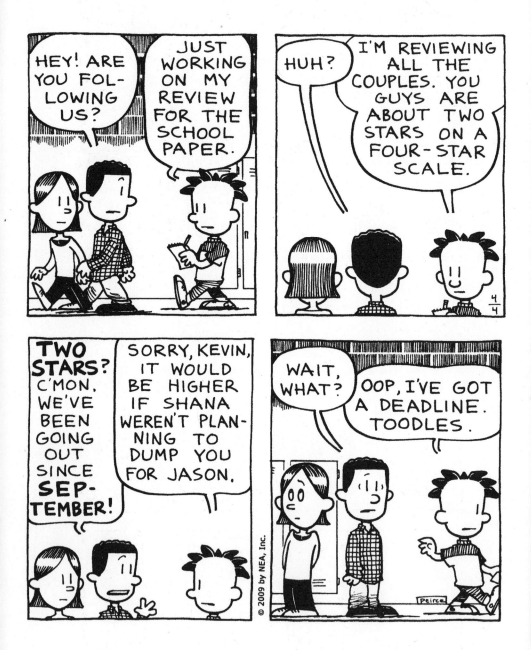

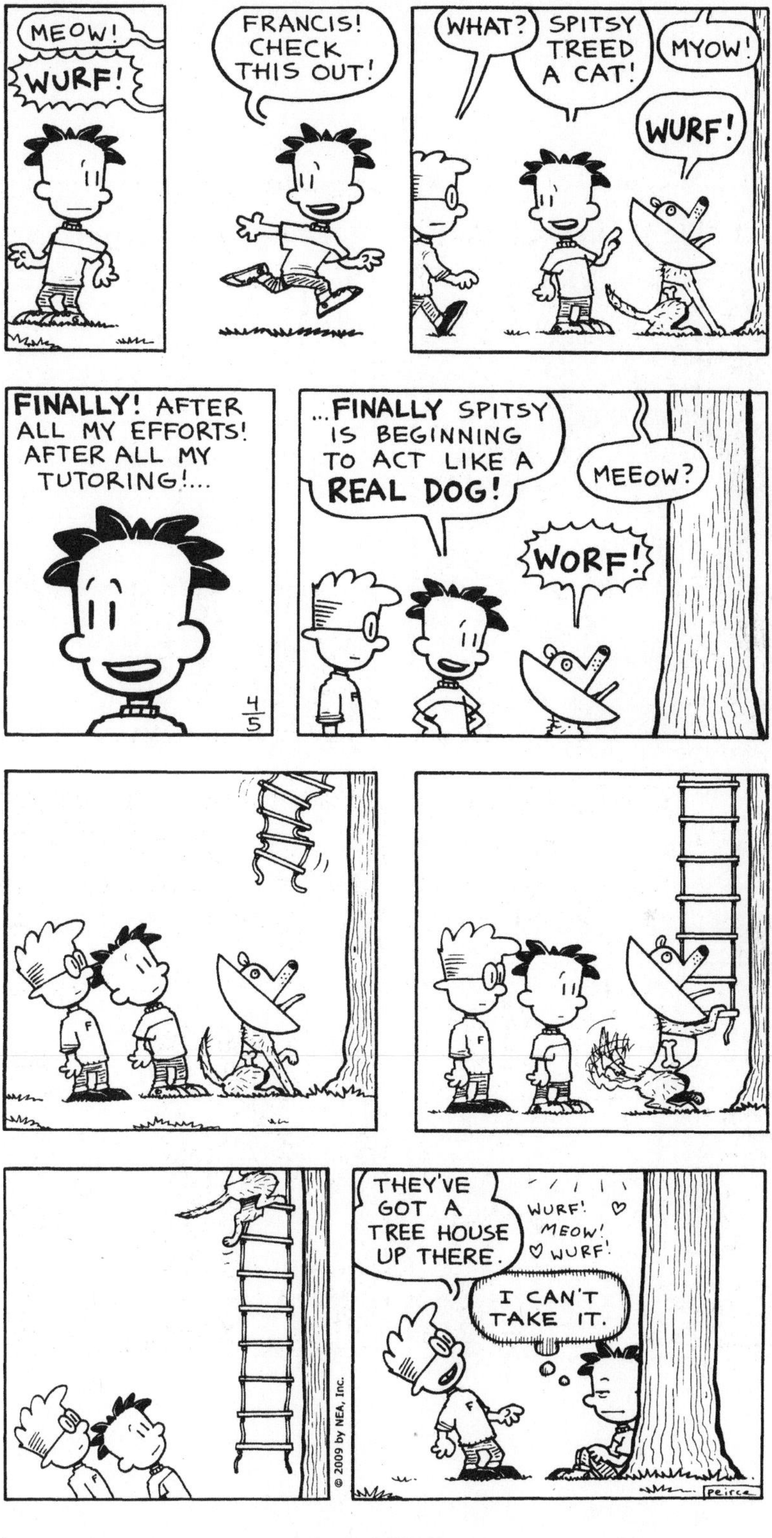
MEOW!
WURF!
FRANCIS! CHECK THIS OUT!
WHAT?
SPITSY TREED A CAT!
MYOW!
WURF!
FINALLY! AFTER ALL MY EFFORTS! AFTER ALL MY TUTORING!...
4/5
...FINALLY SPITSY IS BEGINNING TO ACT LIKE A REAL DOG!
MEEOW?
WORF!
THEY'VE GOT A TREE HOUSE UP THERE.
WURF! MEOW! WURF!
I CAN'T TAKE IT.
© 2009 by NEA, Inc.
peirce

LEGGO MY MOJO

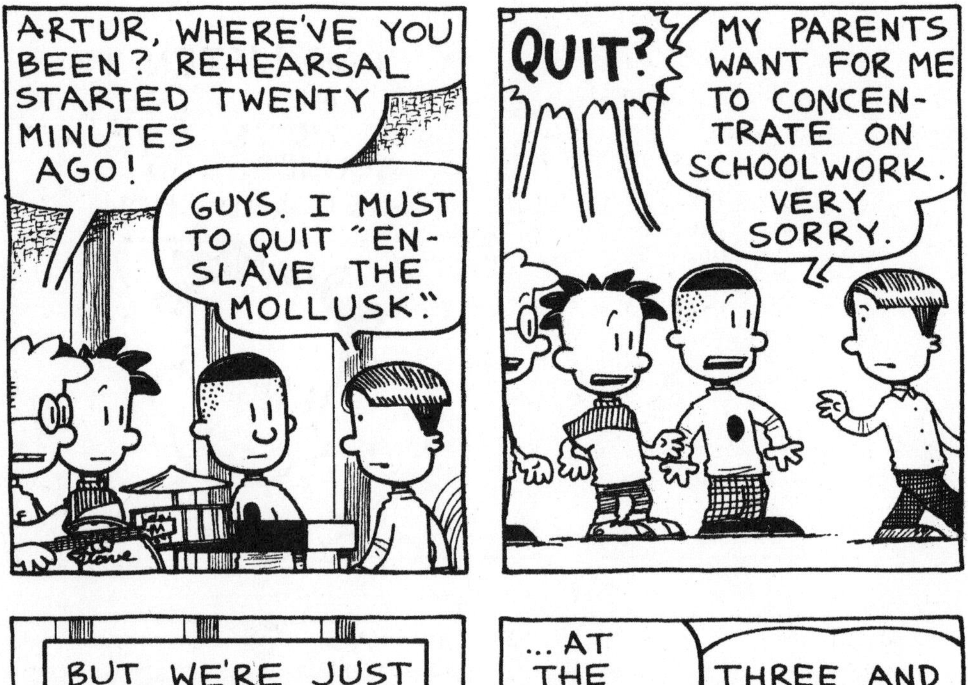

ARTUR, WHERE'VE YOU BEEN? REHEARSAL STARTED TWENTY MINUTES AGO!
GUYS. I MUST TO QUIT "ENSLAVE THE MOLLUSK."
QUIT?
MY PARENTS WANT FOR ME TO CONCENTRATE ON SCHOOLWORK. VERY SORRY.
BUT WE'RE JUST STARTING TO GET **GOOD**!
... AT THE THREE SONGS WE ACTUALLY KNOW.
THREE AND A HALF! "BAA, BAA, BLACK SHEEP" IS REALLY COMING ALONG!
© 2009 by NEA, Inc.
4/6
Peirce

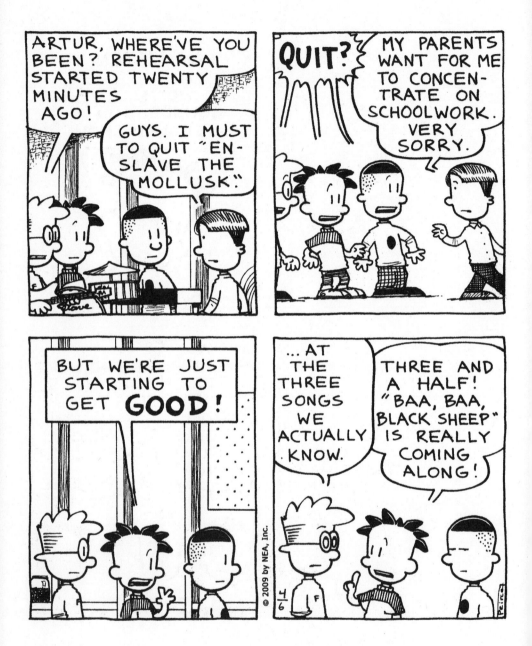

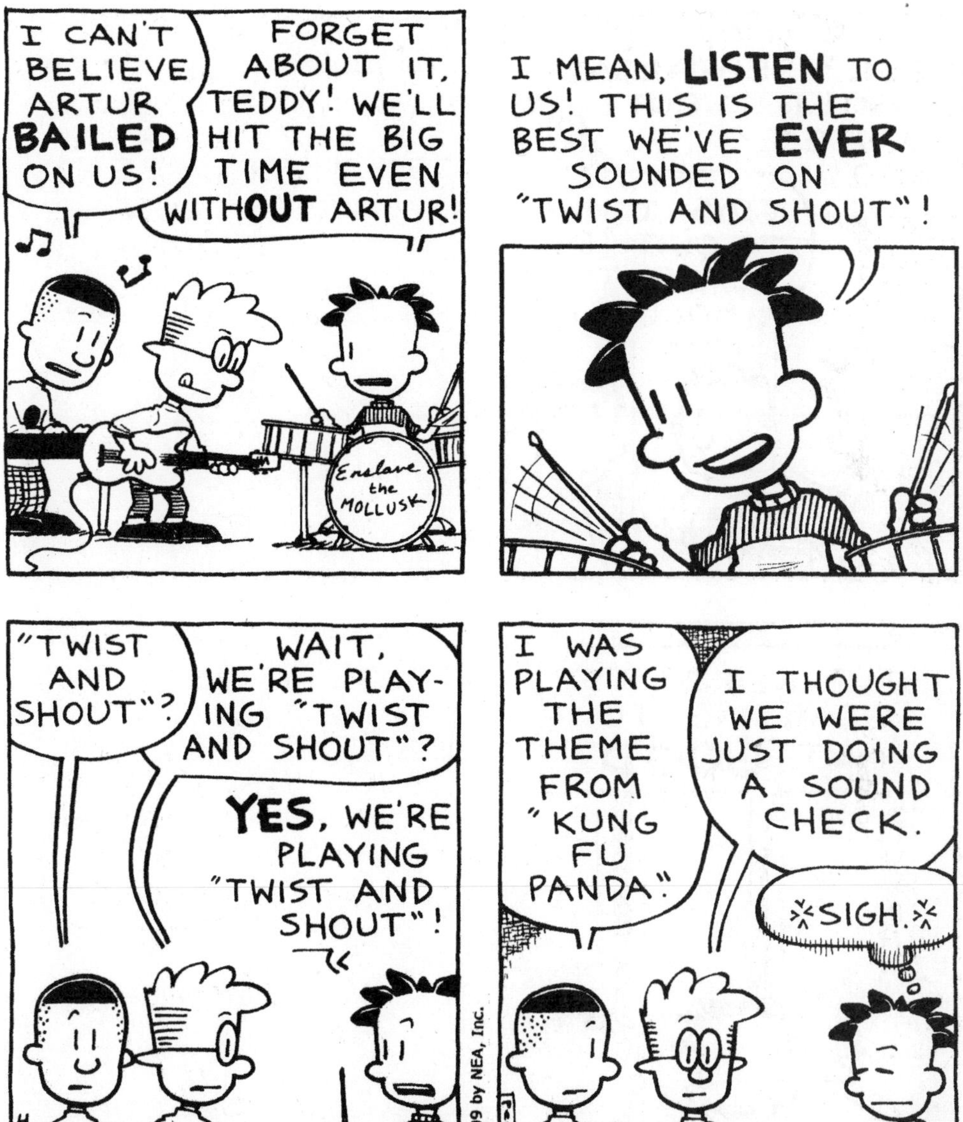
I CAN'T BELIEVE ARTUR BAILED ON US!
FORGET ABOUT IT, TEDDY! WE'LL HIT THE BIG TIME EVEN WITHOUT ARTUR!
Enslave the MOLLUSK
I MEAN, LISTEN TO US! THIS IS THE BEST WE'VE EVER SOUNDED ON "TWIST AND SHOUT"!
"TWIST AND SHOUT"?
WAIT, WE'RE PLAYING "TWIST AND SHOUT"?
YES, WE'RE PLAYING "TWIST AND SHOUT"!
I WAS PLAYING THE THEME FROM "KUNG FU PANDA."
I THOUGHT WE WERE JUST DOING A SOUND CHECK.
SIGH.
4/7
© 2009 by NEA, Inc.
Peirce

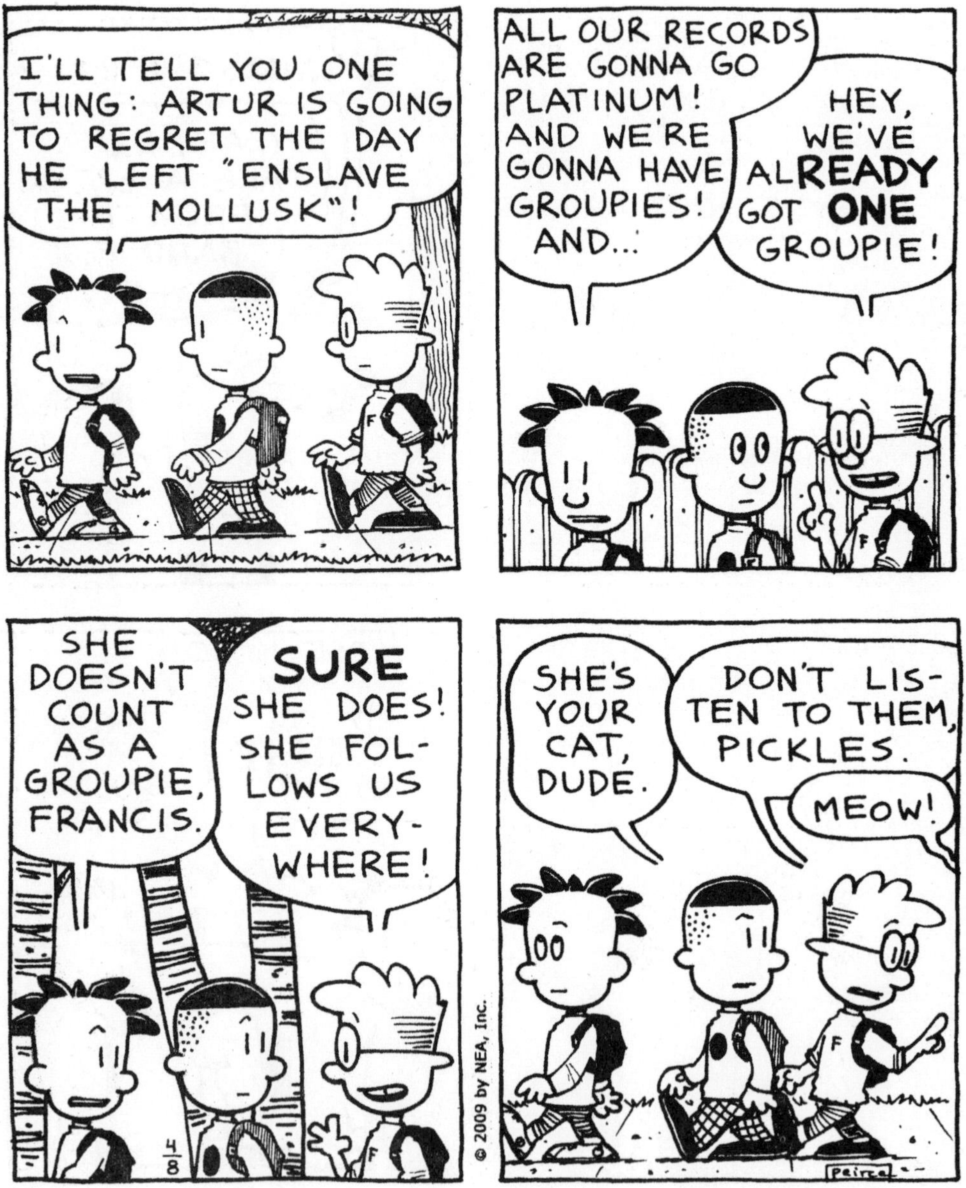

I'LL TELL YOU ONE THING: ARTUR IS GOING TO REGRET THE DAY HE LEFT "ENSLAVE THE MOLLUSK"!
ALL OUR RECORDS ARE GONNA GO PLATINUM! AND WE'RE GONNA HAVE GROUPIES! AND...
HEY, WE'VE ALREADY GOT ONE GROUPIE!
SHE DOESN'T COUNT AS A GROUPIE, FRANCIS.
SURE SHE DOES! SHE FOLLOWS US EVERYWHERE!
4/8
© 2009 by NEA, Inc.
SHE'S YOUR CAT, DUDE.
DON'T LISTEN TO THEM, PICKLES.
MEOW!
PEIRCE

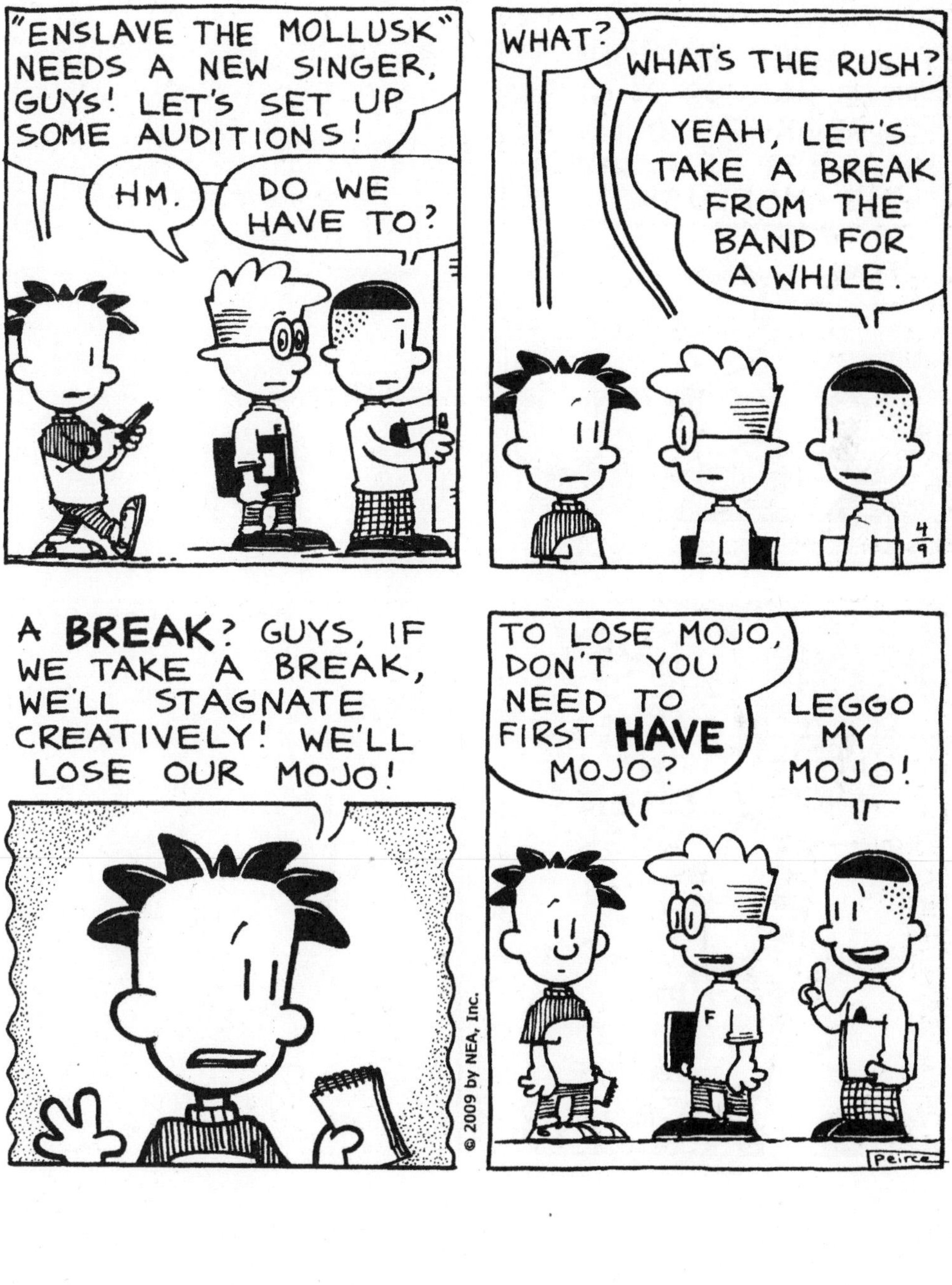
"ENSLAVE THE MOLLUSK" NEEDS A NEW SINGER, GUYS! LET'S SET UP SOME AUDITIONS!
HM.
DO WE HAVE TO?
WHAT?
WHAT'S THE RUSH?
YEAH, LET'S TAKE A BREAK FROM THE BAND FOR A WHILE.
4/9
A **BREAK**? GUYS, IF WE TAKE A BREAK, WE'LL STAGNATE CREATIVELY! WE'LL LOSE OUR MOJO!
© 2009 by NEA, Inc.
TO LOSE MOJO, DON'T YOU NEED TO FIRST **HAVE** MOJO?
LEGGO MY MOJO!
Peirce

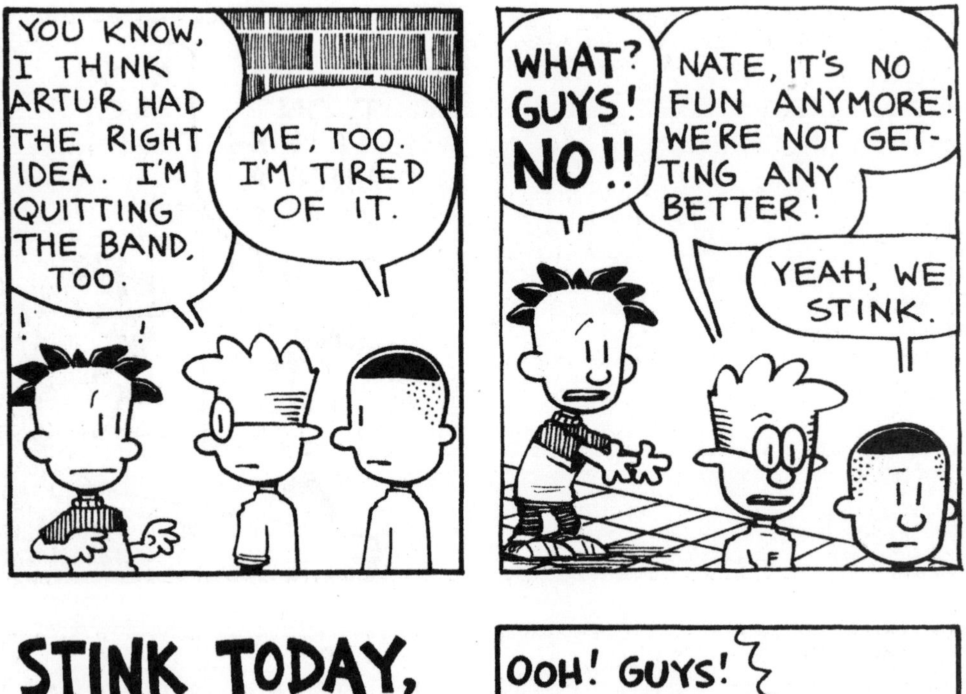
YOU KNOW, I THINK ARTUR HAD THE RIGHT IDEA. I'M QUITTING THE BAND, TOO.
ME, TOO. I'M TIRED OF IT.
!   !
WHAT? GUYS! NO!!
NATE, IT'S NO FUN ANYMORE! WE'RE NOT GETTING ANY BETTER!
YEAH, WE STINK.
STINK TODAY, ROCK TOMORROW!
4/10
© 2009 by NEA, Inc.
OOH! GUYS! HEAR THAT? THAT'S A SONG TITLE!
LET IT GO, MAN.
Peirce

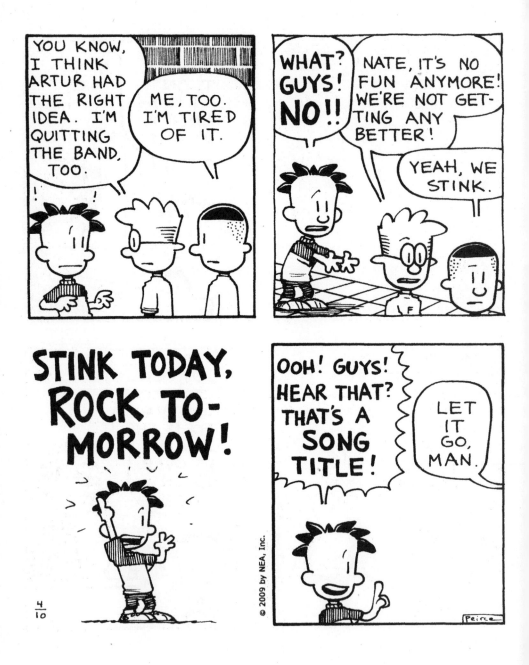

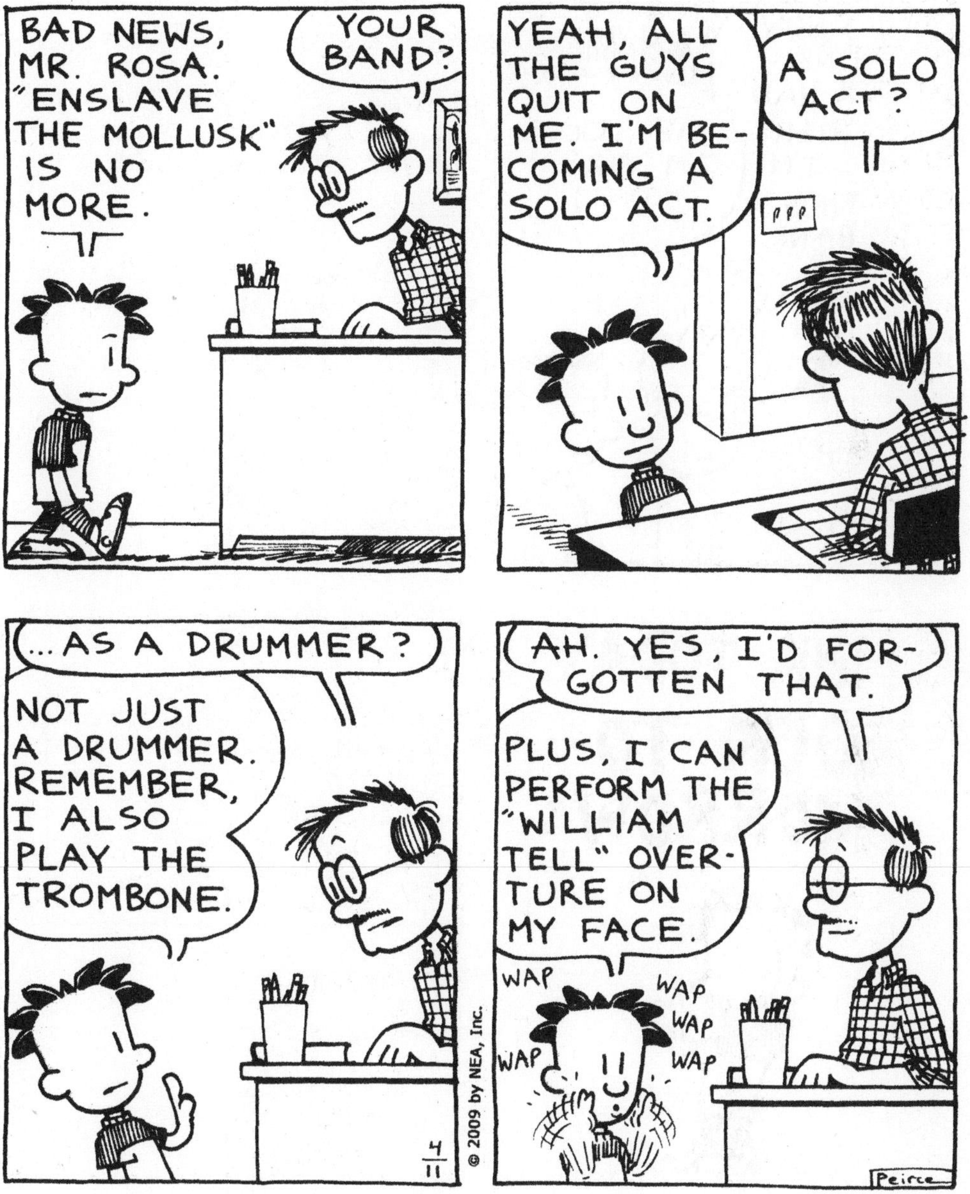
BAD NEWS, MR. ROSA. "ENSLAVE THE MOLLUSK" IS NO MORE.
YOUR BAND?
YEAH, ALL THE GUYS QUIT ON ME. I'M BE-COMING A SOLO ACT.
A SOLO ACT?
...AS A DRUMMER?
NOT JUST A DRUMMER. REMEMBER, I ALSO PLAY THE TROMBONE.
AH. YES, I'D FOR-GOTTEN THAT.
PLUS, I CAN PERFORM THE "WILLIAM TELL" OVER-TURE ON MY FACE.
WAP
WAP
WAP
WAP
WAP
© 2009 by NEA, Inc.
4/11
Peirce

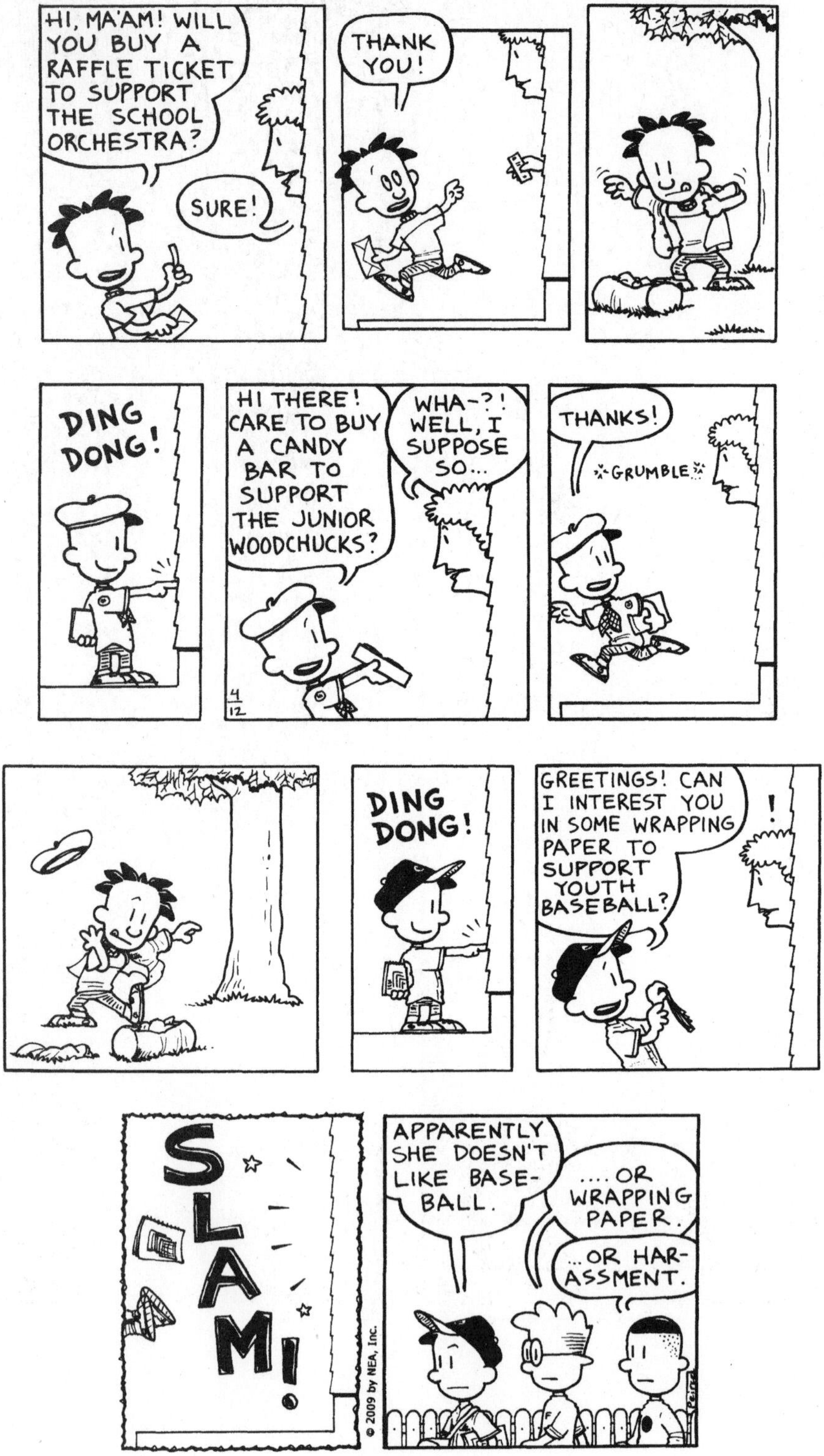
HI, MA'AM! WILL YOU BUY A RAFFLE TICKET TO SUPPORT THE SCHOOL ORCHESTRA?
SURE!
THANK YOU!
DING DONG!
HI THERE! CARE TO BUY A CANDY BAR TO SUPPORT THE JUNIOR WOODCHUCKS?
WHA-?! WELL, I SUPPOSE SO...
4/12
THANKS!
GRUMBLE
DING DONG!
GREETINGS! CAN I INTEREST YOU IN SOME WRAPPING PAPER TO SUPPORT YOUTH BASEBALL?
!
SLAM!
© 2009 by NEA, Inc.
APPARENTLY SHE DOESN'T LIKE BASE-BALL.
....OR WRAPPING PAPER.
...OR HAR-ASSMENT.

GENIUS MODE

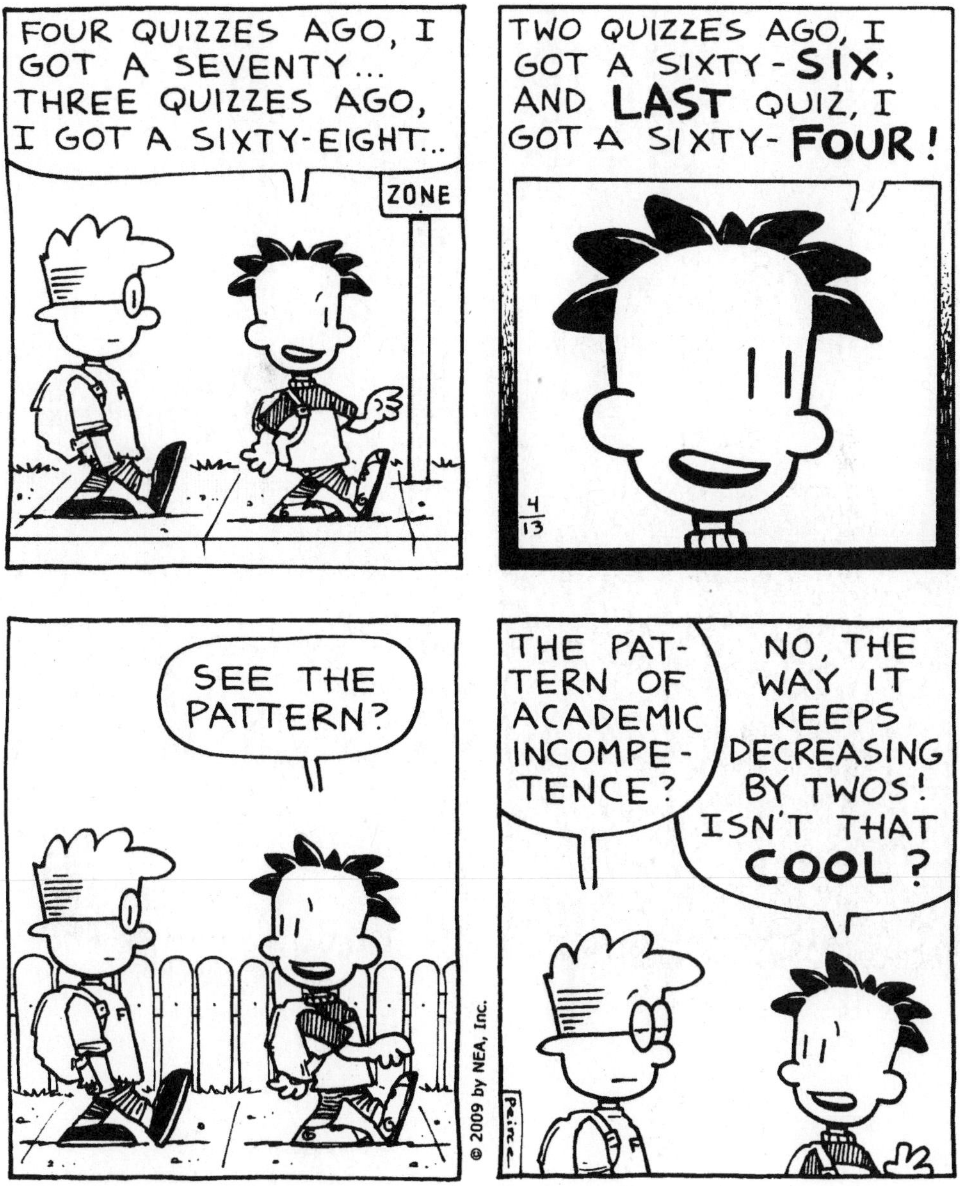
FOUR QUIZZES AGO, I GOT A SEVENTY... THREE QUIZZES AGO, I GOT A SIXTY-EIGHT...
ZONE
TWO QUIZZES AGO, I GOT A SIXTY-SIX. AND LAST QUIZ, I GOT A SIXTY-FOUR!
4/13
SEE THE PATTERN?
THE PATTERN OF ACADEMIC INCOMPETENCE?
NO, THE WAY IT KEEPS DECREASING BY TWOS! ISN'T THAT COOL?
© 2009 by NEA, Inc.
Peirce

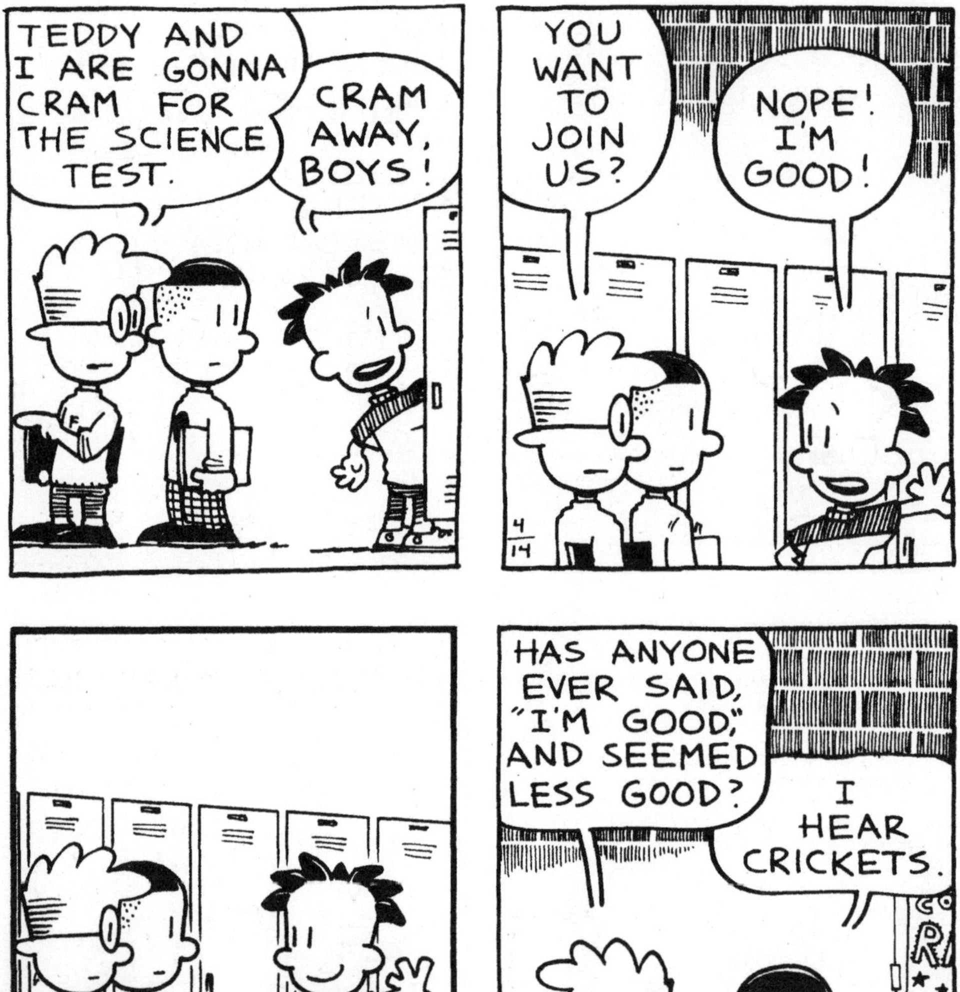
TEDDY AND I ARE GONNA CRAM FOR THE SCIENCE TEST.
CRAM AWAY, BOYS!
YOU WANT TO JOIN US?
NOPE! I'M GOOD!
4/14
HAS ANYONE EVER SAID, "I'M GOOD," AND SEEMED LESS GOOD?
I HEAR CRICKETS.
Peirce

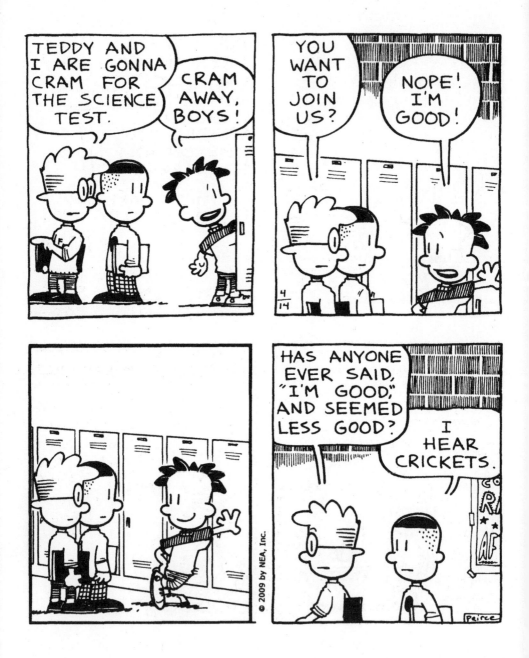

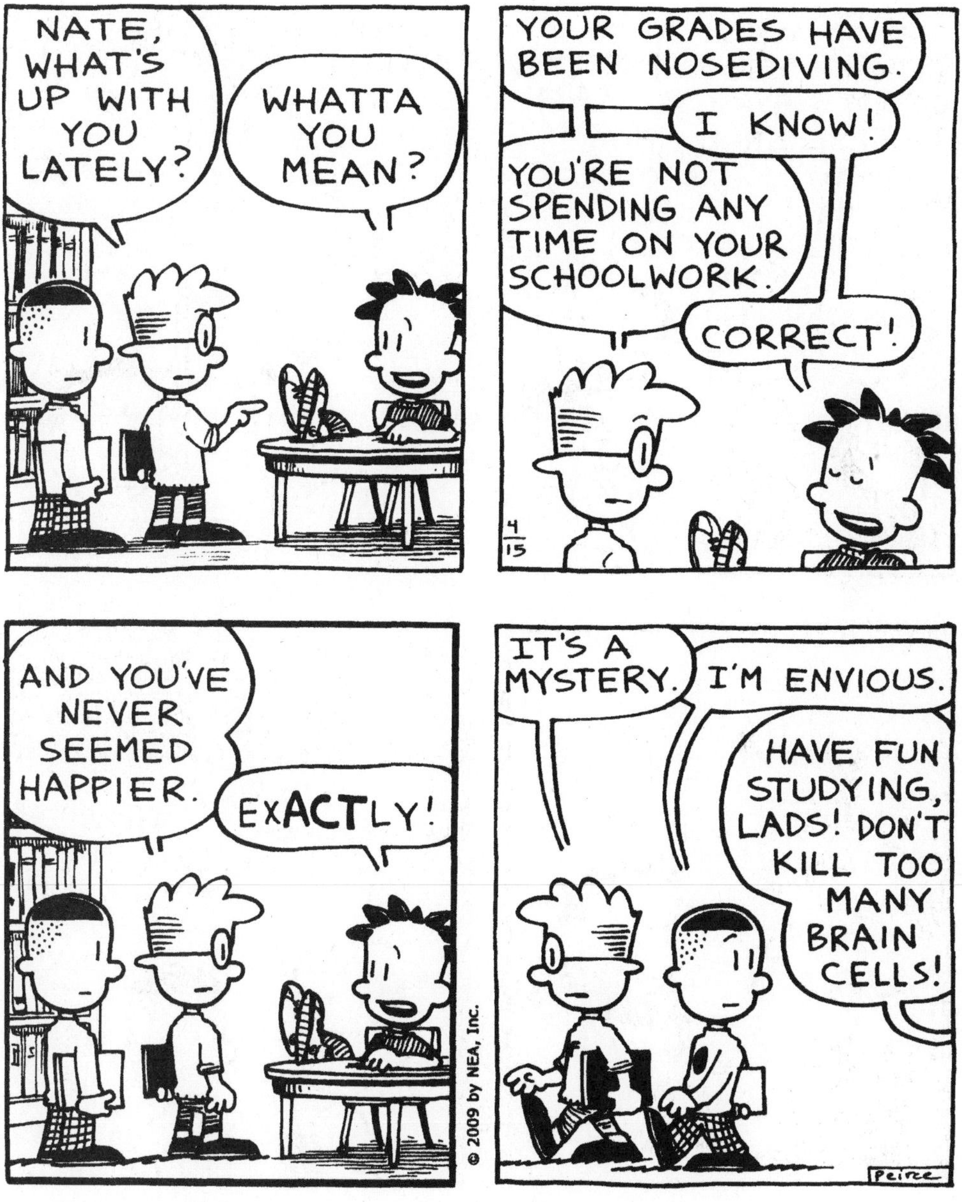
NATE, WHAT'S UP WITH YOU LATELY?
WHATTA YOU MEAN?
YOUR GRADES HAVE BEEN NOSEDIVING.
I KNOW!
YOU'RE NOT SPENDING ANY TIME ON YOUR SCHOOLWORK.
CORRECT!
4/15
AND YOU'VE NEVER SEEMED HAPPIER.
ExACTLY!
© 2009 by NEA, Inc.
IT'S A MYSTERY.
I'M ENVIOUS.
HAVE FUN STUDYING, LADS! DON'T KILL TOO MANY BRAIN CELLS!
Peirce

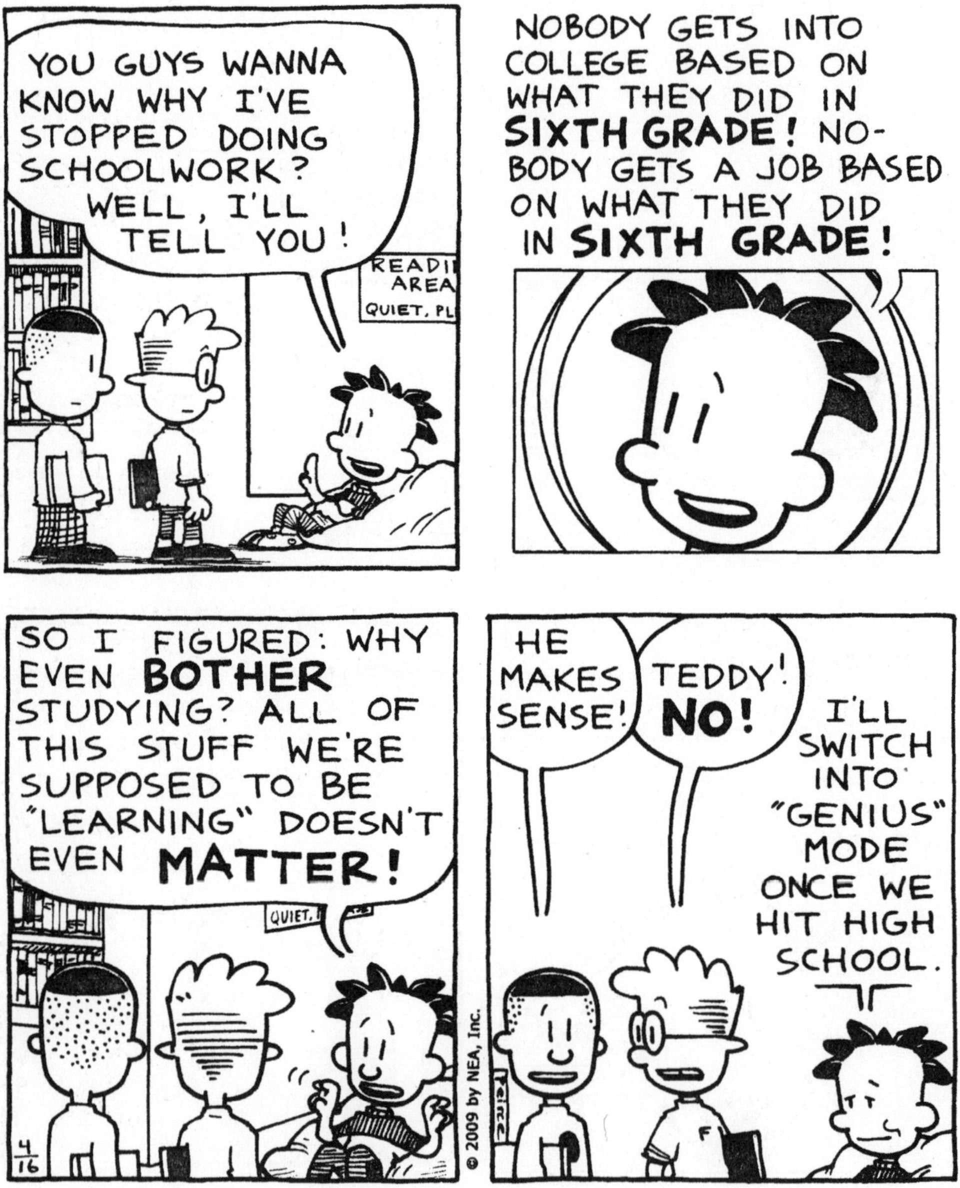
YOU GUYS WANNA KNOW WHY I'VE STOPPED DOING SCHOOLWORK? WELL, I'LL TELL YOU!
READI AREA QUIET, PL
NOBODY GETS INTO COLLEGE BASED ON WHAT THEY DID IN SIXTH GRADE! NOBODY GETS A JOB BASED ON WHAT THEY DID IN SIXTH GRADE!
SO I FIGURED: WHY EVEN BOTHER STUDYING? ALL OF THIS STUFF WE'RE SUPPOSED TO BE "LEARNING" DOESN'T EVEN MATTER!
4/16
© 2009 by NEA, Inc.
HE MAKES SENSE!
TEDDY! NO!
I'LL SWITCH INTO "GENIUS" MODE ONCE WE HIT HIGH SCHOOL.

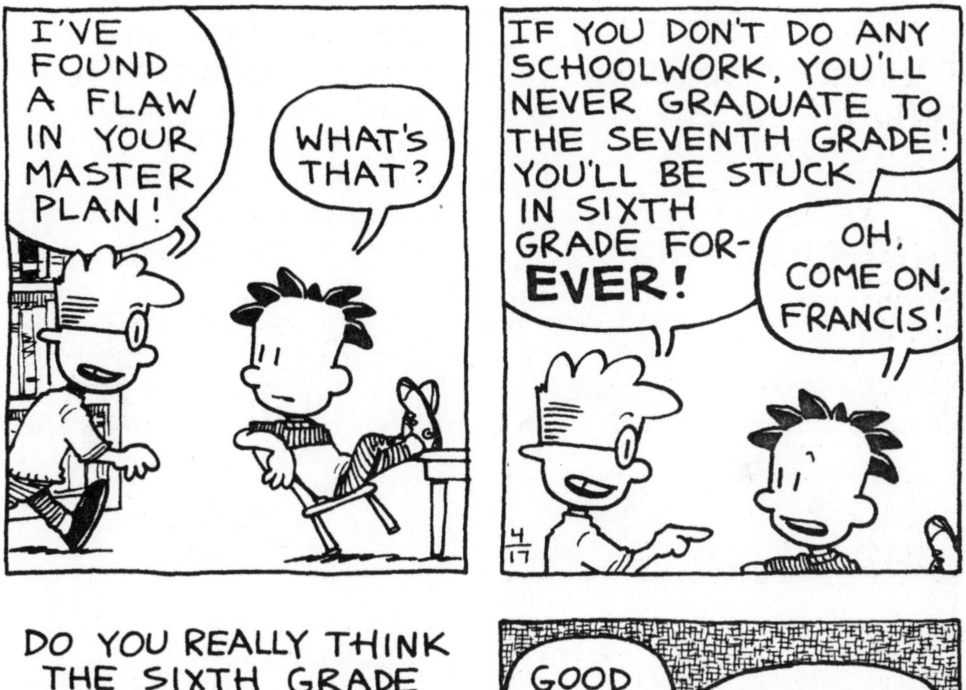
I'VE FOUND A FLAW IN YOUR MASTER PLAN!
WHAT'S THAT?
IF YOU DON'T DO ANY SCHOOLWORK, YOU'LL NEVER GRADUATE TO THE SEVENTH GRADE! YOU'LL BE STUCK IN SIXTH GRADE FOR-EVER!
OH, COME ON, FRANCIS!
DO YOU REALLY THINK THE SIXTH GRADE TEACHERS WOULD CHOOSE TO KEEP ME AROUND WHEN THEY COULD PASS ME UP TO SEVENTH GRADE?
GOOD POINT.
I'VE GOT 'EM RIGHT WHERE I WANT 'EM.
4/17
© 2009 by NEA, Inc.
Peirce

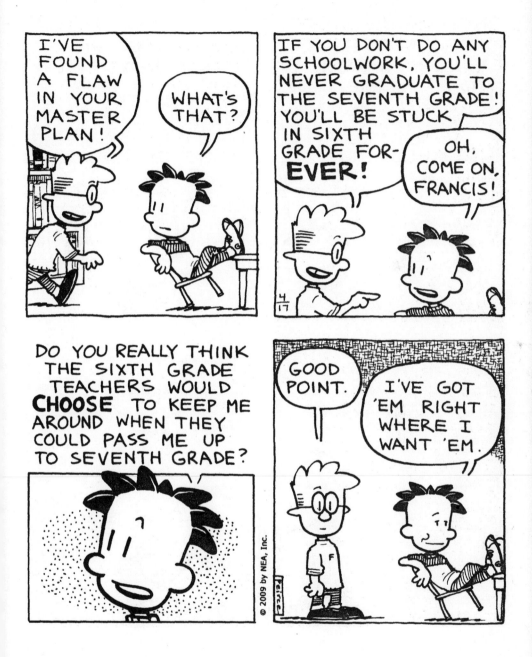

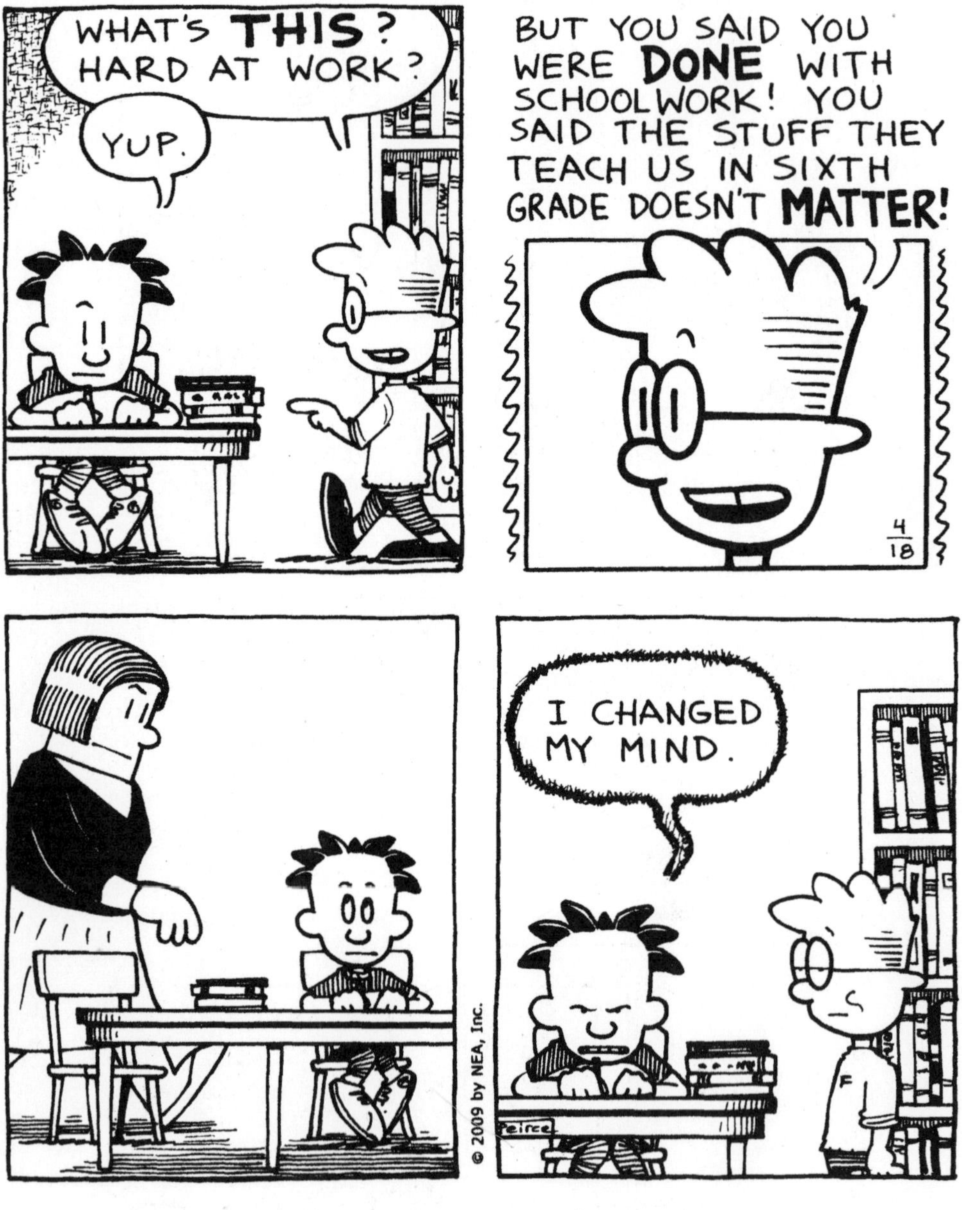
WHAT'S **THIS**? HARD AT WORK?
YUP.
BUT YOU SAID YOU WERE **DONE** WITH SCHOOLWORK! YOU SAID THE STUFF THEY TEACH US IN SIXTH GRADE DOESN'T **MATTER!**
4/18
© 2009 by NEA, Inc.
I CHANGED MY MIND.
Peirce

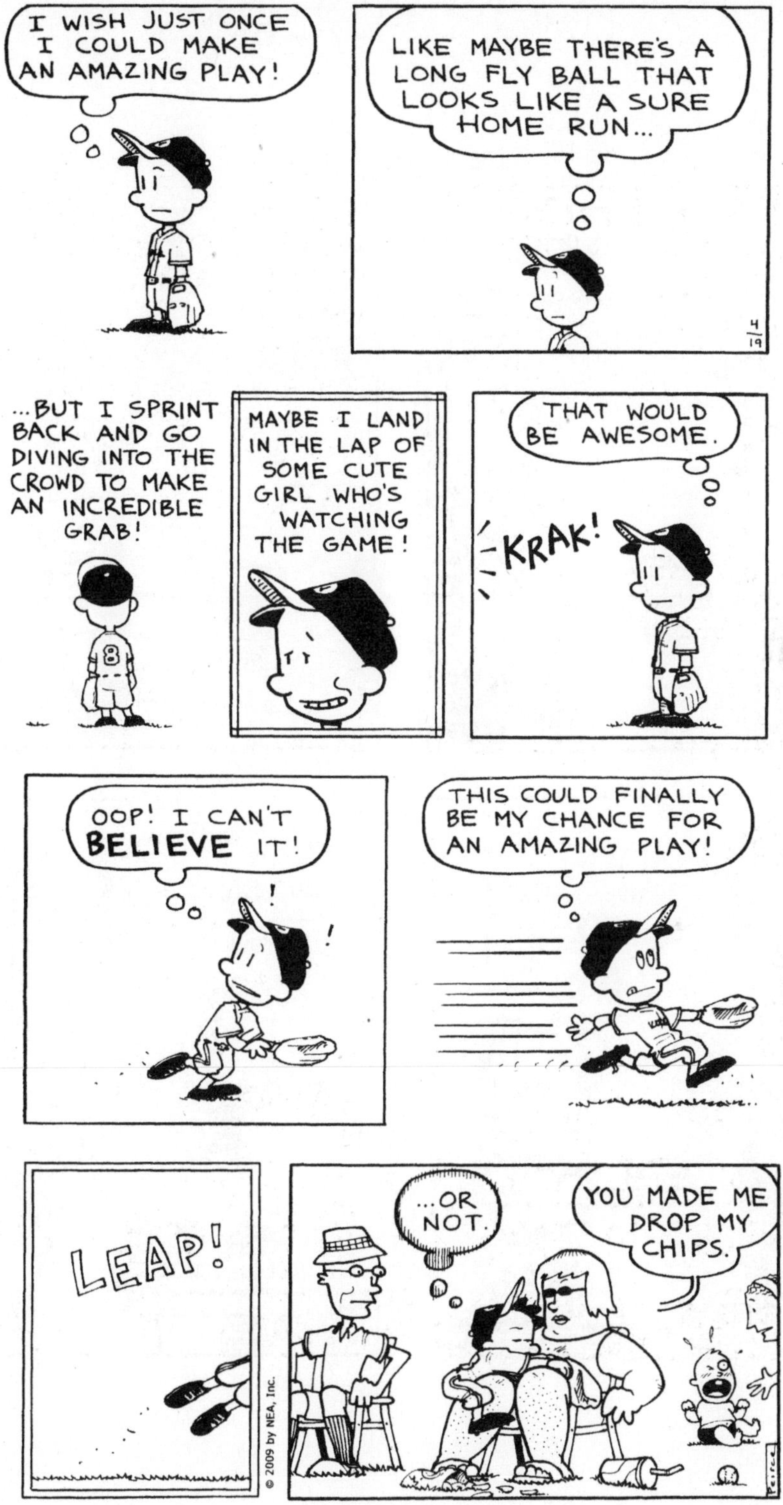
I WISH JUST ONCE I COULD MAKE AN AMAZING PLAY!
LIKE MAYBE THERE'S A LONG FLY BALL THAT LOOKS LIKE A SURE HOME RUN...
4/19
...BUT I SPRINT BACK AND GO DIVING INTO THE CROWD TO MAKE AN INCREDIBLE GRAB!
MAYBE I LAND IN THE LAP OF SOME CUTE GIRL WHO'S WATCHING THE GAME!
THAT WOULD BE AWESOME.
KRAK!
OOP! I CAN'T BELIEVE IT!
!
!
THIS COULD FINALLY BE MY CHANCE FOR AN AMAZING PLAY!
LEAP!
© 2009 by NEA, Inc.
...OR NOT.
YOU MADE ME DROP MY CHIPS.

OO, LA, LA!

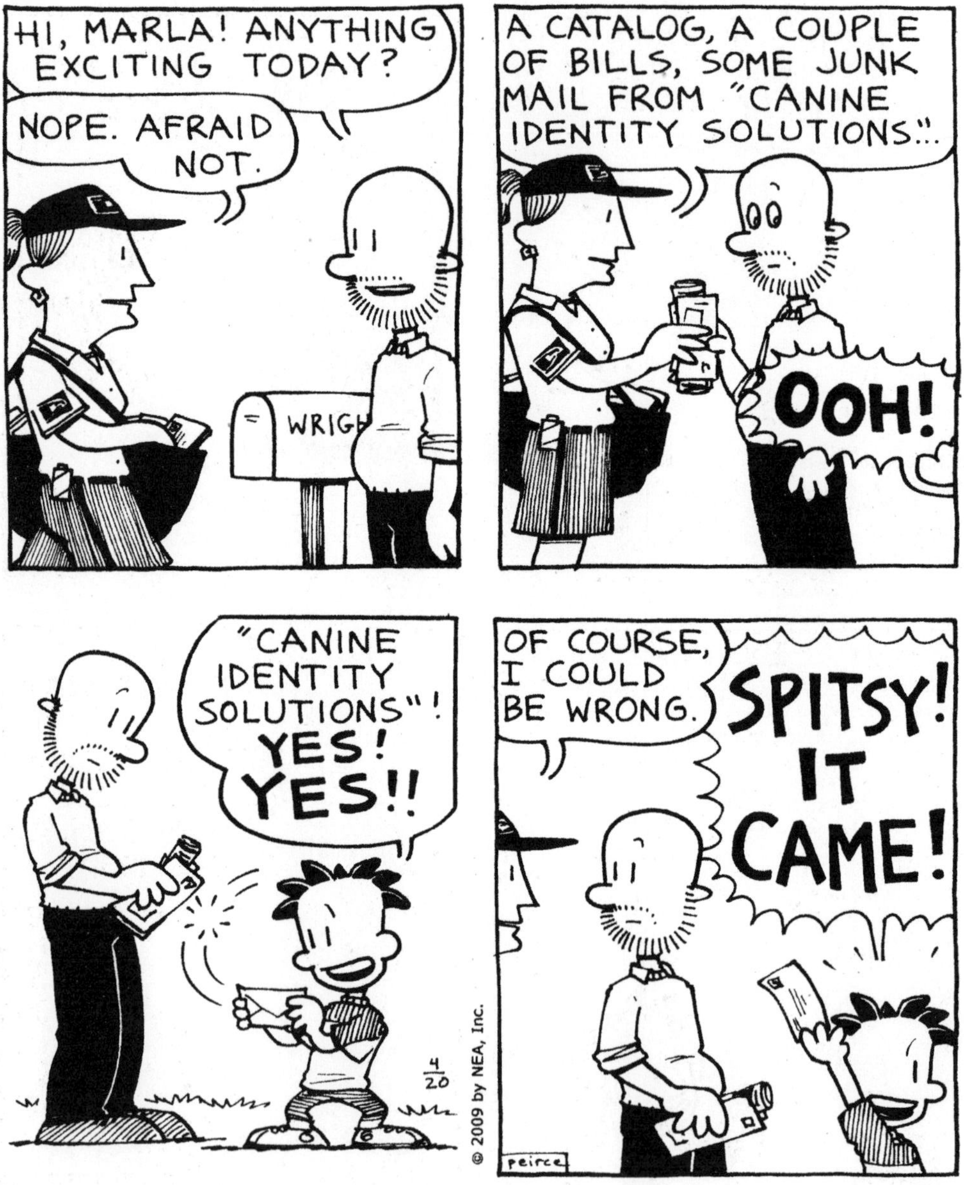

HI, MARLA! ANYTHING EXCITING TODAY?
NOPE. AFRAID NOT.
WRIGH
A CATALOG, A COUPLE OF BILLS, SOME JUNK MAIL FROM "CANINE IDENTITY SOLUTIONS."
OOH!
"CANINE IDENTITY SOLUTIONS"! YES! YES!!
4/20
© 2009 by NEA, Inc.
OF COURSE, I COULD BE WRONG.
SPITSY! IT CAME!
peirce

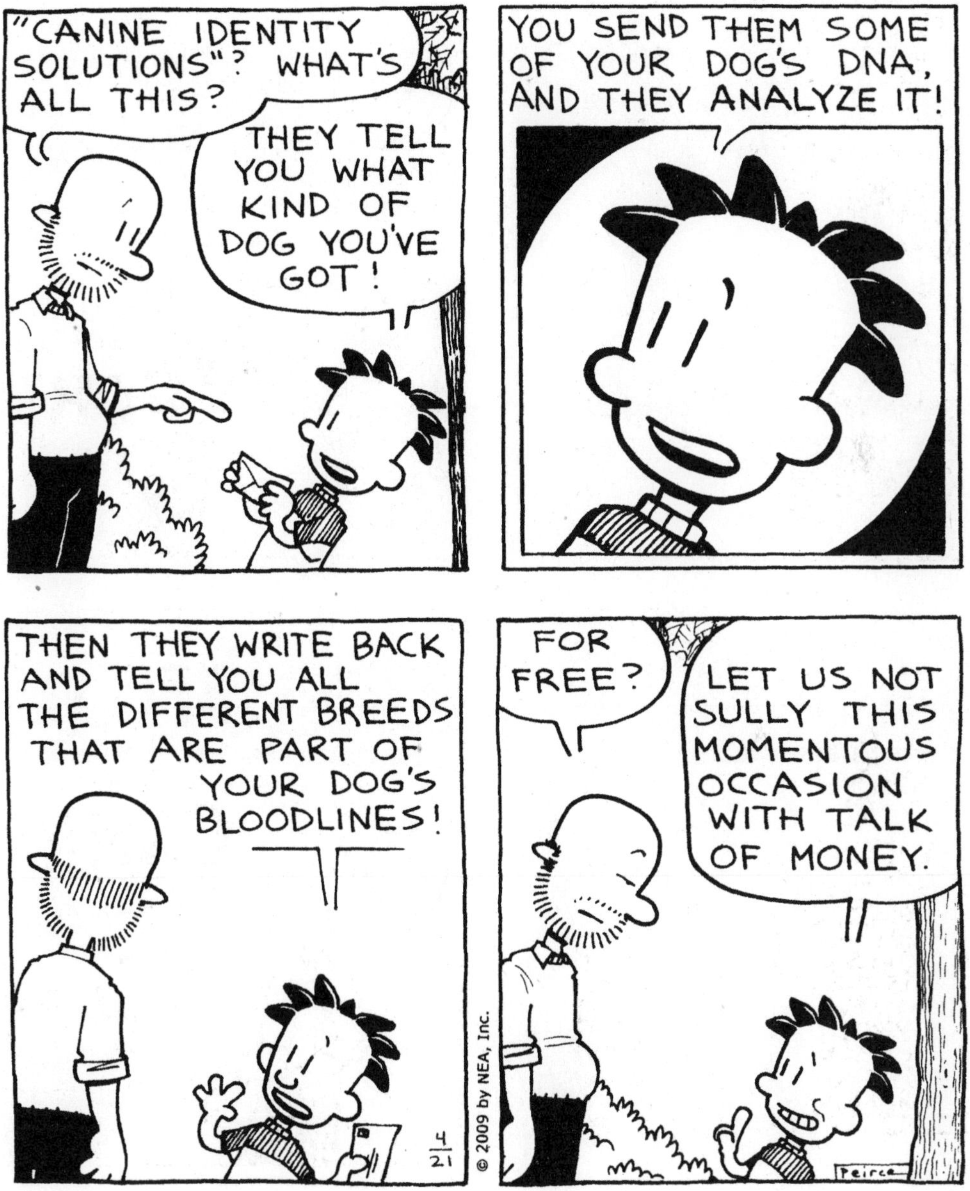
"CANINE IDENTITY SOLUTIONS"? WHAT'S ALL THIS?
THEY TELL YOU WHAT KIND OF DOG YOU'VE GOT!
YOU SEND THEM SOME OF YOUR DOG'S DNA, AND THEY ANALYZE IT!
THEN THEY WRITE BACK AND TELL YOU ALL THE DIFFERENT BREEDS THAT ARE PART OF YOUR DOG'S BLOODLINES!
FOR FREE?
LET US NOT SULLY THIS MOMENTOUS OCCASION WITH TALK OF MONEY.
4/21
© 2009 by NEA, Inc.
Peirce

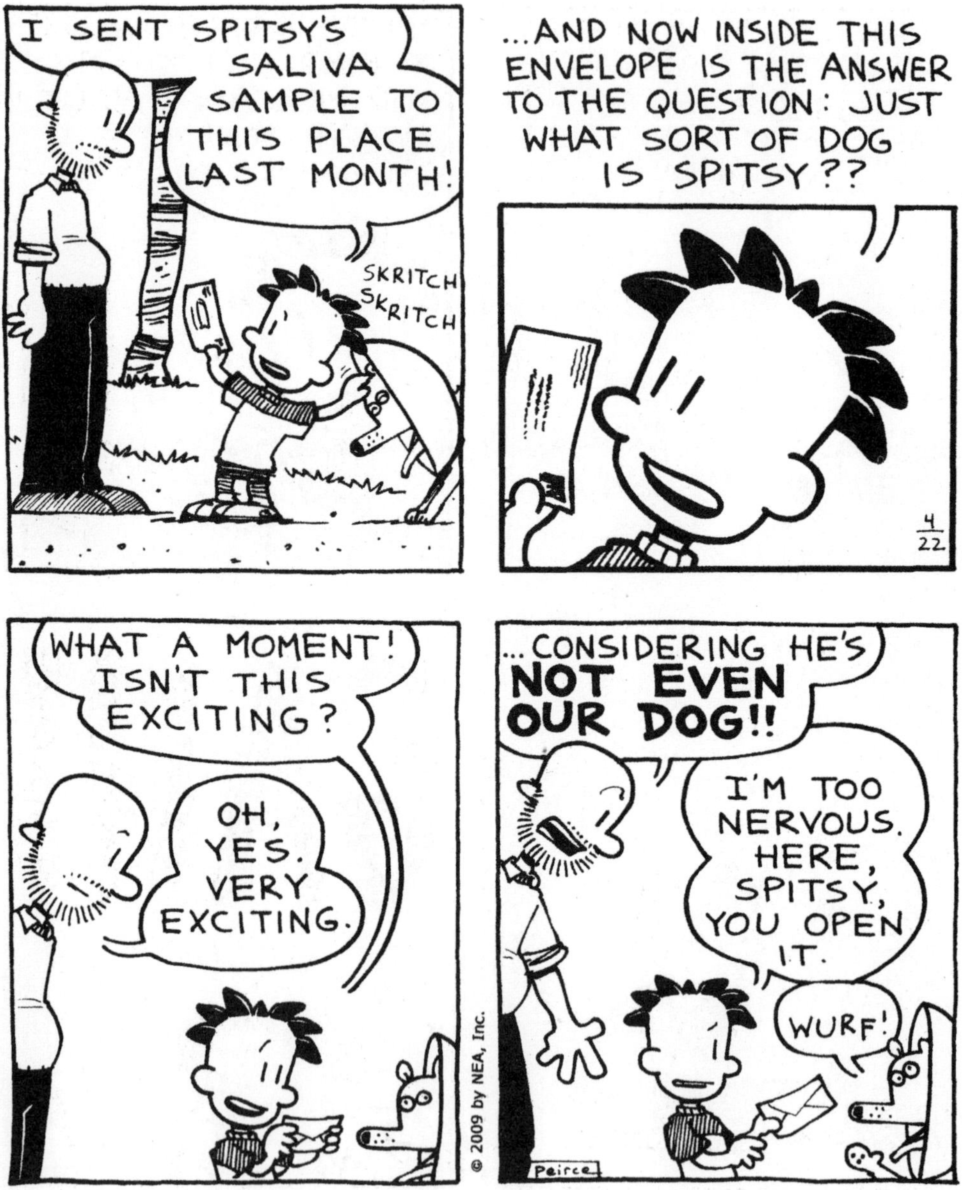

I SENT SPITSY'S SALIVA SAMPLE TO THIS PLACE LAST MONTH!
SKRITCH SKRITCH
...AND NOW INSIDE THIS ENVELOPE IS THE ANSWER TO THE QUESTION: JUST WHAT SORT OF DOG IS SPITSY??
4/22
WHAT A MOMENT! ISN'T THIS EXCITING?
OH, YES. VERY EXCITING.
© 2009 by NEA, Inc.
...CONSIDERING HE'S **NOT EVEN OUR DOG!!**
I'M TOO NERVOUS. HERE, SPITSY, YOU OPEN IT.
WURF!
Peirce

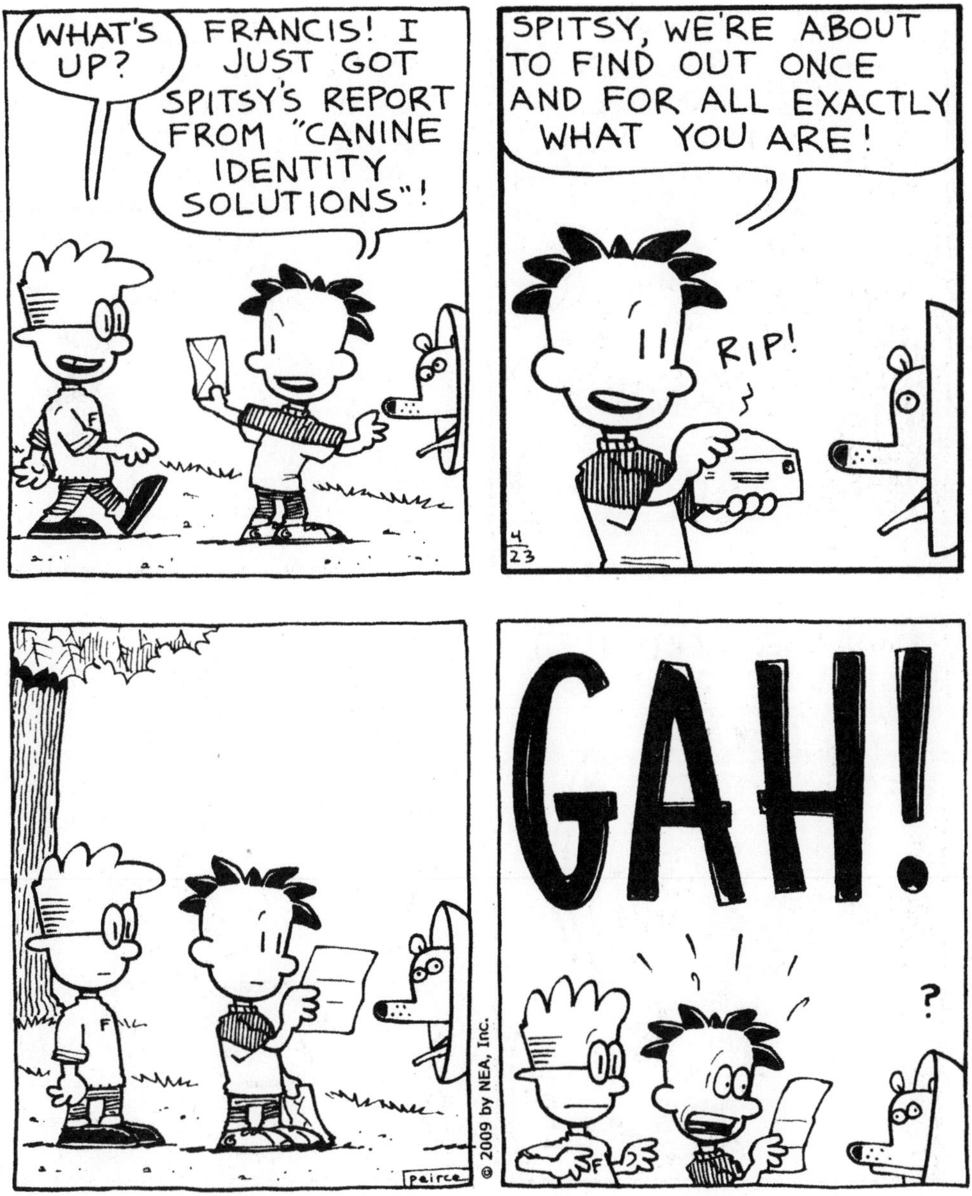

WHAT'S UP?
FRANCIS! I JUST GOT SPITSY'S REPORT FROM "CANINE IDENTITY SOLUTIONS"!
SPITSY, WE'RE ABOUT TO FIND OUT ONCE AND FOR ALL EXACTLY WHAT YOU ARE!
RIP!
4
23
peirce
© 2009 by NEA, Inc.
GAH!
?

WHAT'S WRONG?

SPITSY'S REPORT FROM "CANINE IDENTITY SOLUTIONS," **THAT'S** WHAT'S WRONG!

"DEAR SIR: DUE TO INCONSISTENCIES IN THE SALIVA SAMPLE YOU SENT, WE ARE UNABLE TO PROVIDE A COMPLETE ANALYSIS OF YOUR DOG'S DNA."

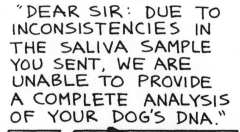

4/24

"THE ONLY BREED WE WERE ABLE TO ISOLATE AND IDENTIFY WITH 100 PERCENT ACCURACY IS: **FRENCH POODLE**"!!

Peirce

© 2009 by NEA, Inc.

SPITSY! BONJOUR!

WURF!

I CAN'T TAKE IT.

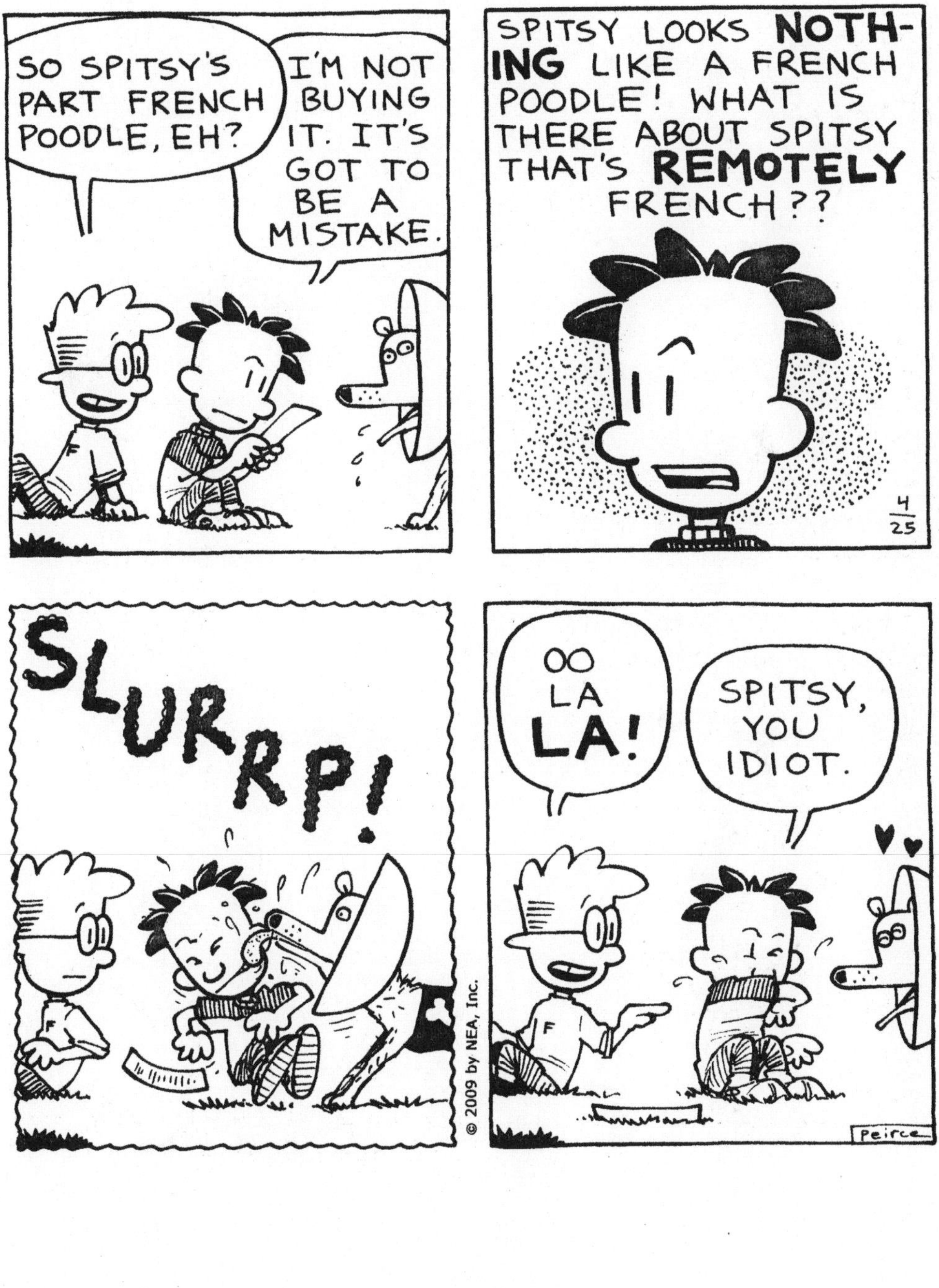
SO SPITSY'S PART FRENCH POODLE, EH?
I'M NOT BUYING IT. IT'S GOT TO BE A MISTAKE.
SPITSY LOOKS **NOTHING** LIKE A FRENCH POODLE! WHAT IS THERE ABOUT SPITSY THAT'S **REMOTELY** FRENCH??
4/25
SLURRP!
© 2009 by NEA, Inc.
OO LA **LA!**
SPITSY, YOU IDIOT.
Peirce

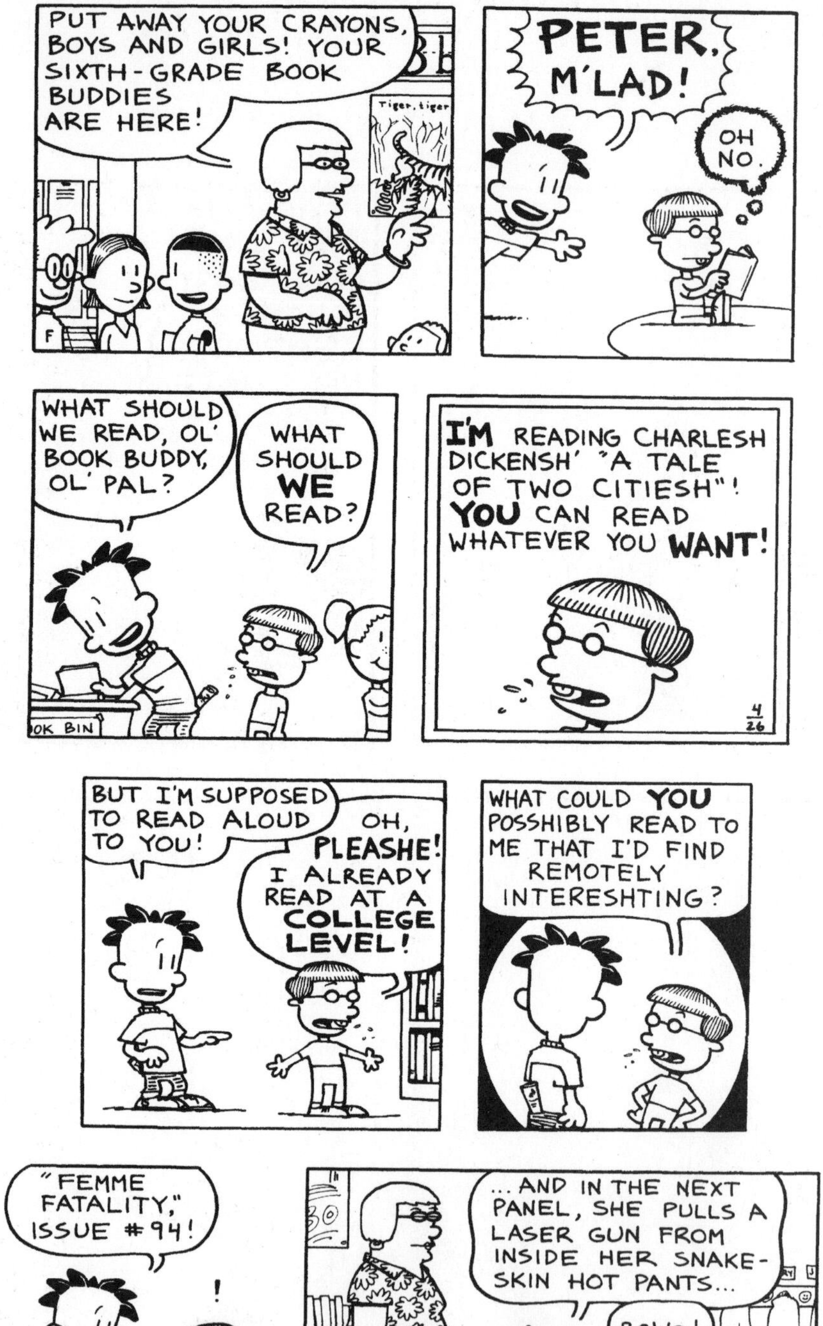
PUT AWAY YOUR CRAYONS, BOYS AND GIRLS! YOUR SIXTH-GRADE BOOK BUDDIES ARE HERE!
Tiger, tiger
PETER, M'LAD!
OH NO.
WHAT SHOULD WE READ, OL' BOOK BUDDY, OL' PAL?
WHAT SHOULD WE READ?
OK BIN
I'M READING CHARLESH DICKENSH' "A TALE OF TWO CITIESH"! YOU CAN READ WHATEVER YOU WANT!
4/26
BUT I'M SUPPOSED TO READ ALOUD TO YOU!
OH, PLEASHE! I ALREADY READ AT A COLLEGE LEVEL!
WHAT COULD YOU POSSHIBLY READ TO ME THAT I'D FIND REMOTELY INTERESHTING?
"FEMME FATALITY," ISSUE #94!
!
... AND IN THE NEXT PANEL, SHE PULLS A LASER GUN FROM INSIDE HER SNAKE-SKIN HOT PANTS...
ROWR!
© 2009 by NEA, Inc.
Peirce

A NOVEL IDEA

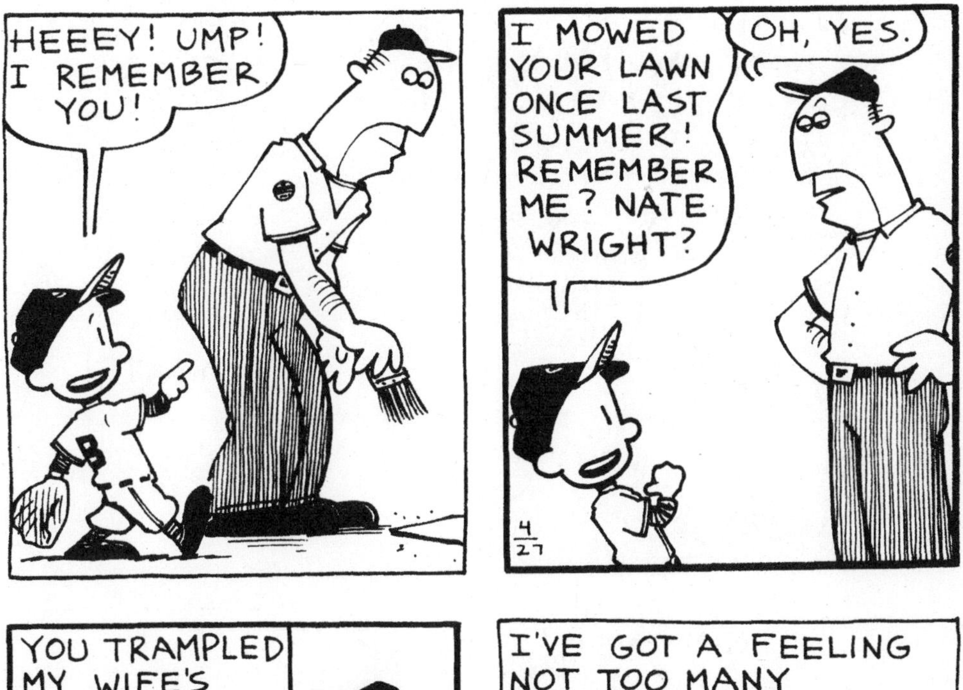
HEEEY! UMP! I REMEMBER YOU!
I MOWED YOUR LAWN ONCE LAST SUMMER! REMEMBER ME? NATE WRIGHT?
OH, YES.
4/27
YOU TRAMPLED MY WIFE'S FLOWER BEDS, THEN RAN MY MOWER OVER A ROCK AND BROKE THE BLADE.
© 2009 by NEA, Inc.
I'VE GOT A FEELING NOT TOO MANY CLOSE CALLS WILL GO **YOUR** WAY TODAY!
HMPH.
Peirce

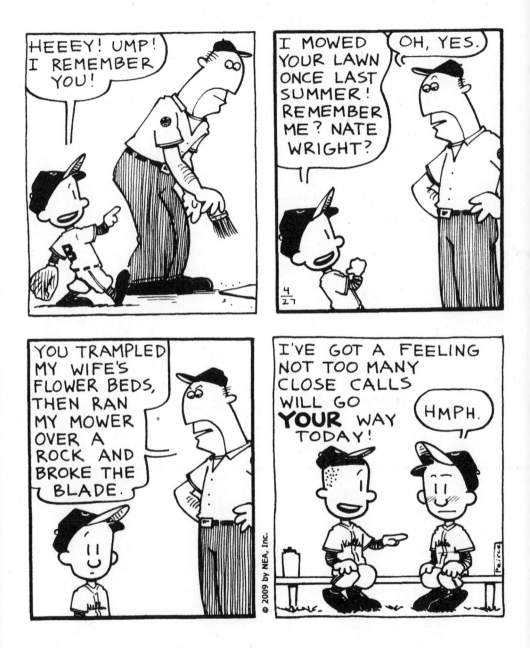

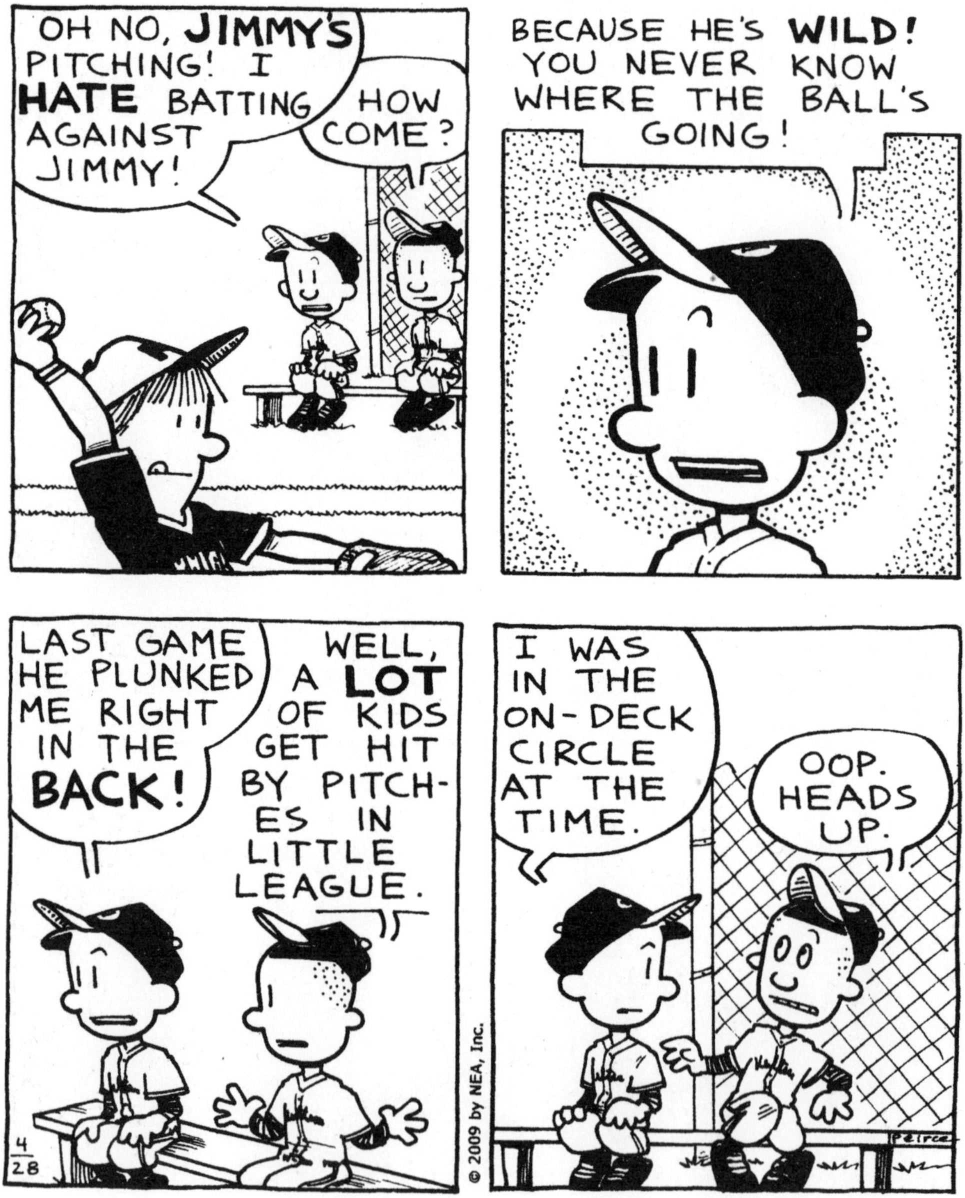
OH NO, **JIMMY'S** PITCHING! I **HATE** BATTING AGAINST JIMMY!
HOW COME?
BECAUSE HE'S **WILD**! YOU NEVER KNOW WHERE THE BALL'S GOING!
LAST GAME HE PLUNKED ME RIGHT IN THE **BACK**!
WELL, A **LOT** OF KIDS GET HIT BY PITCH-ES IN LITTLE LEAGUE.
I WAS IN THE ON-DECK CIRCLE AT THE TIME.
OOP. HEADS UP.
4 28
PEIRCE
© 2009 by NEA, Inc.

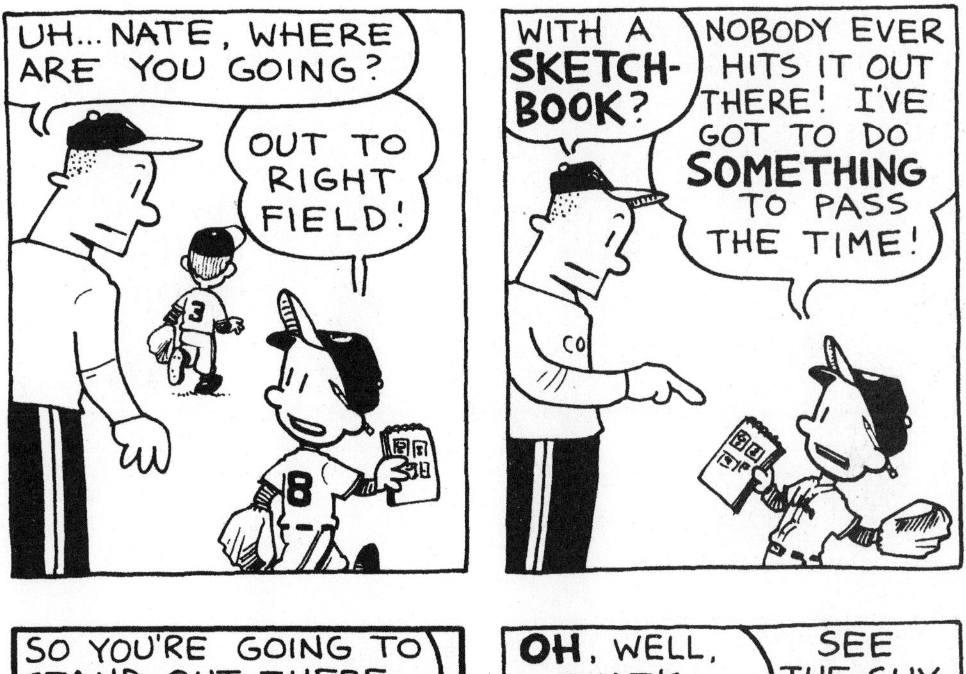
UH... NATE, WHERE ARE YOU GOING?
OUT TO RIGHT FIELD!
WITH A **SKETCH-BOOK**?
NOBODY EVER HITS IT OUT THERE! I'VE GOT TO DO **SOMETHING** TO PASS THE TIME!
SO YOU'RE GOING TO STAND OUT THERE **DRAWING COMICS**?
NOT JUST COMICS! IT'S A **GRAPHIC NOVEL**!
OH, WELL, THAT'S **DIFFERENT**!
SEE THE GUY WITH SMOKE COMING OUT OF HIS EARS? THAT'S **YOU**!
COACH
4/29
Peirce

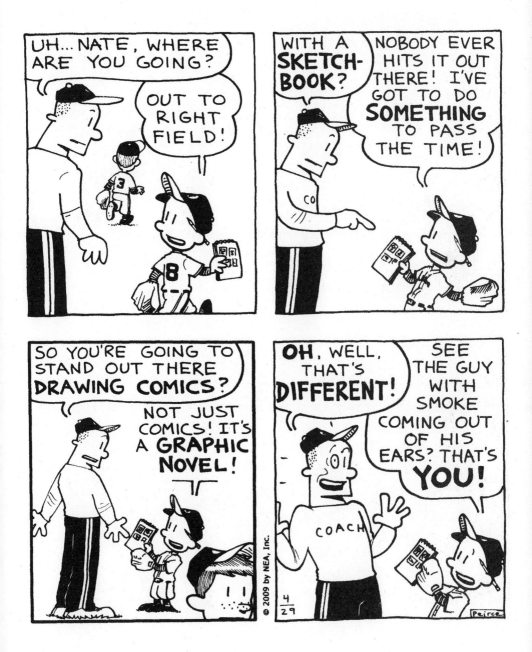

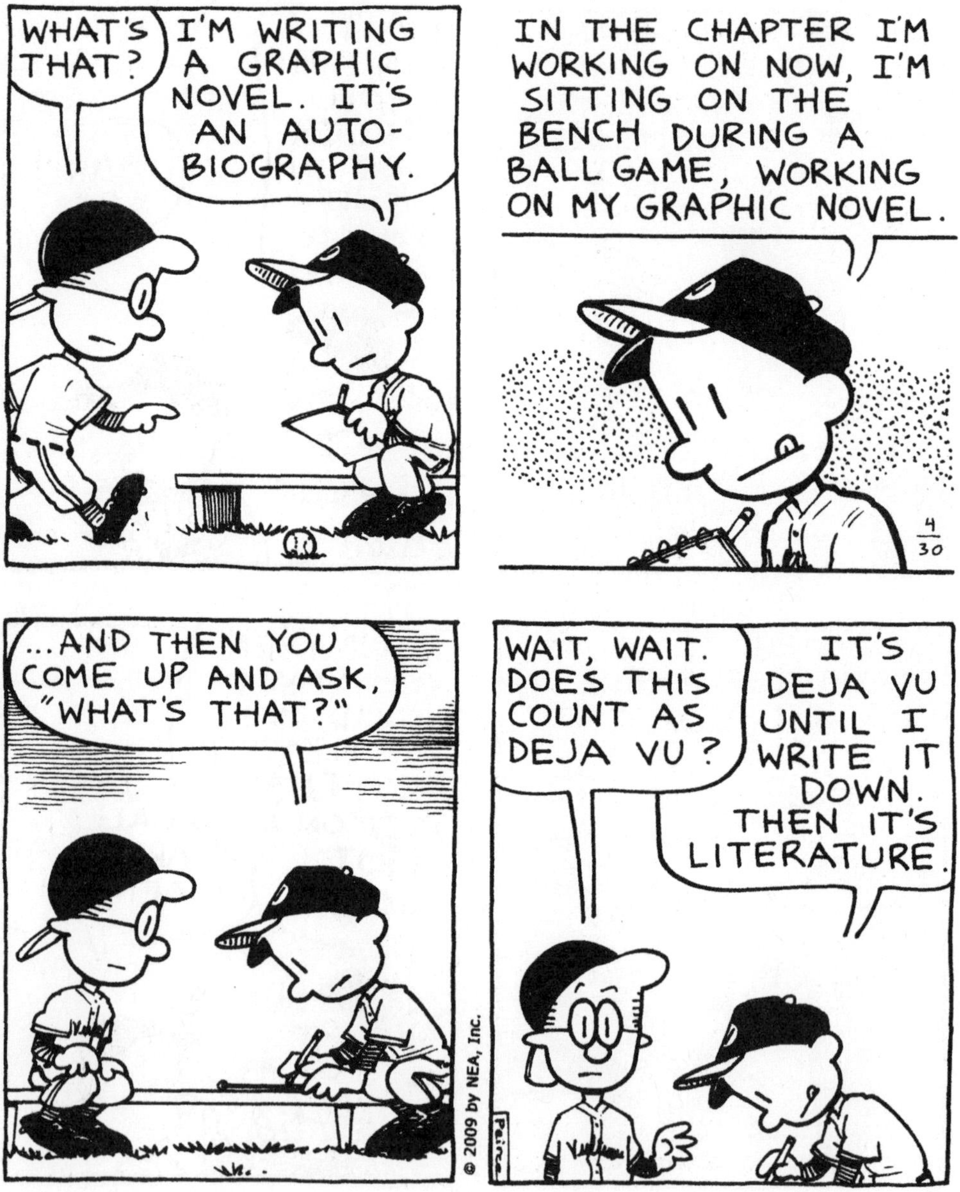
WHAT'S THAT?
I'M WRITING A GRAPHIC NOVEL. IT'S AN AUTO-BIOGRAPHY.
IN THE CHAPTER I'M WORKING ON NOW, I'M SITTING ON THE BENCH DURING A BALL GAME, WORKING ON MY GRAPHIC NOVEL.
4/30
...AND THEN YOU COME UP AND ASK, "WHAT'S THAT?"
WAIT, WAIT. DOES THIS COUNT AS DEJA VU?
IT'S DEJA VU UNTIL I WRITE IT DOWN. THEN IT'S LITERATURE.
© 2009 by NEA, Inc.
Paige

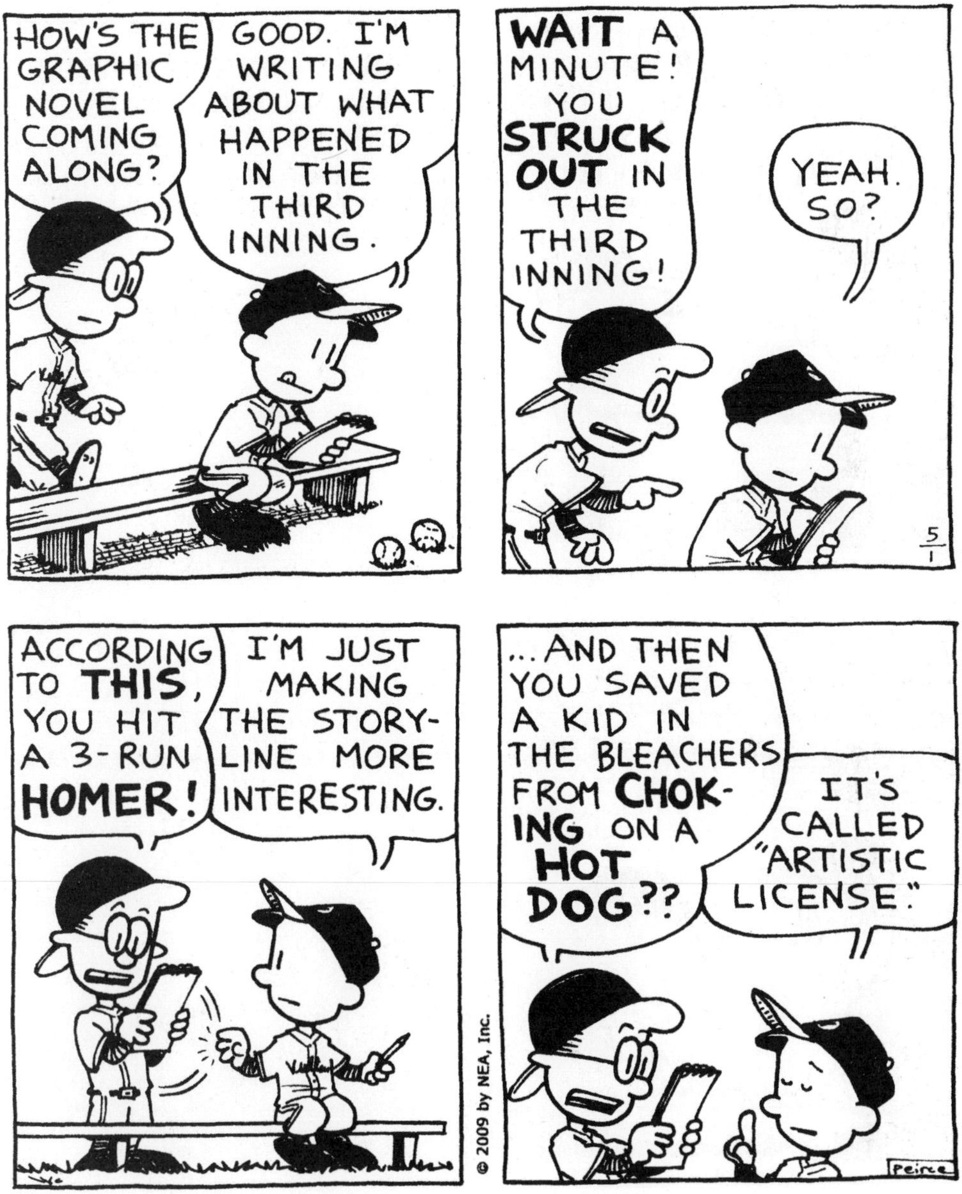
HOW'S THE GRAPHIC NOVEL COMING ALONG?
GOOD. I'M WRITING ABOUT WHAT HAPPENED IN THE THIRD INNING.
WAIT A MINUTE! YOU STRUCK OUT IN THE THIRD INNING!
YEAH. SO?
5/1
ACCORDING TO THIS, YOU HIT A 3-RUN HOMER!
I'M JUST MAKING THE STORY-LINE MORE INTERESTING.
...AND THEN YOU SAVED A KID IN THE BLEACHERS FROM CHOK-ING ON A HOT DOG??
IT'S CALLED "ARTISTIC LICENSE."
peirce
© 2009 by NEA, Inc.

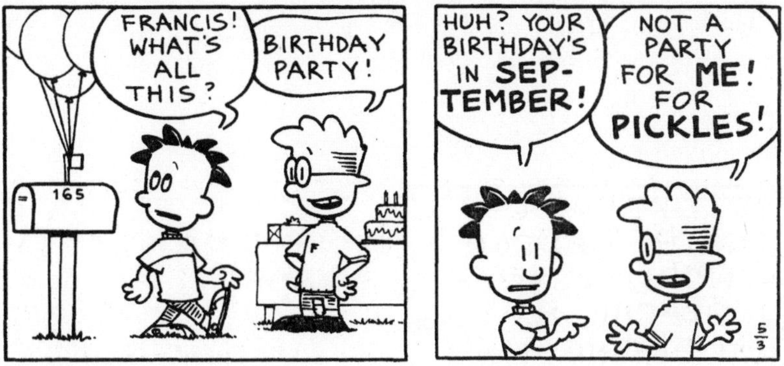
FRANCIS! WHAT'S ALL THIS?
BIRTHDAY PARTY!
HUH? YOUR BIRTHDAY'S IN SEPTEMBER!
NOT A PARTY FOR ME! FOR PICKLES!
5/3

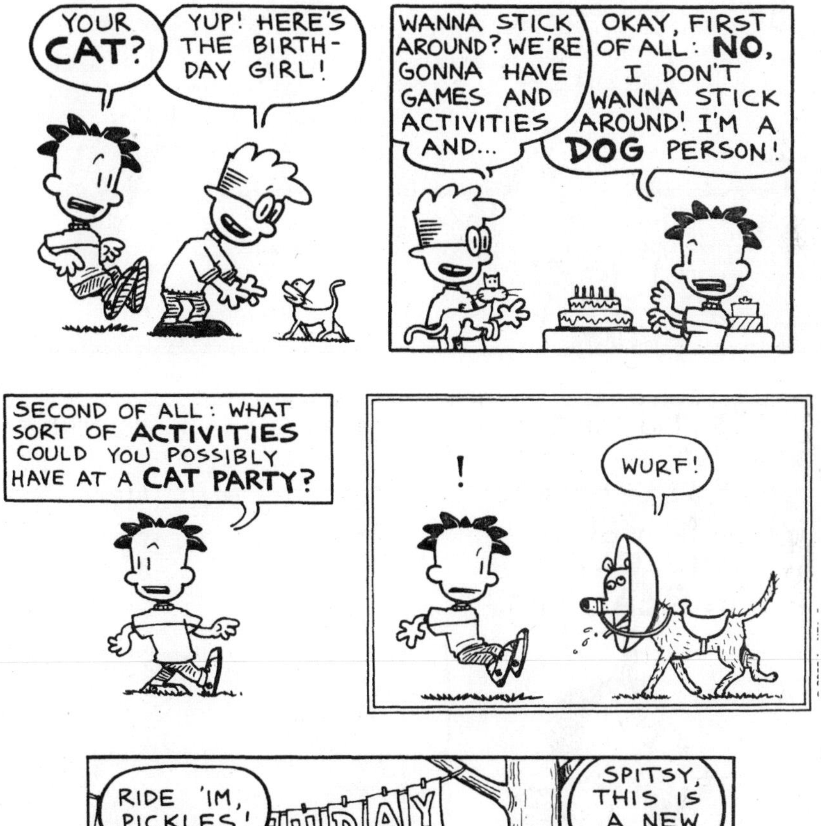
YOUR CAT?
YUP! HERE'S THE BIRTHDAY GIRL!
WANNA STICK AROUND? WE'RE GONNA HAVE GAMES AND ACTIVITIES AND...
OKAY, FIRST OF ALL: NO, I DON'T WANNA STICK AROUND! I'M A DOG PERSON!
SECOND OF ALL: WHAT SORT OF ACTIVITIES COULD YOU POSSIBLY HAVE AT A CAT PARTY?
!
WURF!
RIDE 'IM, PICKLES!
THDAY
SPITSY, THIS IS A NEW LOW.
© 2009 by NEA, Inc.
Peirce

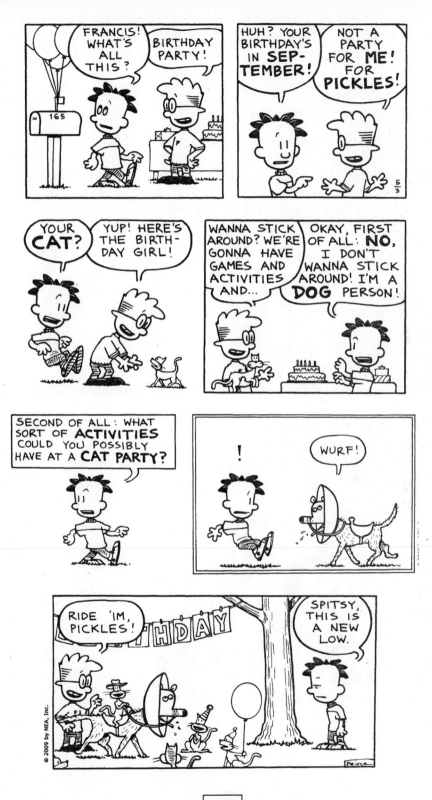

SUGAR BUZZ

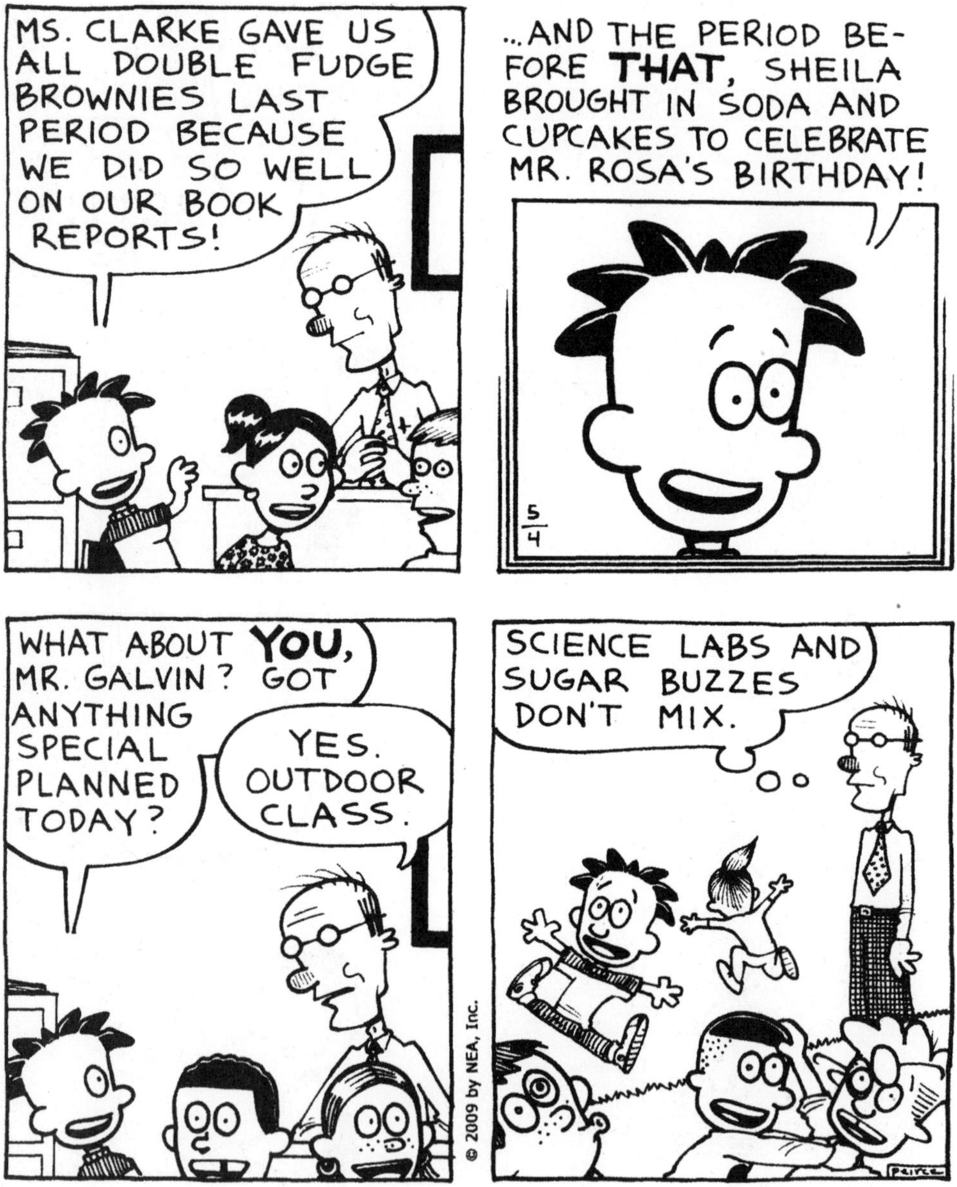
MS. CLARKE GAVE US ALL DOUBLE FUDGE BROWNIES LAST PERIOD BECAUSE WE DID SO WELL ON OUR BOOK REPORTS!
...AND THE PERIOD BEFORE **THAT**, SHEILA BROUGHT IN SODA AND CUPCAKES TO CELEBRATE MR. ROSA'S BIRTHDAY!
5/4
WHAT ABOUT **YOU**, MR. GALVIN? GOT ANYTHING SPECIAL PLANNED TODAY?
YES. OUTDOOR CLASS.
© 2009 by NEA, Inc.
SCIENCE LABS AND SUGAR BUZZES DON'T MIX.

NATE MAKES THE GRADE

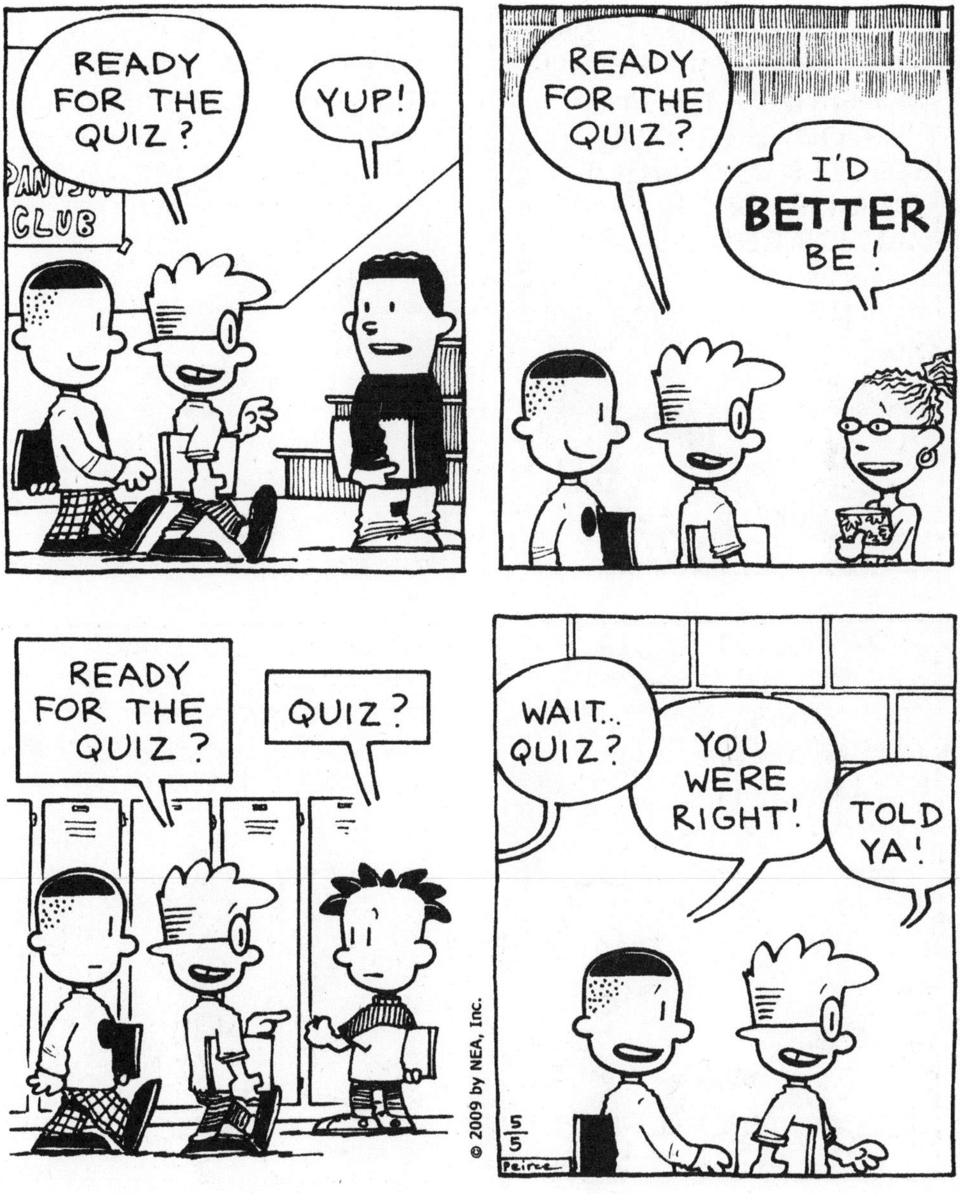
CLUB
READY FOR THE QUIZ?
YUP!
READY FOR THE QUIZ?
I'D **BETTER** BE!
READY FOR THE QUIZ?
QUIZ?
WAIT.. QUIZ?
YOU WERE RIGHT!
TOLD YA!
© 2009 by NEA, Inc.
5/5
Peirce

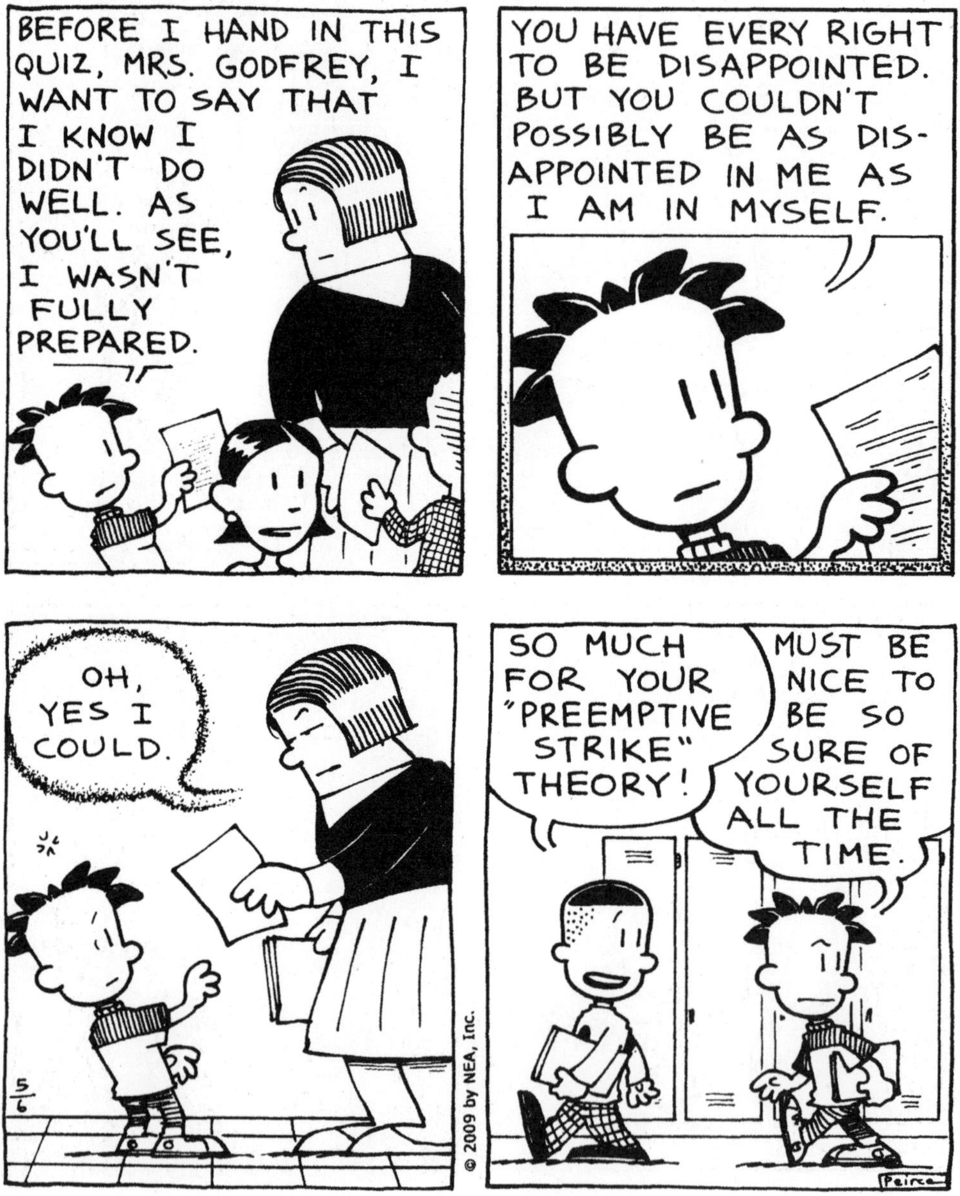
BEFORE I HAND IN THIS QUIZ, MRS. GODFREY, I WANT TO SAY THAT I KNOW I DIDN'T DO WELL. AS YOU'LL SEE, I WASN'T FULLY PREPARED.
YOU HAVE EVERY RIGHT TO BE DISAPPOINTED. BUT YOU COULDN'T POSSIBLY BE AS DISAPPOINTED IN ME AS I AM IN MYSELF.
OH, YES I COULD.
5/6
© 2009 by NEA, Inc.
SO MUCH FOR YOUR "PREEMPTIVE STRIKE" THEORY!
MUST BE NICE TO BE SO SURE OF YOURSELF ALL THE TIME.
Peirce

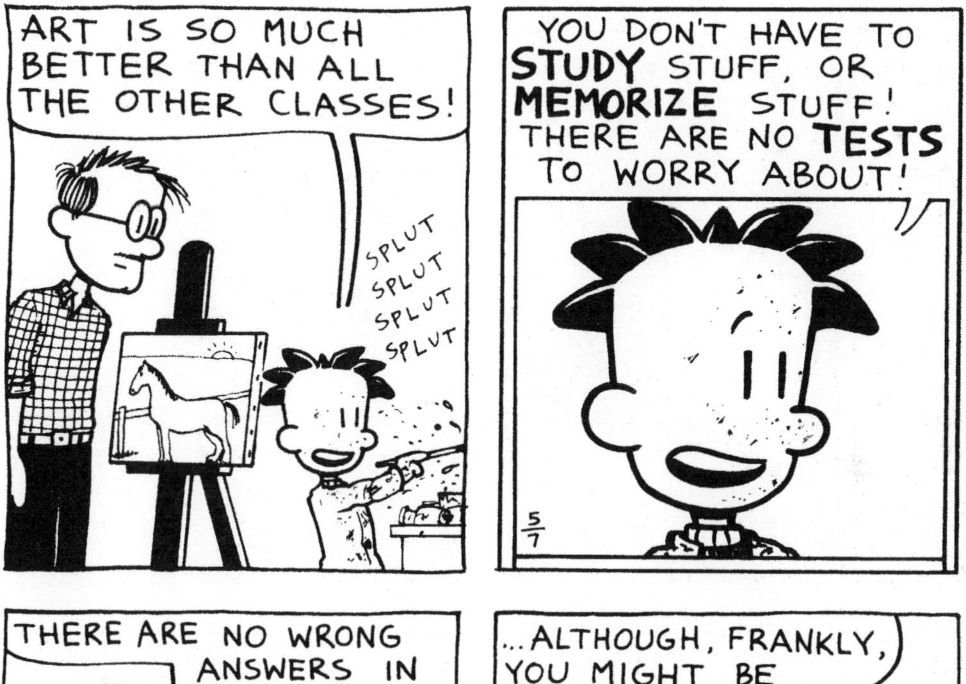
ART IS SO MUCH BETTER THAN ALL THE OTHER CLASSES!
SPLUT SPLUT SPLUT SPLUT
YOU DON'T HAVE TO **STUDY** STUFF, OR **MEMORIZE** STUFF! THERE ARE NO **TESTS** TO WORRY ABOUT!
5/7
THERE ARE NO WRONG ANSWERS IN ART! RIGHT, MR. ROSA?
RIGHT.
© 2009 by NEA, Inc.
...ALTHOUGH, FRANKLY, YOU MIGHT BE PUSHING THE ENVELOPE.
YEP. STAND BACK.

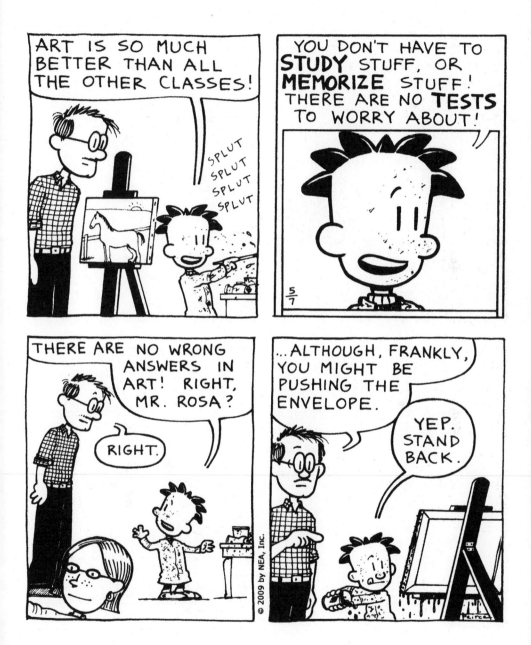

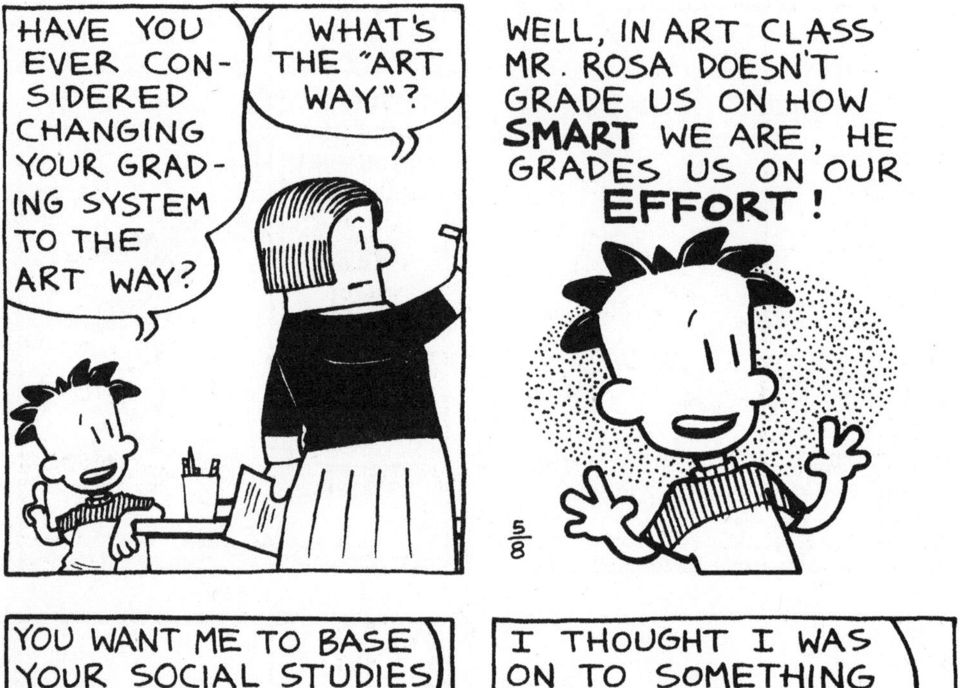
HAVE YOU EVER CONSIDERED CHANGING YOUR GRADING SYSTEM TO THE ART WAY?
WHAT'S THE "ART WAY"?
WELL, IN ART CLASS MR. ROSA DOESN'T GRADE US ON HOW **SMART** WE ARE, HE GRADES US ON OUR **EFFORT**!
5/8
YOU WANT ME TO BASE YOUR SOCIAL STUDIES GRADE ON HOW HARD YOU TRY?
YOU?
© 2009 by NEA, Inc.
I THOUGHT I WAS ON TO SOMETHING UNTIL THAT LAST "YOU."
Peirce

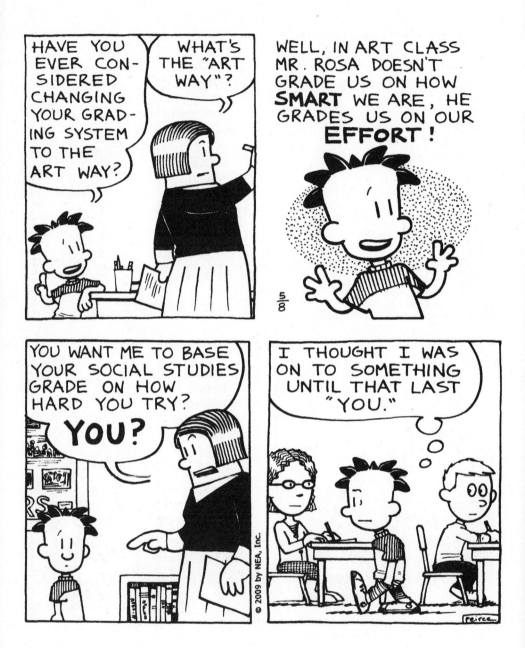

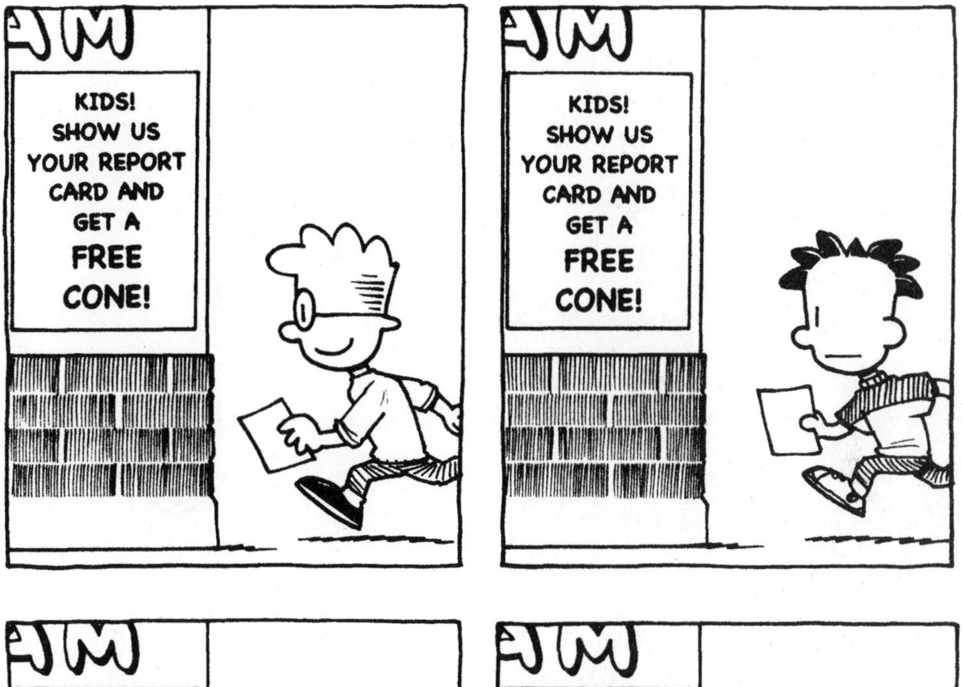
KIDS! SHOW US YOUR REPORT CARD AND GET A FREE CONE!
KIDS! SHOW US YOUR REPORT CARD AND GET A FREE CONE!
KIDS! SHOW US YOUR REPORT CARD AND GET A FREE CONE!
KIDS! SHOW US YOUR REPORT CARD AND GET A FREE CONE!
© 2009 by NEA, Inc.
5/9
Peirce

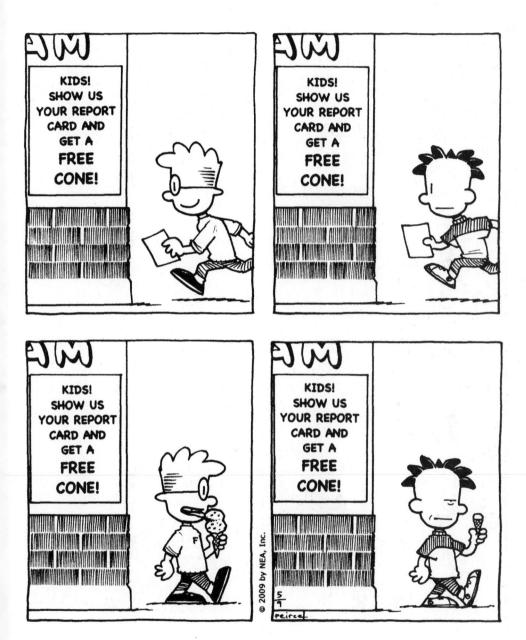

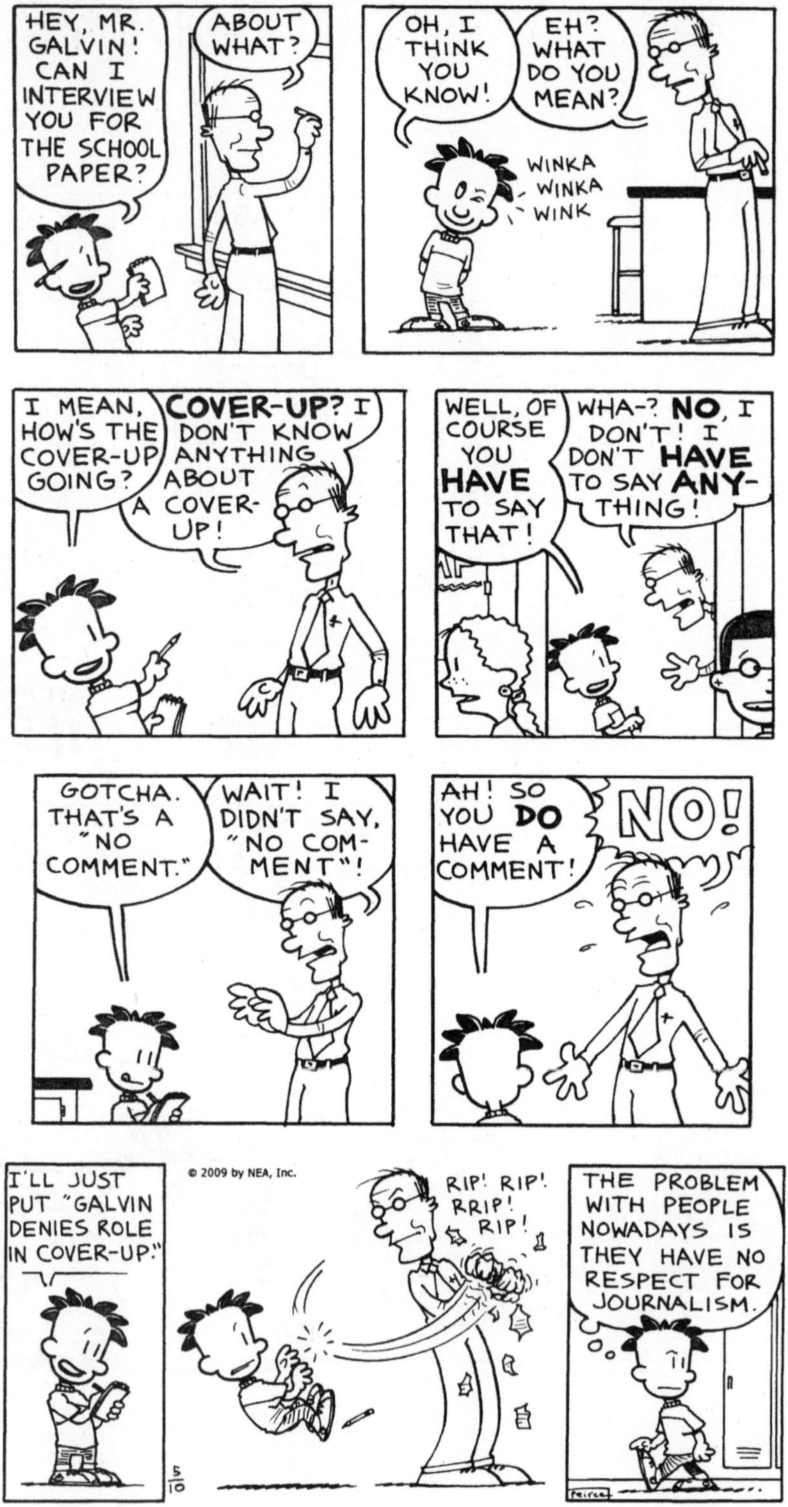
HEY, MR. GALVIN! CAN I INTERVIEW YOU FOR THE SCHOOL PAPER?
ABOUT WHAT?
OH, I THINK YOU KNOW!
EH? WHAT DO YOU MEAN?
WINKA WINKA WINK
I MEAN, HOW'S THE COVER-UP GOING?
COVER-UP? I DON'T KNOW ANYTHING ABOUT A COVER-UP!
WELL, OF COURSE YOU HAVE TO SAY THAT!
WHA-? NO, I DON'T! I DON'T HAVE TO SAY ANY-THING!
GOTCHA. THAT'S A "NO COMMENT."
WAIT! I DIDN'T SAY, "NO COM-MENT"!
AH! SO YOU DO HAVE A COMMENT!
NO!
I'LL JUST PUT "GALVIN DENIES ROLE IN COVER-UP."
© 2009 by NEA, Inc.
RIP! RIP! RRIP! RIP!
5/10
THE PROBLEM WITH PEOPLE NOWADAYS IS THEY HAVE NO RESPECT FOR JOURNALISM.
peirce

WHO'S YOUR CADDY?

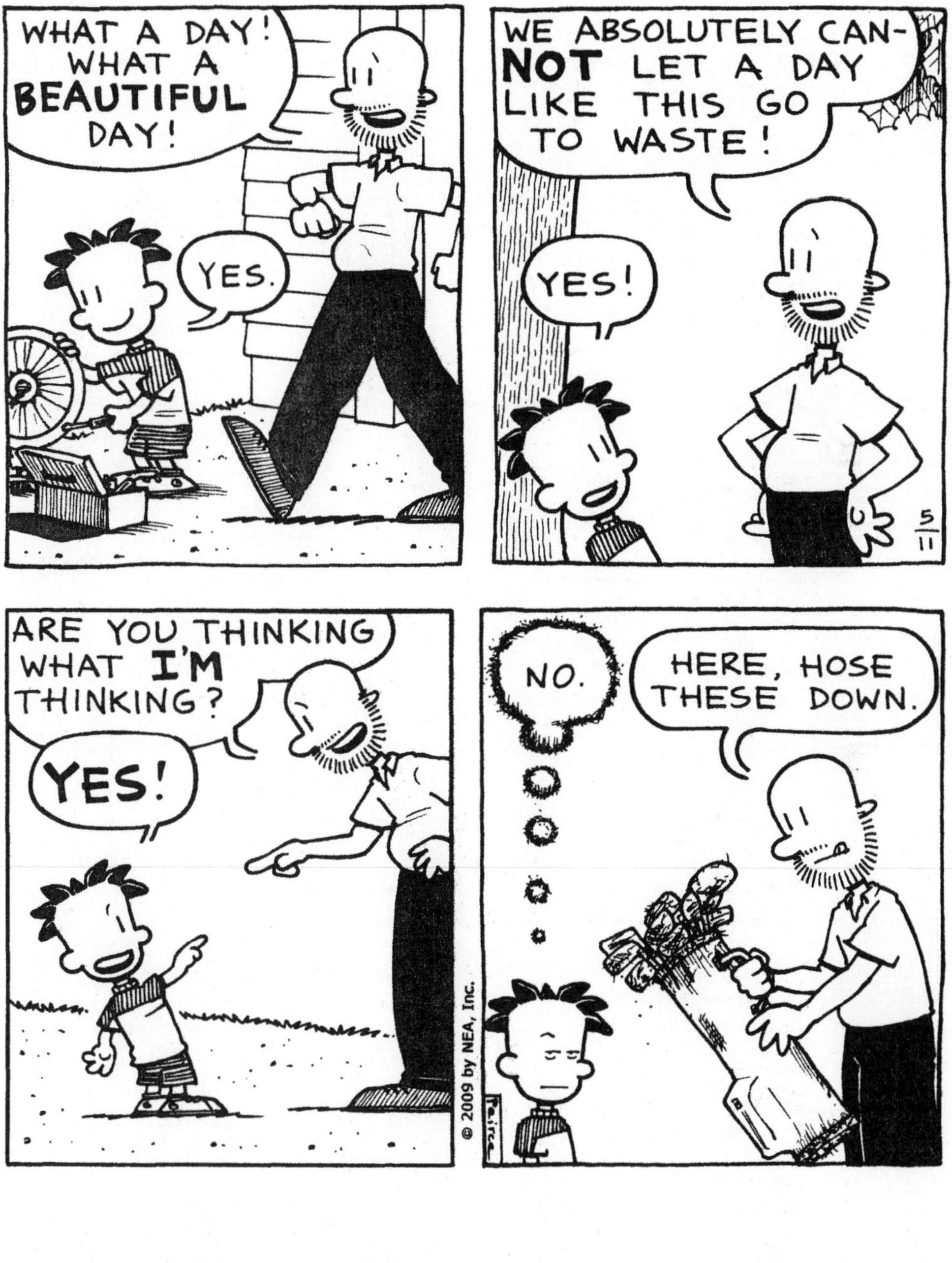
WHAT A DAY! WHAT A **BEAUTIFUL** DAY!
YES.
WE ABSOLUTELY CAN**NOT** LET A DAY LIKE THIS GO TO WASTE!
YES!
5/11
ARE YOU THINKING WHAT **I'M** THINKING?
YES!
© 2009 by NEA, Inc.
NO.
HERE, HOSE THESE DOWN.
Peirce

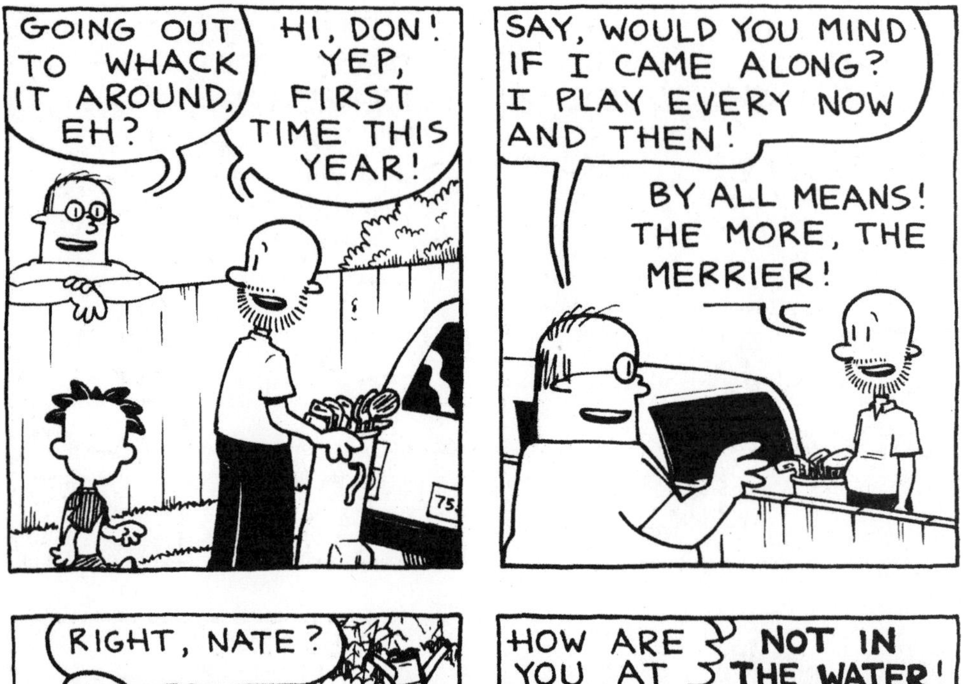
GOING OUT TO WHACK IT AROUND, EH?
HI, DON! YEP, FIRST TIME THIS YEAR!
75
SAY, WOULD YOU MIND IF I CAME ALONG? I PLAY EVERY NOW AND THEN!
BY ALL MEANS! THE MORE, THE MERRIER!
RIGHT, NATE?
ABSOLUTELY.
5 12
© 2009 by NEA, Inc.
HOW ARE YOU AT BALL RE-TRIEVAL?
NOT IN THE WATER! NOT IN THE WATER!
1ST TEE
Peirce

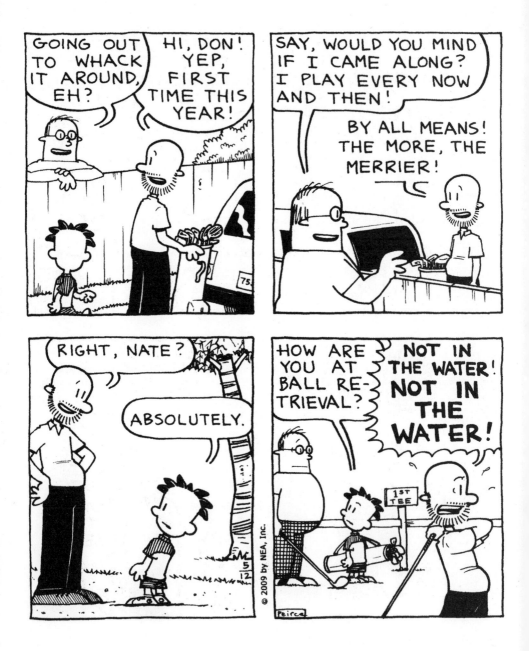

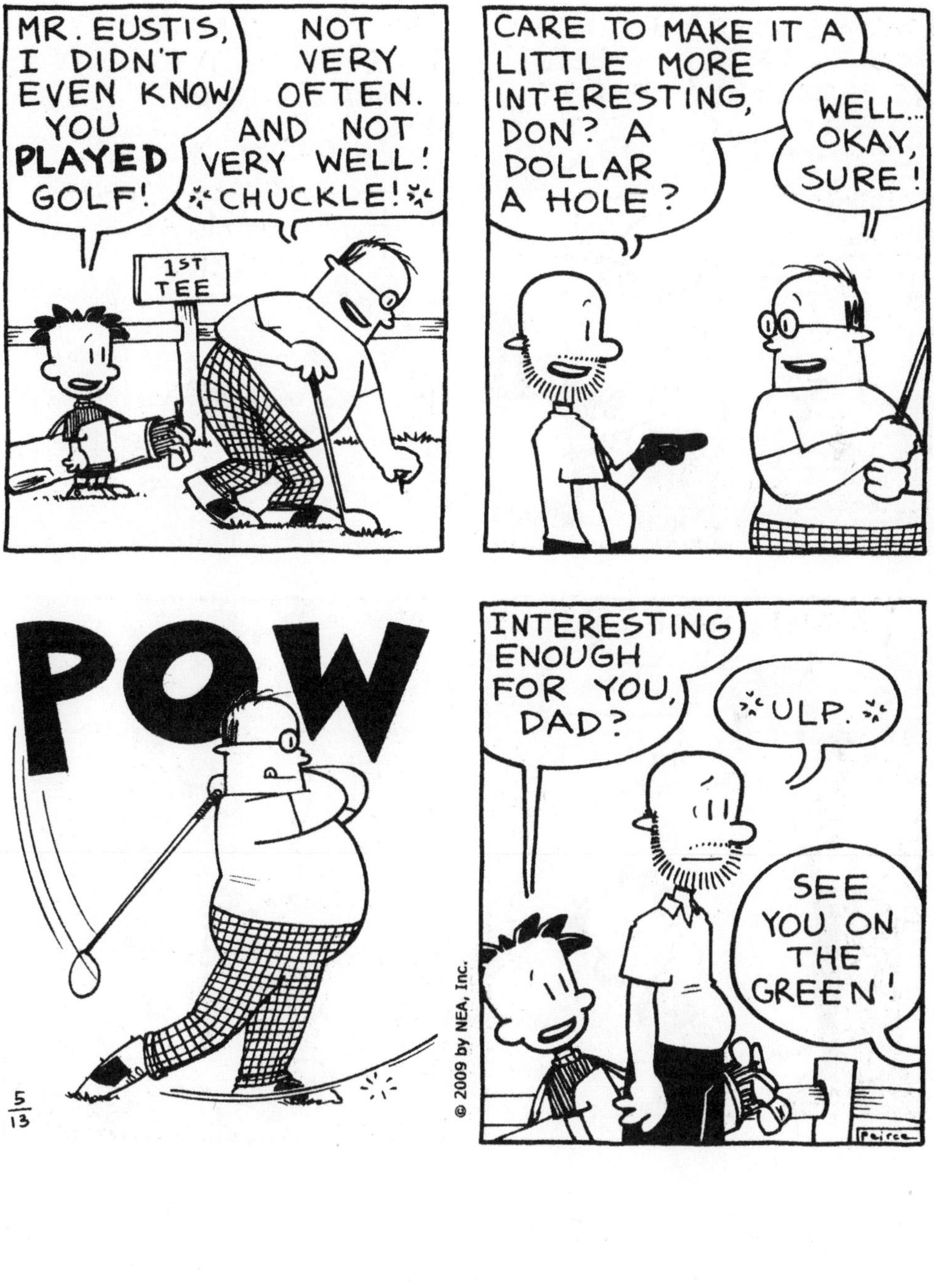
MR. EUSTIS, I DIDN'T EVEN KNOW YOU **PLAYED** GOLF!
NOT VERY OFTEN. AND NOT VERY WELL! CHUCKLE!
1ST TEE
CARE TO MAKE IT A LITTLE MORE INTERESTING, DON? A DOLLAR A HOLE?
WELL... OKAY, SURE!
POW
INTERESTING ENOUGH FOR YOU, DAD?
ULP.
SEE YOU ON THE GREEN!
5/13
© 2009 by NEA, Inc.
Peirce

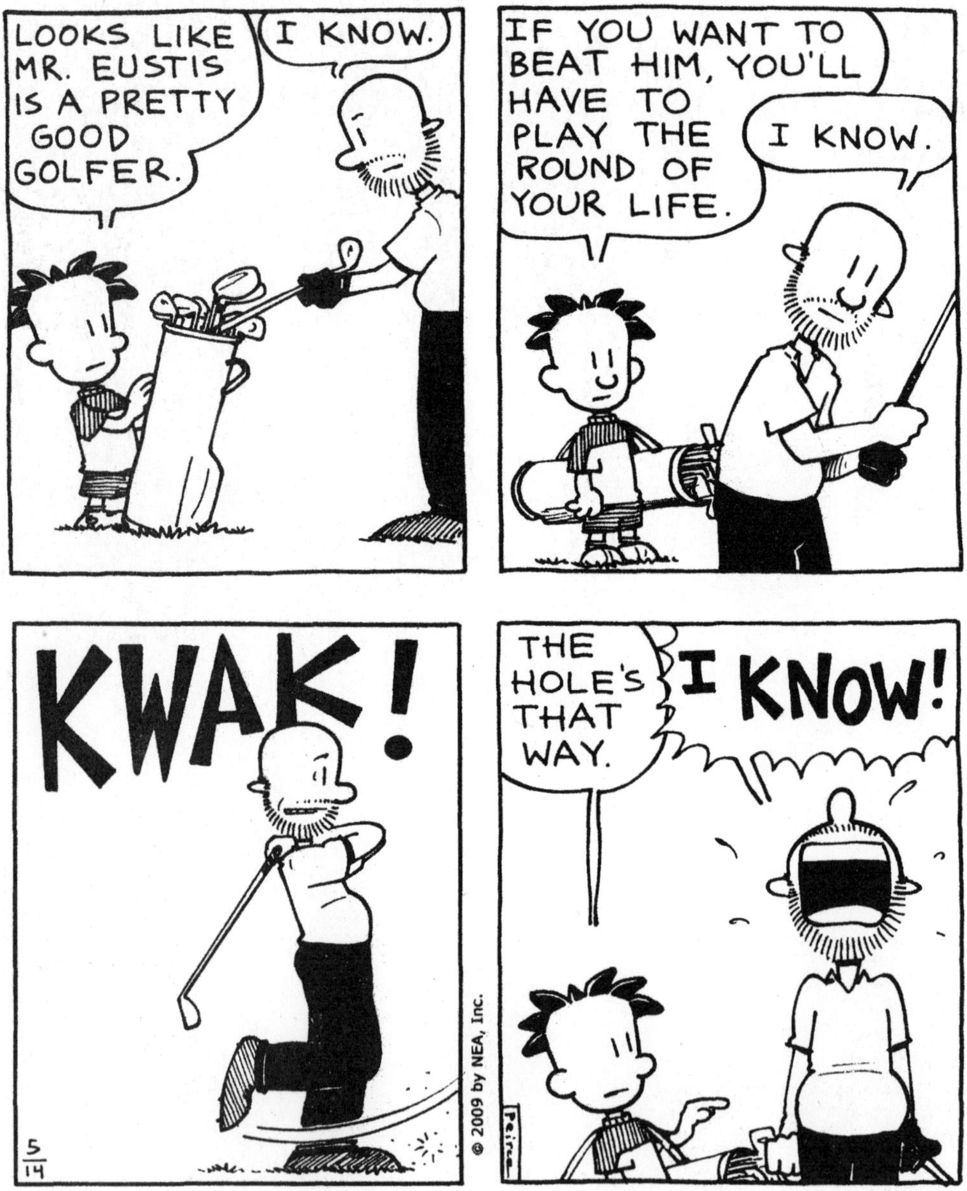
LOOKS LIKE MR. EUSTIS IS A PRETTY GOOD GOLFER.
I KNOW.
IF YOU WANT TO BEAT HIM, YOU'LL HAVE TO PLAY THE ROUND OF YOUR LIFE.
I KNOW.
KWAK!
5/14
© 2009 by NEA, Inc.
THE HOLE'S THAT WAY.
I KNOW!
Peirce

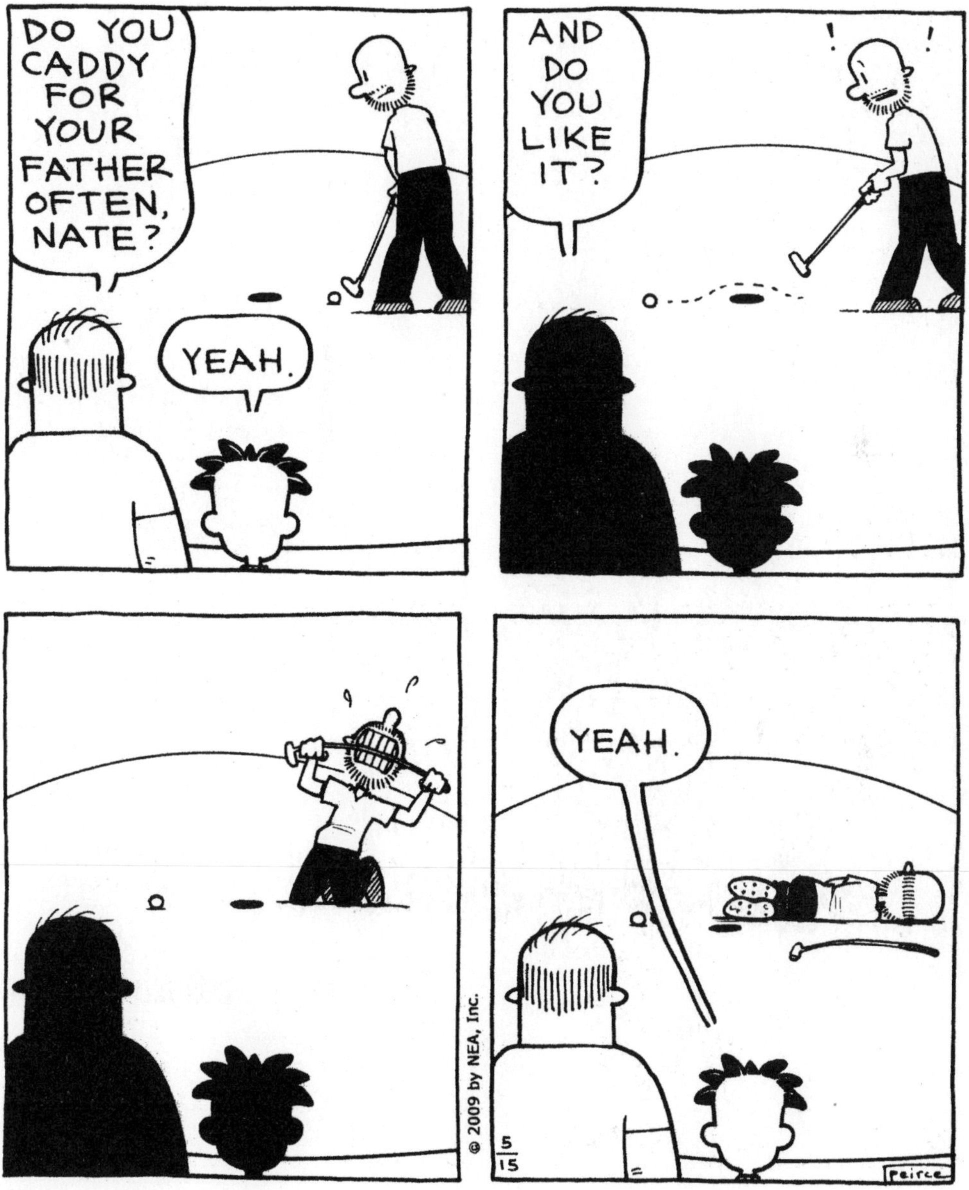
DO YOU CADDY FOR YOUR FATHER OFTEN, NATE?
YEAH.
AND DO YOU LIKE IT?
!
!
YEAH.
© 2009 by NEA, Inc.
5/15
peirce

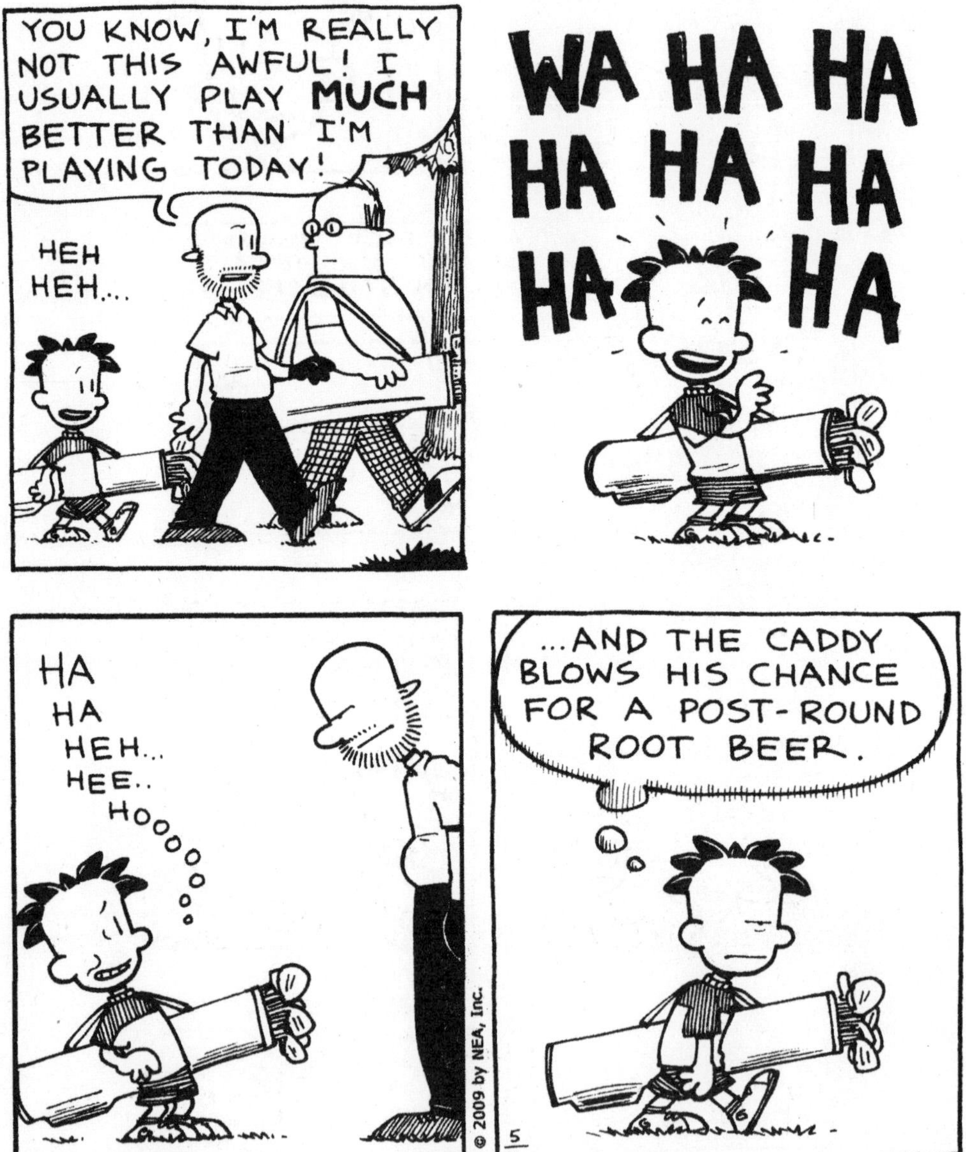
YOU KNOW, I'M REALLY NOT THIS AWFUL! I USUALLY PLAY **MUCH** BETTER THAN I'M PLAYING TODAY!
HEH HEH....
WA HA HA HA HA HA HA HA HA
HA HA HEH... HEE.. HOOOOOOO
© 2009 by NEA, Inc.
...AND THE CADDY BLOWS HIS CHANCE FOR A POST-ROUND ROOT BEER.
5/16
Peirce

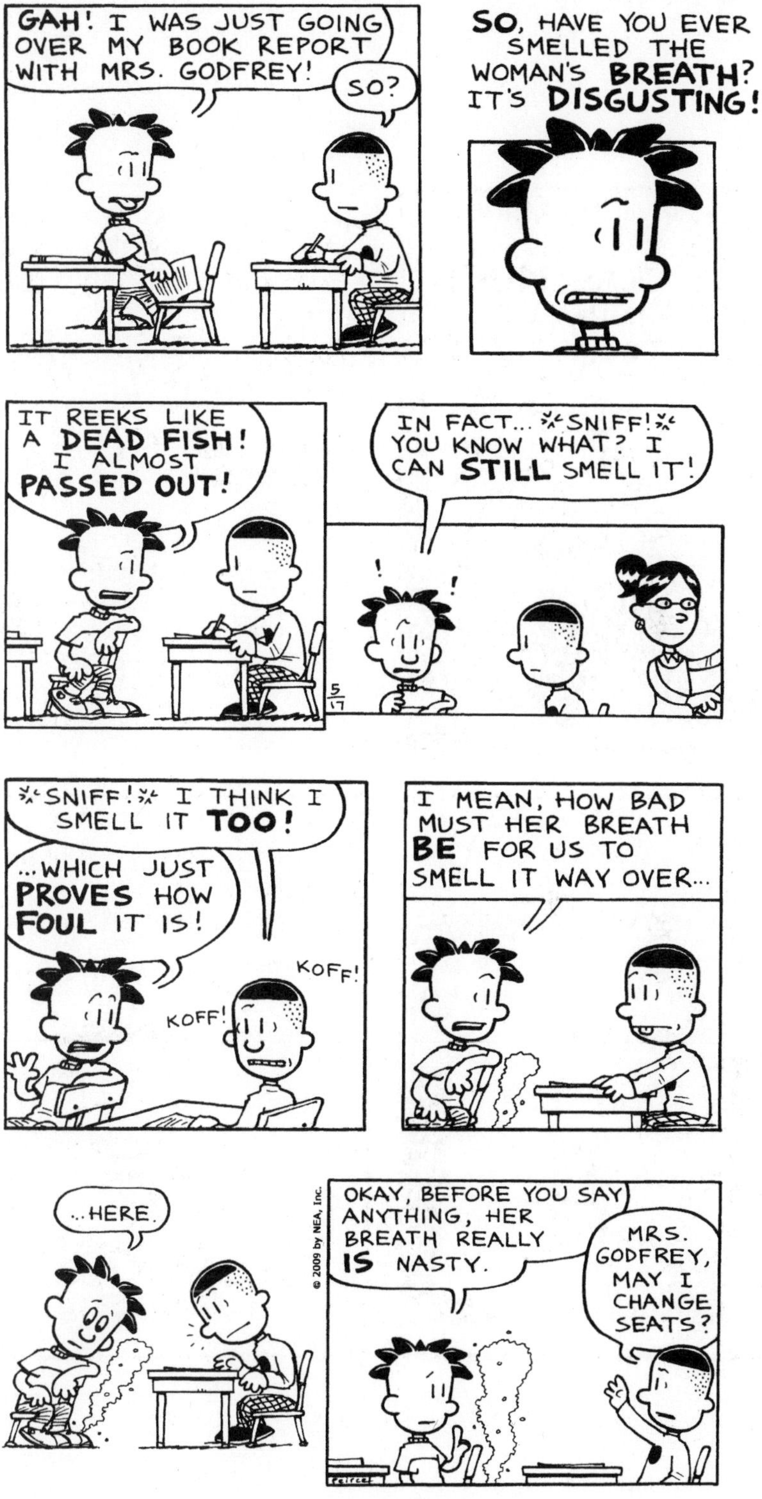
GAH! I WAS JUST GOING OVER MY BOOK REPORT WITH MRS. GODFREY!
SO?
SO, HAVE YOU EVER SMELLED THE WOMAN'S BREATH? IT'S DISGUSTING!
IT REEKS LIKE A DEAD FISH! I ALMOST PASSED OUT!
IN FACT... *SNIFF!* YOU KNOW WHAT? I CAN STILL SMELL IT!
5/17
!
!
SNIFF! I THINK I SMELL IT TOO!
...WHICH JUST PROVES HOW FOUL IT IS!
KOFF!
KOFF!
I MEAN, HOW BAD MUST HER BREATH BE FOR US TO SMELL IT WAY OVER...
...HERE.
© 2009 by NEA, Inc.
OKAY, BEFORE YOU SAY ANYTHING, HER BREATH REALLY IS NASTY.
MRS. GODFREY, MAY I CHANGE SEATS?
Peirce

25...AND COUNTING

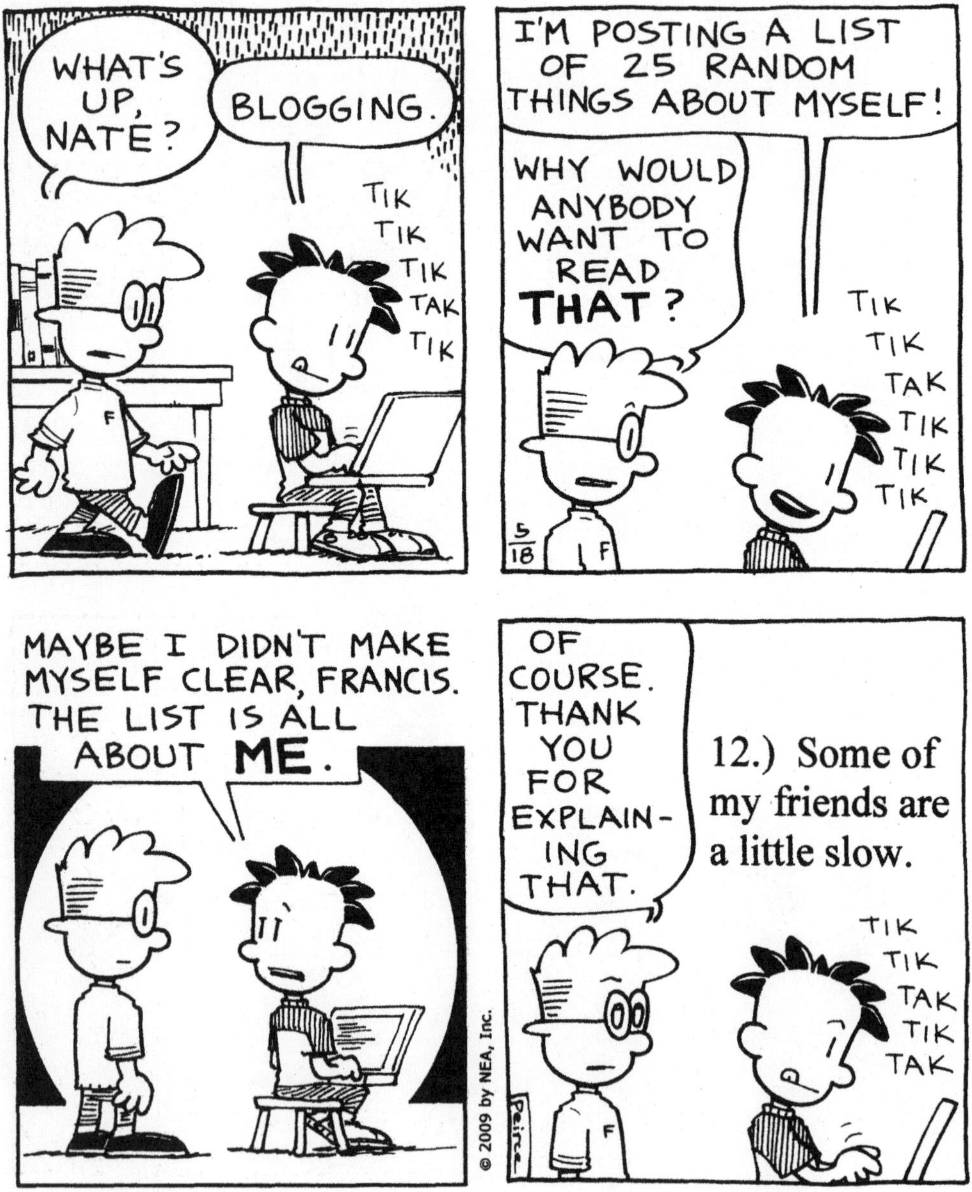
WHAT'S UP, NATE?
BLOGGING.
TIK TIK TIK TAK TIK
I'M POSTING A LIST OF 25 RANDOM THINGS ABOUT MYSELF!
WHY WOULD ANYBODY WANT TO READ **THAT**?
TIK TIK TAK TIK TIK TIK
5/18
MAYBE I DIDN'T MAKE MYSELF CLEAR, FRANCIS. THE LIST IS ALL ABOUT **ME**.
© 2009 by NEA, Inc.
Peirce
OF COURSE. THANK YOU FOR EXPLAINING THAT.
12.) Some of my friends are a little slow.
TIK TIK TAK TIK TAK

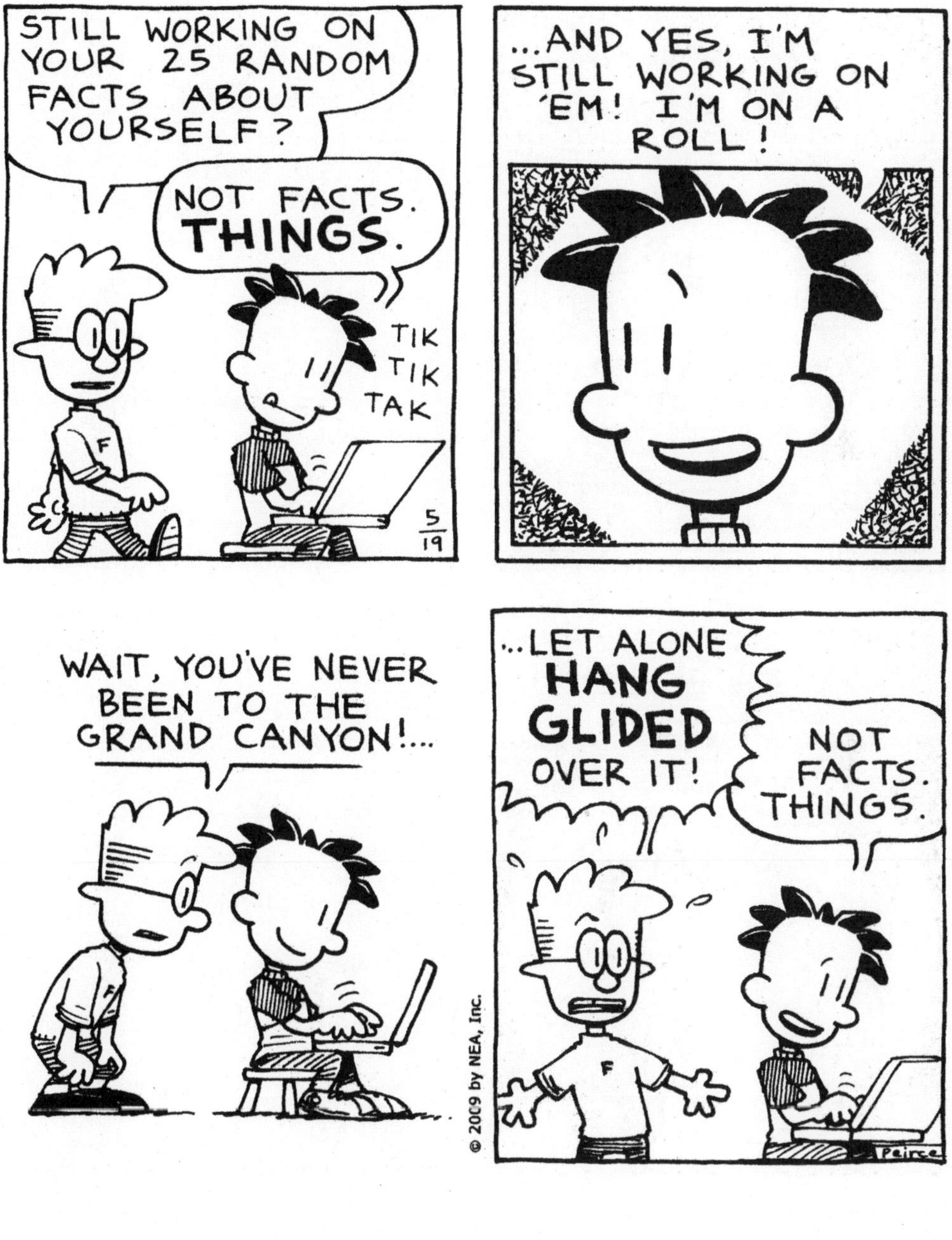
STILL WORKING ON YOUR 25 RANDOM FACTS ABOUT YOURSELF?
NOT FACTS. **THINGS**.
TIK TIK TAK
5/19
...AND YES, I'M STILL WORKING ON 'EM! I'M ON A ROLL!
WAIT, YOU'VE NEVER BEEN TO THE GRAND CANYON!...
...LET ALONE **HANG GLIDED** OVER IT!
NOT FACTS. THINGS.
Peirce
© 2009 by NEA, Inc.

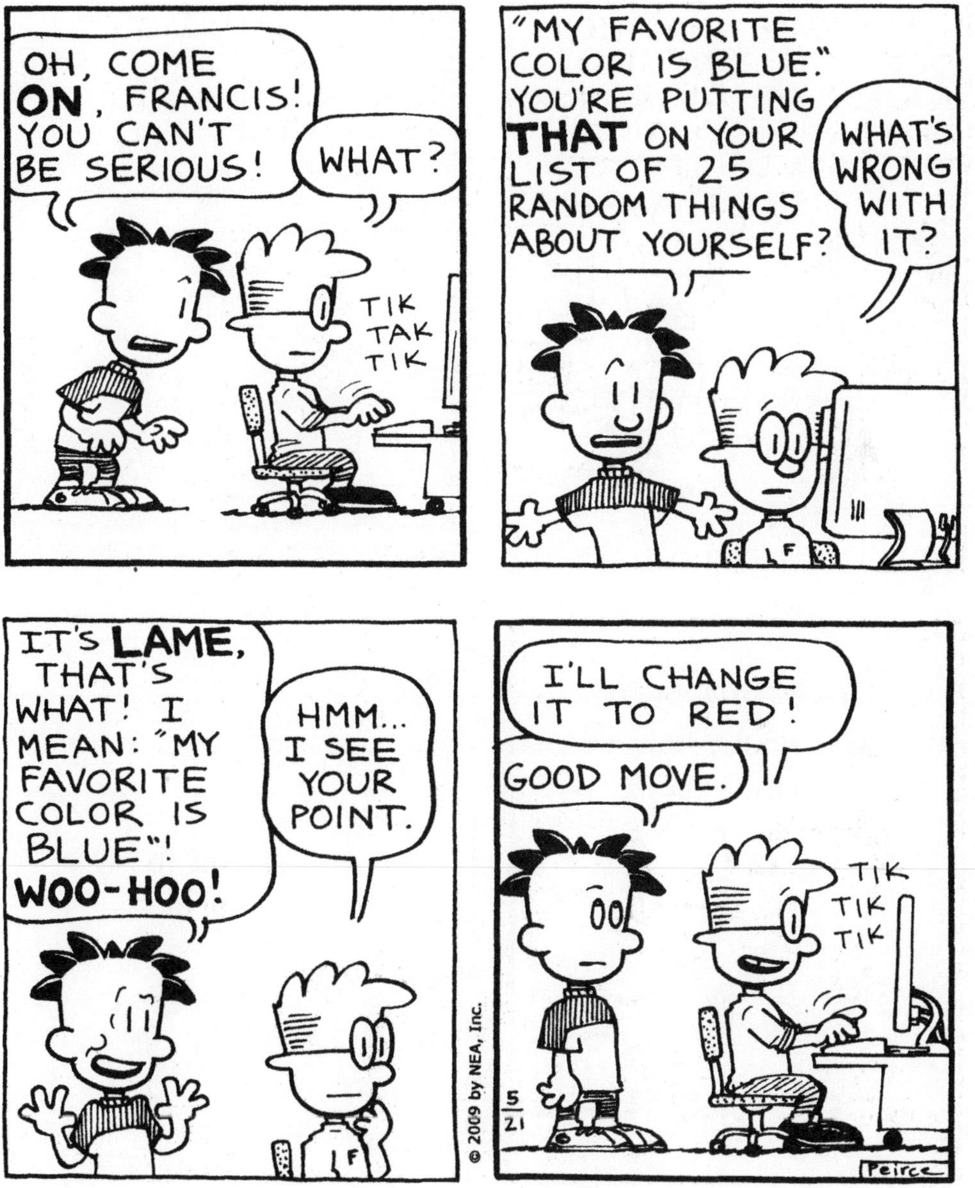
OH, COME **ON**, FRANCIS! YOU CAN'T BE SERIOUS!
WHAT?
TIK TAK TIK
"MY FAVORITE COLOR IS BLUE." YOU'RE PUTTING **THAT** ON YOUR LIST OF 25 RANDOM THINGS ABOUT YOURSELF?
WHAT'S WRONG WITH IT?
IT'S **LAME**, THAT'S WHAT! I MEAN: "MY FAVORITE COLOR IS BLUE"! **WOO-HOO**!
HMM... I SEE YOUR POINT.
I'LL CHANGE IT TO RED!
GOOD MOVE.
TIK TIK TIK
© 2009 by NEA, Inc.
5/21
Peirce

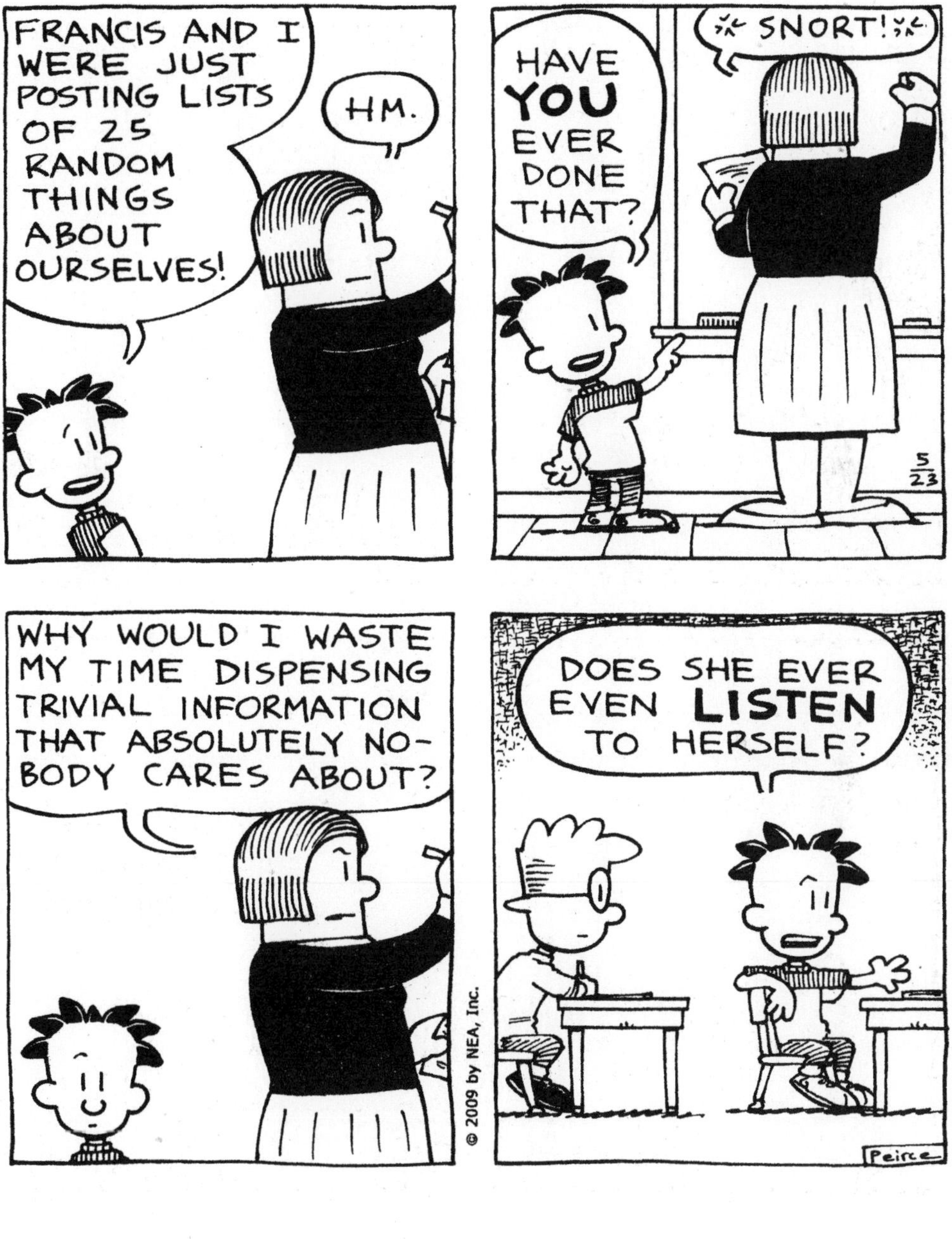
FRANCIS AND I WERE JUST POSTING LISTS OF 25 RANDOM THINGS ABOUT OURSELVES!
HM.
HAVE **YOU** EVER DONE THAT?
SNORT!
5/23
WHY WOULD I WASTE MY TIME DISPENSING TRIVIAL INFORMATION THAT ABSOLUTELY NO-BODY CARES ABOUT?
© 2009 by NEA, Inc.
DOES SHE EVER EVEN **LISTEN** TO HERSELF?
Peirce

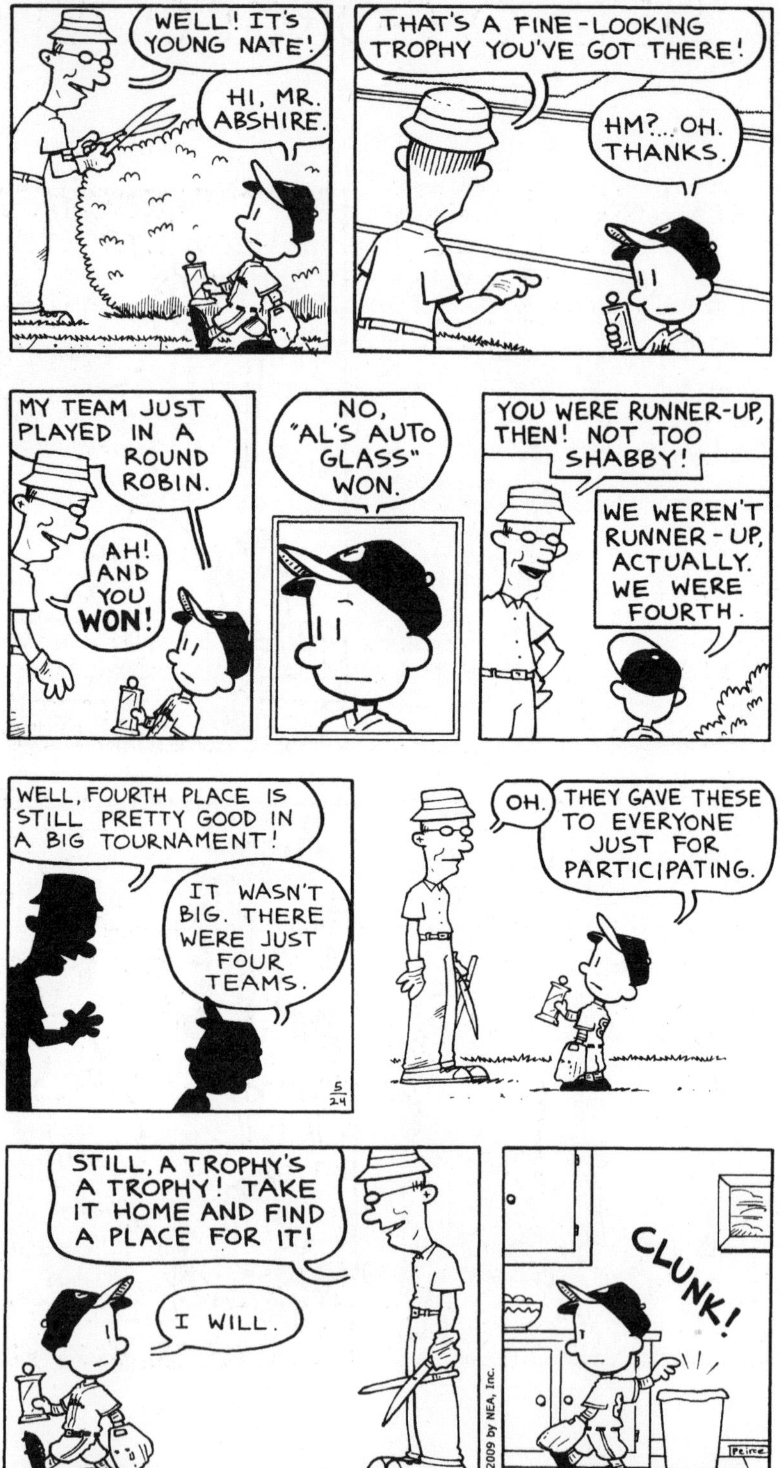
WELL! IT'S YOUNG NATE!
HI, MR. ABSHIRE.
THAT'S A FINE-LOOKING TROPHY YOU'VE GOT THERE!
HM?... OH. THANKS.
MY TEAM JUST PLAYED IN A ROUND ROBIN.
AH! AND YOU **WON**!
NO, "AL'S AUTO GLASS" WON.
YOU WERE RUNNER-UP, THEN! NOT TOO SHABBY!
WE WEREN'T RUNNER-UP, ACTUALLY. WE WERE FOURTH.
WELL, FOURTH PLACE IS STILL PRETTY GOOD IN A BIG TOURNAMENT!
IT WASN'T BIG. THERE WERE JUST FOUR TEAMS.
5/24
OH.
THEY GAVE THESE TO EVERYONE JUST FOR PARTICIPATING.
STILL, A TROPHY'S A TROPHY! TAKE IT HOME AND FIND A PLACE FOR IT!
I WILL.
CLUNK!
Peirce

HELLO, GORGEOUS!

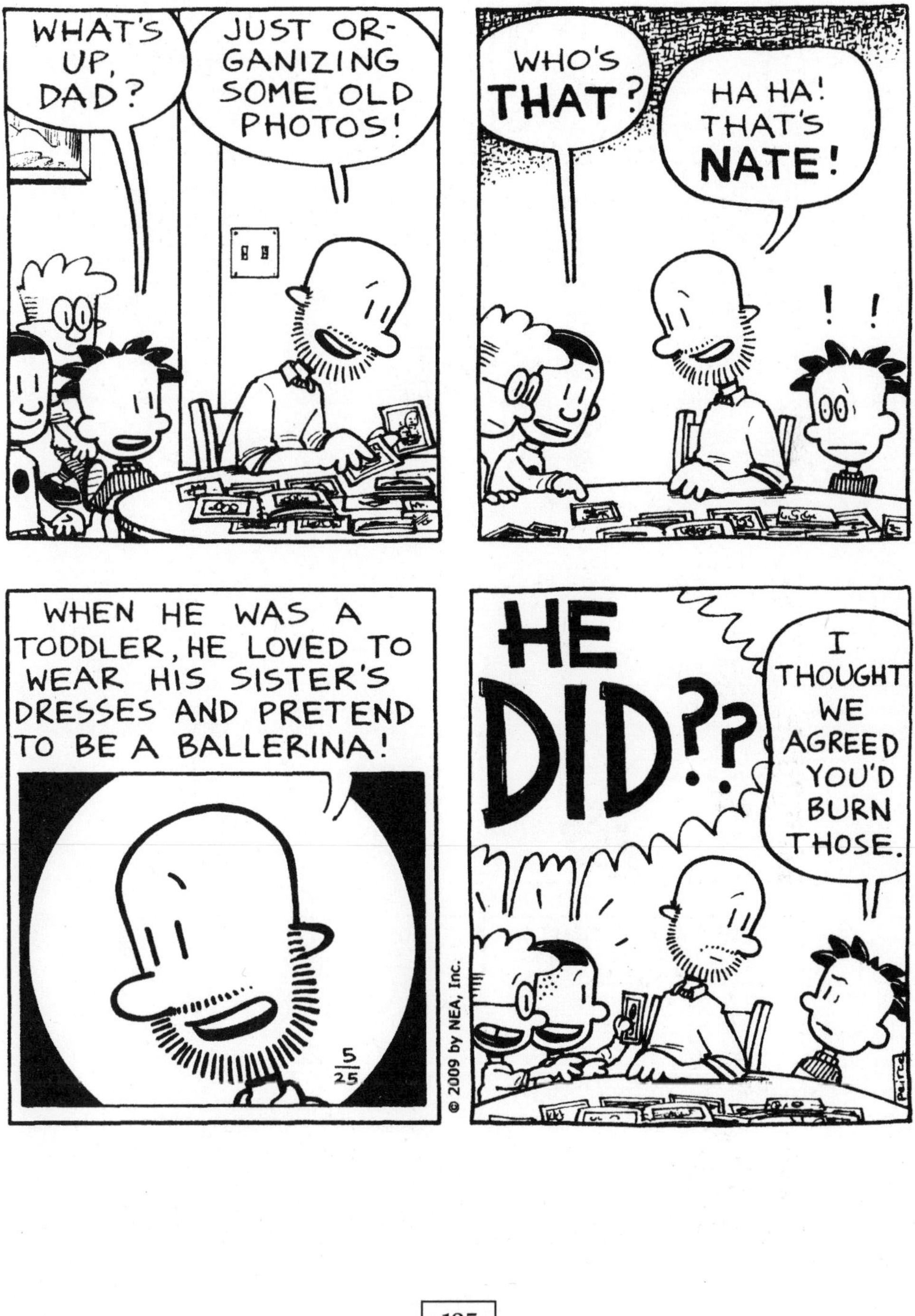
WHAT'S UP, DAD?
JUST ORGANIZING SOME OLD PHOTOS!
WHO'S **THAT**?
HA HA! THAT'S **NATE**!
! !
WHEN HE WAS A TODDLER, HE LOVED TO WEAR HIS SISTER'S DRESSES AND PRETEND TO BE A BALLERINA!
5/25
© 2009 by NEA, Inc.
HE DID??
I THOUGHT WE AGREED YOU'D BURN THOSE.
PEIRCE

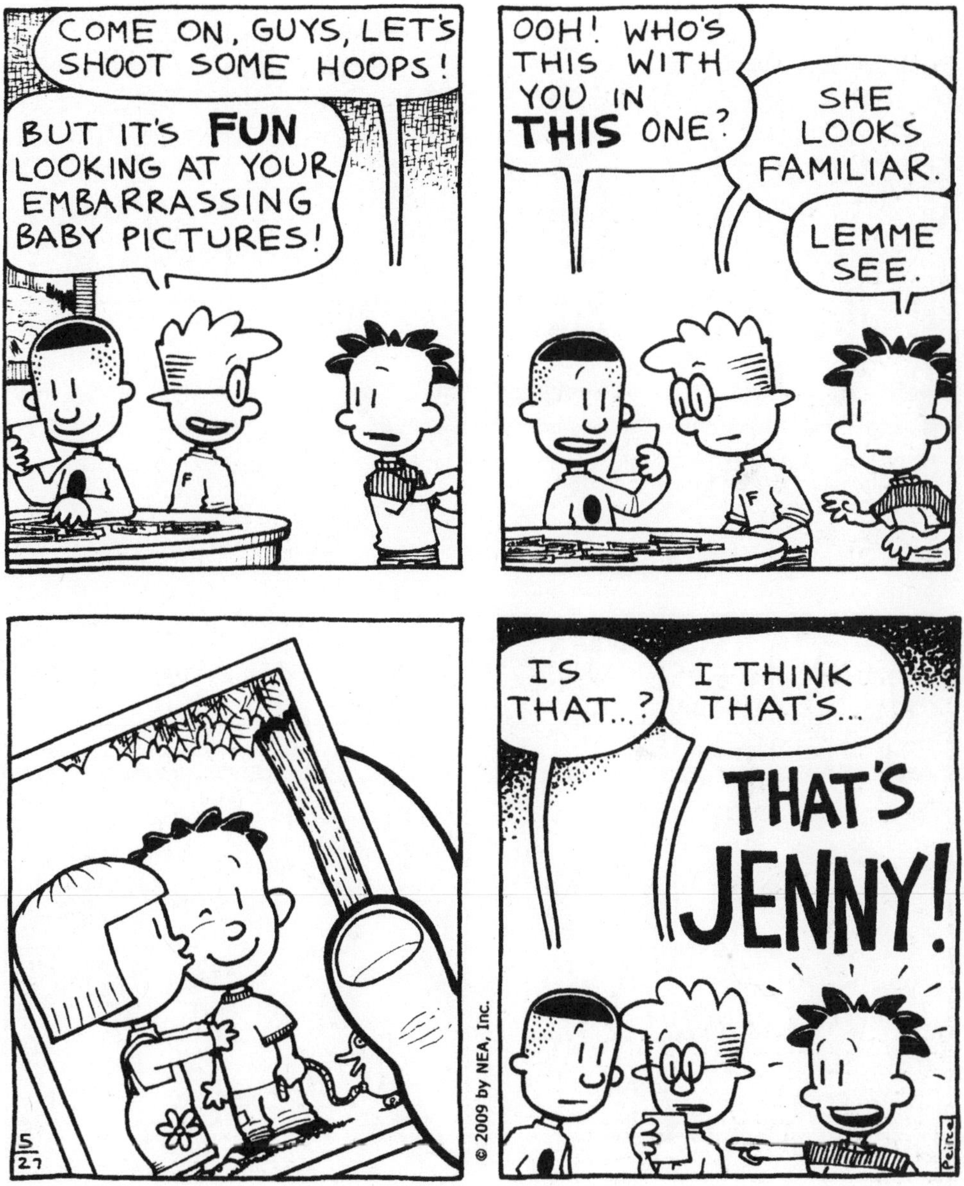
COME ON, GUYS, LET'S SHOOT SOME HOOPS!
BUT IT'S **FUN** LOOKING AT YOUR EMBARRASSING BABY PICTURES!
OOH! WHO'S THIS WITH YOU IN **THIS** ONE?
SHE LOOKS FAMILIAR.
LEMME SEE.
5/27
IS THAT..?
I THINK THAT'S...
THAT'S JENNY!
© 2009 by NEA, Inc.
Peirce

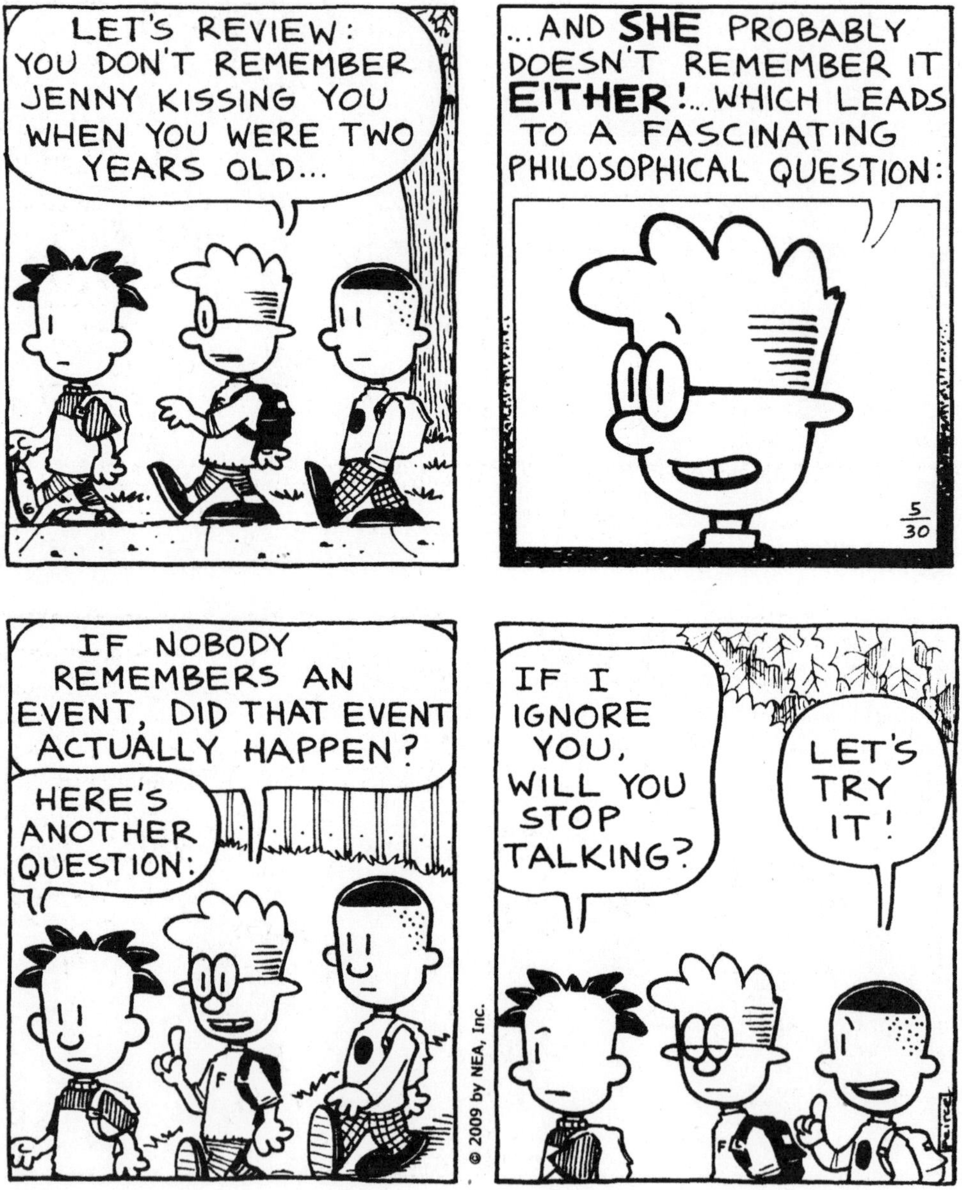
LET'S REVIEW: YOU DON'T REMEMBER JENNY KISSING YOU WHEN YOU WERE TWO YEARS OLD...
...AND SHE PROBABLY DOESN'T REMEMBER IT EITHER!... WHICH LEADS TO A FASCINATING PHILOSOPHICAL QUESTION:
5/30
IF NOBODY REMEMBERS AN EVENT, DID THAT EVENT ACTUALLY HAPPEN?
HERE'S ANOTHER QUESTION:
IF I IGNORE YOU, WILL YOU STOP TALKING?
LET'S TRY IT!
© 2009 by NEA, Inc.

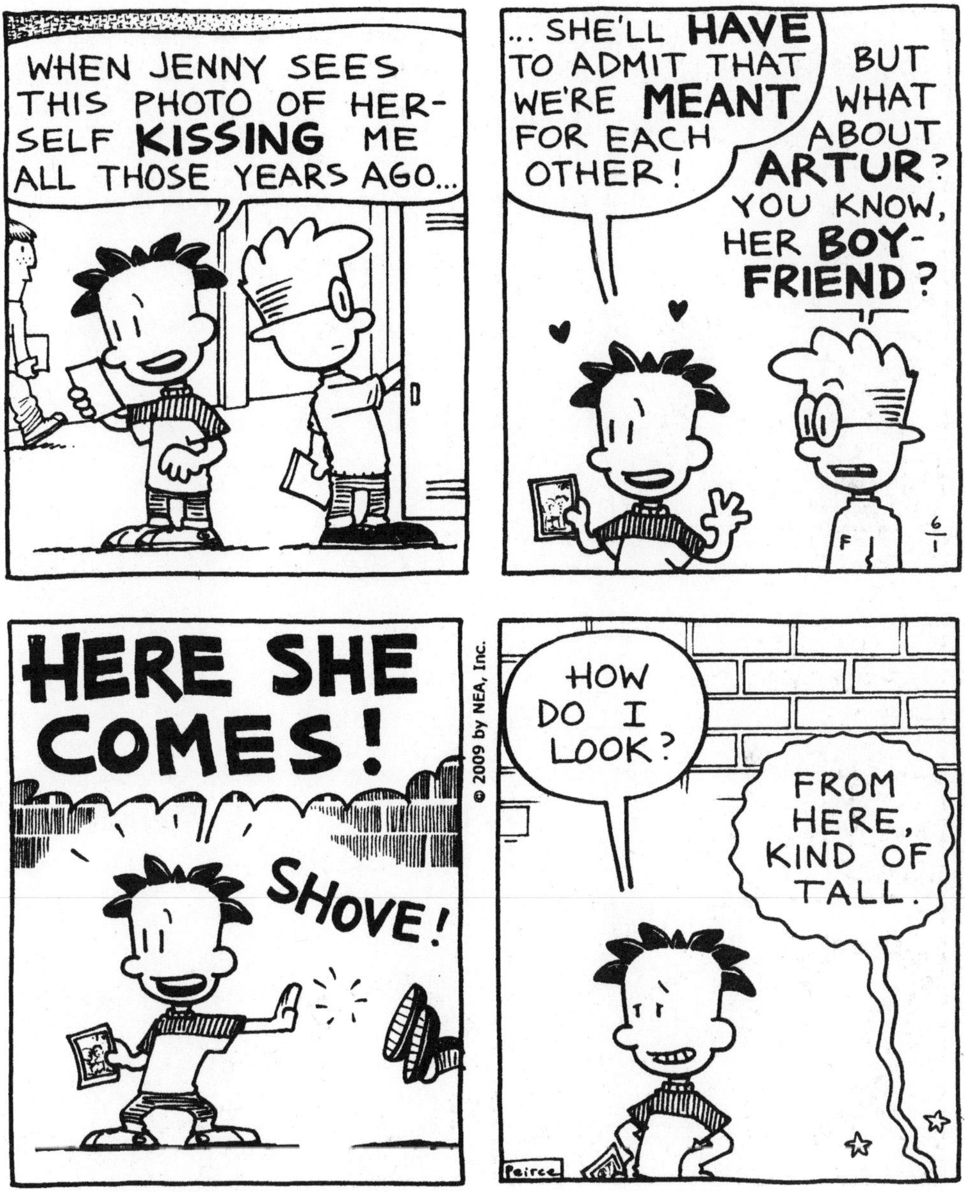
WHEN JENNY SEES THIS PHOTO OF HER-SELF KISSING ME ALL THOSE YEARS AGO...
... SHE'LL HAVE TO ADMIT THAT WE'RE MEANT FOR EACH OTHER!
BUT WHAT ABOUT ARTUR? YOU KNOW, HER BOY-FRIEND?
HERE SHE COMES!
SHOVE!
HOW DO I LOOK?
FROM HERE, KIND OF TALL.
© 2009 by NEA, Inc.
Peirce

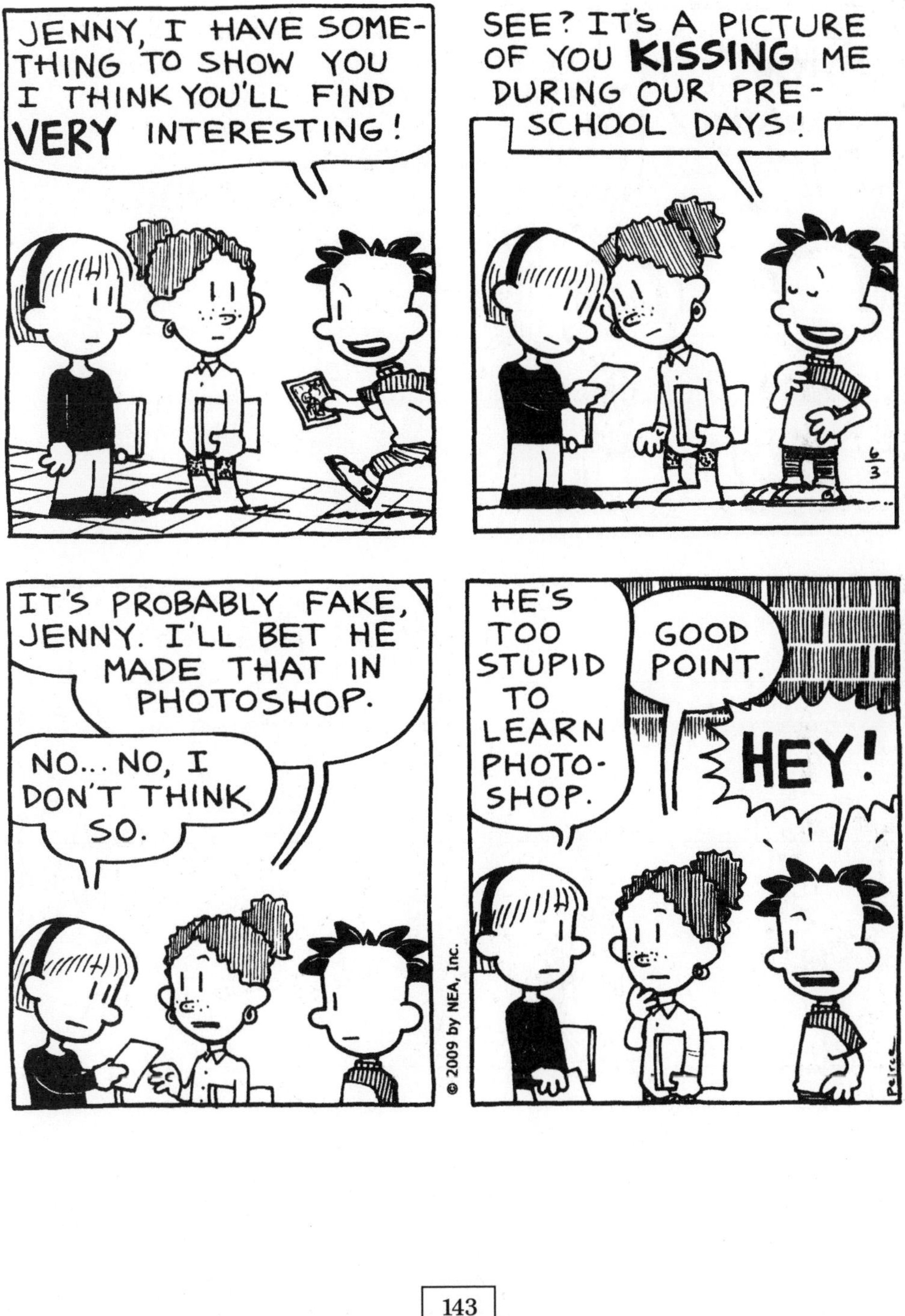
JENNY, I HAVE SOMETHING TO SHOW YOU I THINK YOU'LL FIND **VERY** INTERESTING!
SEE? IT'S A PICTURE OF YOU **KISSING** ME DURING OUR PRE-SCHOOL DAYS!
6/3
IT'S PROBABLY FAKE, JENNY. I'LL BET HE MADE THAT IN PHOTOSHOP.
NO... NO, I DON'T THINK SO.
© 2009 by NEA, Inc.
HE'S TOO STUPID TO LEARN PHOTOSHOP.
GOOD POINT.
HEY!
Peirce

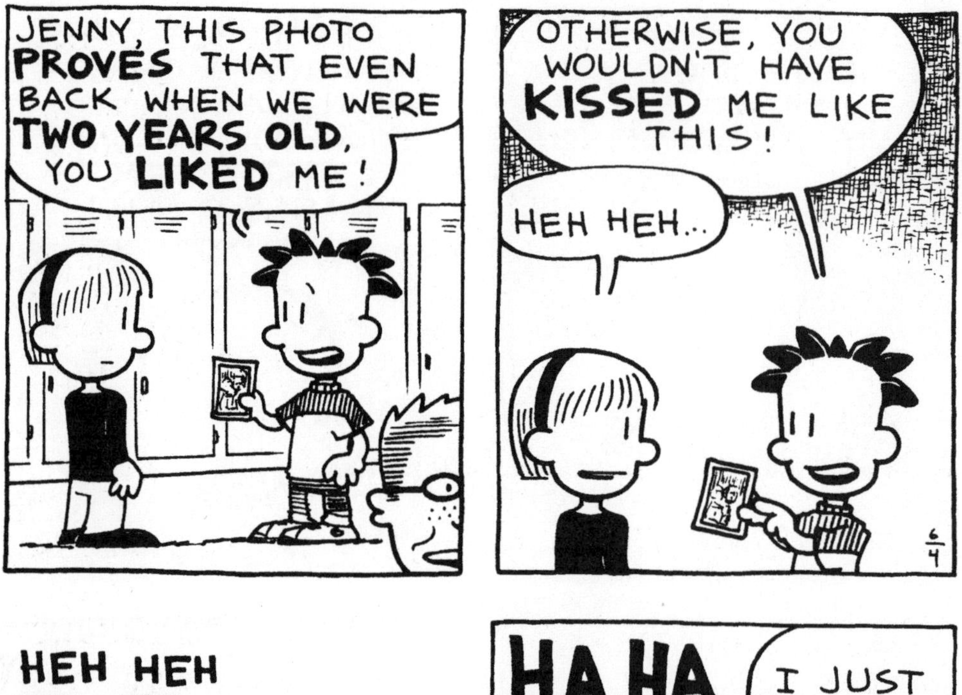
JENNY, THIS PHOTO **PROVES** THAT EVEN BACK WHEN WE WERE **TWO YEARS OLD**, YOU **LIKED** ME!
OTHERWISE, YOU WOULDN'T HAVE **KISSED** ME LIKE THIS!
HEH HEH...
HEH HEH
HA HA HA
HA HA HA
HA
HA HA
HA HA HA
HA HA
HA
I JUST TOLD HER A REALLY FUNNY "KNOCK-KNOCK" JOKE.
PEIRCE

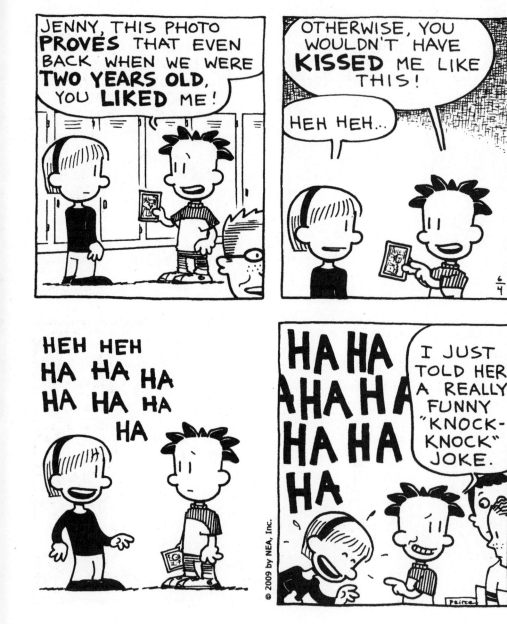

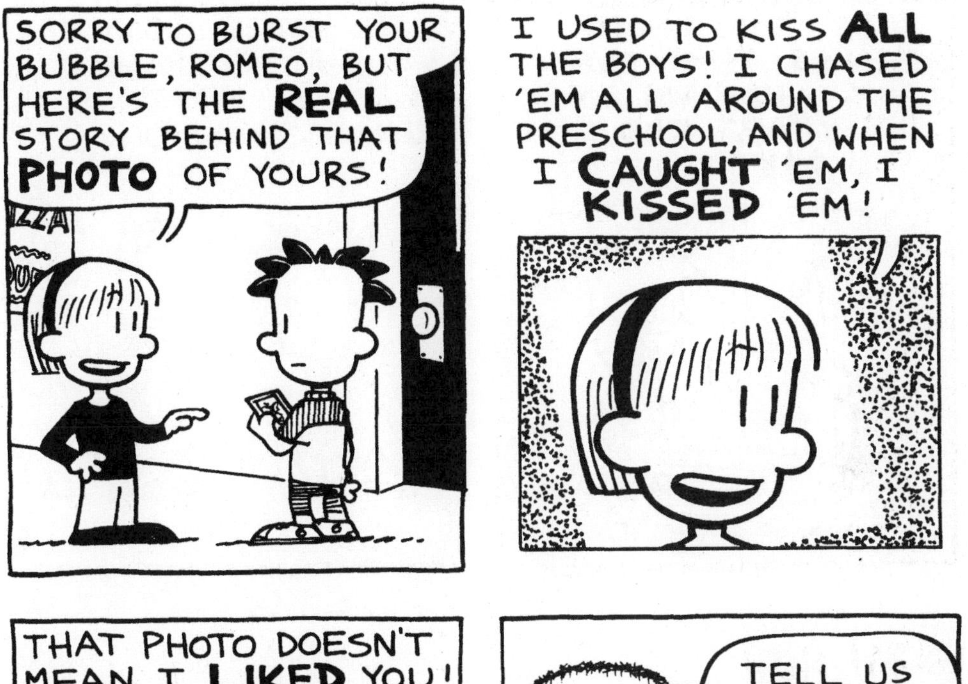
SORRY TO BURST YOUR BUBBLE, ROMEO, BUT HERE'S THE **REAL** STORY BEHIND THAT **PHOTO** OF YOURS!
I USED TO KISS **ALL** THE BOYS! I CHASED 'EM ALL AROUND THE PRESCHOOL, AND WHEN I **CAUGHT** 'EM, I **KISSED** 'EM!
THAT PHOTO DOESN'T MEAN I **LIKED** YOU! IT MEANS I COULD **RUN** FASTER THAN YOU COULD!
I'M SLOW.
TELL US SOMETHING WE **DIDN'T** KNOW!
© 2009 by NEA, Inc.
Peirce

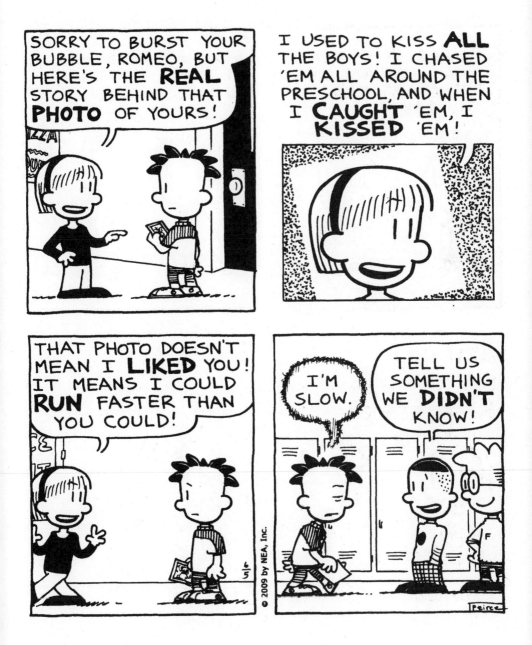

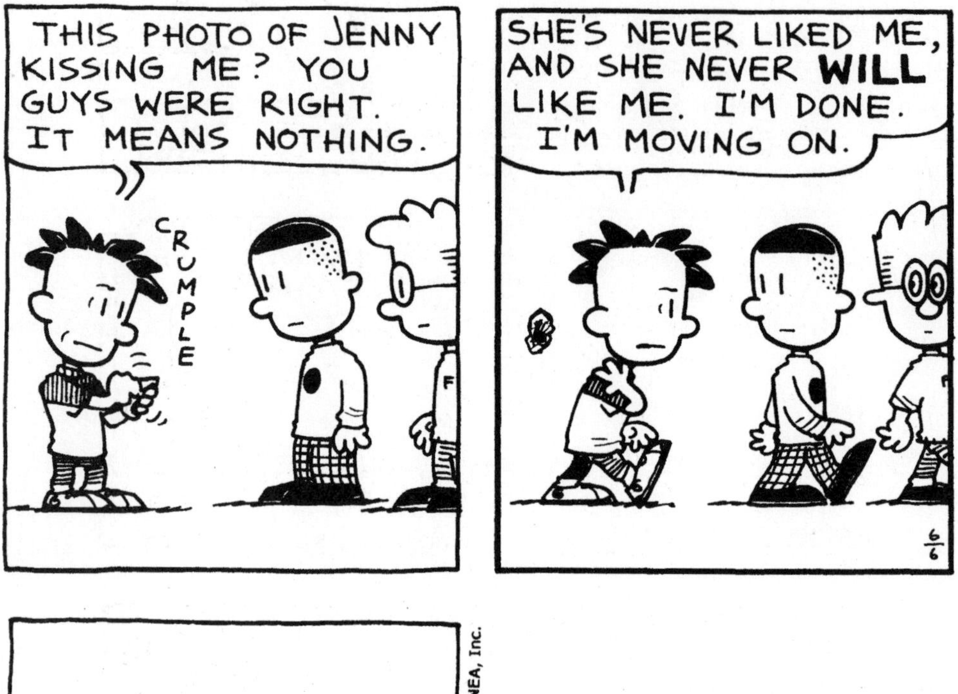
THIS PHOTO OF JENNY KISSING ME? YOU GUYS WERE RIGHT. IT MEANS NOTHING.
CRUMPLE
SHE'S NEVER LIKED ME, AND SHE NEVER **WILL** LIKE ME. I'M DONE. I'M MOVING ON.
6/6
Peirce

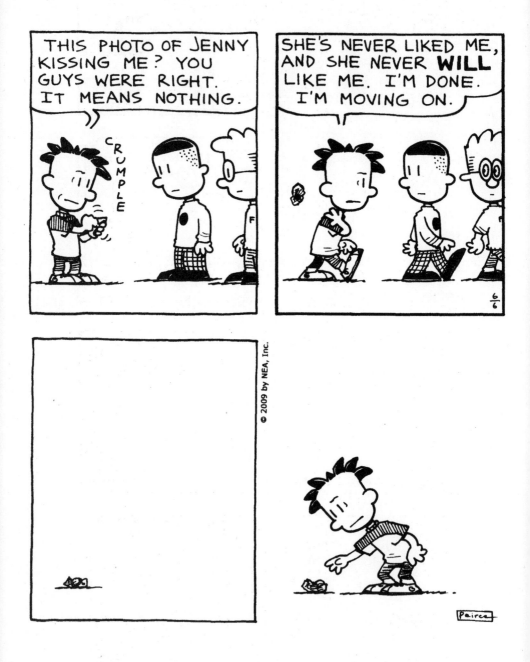

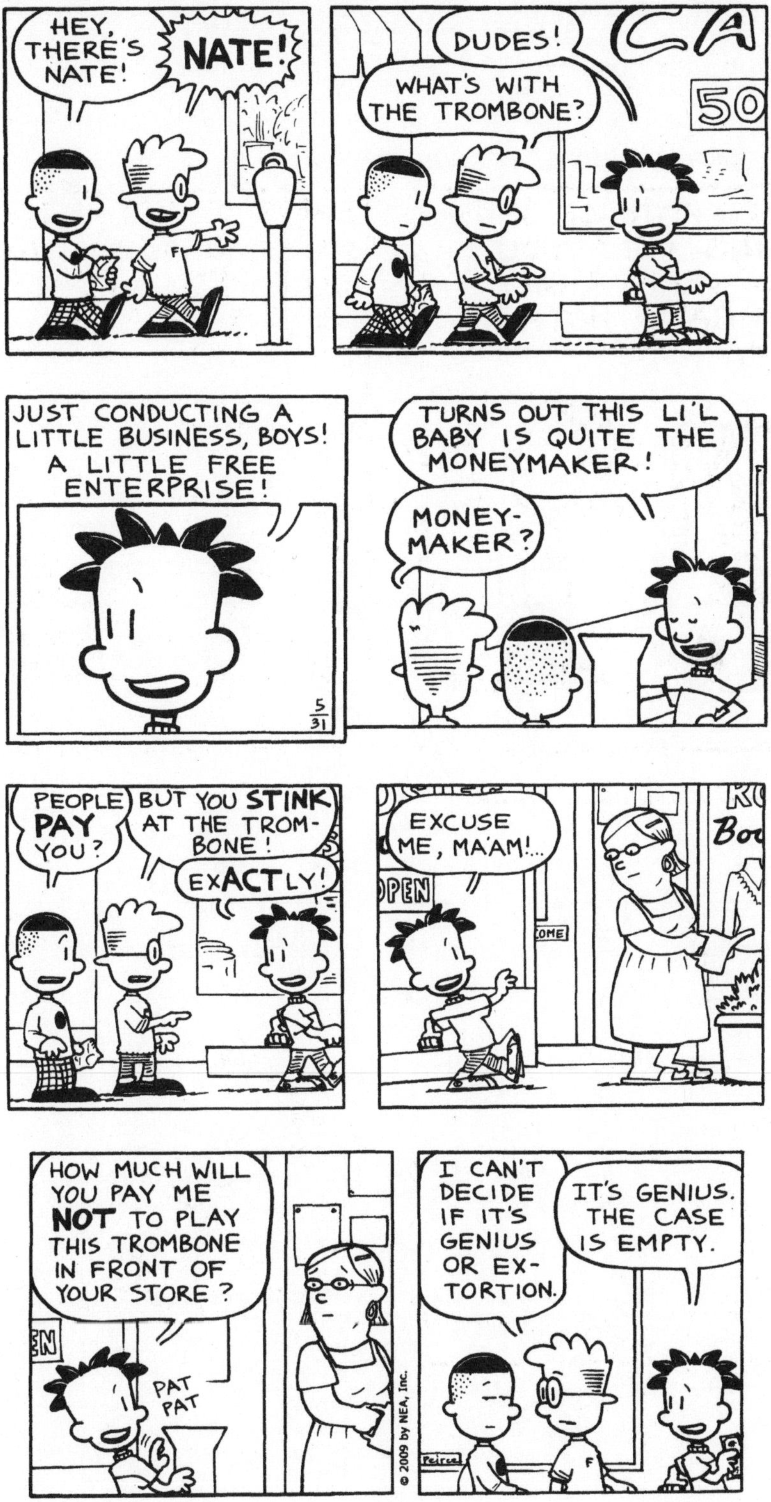
HEY, THERE'S NATE!
NATE!
DUDES!
WHAT'S WITH THE TROMBONE?
JUST CONDUCTING A LITTLE BUSINESS, BOYS! A LITTLE FREE ENTERPRISE!
5/31
TURNS OUT THIS LI'L BABY IS QUITE THE MONEYMAKER!
MONEY-MAKER?
PEOPLE PAY YOU?
BUT YOU STINK AT THE TROM-BONE!
EXACTLY!
EXCUSE ME, MA'AM!...
OPEN
HOW MUCH WILL YOU PAY ME NOT TO PLAY THIS TROMBONE IN FRONT OF YOUR STORE?
PAT PAT
© 2009 by NEA, Inc.
I CAN'T DECIDE IF IT'S GENIUS OR EX-TORTION.
IT'S GENIUS. THE CASE IS EMPTY.
Peirce

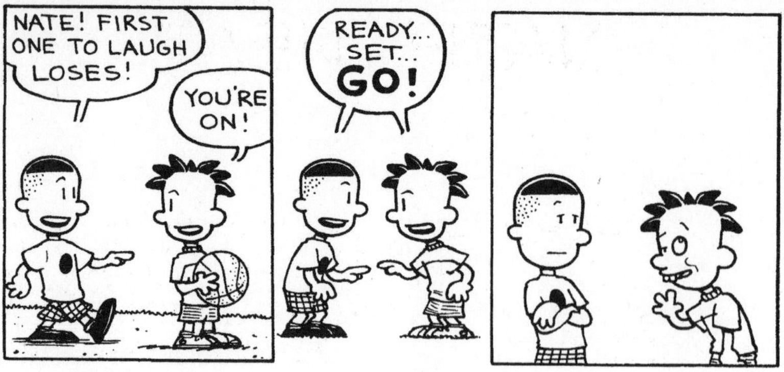
NATE! FIRST ONE TO LAUGH LOSES!
YOU'RE ON!
READY... SET... GO!

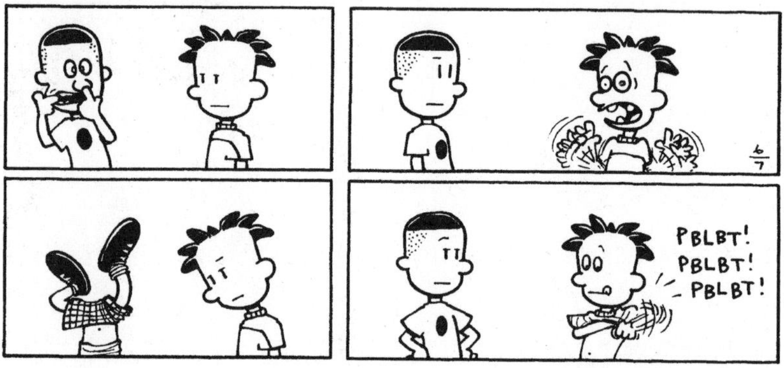
PBLBT! PBLBT! PBLBT!

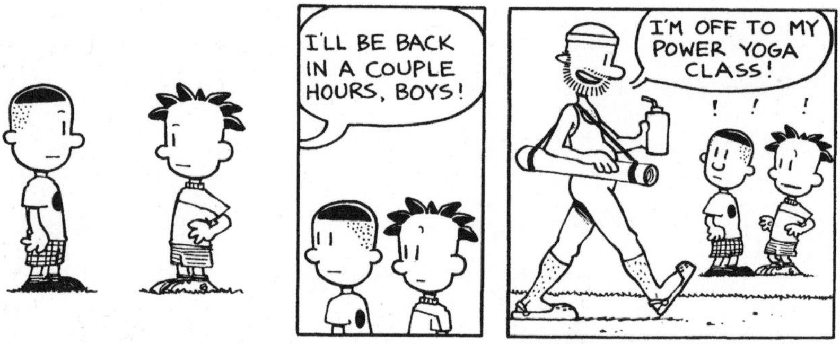
I'LL BE BACK IN A COUPLE HOURS, BOYS!
I'M OFF TO MY POWER YOGA CLASS!
! ! !

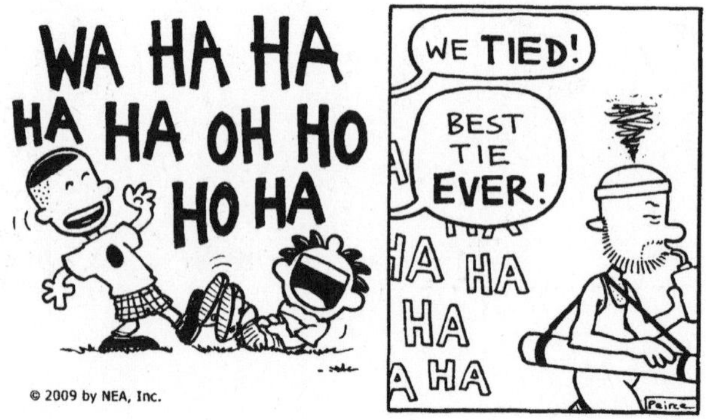
WA HA HA HA HA OH HO HO HA
WE TIED!
BEST TIE EVER!
HA HA
HA
HA HA

NATE ≠ NEAT

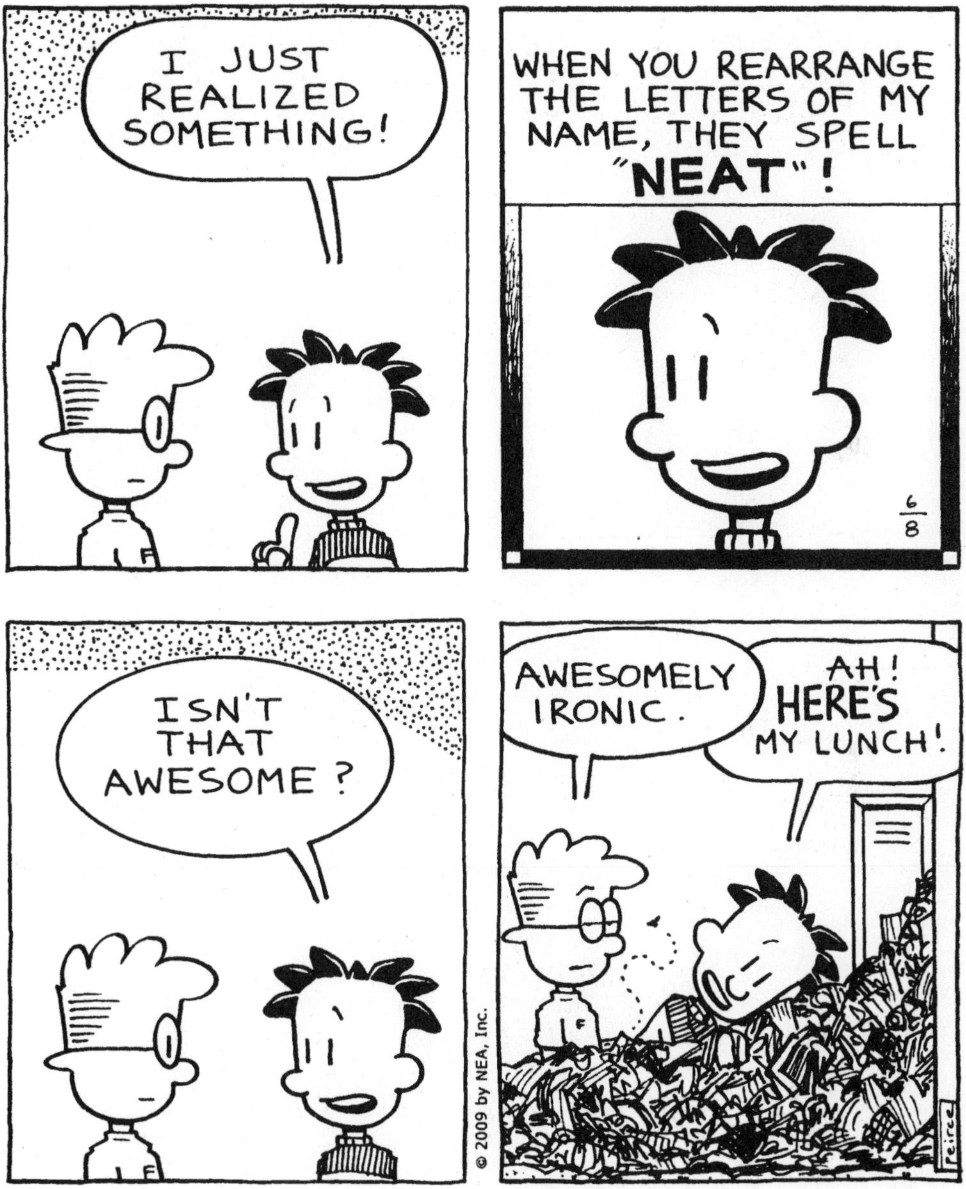
I JUST REALIZED SOMETHING!
WHEN YOU REARRANGE THE LETTERS OF MY NAME, THEY SPELL "NEAT"!
6/8
ISN'T THAT AWESOME?
© 2009 by NEA, Inc.
AWESOMELY IRONIC.
AH! HERE'S MY LUNCH!
peirce

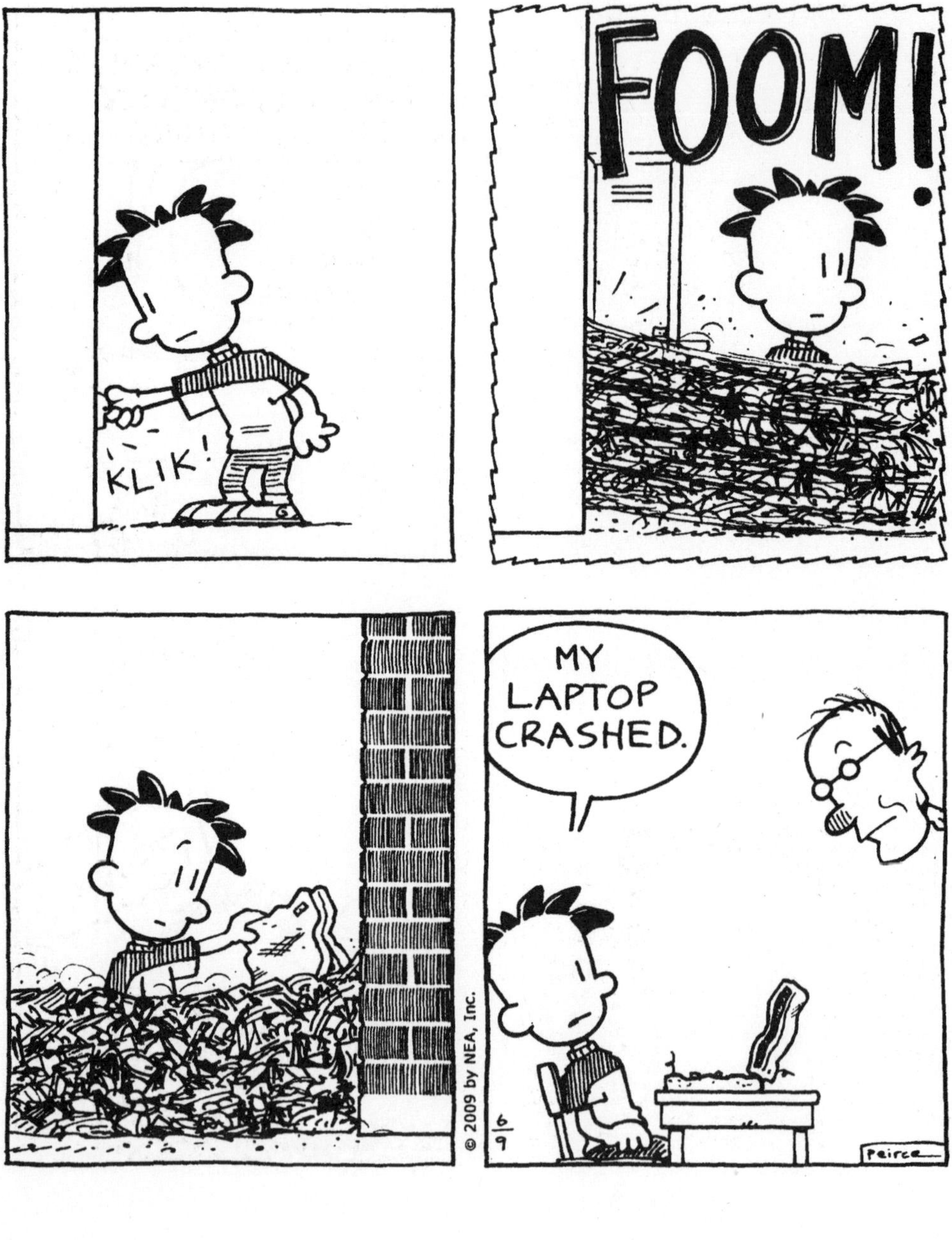
KLIK!
FOOM!
© 2009 by NEA, Inc.
6/9
MY LAPTOP CRASHED.
Peirce

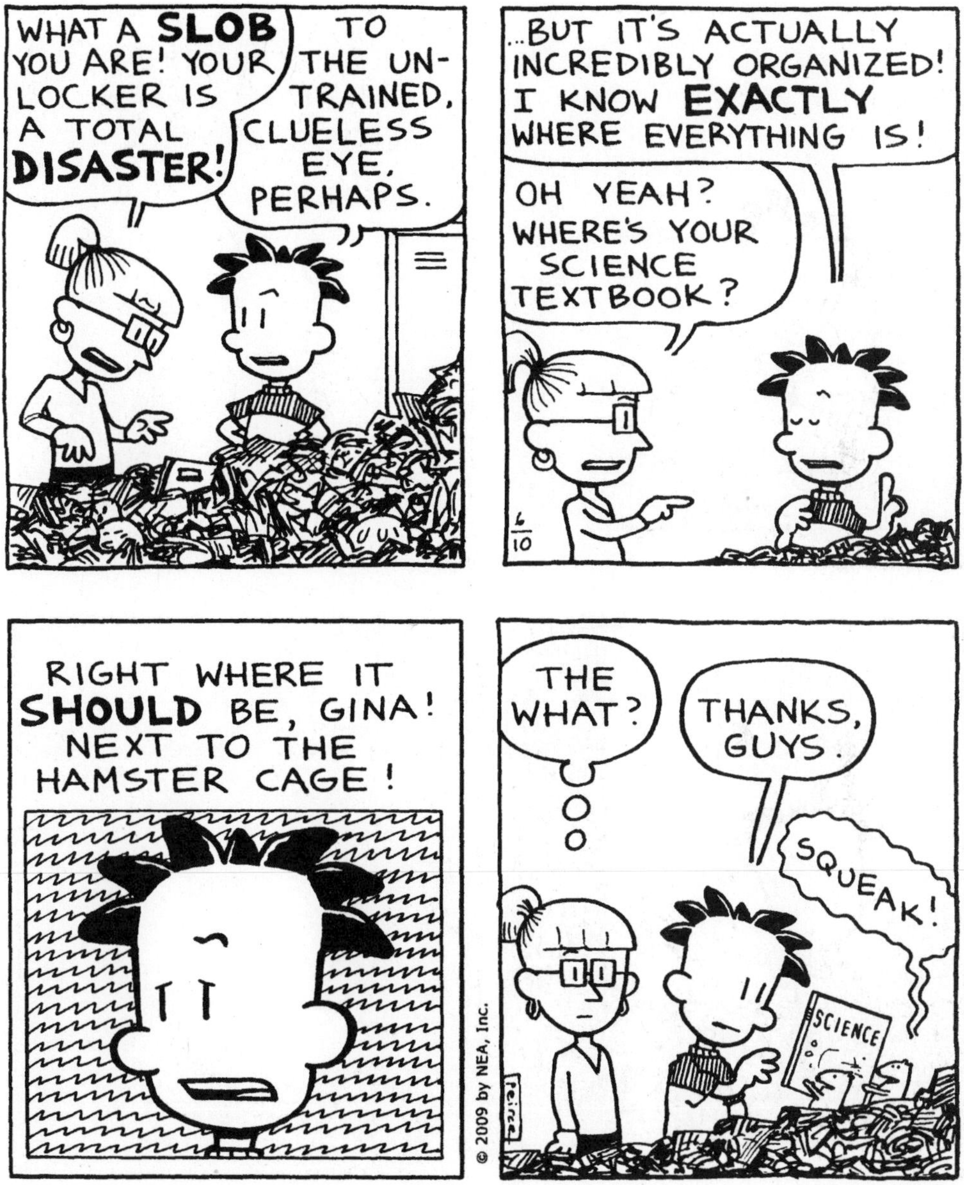
WHAT A SLOB YOU ARE! YOUR LOCKER IS A TOTAL DISASTER!
TO THE UN-TRAINED, CLUELESS EYE, PERHAPS.
...BUT IT'S ACTUALLY INCREDIBLY ORGANIZED! I KNOW EXACTLY WHERE EVERYTHING IS!
OH YEAH? WHERE'S YOUR SCIENCE TEXTBOOK?
6/10
RIGHT WHERE IT SHOULD BE, GINA! NEXT TO THE HAMSTER CAGE!
THE WHAT?
THANKS, GUYS.
SQUEAK!
SCIENCE
peirce

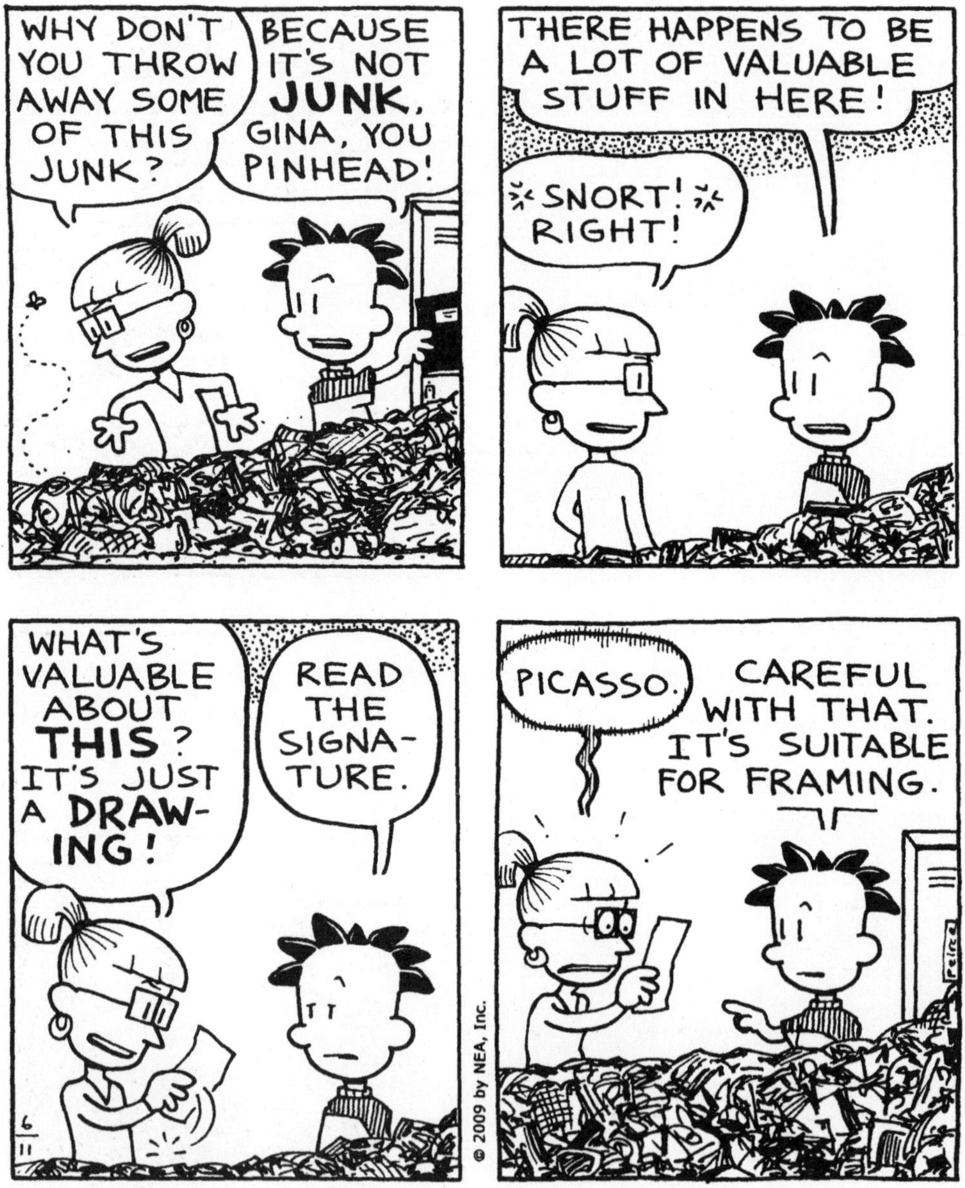
WHY DON'T YOU THROW AWAY SOME OF THIS JUNK?
BECAUSE IT'S NOT **JUNK**, GINA, YOU PINHEAD!
THERE HAPPENS TO BE A LOT OF VALUABLE STUFF IN HERE!
SNORT! RIGHT!
WHAT'S VALUABLE ABOUT **THIS**? IT'S JUST A **DRAWING**!
READ THE SIGNATURE.
PICASSO.
CAREFUL WITH THAT. IT'S SUITABLE FOR FRAMING.
6/11
© 2009 by NEA, Inc.

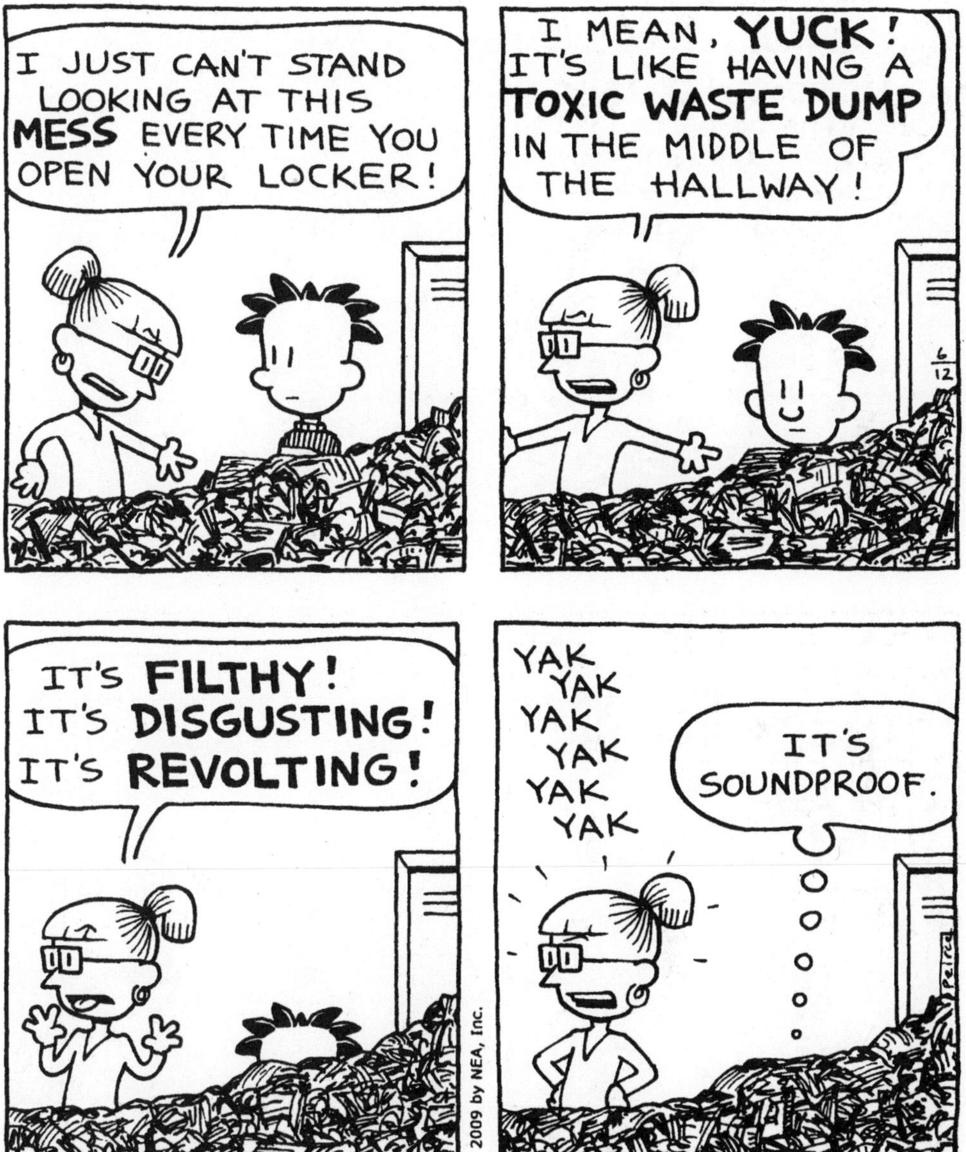
I JUST CAN'T STAND LOOKING AT THIS MESS EVERY TIME YOU OPEN YOUR LOCKER!
I MEAN, YUCK! IT'S LIKE HAVING A TOXIC WASTE DUMP IN THE MIDDLE OF THE HALLWAY!
IT'S FILTHY! IT'S DISGUSTING! IT'S REVOLTING!
YAK YAK YAK YAK YAK YAK
IT'S SOUNDPROOF.

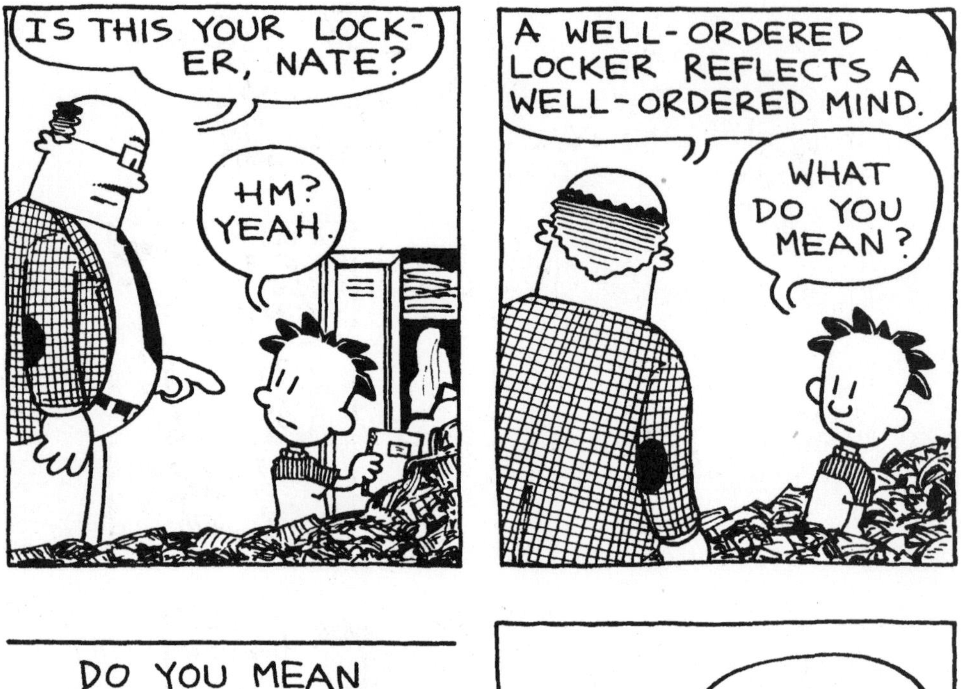
IS THIS YOUR LOCKER, NATE?
HM? YEAH.
A WELL-ORDERED LOCKER REFLECTS A WELL-ORDERED MIND.
WHAT DO YOU MEAN?
DO YOU MEAN THAT I... UH... ARE YOU.... DOES THAT...?
6/13
I FORGOT WHAT I WAS GOING TO SAY.

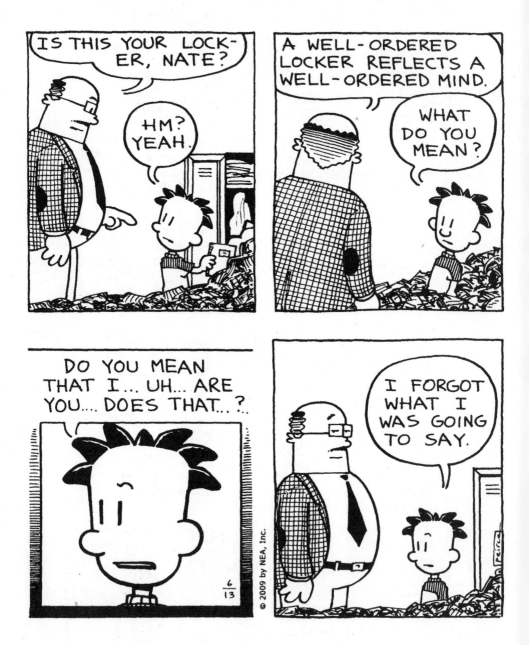

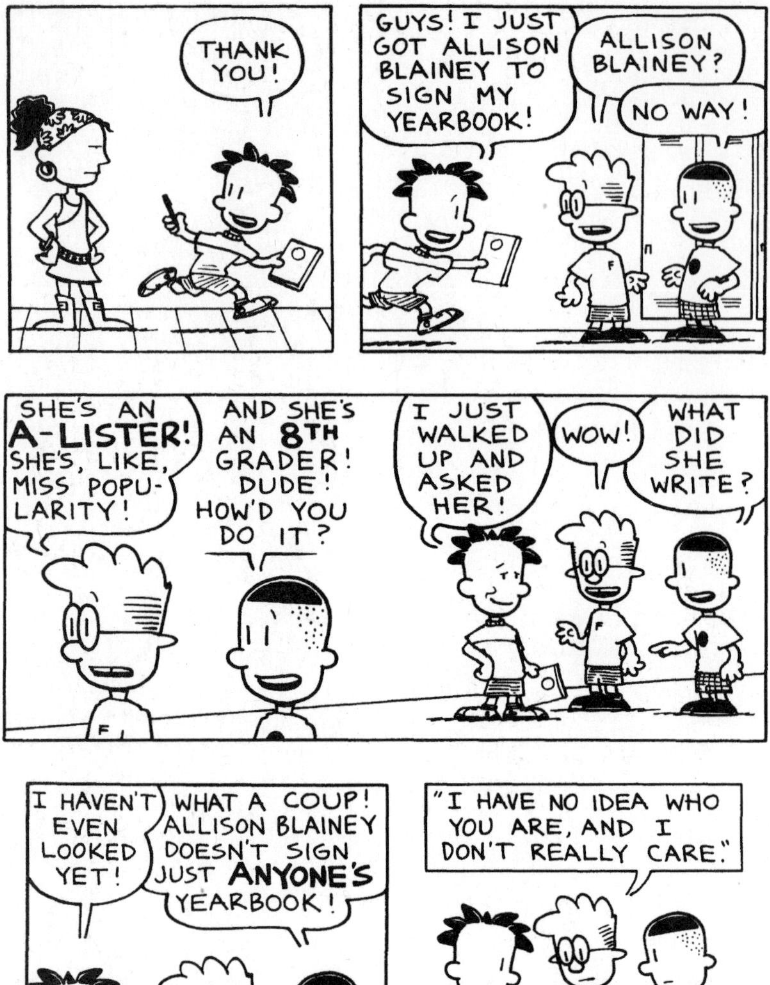
THANK YOU!
GUYS! I JUST GOT ALLISON BLAINEY TO SIGN MY YEARBOOK!
ALLISON BLAINEY?
NO WAY!
SHE'S AN **A-LISTER!** SHE'S, LIKE, MISS POPULARITY!
AND SHE'S AN **8TH** GRADER! DUDE! HOW'D YOU DO IT?
I JUST WALKED UP AND ASKED HER!
WOW!
WHAT DID SHE WRITE?
I HAVEN'T EVEN LOOKED YET!
WHAT A COUP! ALLISON BLAINEY DOESN'T SIGN JUST **ANYONE'S** YEARBOOK!
"I HAVE NO IDEA WHO YOU ARE, AND I DON'T REALLY CARE."
ON THE BRIGHT SIDE, IT'S MORE MEMORABLE THAN "HAVE A GREAT SUMMER"!
I LIKE THE WAY SHE DOTS HER I'S WITH LITTLE SMILEY FACES!
6/21
© 2009 by NEA, Inc.
PEIRCE

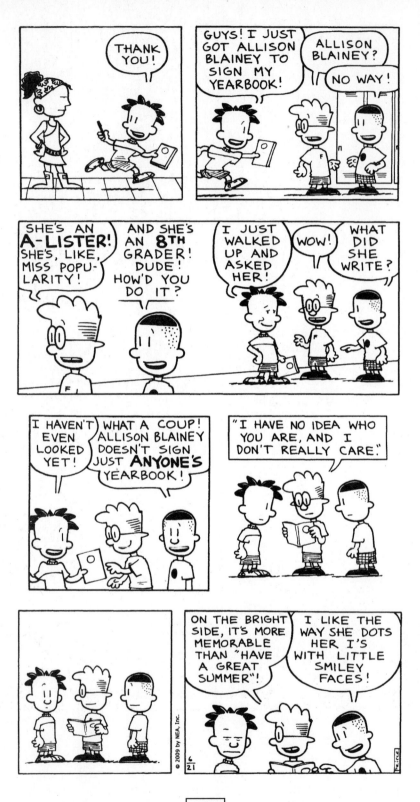

BEAT THE HEAT

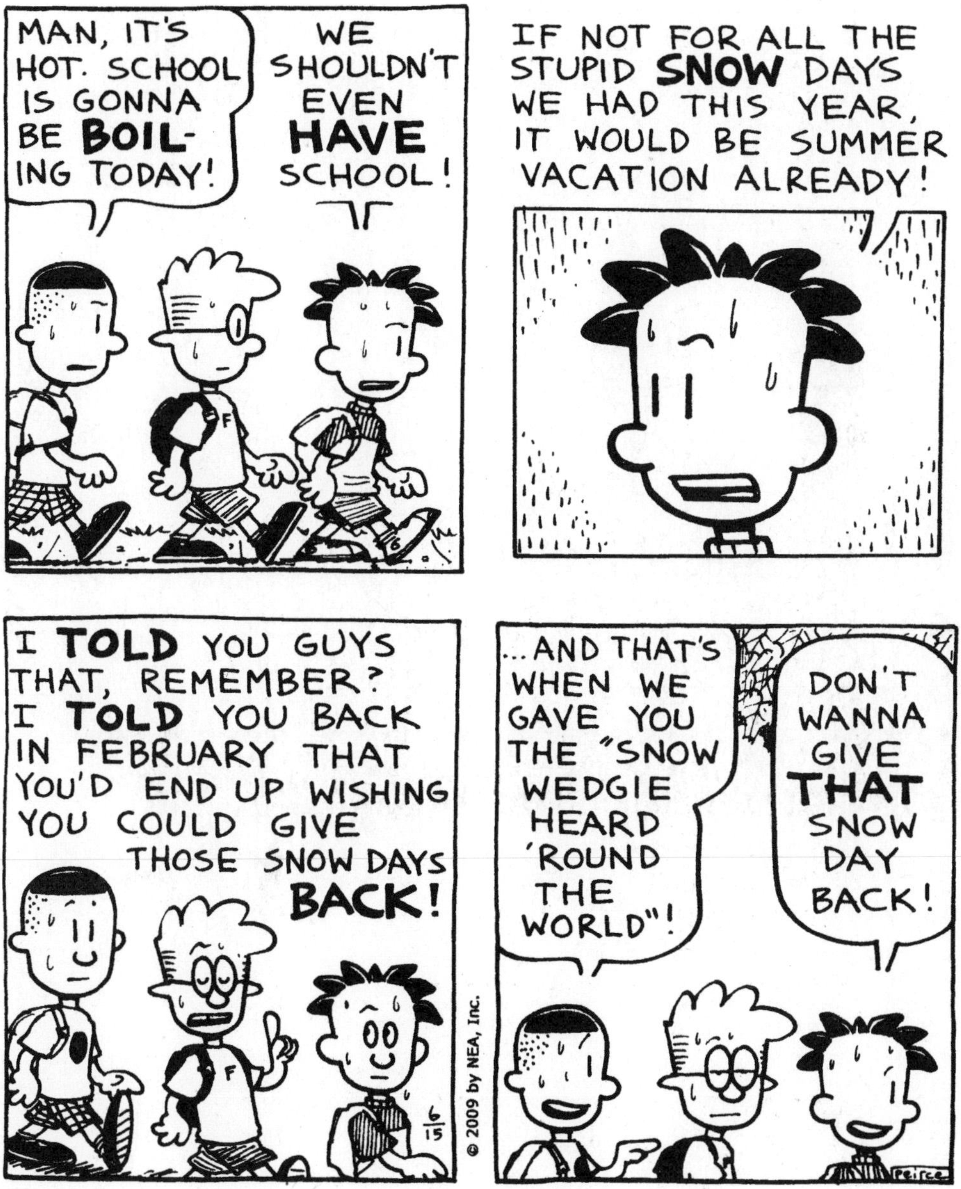
MAN, IT'S HOT. SCHOOL IS GONNA BE **BOIL**-ING TODAY!
WE SHOULDN'T EVEN **HAVE** SCHOOL!
IF NOT FOR ALL THE STUPID **SNOW** DAYS WE HAD THIS YEAR, IT WOULD BE SUMMER VACATION ALREADY!
I **TOLD** YOU GUYS THAT, REMEMBER? I **TOLD** YOU BACK IN FEBRUARY THAT YOU'D END UP WISHING YOU COULD GIVE THOSE SNOW DAYS **BACK**!
6/15
© 2009 by NEA, Inc.
...AND THAT'S WHEN WE GAVE YOU THE "SNOW WEDGIE HEARD 'ROUND THE WORLD"!
DON'T WANNA GIVE **THAT** SNOW DAY BACK!
peirce

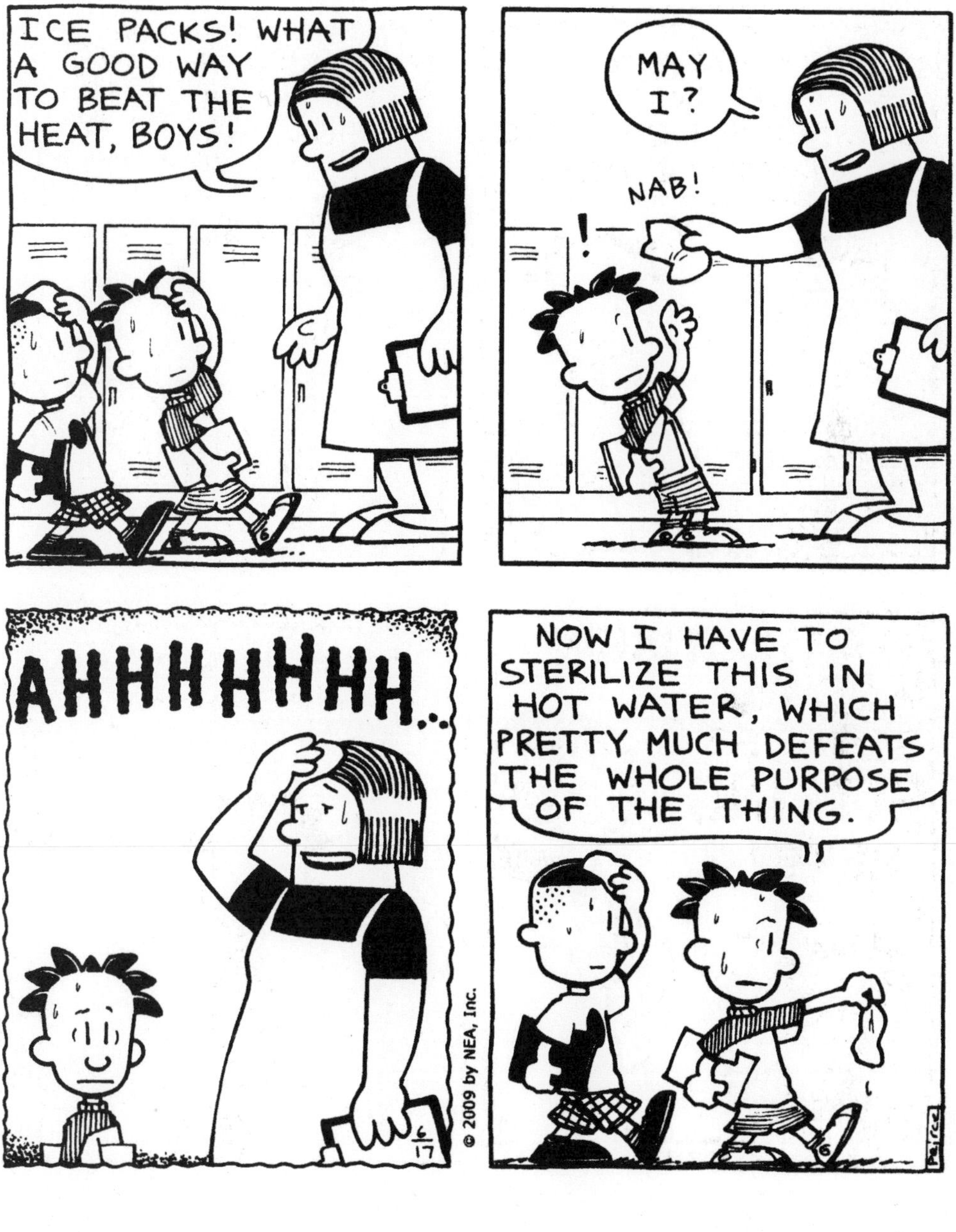
ICE PACKS! WHAT A GOOD WAY TO BEAT THE HEAT, BOYS!
MAY I?
NAB!
!
AHHHHHHH...
NOW I HAVE TO STERILIZE THIS IN HOT WATER, WHICH PRETTY MUCH DEFEATS THE WHOLE PURPOSE OF THE THING.
Peirce

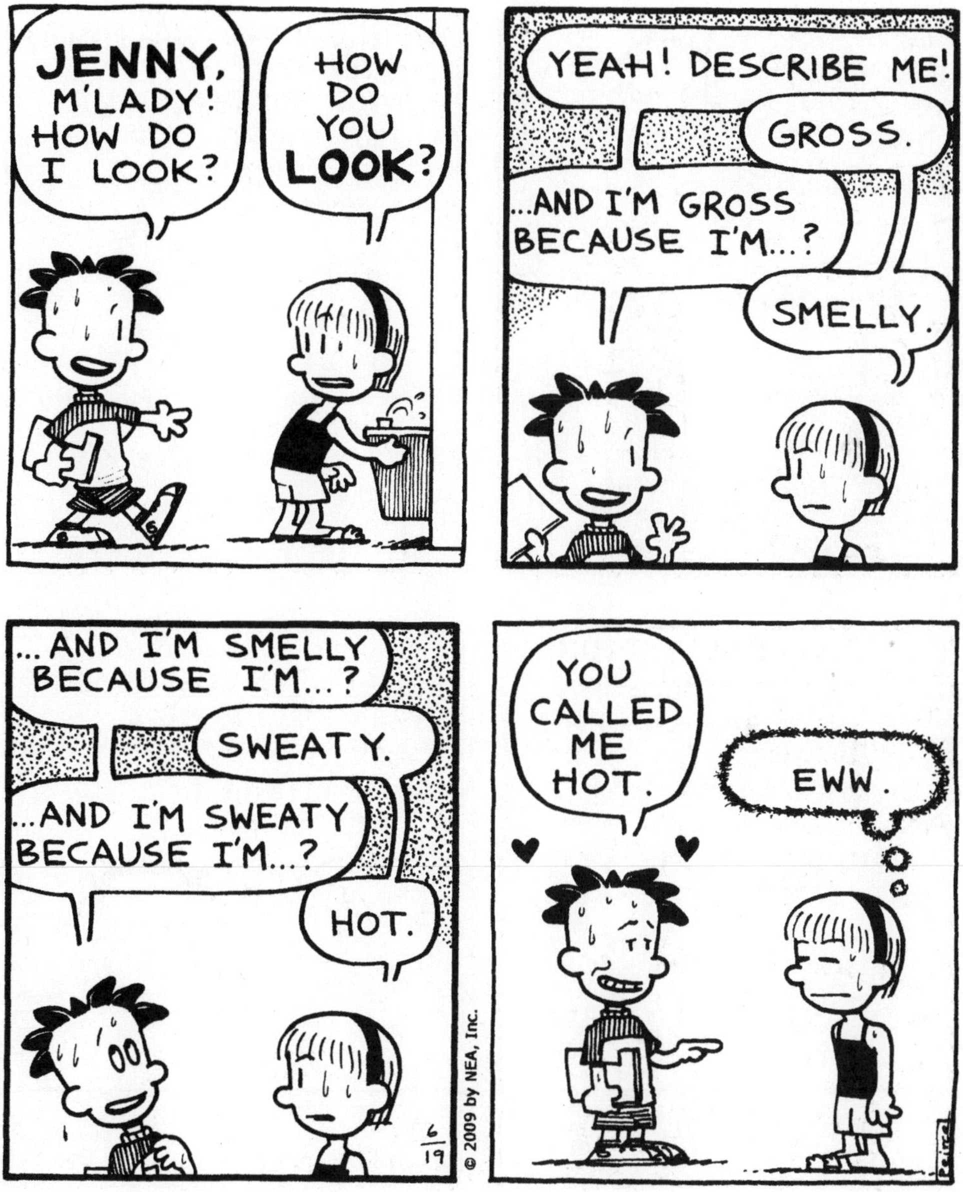
JENNY, M'LADY! HOW DO I LOOK?
HOW DO YOU LOOK?
YEAH! DESCRIBE ME!
GROSS.
...AND I'M GROSS BECAUSE I'M...?
SMELLY.
...AND I'M SMELLY BECAUSE I'M...?
SWEATY.
...AND I'M SWEATY BECAUSE I'M...?
HOT.
6/19
© 2009 by NEA, Inc.
YOU CALLED ME HOT.
EWW.

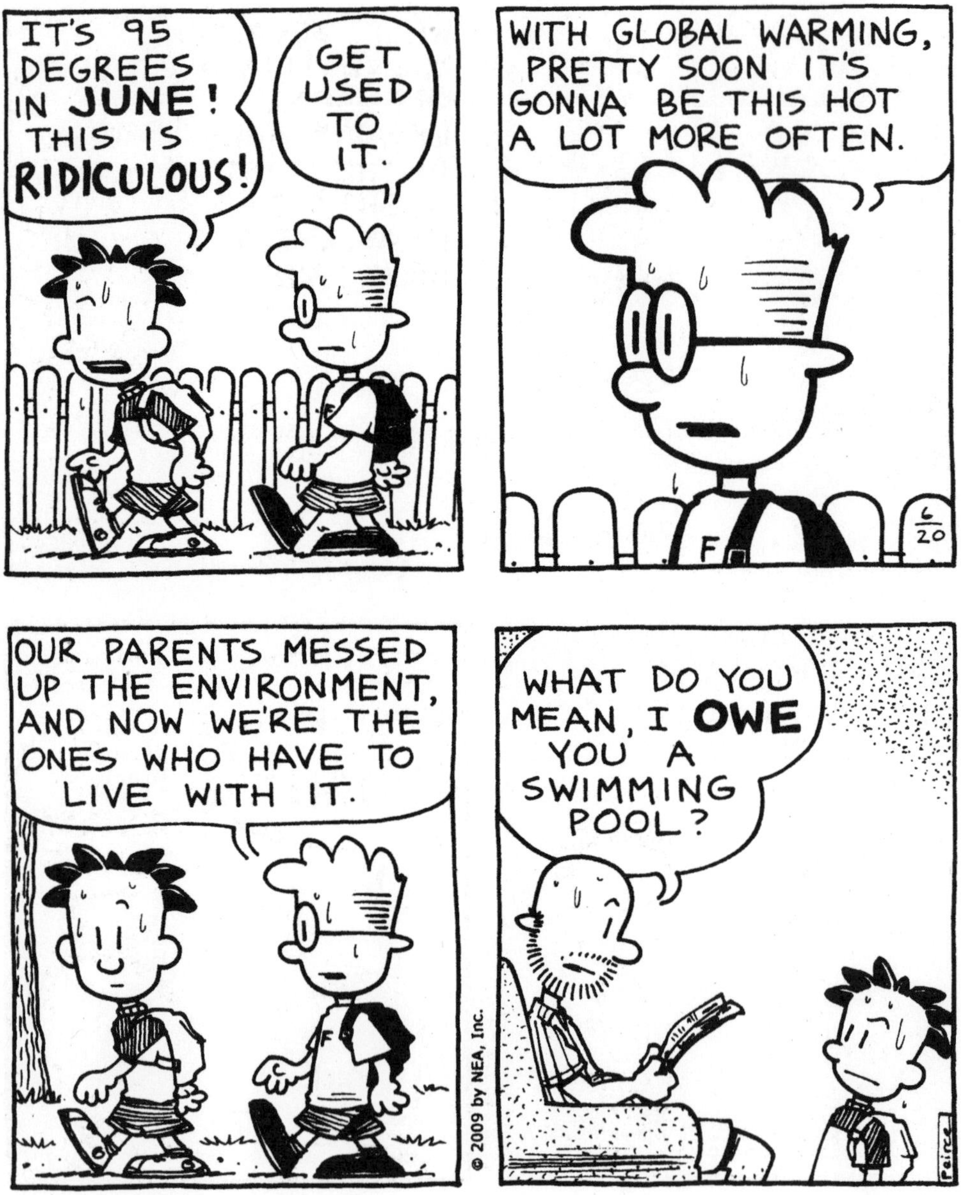
IT'S 95 DEGREES IN JUNE! THIS IS RIDICULOUS!
GET USED TO IT.
WITH GLOBAL WARMING, PRETTY SOON IT'S GONNA BE THIS HOT A LOT MORE OFTEN.
6/20
OUR PARENTS MESSED UP THE ENVIRONMENT, AND NOW WE'RE THE ONES WHO HAVE TO LIVE WITH IT.
WHAT DO YOU MEAN, I OWE YOU A SWIMMING POOL?
© 2009 by NEA, Inc.
Peirce

WATCH AND LEARN

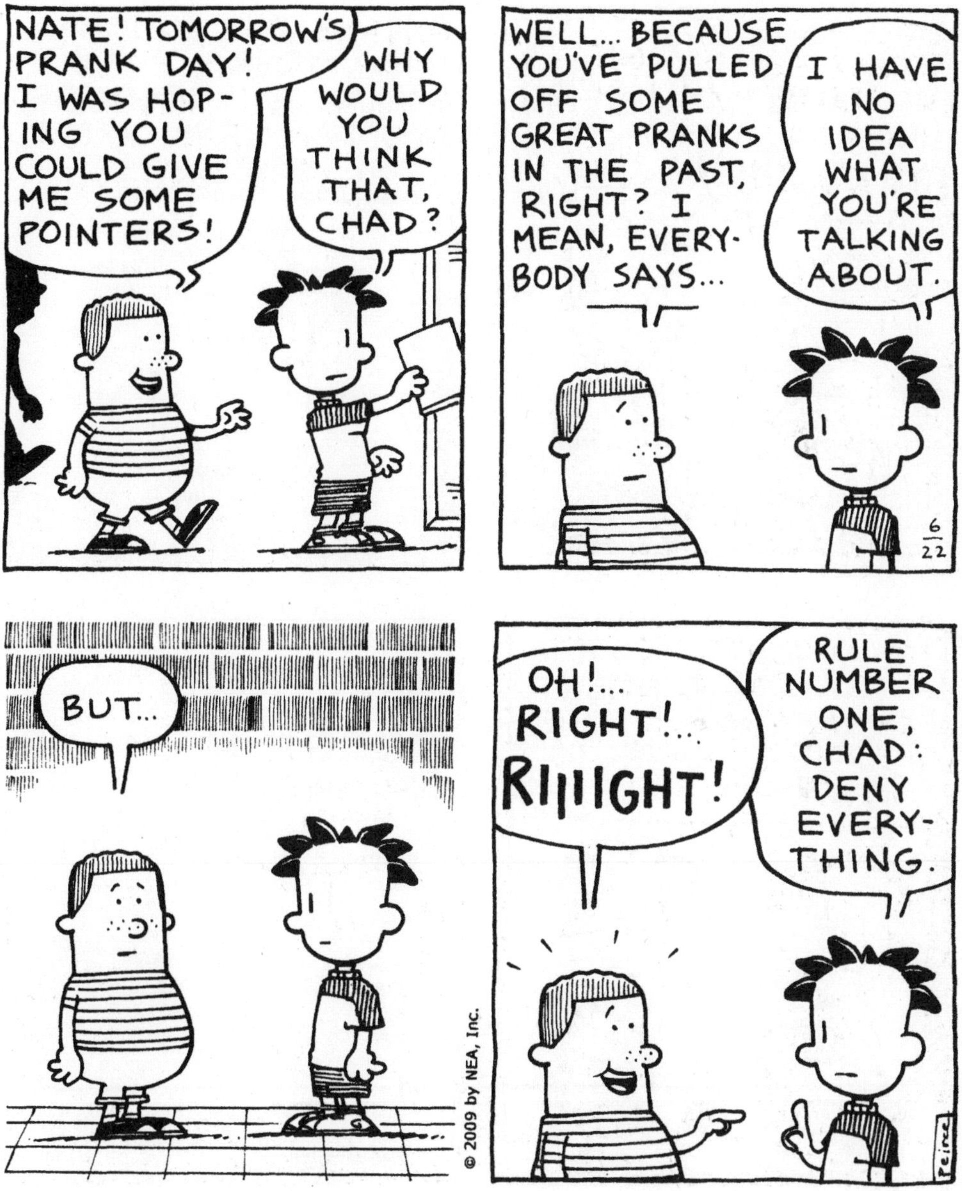
NATE! TOMORROW'S PRANK DAY! I WAS HOPING YOU COULD GIVE ME SOME POINTERS!
WHY WOULD YOU THINK THAT, CHAD?
WELL... BECAUSE YOU'VE PULLED OFF SOME GREAT PRANKS IN THE PAST, RIGHT? I MEAN, EVERYBODY SAYS...
I HAVE NO IDEA WHAT YOU'RE TALKING ABOUT.
6/22
BUT...
OH!... RIGHT!... RIIIIGHT!
RULE NUMBER ONE, CHAD: DENY EVERYTHING.
Peirce

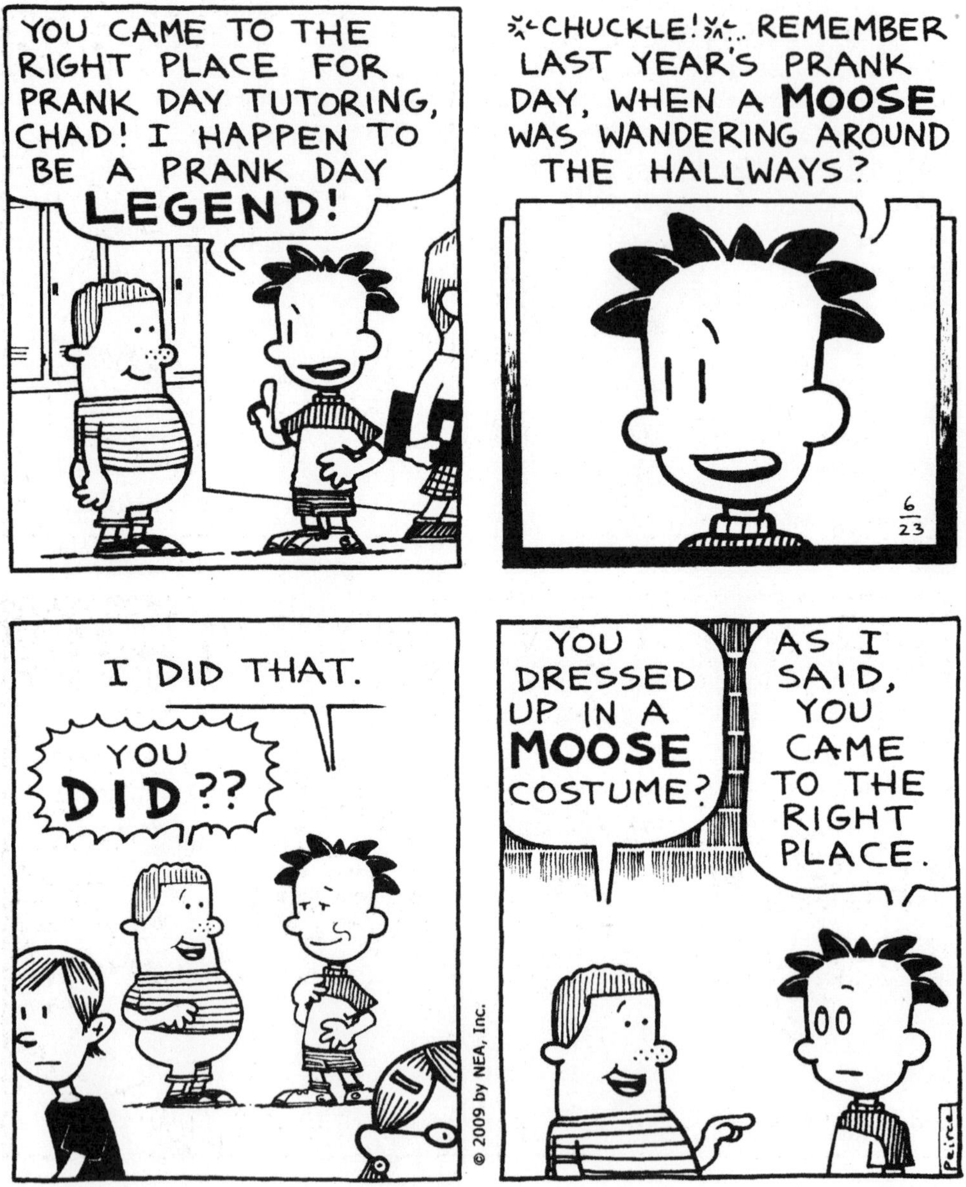
YOU CAME TO THE RIGHT PLACE FOR PRANK DAY TUTORING, CHAD! I HAPPEN TO BE A PRANK DAY LEGEND!
CHUCKLE! REMEMBER LAST YEAR'S PRANK DAY, WHEN A MOOSE WAS WANDERING AROUND THE HALLWAYS?
6/23
I DID THAT.
YOU DID??
YOU DRESSED UP IN A MOOSE COSTUME?
AS I SAID, YOU CAME TO THE RIGHT PLACE.
© 2009 by NEA, Inc.
Peirce

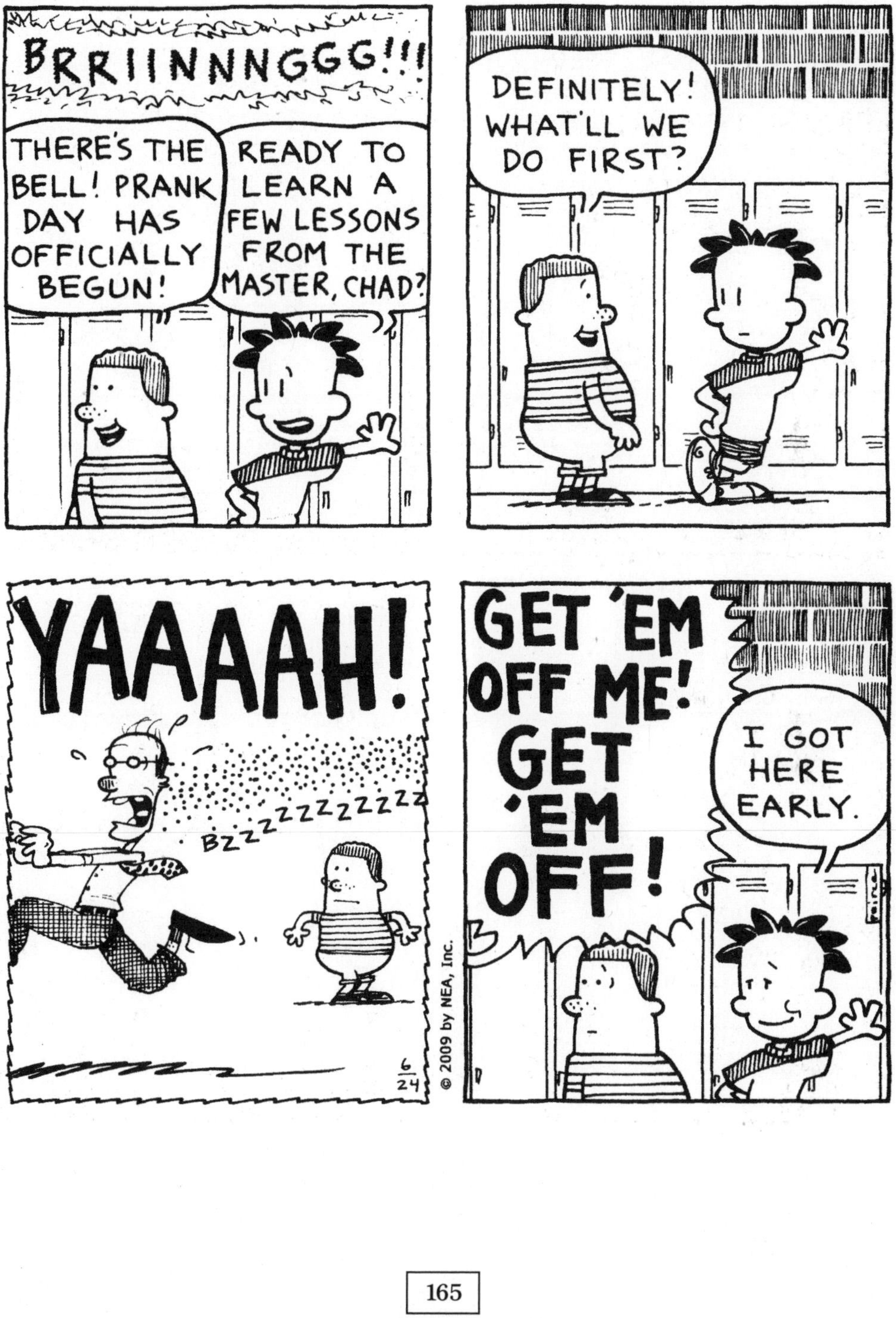
BRRIINNNGGG!!!
THERE'S THE BELL! PRANK DAY HAS OFFICIALLY BEGUN!
READY TO LEARN A FEW LESSONS FROM THE MASTER, CHAD?
DEFINITELY! WHAT'LL WE DO FIRST?
YAAAAH!
BZZZZZZZZZZZ
GET 'EM OFF ME! GET 'EM OFF!
I GOT HERE EARLY.
6/24
© 2009 by NEA, Inc.

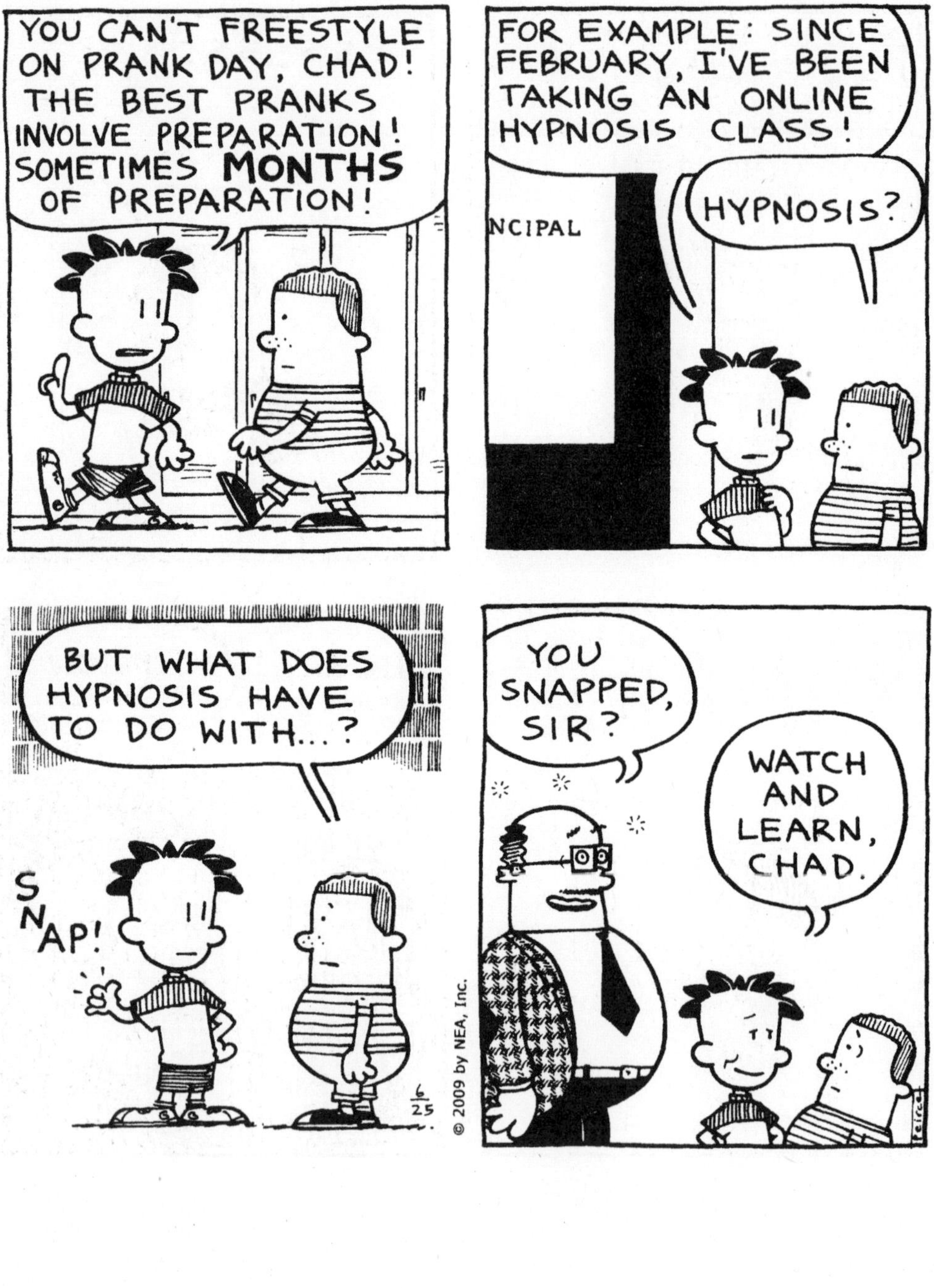
YOU CAN'T FREESTYLE ON PRANK DAY, CHAD! THE BEST PRANKS INVOLVE PREPARATION! SOMETIMES MONTHS OF PREPARATION!
FOR EXAMPLE: SINCE FEBRUARY, I'VE BEEN TAKING AN ONLINE HYPNOSIS CLASS!
NCIPAL
HYPNOSIS?
BUT WHAT DOES HYPNOSIS HAVE TO DO WITH...?
SNAP!
6/25
© 2009 by NEA, Inc.
YOU SNAPPED, SIR?
WATCH AND LEARN, CHAD.

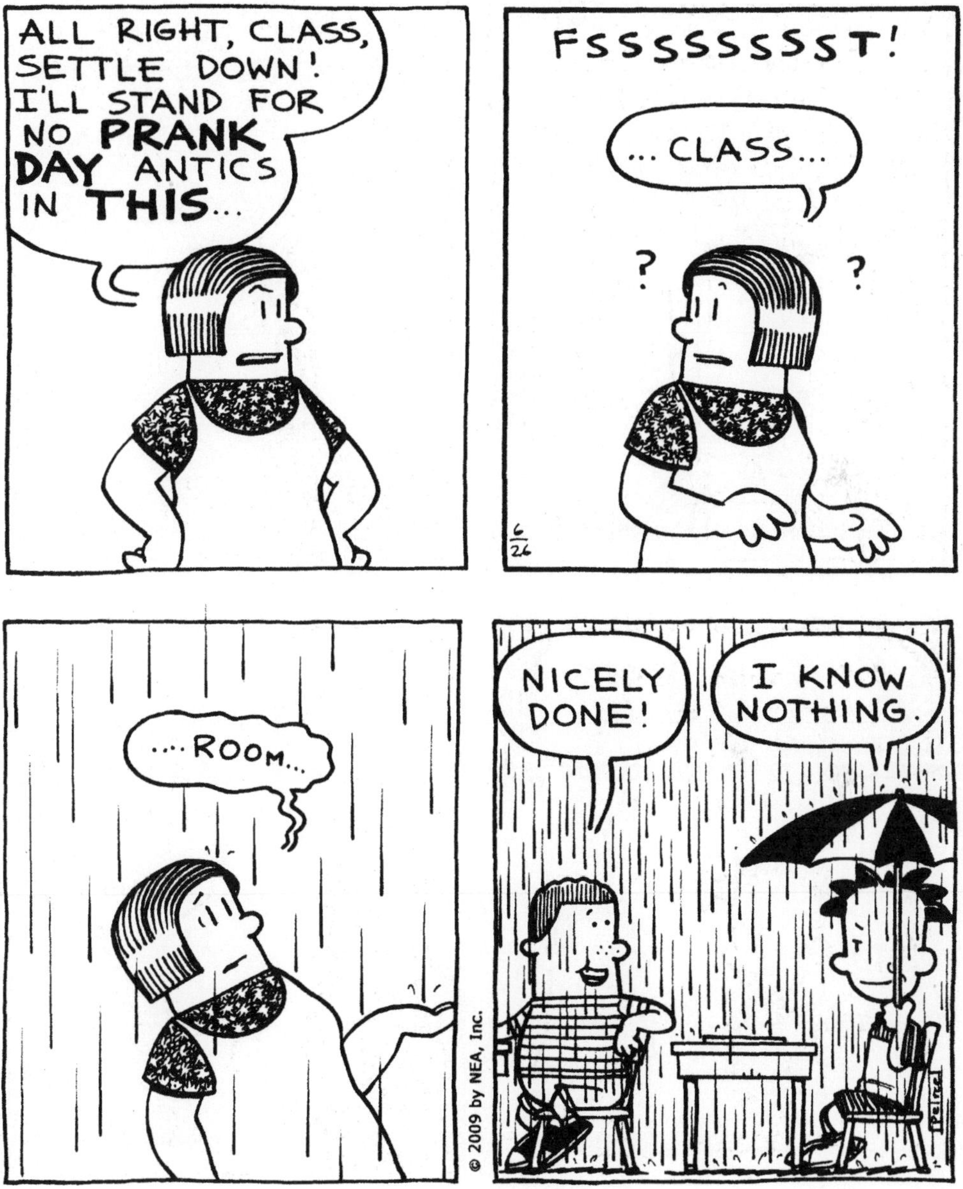
ALL RIGHT, CLASS, SETTLE DOWN! I'LL STAND FOR NO **PRANK DAY** ANTICS IN **THIS**...
FSSSSSSSST!
...CLASS...
?
?
6/26
....ROOM...
NICELY DONE!
I KNOW NOTHING.
PEIRCE

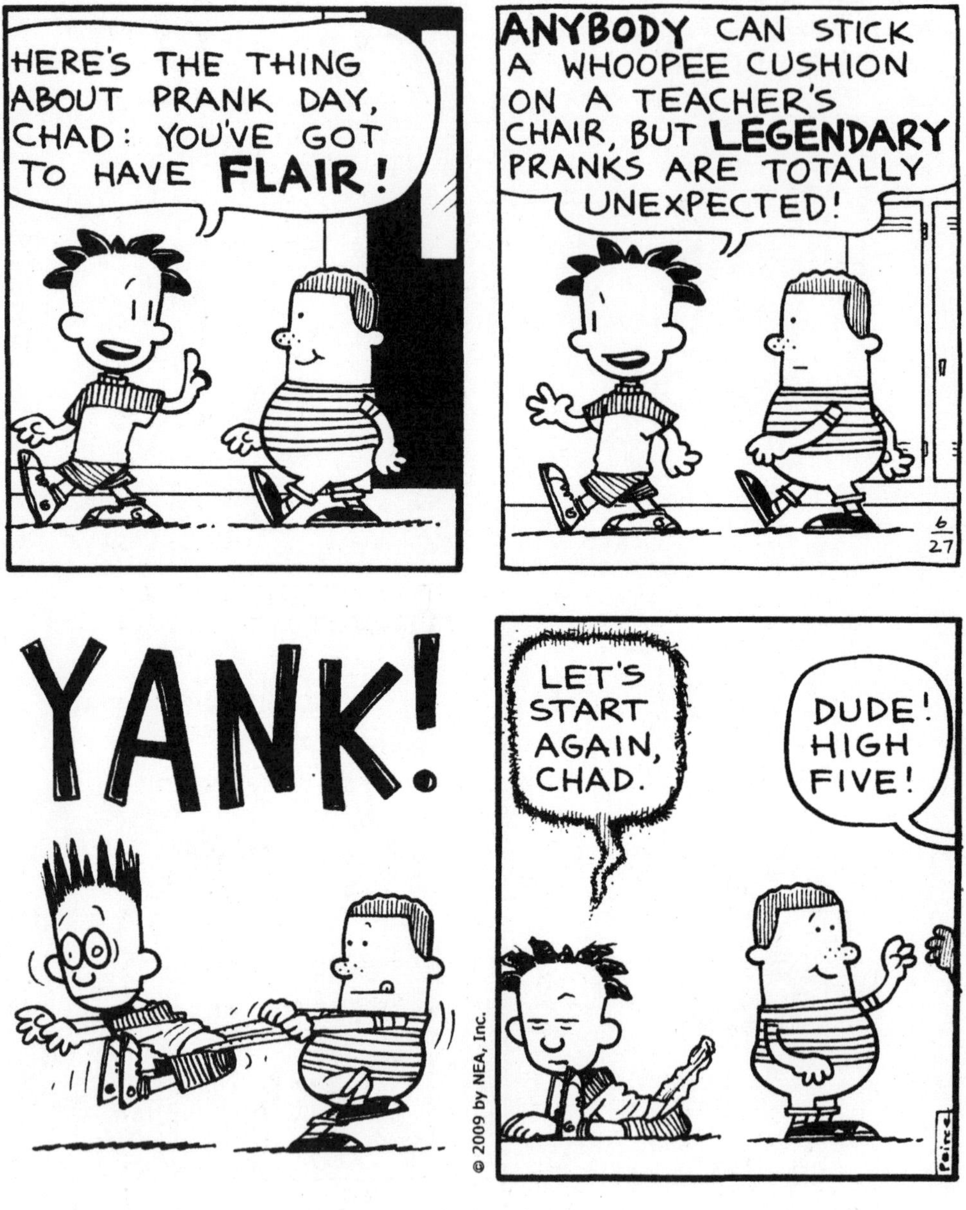
HERE'S THE THING ABOUT PRANK DAY, CHAD: YOU'VE GOT TO HAVE FLAIR!
ANYBODY CAN STICK A WHOOPEE CUSHION ON A TEACHER'S CHAIR, BUT LEGENDARY PRANKS ARE TOTALLY UNEXPECTED!
6/27
YANK!
LET'S START AGAIN, CHAD.
DUDE! HIGH FIVE!
Peirce

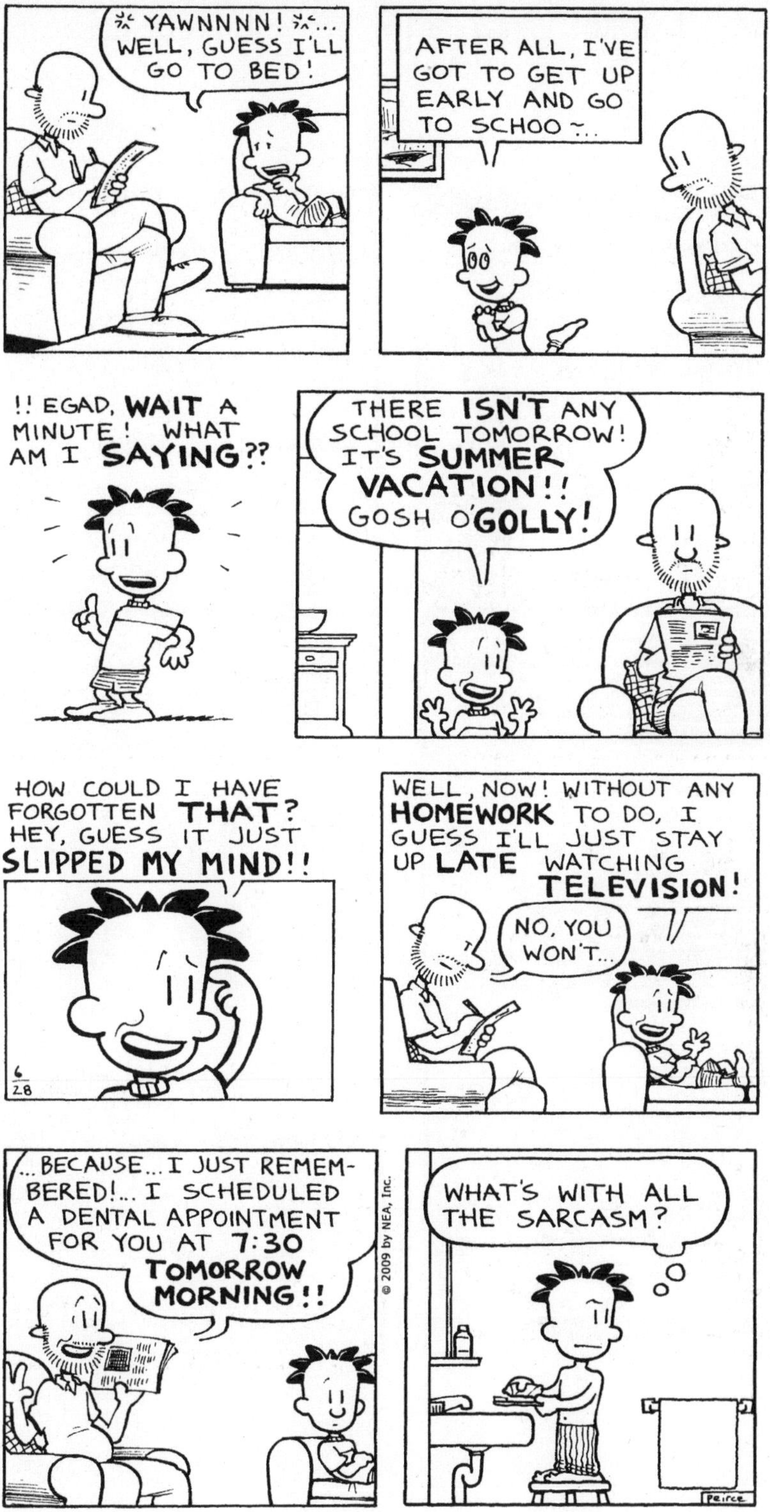

YAWNNNN!... WELL, GUESS I'LL GO TO BED!
AFTER ALL, I'VE GOT TO GET UP EARLY AND GO TO SCHOO~...
!! EGAD, WAIT A MINUTE! WHAT AM I SAYING??
THERE ISN'T ANY SCHOOL TOMORROW! IT'S SUMMER VACATION!! GOSH O'GOLLY!
HOW COULD I HAVE FORGOTTEN THAT? HEY, GUESS IT JUST SLIPPED MY MIND!!
6/28
WELL, NOW! WITHOUT ANY HOMEWORK TO DO, I GUESS I'LL JUST STAY UP LATE WATCHING TELEVISION!
NO, YOU WON'T...
...BECAUSE... I JUST REMEMBERED!... I SCHEDULED A DENTAL APPOINTMENT FOR YOU AT 7:30 TOMORROW MORNING!!
© 2009 by NEA, Inc.
WHAT'S WITH ALL THE SARCASM?
Peirce

THREE IN A TREE

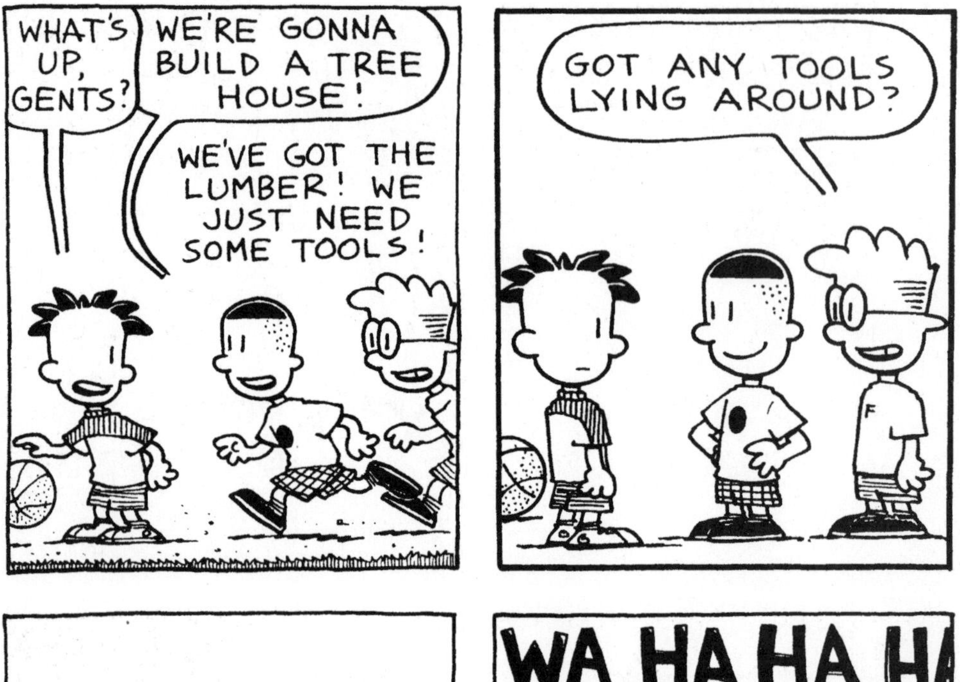
WHAT'S UP, GENTS?
WE'RE GONNA BUILD A TREE HOUSE!
WE'VE GOT THE LUMBER! WE JUST NEED SOME TOOLS!
GOT ANY TOOLS LYING AROUND?
WA HA HA HA HA HA HA HA HA HA HA HA
I HOPE THEY SMASH THEIR LITTLE THUMBS.
6/29
Peirce

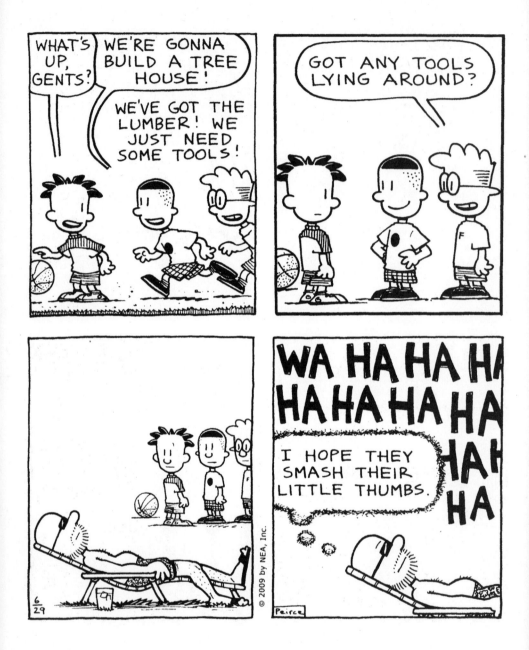

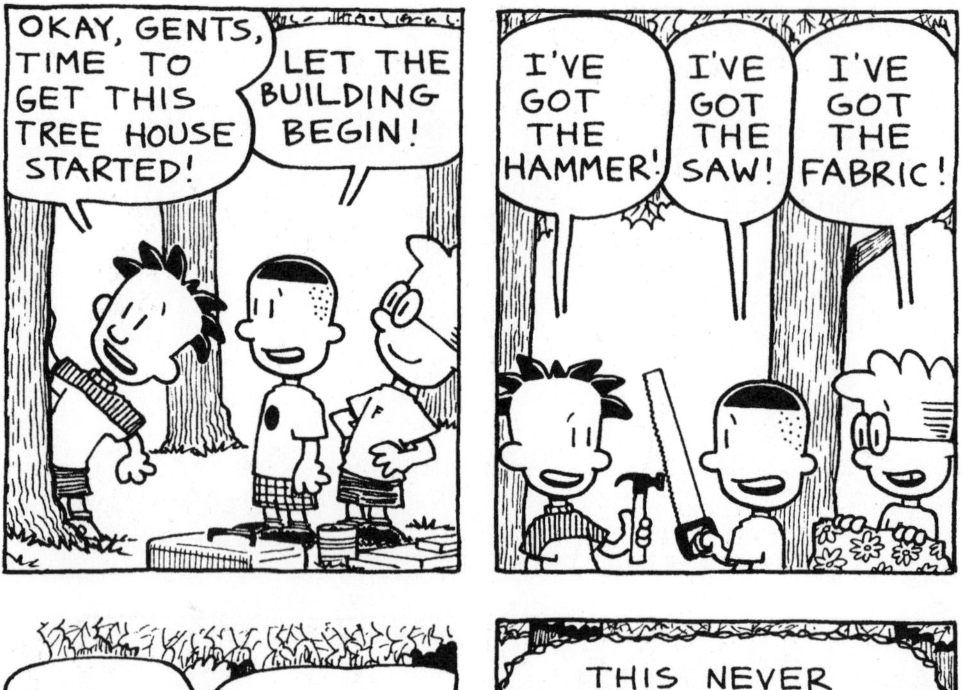
OKAY, GENTS, TIME TO GET THIS TREE HOUSE STARTED!
LET THE BUILDING BEGIN!
I'VE GOT THE HAMMER!
I'VE GOT THE SAW!
I'VE GOT THE FABRIC!
FABRIC?
FOR CURTAINS!
© 2009 by NEA, Inc.
THIS NEVER HAPPENS ON "DESIGN ON A DIME."

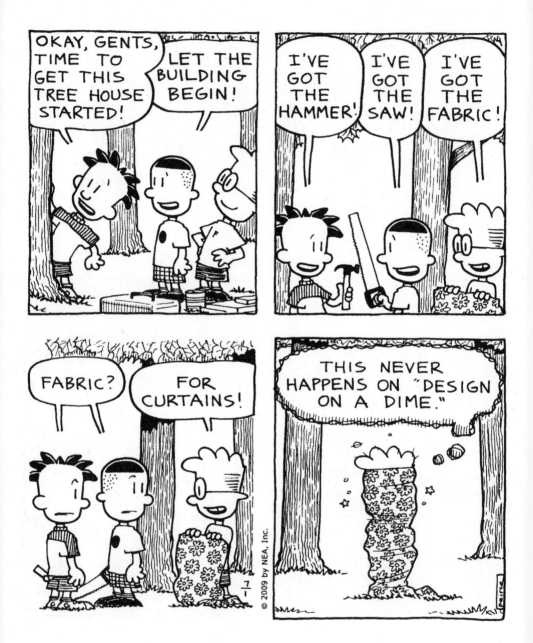

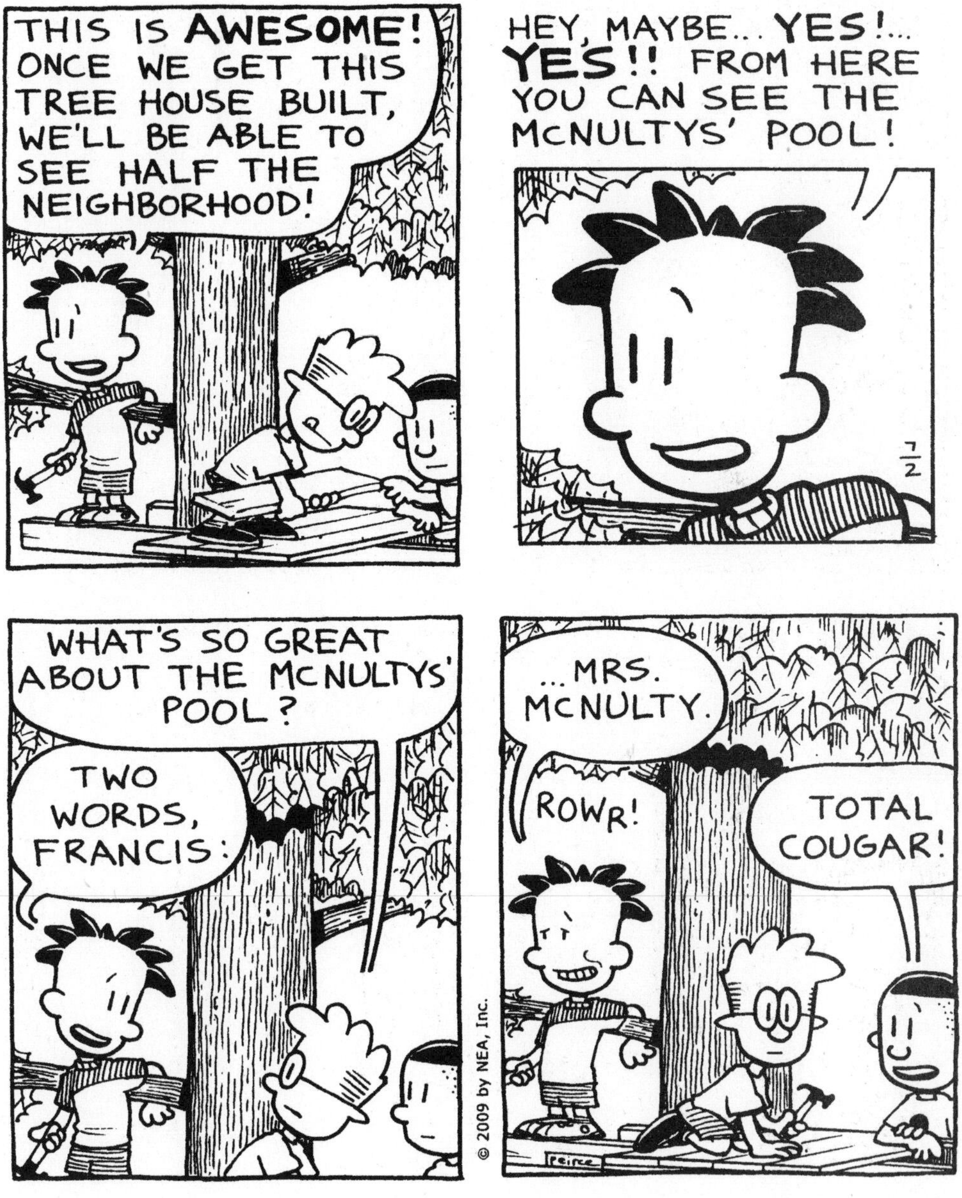
THIS IS **AWESOME**! ONCE WE GET THIS TREE HOUSE BUILT, WE'LL BE ABLE TO SEE HALF THE NEIGHBORHOOD!
HEY, MAYBE... **YES**!... **YES**!! FROM HERE YOU CAN SEE THE McNULTYS' POOL!
7/2
WHAT'S SO GREAT ABOUT THE McNULTYS' POOL?
TWO WORDS, FRANCIS:
...MRS. McNULTY.
ROWR!
TOTAL COUGAR!
PEIRCE

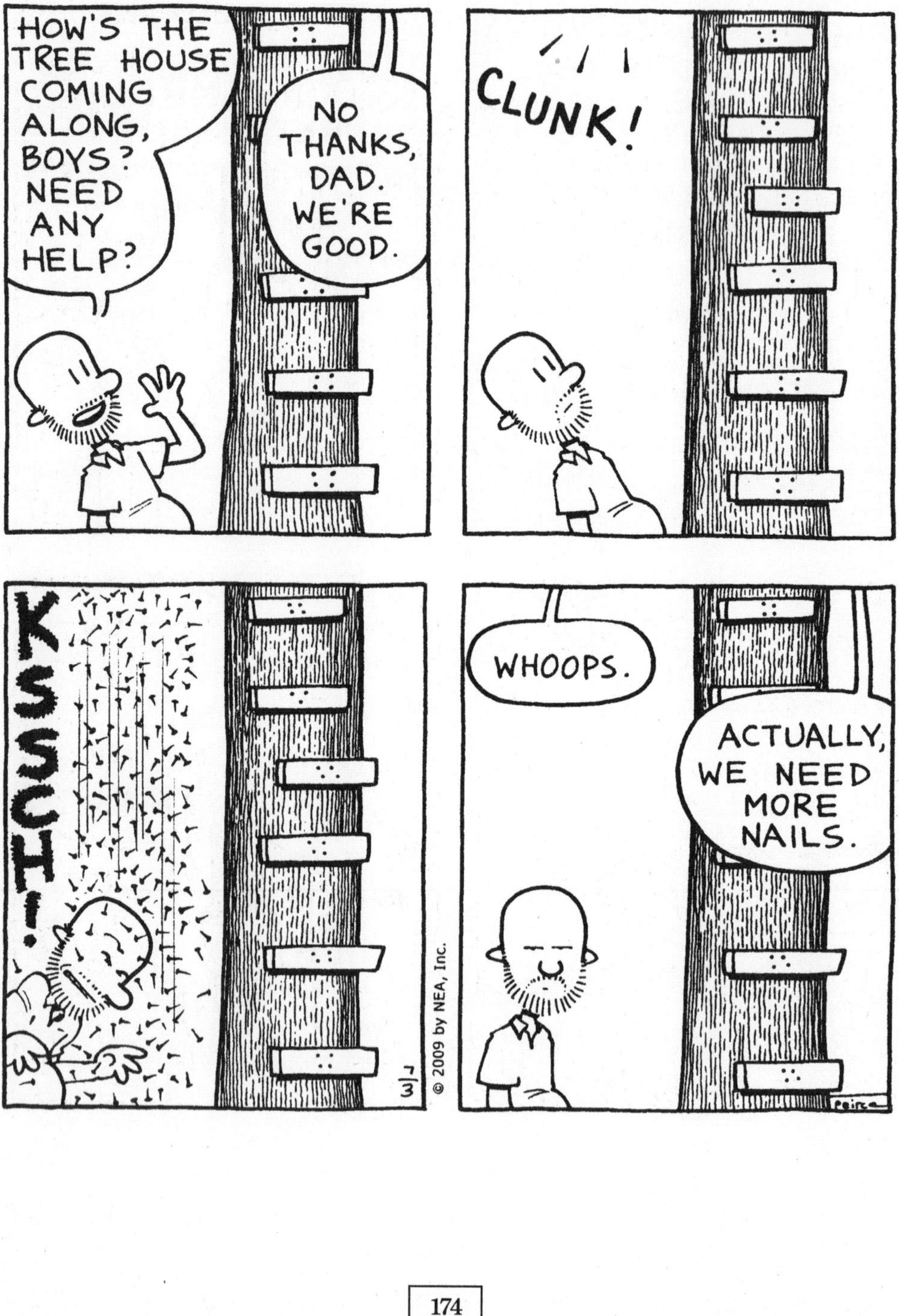
HOW'S THE TREE HOUSE COMING ALONG, BOYS? NEED ANY HELP?
NO THANKS, DAD. WE'RE GOOD.
CLUNK!
KSSCH!
WHOOPS.
ACTUALLY, WE NEED MORE NAILS.
3/7
© 2009 by NEA, Inc.
Peirce

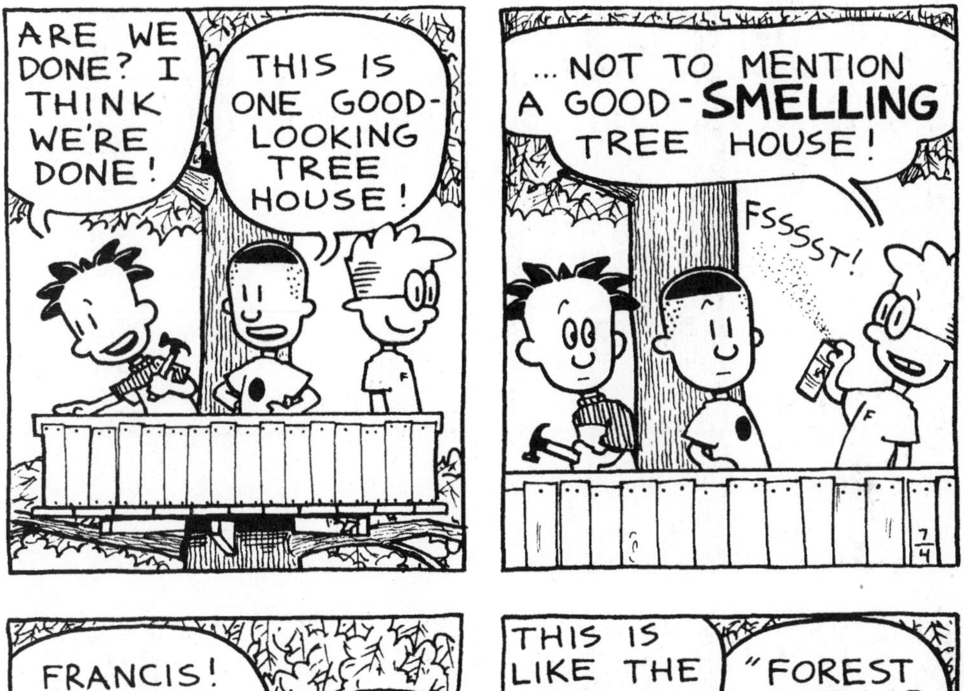
ARE WE DONE? I THINK WE'RE DONE!
THIS IS ONE GOOD-LOOKING TREE HOUSE!
...NOT TO MENTION A GOOD-SMELLING TREE HOUSE!
FSSSSST!
FRANCIS! IS THAT AIR FRESH-ENER?
YUP!
THIS IS LIKE THE TIME YOU BROUGHT PLACEMATS ON OUR CAMPING TRIP.
"FOREST PINE"?? DUDE, THIS IS AN OAK TREE!
Peirce
© 2009 by NEA, Inc.

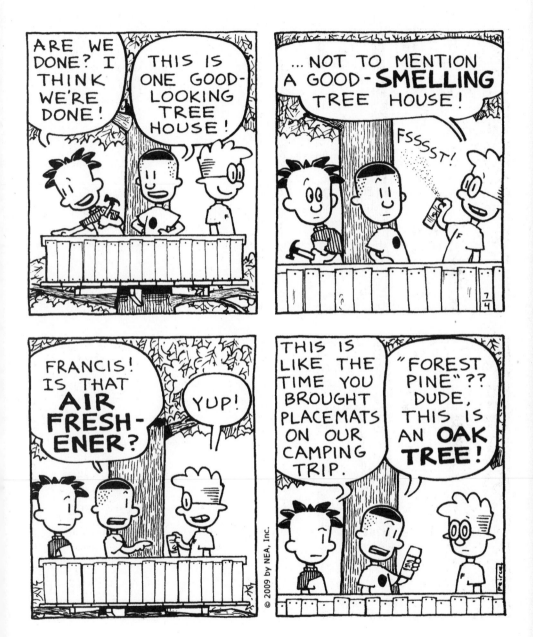

WHAT A CARD

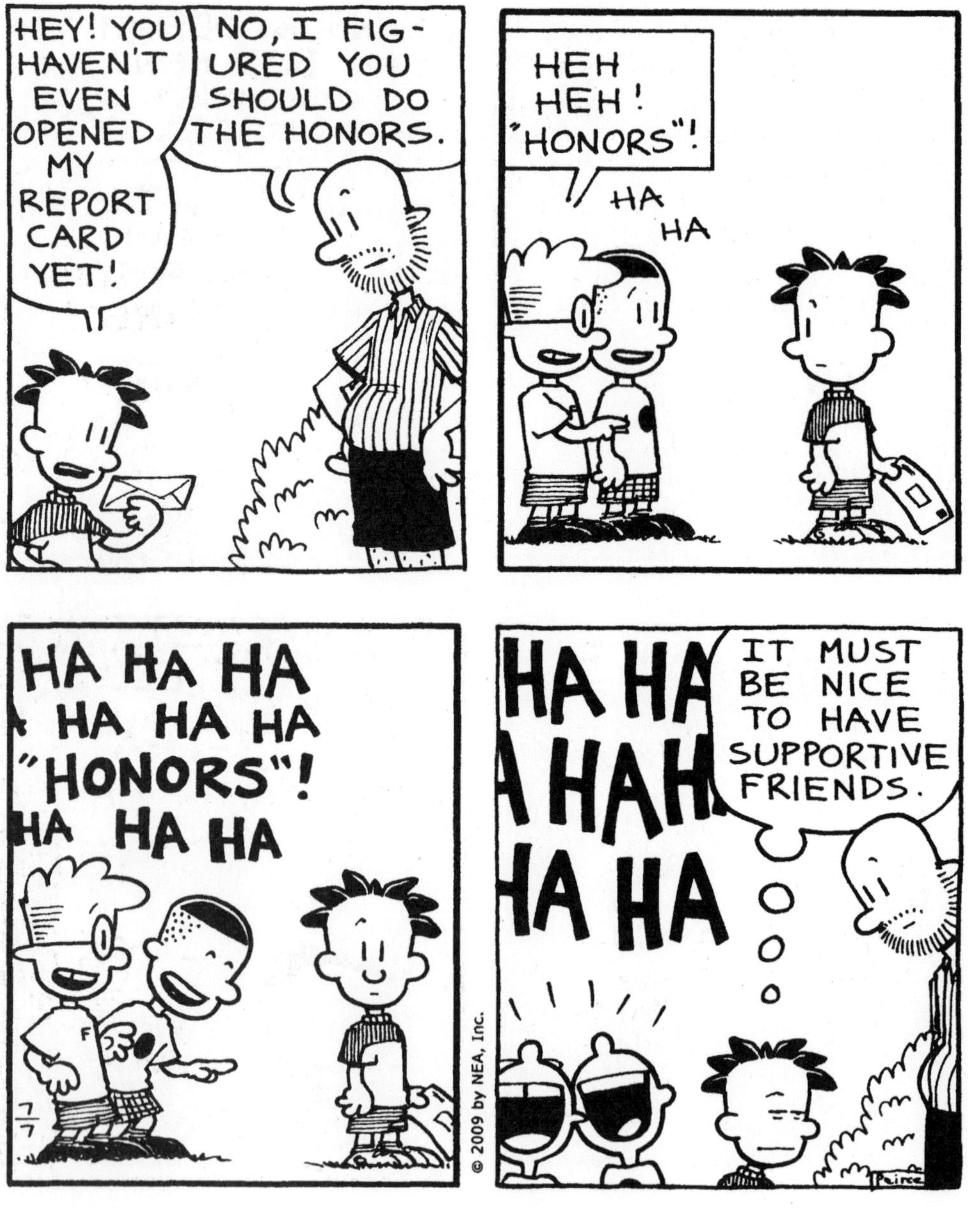

HEY! YOU HAVEN'T EVEN OPENED MY REPORT CARD YET!
NO, I FIGURED YOU SHOULD DO THE HONORS.
HEH HEH! "HONORS"!
HA HA
HA HA HA HA HA HA "HONORS"! HA HA HA
IT MUST BE NICE TO HAVE SUPPORTIVE FRIENDS.
HA HA HA HA HA HA
7/7
© 2009 by NEA, Inc.
Peirce

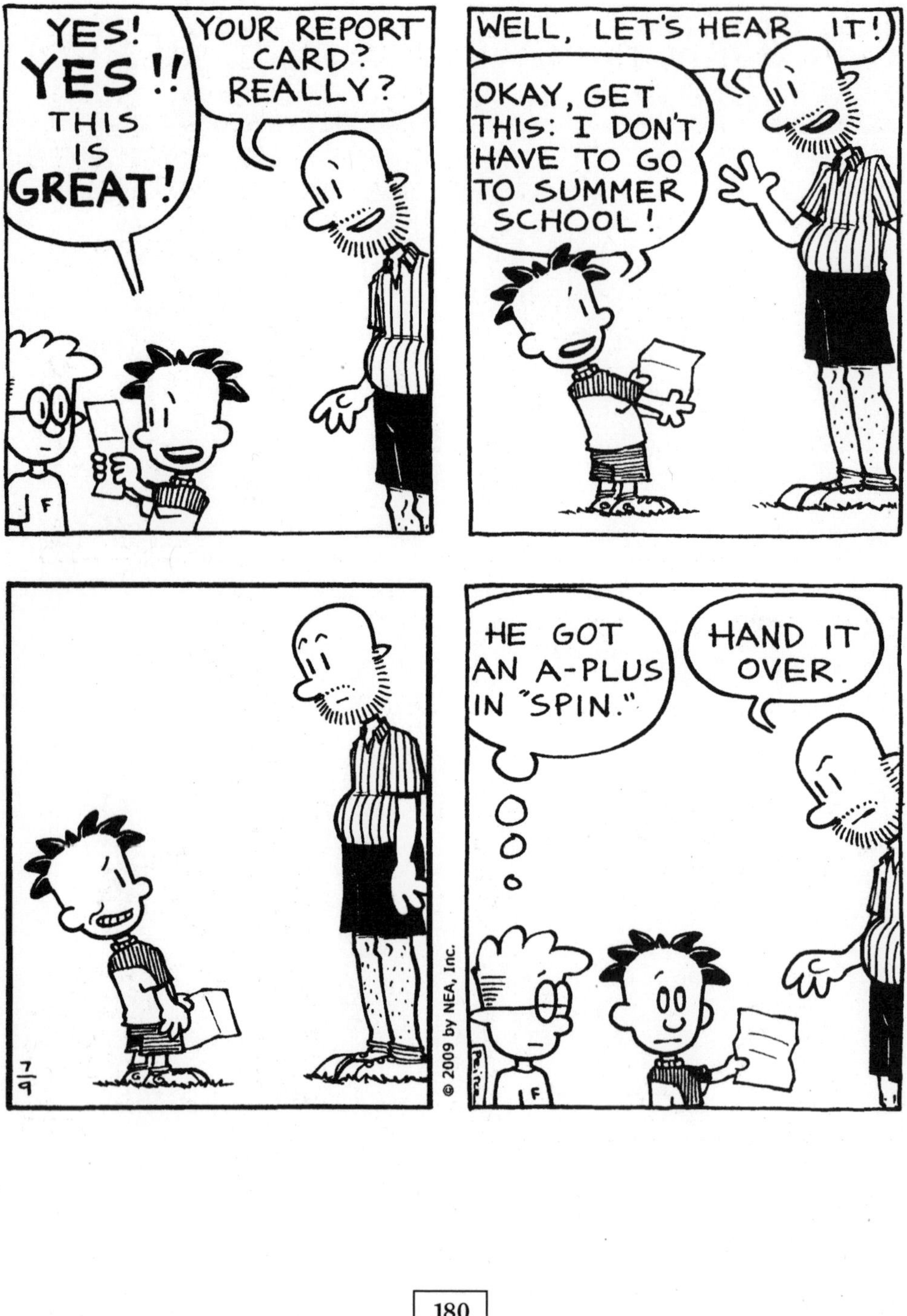
YES! YES!! THIS IS GREAT!
YOUR REPORT CARD? REALLY?
WELL, LET'S HEAR IT!
OKAY, GET THIS: I DON'T HAVE TO GO TO SUMMER SCHOOL!
HE GOT AN A-PLUS IN "SPIN."
HAND IT OVER.
7/9
© 2009 by NEA, Inc.

THE JOY OF READING

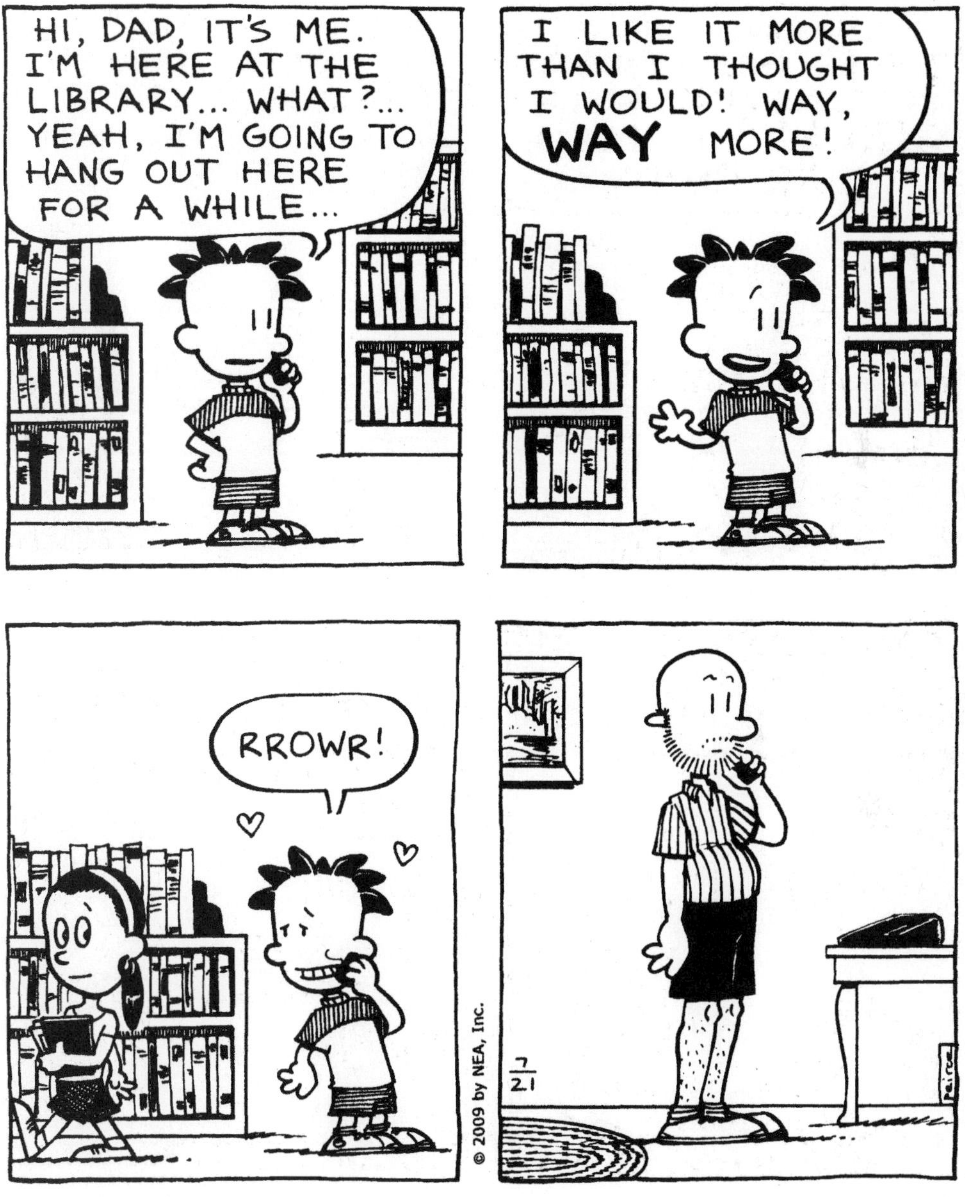
HI, DAD, IT'S ME. I'M HERE AT THE LIBRARY... WHAT?... YEAH, I'M GOING TO HANG OUT HERE FOR A WHILE...
I LIKE IT MORE THAN I THOUGHT I WOULD! WAY, **WAY** MORE!
RROWR!
7/21
PEIRCE

THAT'S GOOD. READING IS IMPORTANT. PEOPLE JUST DON'T REALIZE HOW IMPORTANT IT IS TO READ. OR, AS I'VE OFTEN SAID...

GAME ON!

MR. ROSA GETS THE SCOOP

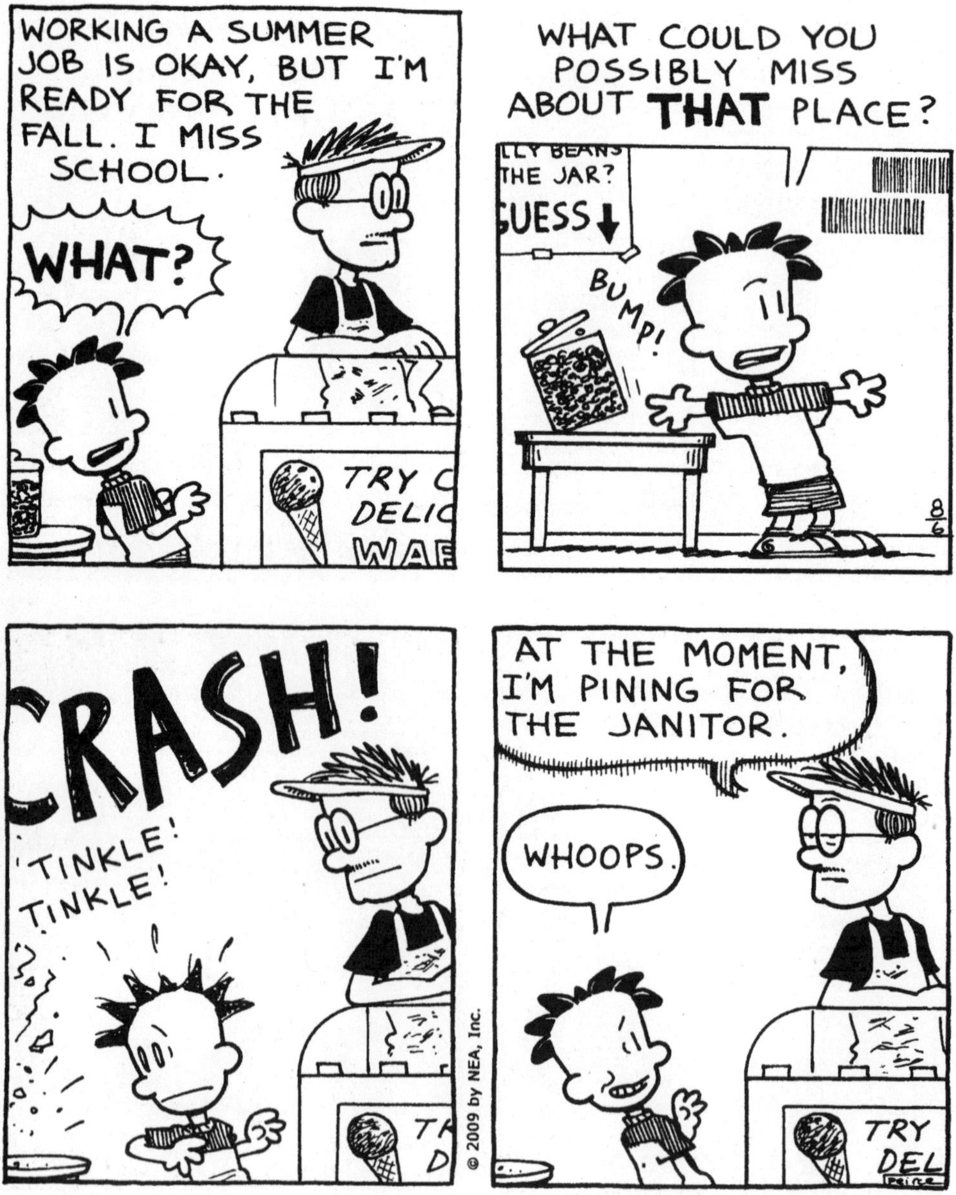
WORKING A SUMMER JOB IS OKAY, BUT I'M READY FOR THE FALL. I MISS SCHOOL.
WHAT?
TRY
DELIC
WHAT COULD YOU POSSIBLY MISS ABOUT **THAT** PLACE?
THE JAR?
GUESS
BUMP!
8/6
CRASH!
TINKLE! TINKLE!
AT THE MOMENT, I'M PINING FOR THE JANITOR.
WHOOPS.
TRY
DEL
© 2009 by NEA, Inc.

THIS JUST IN!

Everything Nate does is newsworthy—at least in his mind!
Write your own headlines for some of Nate's all-star moments!

EXTRA! EXTRA! Match each sketch to its Sunday strip!

Comic A goes on page _____.

Comic B goes on page _____.

Comic C goes on page _____.

Comic D goes on page _____.

WHAT HAPPENS NEXT?

Come up with the next scene using Nate's Sunday strip sketches as inspiration!

(A)

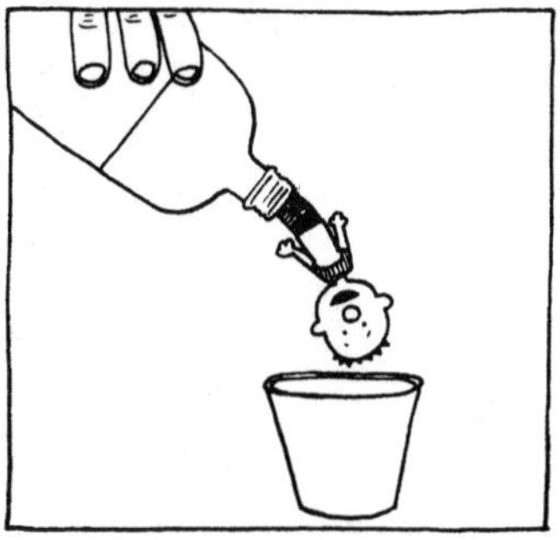

(B)

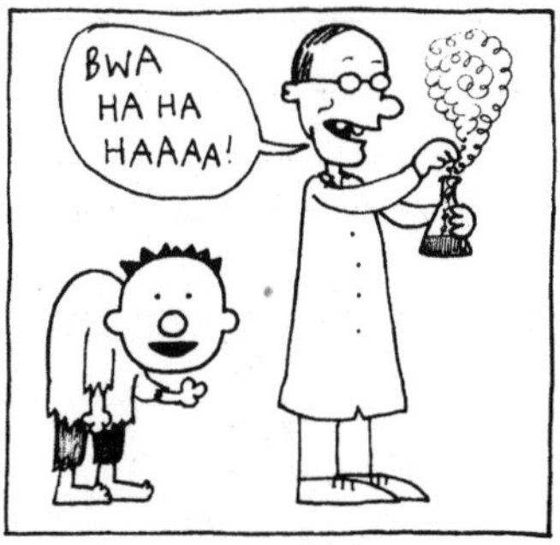
BWA HA HA HAAAA!

(C)

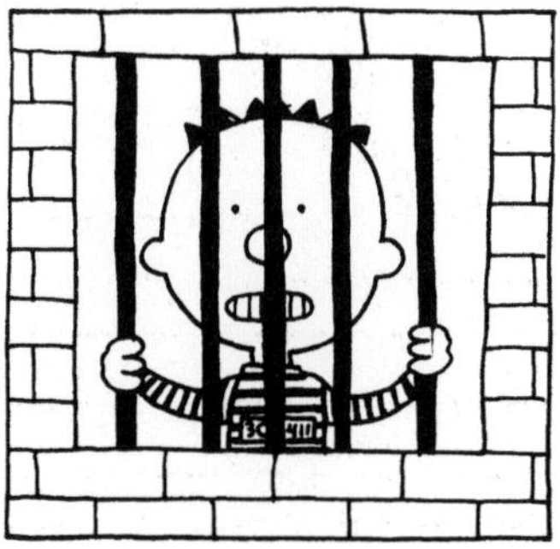

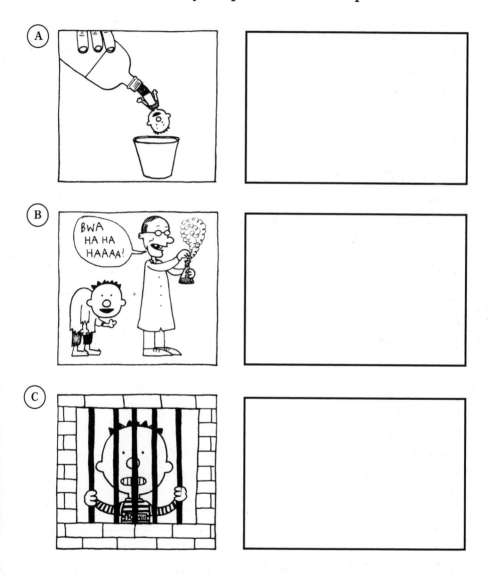

Bonus: Can you match each sketch to the original comic?

Comic A goes on page ____________.

Comic B goes on page ____________.

Comic C goes on page ____________.

Answers: A: p. 1; B: p. 8; C: p. 15.

WHAT A _____!
(YOU FILL IN THE BLANK)

Can you make up an awesome and hilarious story
based on Nate's drawings below?

For added silliness, use these words in your story!

fence	tomato
parachute	emergency
headline	turtle
marshmallow	cat
faint	crazy
firefighter	lightning

What a day! First, Nate . . .

"ZONED" OUT!

You know what? Only a week ago, my life totally stunk.

ExCUSE me, but the CORRECT word would be "stank."

Okay, then — it STANK. Gina was being her usual know-it-all self...

nuzzle nuzzle

Ugh.

Artur and Jenny were going overboard with the PDOs...

(*Public Displays of Obnoxiousness)

And worst of all: last week, REPORT CARDS got mailed home.

Ellen, I can't BELIEVE these GRADES!

Nate, I can't BELIEVE these grades.

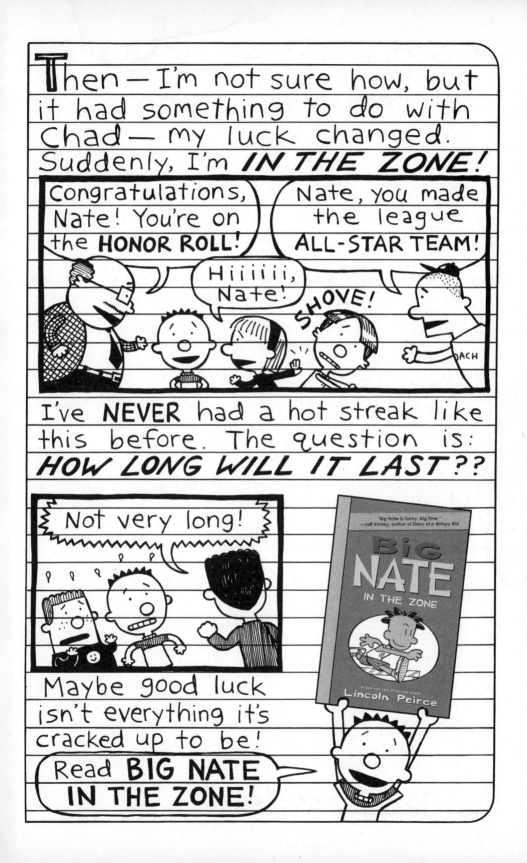

Lincoln Peirce

(pronounced "purse") is a cartoonist/writer and *New York Times* bestselling author of the hilarious Big Nate book series (www.bignatebooks.com), now published in twenty-five countries worldwide and available as ebooks and audiobooks and as an app, Big Nate: Comix by U! He is also the creator of the comic strip *Big Nate*. It appears in over two hundred and fifty U.S. newspapers and online daily at www.gocomics.com/bignate. Lincoln's boyhood idol was Charles Schulz of *Peanuts* fame, but his main inspiration for Big Nate has always been his own experience as a sixth grader. Just like Nate, Lincoln loves comics, ice hockey, and Cheez Doodles (and dislikes cats, figure skating, and egg salad). His Big Nate books have been featured on *Good Morning America* and in the *Boston Globe*, the *Los Angeles Times*, *USA Today*, and the *Washington Post*. He has also written for Cartoon Network and Nickelodeon. Lincoln lives with his wife and two children in Portland, Maine.

FRANCIS RATES ALL THE BIG NATE BOOKS!

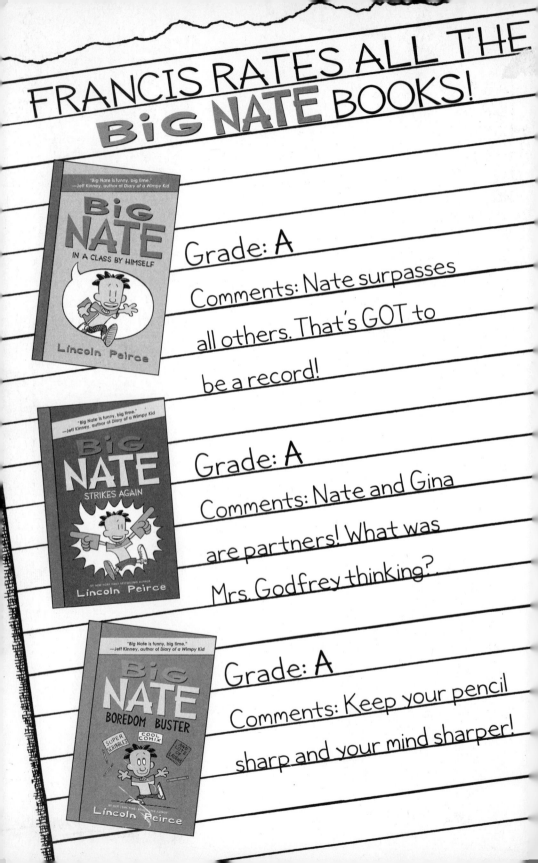

"Big Nate is funny, big time."
—Jeff Kinney, author of Diary of a Wimpy Kid
BIG NATE
IN A CLASS BY HIMSELF
Lincoln Peirce

Grade: A

Comments: Nate surpasses all others. That's GOT to be a record!

"Big Nate is funny, big time."
—Jeff Kinney, author of Diary of a Wimpy Kid
BIG NATE
STRIKES AGAIN
Lincoln Peirce

Grade: A

Comments: Nate and Gina are partners! What was Mrs. Godfrey thinking?

"Big Nate is funny, big time."
—Jeff Kinney, author of Diary of a Wimpy Kid
BIG NATE
BOREDOM BUSTER
SUPER SCRIBBLES
COOL COMIX
AND LOTS OF LAUGHS
Lincoln Peirce

Grade: A

Comments: Keep your pencil sharp and your mind sharper!